Jonathan Harker 'made search among the books' in the British Museum Library, before setting off on his fateful journey to Transylvania – so it is fitting that this exciting new anthology of short vampire fiction *Visions of the Vampire* should be published over a century later by that very same institution. It digs deeper and wider than the standard collections – to resurrect not just the traditional *grands saigneurs* but more up-to-date haematodipsomaniacs as well, some of them dazed and confused rather than predatory. Clearly, to judge by *Visions of the Vampire*, the old dreams have not died – they've shifted shape, moved with the anxieties of the times, and spread their wings...

Sir Christopher Frayling
Writer, broadcaster and author of
Vampyres – from Count Dracula to Vampirella

VISIONS

of the

VAMPIRE

VISIONS
of the
VAMPIRE

Two Centuries of Immortal Tales

Edited by

SORCHA NÍ FHLAINN

and

XAVIER ALDANA REYES

THE BRITISH LIBRARY

This collection first published in 2020 by
The British Library
96 Euston Road
London NW1 2DB

Introduction © 2020 Sorcha Ní Fhlainn and Xavier Aldana Reyes

'The Family of the Vourdalak' translated by Christopher Frayling
© 1976 Christopher Frayling. Reproduced with permission of HLA Agency.

'The Lady of the House of Love' © 1975 Angela Carter.
Reprinted with permission of Rogers, Coleridge and White.

'The Master of Rampling Gate' © 1984 Anne Rice. Reprinted with permission of the author.

'Advocates' © 1991 Suzy McKee Charnas and Chelsea Quinn Yarbro.
Reprinted with the permission of the authors.

'Let the Old Dreams Die' © 2011 John Ajvide Lindqvist, English translation by Marlaine
Delargy © 2011 Text Publishing. Reprinted with the permission of rightsholders Text
Publishing (www.textpublishing.com.au), St. Martin's Press (www.us.macmillan.com/smp)
and Quercus Books (www.quercusbooks.co.uk).

Dates attributed to each story relate to first publication.

Cataloguing in Publication Data
A catalogue record for this publication is available from the British Library

ISBN 978 0 7123 5392 2

Cover design by Mauricio Villamayor with illustration by Sandra Gómez.

Text design and typesetting by Tetragon, London.
Printed in Malta by Gutenberg Press.

CONTENTS

INTRODUCTION

In January 2020, the BBC released *Dracula*, the latest screen adaptation of the adventures of popular culture's master vampire. A modern reimagining of the quintessential Gothic monster pitted against a female vampire hunter and spanning three centuries, this update of the count's journey from his Romanian castle to contemporary London emphasises that vampire tales are immortal, that they have endured in their almost compulsive retelling and that their basic structures are easily mappable onto different times and places. Vampires, sometimes stalwarts of ancient times and orders, have not simply modernised to inhabit our hyperconnected lives – they have ironically become reflective mirrors. There has certainly been no shortage of vampire fictions pushing this point in the twenty-first century. From the 'real' assimilationist creatures in Charlaine Harris's *The Southern Vampire Mysteries* (2001–13) to Edward Cullen, as the latest iteration of the Byronic hero in Stephenie Meyer's *Twilight* novels (2005–8), and Eli in *Låt den rätte komma in* (*Let the Right One In*, 2004; translated in 2008), who saves twelve-year-old Oskar from death at the hands of school bullies, contemporary vampires channel lust and fantasies of dominance as easily as they negotiate concerns about isolation, marginalisation, essential economic inequalities and the difficult search for empathy and deeper understanding. In this respect, new vampires do not mark a significant departure; they continue to engage with ideas already emerging from foundational texts of the nineteenth century like John William Polidori's 'The Vampyre' (1819), included in this collection, and the penny dreadful *Varney the Vampire; or, The Feast of Blood* (1845–7). In fact, it is possible to see the evolution of vampire depictions as indicative of changes to our social landscape and of evolving attitudes around sexuality, faith and nationality.

But what is a vampire? Folkloric accounts significantly predate their fictional counterparts. Preventive action was once undertaken to ensure that a corpse did not rise from its grave to wreak havoc on small communities. Methods of protection from, and disposal of, presumed revenants included burials at crossroads (to disorientate the quickened corpse); the removal of the heart; in Asia, the scattering of sand or rice around a grave (thereby forcing the vampire to count each individual grain); pushing a large stone into the suspect's mouth, as found in the west of Ireland; or, in Bulgaria, pinning the body to the ground through the heart with iron stakes. As diverse as the rites to warn off vampirism were the means by which a healthy person could 'turn'. These ranged from dying alone and being an outlaw to instances of retribution from beyond the grave. Babies born with teeth were at one point deemed to be predisposed to vampirism, as were red-haired children. While most folkloric vampires imbibed blood, others also consumed nail clippings (the Madagascan 'Ramanga') or drained vitality as a floating ball of light (the West African 'Obayifo'). Other vampires bore a single fang to extract blood (the Spanish 'Guaxa'), and others an unusual tongue to feast on the fluids of the sick and dying. The feared condition was not relegated to the masses either: rulers were sometimes dispatched as vampires. In the case of the Abhartach, a despotic ruler in Ulster, his permanent consignment to the grave as a member of the 'neamh-mairbh' (un-dead) could only be ensured through his being stabbed by a sword of yew wood and then buried upside down.

Few of these folkloric creatures have inspired modern versions of the vampires, although their spirit is partially captured in a story like Aleksey Konstantinovich Tolstoy's 'The Family of the Vourdalak' (1884), included in this collection. It is the vampire's entry into cinema that largely informs much of our expectations today. Since the publication of *Dracula*, which almost coincided with the Lumière brothers' development of the cine-matograph in 1895, vampires have been reimagined and represented time and again on the big screen, from Count Orlok in *Nosferatu* (1922) to Universal's suave Bela Lugosi and on to Hammer's racier, technicolour bloodsuckers. Traditional vampires are fetching aristocrats or members of the nobility who live off the blood of others, wear long cloaks and generally mean bad news for humanity. They are selfish and flirtatious, interested, like the deadly plague and foreign threat they symbolise, in using others to extend their life and propagate their ilk. The reader will find echoes of this pervasive model in our volume in stories like 'The Cloak' (1939), by Robert Bloch, Anne Rice's 'The Master of Rampling Gate' (1984) and, naturally, Stoker's own 'Dracula's Guest' (1914), believed to have been the rejected first chapter of his famous novel. That other archetype, the vampiric femme fatale imagined as early as Ernst Raupach's 'Laßt die Todten ruhen!' (1822), or 'Wake Not the Dead!' in its 1823 English translation, and Théophile Gautier's 'La Morte amoureuse' (1836), or 'The Deathly Lover', met with renewed interest after filmmakers started adapting – almost always very loosely and with titillating intent – Sheridan Le Fanu's novella of veiled lesbian desire, 'Carmilla' (1871–2). The female vampire, her dangerous sex appeal literalised in her pleasurable but deadly bite, has persisted in films such as *The Hunger* (1983) and *From Dusk Till Dawn* (1996), and (with a twist) in a story we include here, Angela Carter's 'The Lady of the House of Love' (1975).

In this collection, we take the view that vampires need not be exclu-sively supernatural beings who sleep in coffins, and that their longevity is precisely a consequence of the fact that they have remained protean figures. Some vampires can be very real, and just as dangerous (in Mary Elizabeth Braddon's 'Good Lady Ducayne' (1869) and in Waif Wander's 'The White Maniac' (1867)), while others appear to operate psychically, draining the energy of their victims (in Mary E. Wilkins Freeman's 'Luella Miller' (1903)). Some show very peculiar characteristics, like the ability to be revived by moonlight (in 'The Vampyre') or the incapacity to rest until buried in unhallowed ground (in E. F. Benson's 'The Room in the Tower' (1912)). While zombies have broadly continued to embrace their potential as abject 'Others', vampires have remained close, and sometimes vulnerable, human proxies. Vampires can now elicit sympathy (in John Ajvide Lindqvist's 'Let the Old Dreams Die' (2011), which continues the story of *Let the Right One In*), suffer confusion about their new condition (in P. Schuyler Miller's 'Over the River' (1941)) and even feel the moral need to defend their undead kin on trial (in Suzy McKee Charnas and Chelsea Quinn Yarbro's 'Advocates' (1991)). The screen success of vampire films has given rise to the notion that, a few key novels and novellas aside, vampires are primarily a visual invention. The reality is that there has been a constant stream of short fiction since the publication of 'The Vampyre' that we believe is just as valuable and interesting.

This collection presents stories that have traditionally remained the province of researchers and horror enthusiasts, some tucked away in specialist anthologies or long gone without a reprint. In our selection, we were keen to emphasise the vampire's mutability, as well as its capacity to inhabit different genres and tones. We also wanted to bring attention to little gems that may have flown under the radar. *Visions of the Vampire* is thus intended as an introduction to the literary vampire for the general aficionado and an invitation to enjoy the many permutations of this monster across two centuries. We certainly hope you will take as much pleasure in reading them as we did in putting them together. As a certain Transylvanian gentleman once put it, we 'bid you welcome. Enter freely of your own will, and leave some of the happiness you bring.'

SORCHA NÍ FHLAINN AND XAVIER ALDANA REYES

SORCHA NÍ FHLAINN is Senior Lecturer in Film Studies and American Studies, and a founding member of the Manchester Centre for Gothic Studies at Manchester Metropolitan University. She is the author of *Postmodern Vampires: Film, Fiction and Popular Culture* (2019), and specialises in monster studies, subjectivity and cultural history.

XAVIER ALDANA REYES is Reader in English Literature and Film at Manchester Metropolitan University and a founding member of the Manchester Centre for Gothic Studies. He has edited *Horror: A Literary History* for the British Library, along with collections of stories by Algernon Blackwood, William Hope Hodgson, Sheridan Le Fanu and H. P. Lovecraft.

ACKNOWLEDGEMENTS

The editors would like to thank the British Library's archival team for the sourcing and typesetting of the stories collected in this anthology. We are particularly grateful to Jonny Davidson for his enthusiasm for this project and for his assistance throughout the entire process. Thanks are also due to the fantastic design pairing of Mauricio Villamayor and Sandra Gómez, who developed the arresting cover for this book.

Our friend Ramsey Campbell, who is a true walking encyclopaedia of the horror genre as well as one of its most consummate writers, deserves a special mention for introducing us to P. Schuyler Miller's 'Over the River'. The story's appearance in this collection will hopefully go some way towards addressing its undue neglect.

Finally, we would like to thank our respective partners for their enduring support and love. If 'the blood is the life', then they are our main arteries. We would struggle to continue without them.

The editors would like to dedicate this anthology to the memory of the great scholar Nina Auerbach, whose research taught us so much about vampires and, as she would have it, about ourselves.

'To the jaded eye, all vampires seem alike, but they are wonderful in their versatility.'

THE VAMPYRE

John William Polidori

I T happened that in the midst of the dissipations attendant upon a London winter, there appeared at the various parties of the leaders of the *ton* a nobleman, more remarkable for his singularities, than his rank. He gazed upon the mirth around him, as if he could not participate therein. Apparently, the light laughter of the fair only attracted his attention, that he might by a look quell it, and throw fear into those breasts where thoughtlessness reigned. Those who felt this sensation of awe, could not explain whence it arose: some attributed it to the dead grey eye, which, fixing upon the object's face, did not seem to penetrate, and at one glance to pierce through to the inward workings of the heart; but fell upon the cheek with a leaden ray that weighed upon the skin it could not pass. His peculiarities caused him to be invited to every house; all wished to see him, and those who had been accustomed to violent excitement, and now felt the weight of *ennui*, were pleased at having something in their presence capable of engaging their attention. In spite of the deadly hue of his face, which never gained a warmer tint, either from the blush of modesty, or from the strong emotion of passion, though its form and outline were beautiful, many of the female hunters after notoriety attempted to win his attentions, and gain, at least, some marks of what they might term affection: Lady Mercer, who had been the mockery of every monster shewn in drawing-rooms since her marriage, threw herself in his way, and did all but put on the dress of a mountebank, to attract his notice—though in vain; when she stood before him, though his eyes were apparently fixed upon hers, still it seemed as if they were unperceived; even her unappalled impudence was baffled, and she left the field. But though the common adulteress could not influence even the guidance of his eyes, it was not that the female sex was indifferent to him: yet such was the apparent caution with which he spoke to the virtuous wife and innocent daughter, that few knew he ever addressed himself to females. He had, however, the reputation of a winning tongue; and whether it was that it even overcame the dread of his singular character, or that they were moved by his apparent hatred of vice, he was as often among those females who form the boast of their sex from their domestic virtues, as among those who sully it by their vices.

About the same time, there came to London a young gentleman of the name of Aubrey: he was an orphan left with an only sister in the posses-sion of great wealth, by parents who died while he was yet in childhood. Left also to himself by guardians, who thought it their duty merely to take care of his fortune, while they relinquished the more important charge of his mind to the care of mercenary subalterns, he cultivated more his imag-ination than his judgment. He had, hence, that high romantic feeling of honour and candour, which daily ruins so many milliners' apprentices. He believed all to sympathise with virtue, and thought that vice was thrown in by Providence merely for the picturesque effect of the scene, as we see in romances: he thought that the misery of a cottage merely consisted in the vesting of clothes, which were as warm, but which were better adapted to the painter's eye by their irregular folds and various coloured patches. He thought, in fine, that the dreams of poets were the realities of life. He was handsome, frank, and rich: for these reasons, upon his entering into the gay circles, many mothers surround him, striving which should describe with least truth their languishing or romping favourites: the daughters at the same time, by their brightening countenances when he approached, and by their sparkling eyes, when he opened his lips, soon led him into false notions of his talents and his merit. Attached as he was to the romance of his solitary hours, he was startled at finding, that, except in the tallow and wax candles that flickered, not from the presence of a ghost, but from want of snuffing, there was no foundation in real life for any of that congeries of pleasing pictures and descriptions contained in those volumes, from which he had formed his study. Finding, however, some compensation in his gratified vanity, he was about to relinquish his dreams, when the extraordinary being we have above described, crossed him in his career.

He watched him; and the very impossibility of forming an idea of the character of a man entirely absorbed in himself, who gave few other signs of his observation of external objects, than the tacit assent to their existence, implied by the avoidance of their contact: allowing his imagination to picture every thing that flattered its propensity to extravagant ideas, he soon formed this object into the hero of a romance, and determined to observe the off-spring of his fancy, rather than the person before him. He became acquainted with him, paid him attentions, and so far advanced upon his notice, that his presence was always recognised. He gradually learnt that Lord Ruthven's affairs were embarrassed, and soon found, from the notes of preparation in —— Street, that he was about to travel. Desirous of gaining some informa-tion respecting this singular character, who, till now, had only whetted his curiosity, he hinted to his guardians, that it was time for him to perform the tour, which for many generations has been thought necessary to enable the young to take some rapid steps in the career of vice towards putting them-selves upon an equality with the aged, and not allowing them to appear as if fallen from the skies, wherever scandalous intrigues are mentioned as the subjects of pleasantry or of praise, according to the degree of skill shewn in carrying them on. They consented: and Aubrey immediately mentioning his intentions to Lord Ruthven, was surprised to receive from him a proposal to join him. Flattered by such a mark of esteem from him, who, apparently, had nothing in common with other men, he gladly accepted it, and in a few days they had passed the circling waters.

Hitherto, Aubrey had had no opportunity of studying Lord Ruthven's character, and now he found, that, though many more of his actions were exposed to his view, the results offered different conclusions from the apparent motives to his conduct. His companion was profuse in his liberality; the idle, the vagabond, and the beggar, received from his hand more than enough to relieve their immediate wants. But Aubrey could not avoid remarking, that it was not upon the virtuous, reduced to indigence by the misfortunes attendant even upon virtue, that he bestowed his alms; these were sent from the door with hardly suppressed sneers; but when the profligate came to ask something, not to relieve his wants, but to allow him to wallow in his lust, or to sink him still deeper in his iniquity, he was sent away with rich charity. This was, however, attributed by him to the greater importunity of the vicious, which generally prevails over the retiring bashfulness of the virtuous indigent. There was one circumstance about the charity of his Lordship, which was still more impressed upon his mind: all those upon whom it was bestowed, inevitably found that there was a curse upon it, for they were all either led to the scaffold, or sunk to the lowest and the most abject misery. At Brussels and other towns through which they passed, Aubrey was surprised at the apparent eagerness with which his companion sought for the centres of all fashionable vice; there he entered into all the spirit of the faro table: he betted, and always gambled with success, except where the known sharper was his antagonist, and then he lost even more than he gained; but it was always with the same unchanging face, with which he generally watched the society around: it was not, however, so when he encountered the rash youthful novice, or the luckless father of a numerous family; then his very wish seemed fortune's law—this apparent abstractedness of mind was laid aside, and his eyes sparkled with more fire than that of the cat whilst dallying with the half-dead mouse. In every town, he left the formerly affluent youth, torn from the circle he adorned, cursing, in the solitude of a dungeon, the fate that had drawn him within the reach of this fiend; whilst many a father sat frantic, amidst the speaking looks of mute hungry children, without a single farthing of his late immense wealth, wherewith to buy even sufficient to satisfy their present craving. Yet he took no money from the gambling table; but immediately lost, to the ruiner of many, the last gilder he had just snatched from the convulsive grasp of the innocent: this might but be the result of a certain degree of knowledge, which was not, however, capable of combating the cunning of the more experienced. Aubrey often wished to represent this to his friend, and beg him to resign that charity and pleasure which proved the ruin of all, and did not tend to his own profit; but he delayed it—for each day he hoped his friend would give him some opportunity of speaking frankly and openly to him; however, this never occurred. Lord Ruthven in his carriage, and amidst the various wild and rich scenes of nature, was always the same: his eye spoke less than his lip; and though Aubrey was near the object of his curiosity, he obtained no greater gratification from it than the constant excitement of vainly wishing to break that mystery, which to his exalted imagination began to assume the appearance of something supernatural.

They soon arrived at Rome, and Aubrey for a time lost sight of his companion; he left him in daily attendance upon the morning circle of an Italian countess, whilst he went in search of the memorials of another almost deserted city. Whilst he was thus engaged, letters arrived from England, which he opened with eager impatience; the first was from his sister, breathing nothing but affection; the others were from his guardians, the latter astonished him; if it had before entered into his imagination that there was an evil power resident in his companion, these seemed to give him almost sufficient reason for the belief. His guardians insisted upon his immediately leaving his friend, and urged, that his character was dreadfully vicious, for that the possession of irresistible powers of seduction, rendered his licentious habits more dangerous to society. It had been discovered, that his contempt for the adulteress had not originated in hatred of her character; but that he had required, to enhance his gratification, that his victim, the partner of his guilt, should be hurled from the pinnacle of unsullied virtue, down to the lowest abyss of infamy and degradation: in fine, that all those females whom he had sought, apparently on account of their virtue, had, since his departure, thrown even the mask aside, and had not scrupled to expose the whole deformity of their vices to the public gaze.

Aubrey determined upon leaving one, whose character had not yet shown a single bright point on which to rest the eye. He resolved to invent some plausible pretext for abandoning him altogether, purposing, in the mean while, to watch him more closely, and to let no slight circumstances pass by unnoticed. He entered into the same circle, and soon perceived, that his Lordship was endeavouring to work upon the inexperience of the daughter of the lady whose house he chiefly frequented. In Italy, it is seldom that an unmarried female is met with in society; he was therefore obliged to carry on his plans in secret; but Aubrey's eye followed him in all his windings, and soon discovered that an assignation had been appointed, which would most likely end in the ruin of an innocent, though thoughtless girl. Losing no time, he entered the apartment of Lord Ruthven, and abruptly asked him his intentions with respect to the lady, informing him at the same time that he was aware of his being about to meet her that very night. Lord Ruthven answered that his intentions were such as he supposed all would have upon such an occasion; and upon being pressed whether he intended to marry her, merely laughed. Aubrey retired; and, immediately writing a note to say, that from that moment he must decline accompanying his Lordship in the remainder of their proposed tour, he ordered his servant to seek other apartments, and calling upon the mother of the lady, informed her of all he knew, not only with regard to her daughter, but also concerning the character of his Lordship. The assignation was prevented. Lord Ruthven next day merely sent his servant to notify his complete assent to a separation; but did not hint any suspicion of his plans having been foiled by Aubrey's interposition.

Having left Rome, Aubrey directed his steps towards Greece, and crossing the Peninsula, soon found himself at Athens. He then fixed his residence in the house of a Greek; and soon occupied himself in tracing the faded records of ancient glory upon monuments that apparently, ashamed of chronicling the deeds of freemen only before slaves, had hidden themselves beneath the sheltering soil or many coloured lichen. Under the same roof as himself, existed a being, so beautiful and delicate, that she might have formed the model for a painter, wishing to portray on canvass the promised hope of the faithful in Mahomet's paradise, save that her eyes spoke too much mind for any one to think she could belong to those who had no souls. As she danced upon the plain, or tripped along the mountain's side, one would have thought the gazelle a poor type of her beauties; for who would have exchanged her eye, apparently the eye of animated nature, for that sleepy luxurious look of the animal suited but to the taste of an epicure. The light step of Ianthe often accompanied Aubrey in his search after antiquities, and often would the unconscious girl, engaged in the pursuit of a Kashmere butterfly, show the whole beauty of her form, floating as it were upon the wind, to the eager gaze of him, who forgot the letters he had just deciphered upon an almost effaced tablet, in the contemplation of her sylph-like figure. Often would her tresses falling, as she flitted around, exhibit in the sun's ray such delicately brilliant and swiftly fading hues, as might well excuse the forgetfulness of the antiquary, who let escape from his mind the very object he had before thought of vital importance to the proper interpretation of a passage in Pausanias. But why attempt to describe charms which all feel, but none can appreciate?—It was innocence, youth, and beauty, unaffected by crowded drawing-rooms and stifling balls. Whilst he drew those remains of which he wished to preserve a memorial for his future hours, she would stand by, and watch the magic effects of his pencil, in tracing the scenes of her native place; she would then describe to him the circling dance upon the open plain, would paint to him in all the glowing colours of youthful memory, the marriage pomp she remembered viewing in her infancy; and then, turning to subjects that had evidently made a greater impression upon her mind, would tell him all the supernatural tales of her nurse. Her earnestness and apparent belief of what she narrated, excited the interest even of Aubrey; and often as she told him the tale of the living vampyre, who had passed years amidst his friends, and dearest ties, forced every year, by feeding upon the life of a lovely female to prolong his existence for the ensuing months, his blood would run cold, whilst he attempted to laugh her out of such idle and horrible fantasies; but Ianthe cited to him the names of old men, who had at last detected one living among themselves, after several of their near relatives and children had been found marked with the stamp of the fiend's appetite; and when she found him so incredulous, she begged of him to believe her, for it had been remarked, that those who had dared to question their existence, always had some proof given, which obliged them, with grief and heartbreaking, to confess it was true. She detailed to him the traditional appearance of these monsters, and his horror was increased, by hearing a pretty accurate description of Lord Ruthven; he, however, still persisted in persuading her, that there could be no truth in her fears, though at the same time he wondered at the many coincidences which had all tended to excite a belief in the supernatural power of Lord Ruthven.

Aubrey began to attach himself more and more to Ianthe; her innocence, so contrasted with all the affected virtues of the women among whom he had sought for his vision of romance, won his heart; and while he ridiculed the idea of a young man of English habits, marrying an uneducated Greek girl, still he found himself more and more attached to the almost fairy form before him. He would tear himself at times from her, and, forming a plan for some antiquarian research, he would depart, determined not to return until his object was attained; but he always found it impossible to fix his attention upon the ruins around him, whilst in his mind he retained an image that seemed alone the rightful possessor of his thoughts. Ianthe was unconscious of his love, and was ever the same frank infantile being he had first known. She always seemed to part from him with reluctance; but it was because she had no longer any one with whom she could visit her favourite haunts, whilst her guardian was occupied in sketching or uncovering some fragment which had yet escaped the destructive hand of time. She had appealed to her parents on the subject of Vampyres, and they both, with several present, affirmed their existence, pale with horror at the very name.

8

Soon after, Aubrey determined to proceed upon one of his excursions, which was to detain him for a few hours; when they heard the name of the place, they all at once begged of him not to return at night, as he must necessarily pass through a wood, where no Greek would ever remain, after the day had closed, upon any consideration. They described it as the resort of the vampyres in their nocturnal orgies, and denounced the most heavy evils as impending upon him who dared to cross their path. Aubrey made light of their representations, and tried to laugh them out of the idea; but when he saw them shudder at his daring thus to mock a superior, infernal power, the very name of which apparently made their blood freeze, he was silent.

Next morning Aubrey set off upon his excursion unattended; he was surprised to observe the melancholy face of his host, and was concerned to find that his words, mocking the belief of those horrible fiends, had inspired them with such terror. When he was about to depart, Ianthe came to the side of his horse, and earnestly begged of him to return, ere night allowed the power of these beings to be put in action; he promised. He was, however, so occupied in his research, that he did not perceive that daylight would soon end, and that in the horizon there was one of those specks which, in the warmer climates, so rapidly gather into a tremendous mass, and pour all their rage upon the devoted country. He at last, however, mounted his horse, determined to make up by speed for his delay: but it was too late. Twilight, in these southern climates, is almost unknown; immediately the sun sets, night begins: and ere he had advanced far, the power of the storm was above—its echoing thunders had scarcely an interval of rest; its thick heavy rain forced its way through the canopying foliage, whilst the blue forked lightning seemed to fall and radiate at his very feet. Suddenly his horse took fright, and he was carried with dreadful rapidity through the entangled forest. The animal at last, through fatigue, stopped, and he found, by the glare of lightning, that he was in the neighbourhood of a hovel that hardly lifted itself up from the masses of dead leaves and brushwood which surrounded it. Dismounting, he approached, hoping to find some one to guide him to the town, or at least trusting to obtain shelter from the pelting of the storm. As he approached, the thunders, for a moment silent, allowed him to hear the dreadful shrieks of a woman mingling with the stifled, exultant mockery of a laugh, continued in one almost unbroken sound; he was startled: but, roused by the thunder which again rolled over his head, he, with a sudden effort, forced open the door of the hut. He found himself in utter darkness: the sound, however, guided him. He was apparently unperceived; for, though he called, still the sounds continued, and no notice was taken of him. He found himself in contact with some one, whom he immediately seized; when a voice cried, "Again baffled!" to which a loud laugh succeeded; and he felt himself grappled by one whose strength seemed superhuman: determined to sell his life as dearly as he could, he struggled; but it was in vain: he was lifted from his feet and hurled with enormous force against the ground—his enemy threw himself upon him, and kneeling upon his breast, had placed his hands upon his throat—when the glare of many torches penetrating through the hole that gave light in the day, disturbed him; he instantly rose, and, leaving his prey, rushed through the door, and in a moment the crashing of the branches, as he broke through the wood, was no longer heard. The storm was now still; and Aubrey, incapable of moving, was soon heard by those without. They entered; the light of their torches fell upon the mud walls, and the thatch loaded on every individual straw with heavy flakes of soot. At the desire of Aubrey they searched for her who had attracted him by her cries; he was again left in darkness; but what was his horror, when the light of the torches once more burst upon him, to perceive the airy form of his fair conductress brought in a lifeless corpse. He shut his eyes, hoping that it was but a vision arising from his disturbed imagination; but he again saw the same form, when he unclosed them, stretched by his side. There was no colour upon her cheek, not even upon her lip; yet there was a stillness about her face that seemed almost as attaching as the life that once dwelt there: upon her neck and breast was blood, and upon her throat were the marks of teeth having opened the vein: to this the men pointed, crying, simultaneously struck with horror, "A Vampyre! a Vampyre!" A litter was quickly formed, and Aubrey was laid by the side of her who had lately been to him the object of so many bright and fairy visions, now fallen with the flower of life that had died within her. He knew not what his thoughts were—his mind was benumbed and seemed to shun reflection, and take refuge in vacancy; he held almost unconsciously in his hand a naked dagger of a particular construction, which had been found in the hut. They were soon met by different parties who had been engaged in the search of her whom a mother had missed. Their lamentable cries, as they approached the city, forewarned the parents of some dreadful catastrophe. To describe their grief would be impossible; but when they ascertained the cause of their child's death, they looked at Aubrey, and pointed to the corpse. They were inconsolable; both died broken-hearted.

Aubrey being put to bed was seized with a most violent fever, and was often delirious; in these intervals he would call upon Lord Ruthven and upon Ianthe—by some unaccountable combination he seemed to beg of his former companion to spare the being he loved. At other times he would imprecate maledictions upon his head, and curse him as her destroyer. Lord Ruthven chanced at this time to arrive at Athens, and, from whatever motive, upon hearing of the state of Aubrey, immediately placed himself in the same house, and became his constant attendant. When the latter recovered from his delirium, he was horrified and startled at the sight of him whose image he had now combined with that of a Vampyre; but Lord Ruthven, by his kind words, implying almost repentance for the fault that had caused their separation, and still more by the attention, anxiety, and care which he showed, soon reconciled him to his presence. His Lordship seemed quite changed; he no longer appeared that apathetic being who had so astonished Aubrey; but as soon as his convalescence began to be rapid, he again gradually retired into the same state of mind, and Aubrey perceived no difference from the former man, except that at times he was surprised to meet his gaze fixed intently upon him, with a smile of malicious exultation playing upon his lips: he knew not why, but this smile haunted him. During the last stage of the invalid's recovery, Lord Ruthven was apparently engaged in watching the tideless waves raised by the cooling breeze, or in marking the progress of those orbs, circling, like our world, the moveless sun; indeed, he appeared to wish to avoid the eyes of all.

Aubrey's mind, by this shock, was much weakened, and that elasticity of spirit which had once so distinguished him now seemed to have fled for ever. He was now as much a lover of solitude and silence as Lord Ruthven; but much as he wished for solitude, his mind could not find it in the neighbourhood of Athens; if he sought it amidst the ruins he had formerly frequented, Ianthe's form stood by his side; if he sought it in the woods, her light step would appear wandering amidst the underwood, in quest of the modest violet; then suddenly turning round, would show, to his wild imagination, her pale face and wounded throat, with a meek smile upon her lips. He determined to fly scenes, every feature of which created such bitter associations in his mind. He proposed to Lord Ruthven, to whom he held himself bound by the tender care he had taken of him during his illness, that they should visit those parts of Greece neither had yet seen. They travelled in every direction, and sought every spot to which a recollection could be attached: but though they thus hastened from place to place, yet they seemed not to heed what they gazed upon. They heard much of robbers, but they gradually began to slight these reports, which they imagined were only the invention of individuals, whose interest it was to excite the generosity of those whom they defended from pretended dangers. In consequence of thus neglecting the advice of the inhabitants, on one occasion they travelled with only a few guards, more to serve as guides than as a defence. Upon entering, however, a narrow defile, at the bottom of which was the bed of a torrent, with large masses of rock brought down from the neighbouring precipices, they had reason to repent their negligence; for scarcely were the whole of the party engaged in the narrow pass, when they were startled by the whistling of bullets close to their heads, and by the echoed report of several guns. In an instant their guards had left them, and, placing themselves behind rocks, had begun to fire in the direction whence the report came. Lord Ruthven and Aubrey, imitating their example, retired for a moment behind the sheltering turn of the defile: but ashamed of being thus detained by a foe, who with insulting shouts bade them advance, and being exposed to unresisting slaughter, if any of the robbers should climb above and take them in the rear, they determined at once to rush forward in search of the enemy. Hardly had they lost the shelter of the rock, when Lord Ruthven received a shot in the shoulder, which brought him to the ground. Aubrey hastened to his assistance; and, no longer heeding the contest or his own peril, was soon surprised by seeing the robbers' faces around him—his guards having, upon Lord Ruthven's being wounded, immediately thrown up their arms and surrendered.

By promises of great reward, Aubrey soon induced them to convey his wounded friend to a neighbouring cabin; and having agreed upon a ransom, he was no more disturbed by their presence—they being content merely to guard the entrance till their comrade should return with the promised sum, for which he had an order. Lord Ruthven's strength rapidly decreased; in two days mortification ensued, and death seemed advancing with hasty steps. His conduct and appearance had not changed; he seemed as unconscious of pain as he had been of the objects about him: but towards the close of the last evening, his mind became apparently uneasy, and his eye often fixed upon Aubrey, who was induced to offer his assistance with more than usual earnestness—"Assist me! you may save me—you may do more than that—I mean not my life, I heed the death of my existence as little as that of the passing day; but you may save my honour, your friend's honour."—"How? Tell me how? I would do any thing," replied Aubrey.—"I need but little—my life ebbs apace—I cannot explain the whole—but if you would conceal all you know of me, my honour were free from stain in the world's mouth—and if my death were unknown for some time in England—I—I—but life."—"It shall not be known."—"Swear!" cried the dying man, raising himself with exultant violence, "Swear by all your soul reveres, by all your nature fears, swear that for a year and a day you will not impart your knowledge of my crimes or death to any living being in any way, whatever may happen, or whatever you may see." His eyes seemed bursting from their sockets: "I swear!" said Aubrey; he sunk laughing upon his pillow, and breathed no more.

Aubrey retired to rest, but did not sleep; the many circumstances attending his acquaintance with this man rose upon his mind, and he knew not why; when he remembered his oath a cold shivering came over him, as if from the presentiment of something horrible awaiting him. Rising early in the morning, he was about to enter the hovel in which he had left the corpse, when a robber met him, and informed him that it was no longer there, having been conveyed by himself and comrades, upon his retiring, to the pinnacle of a neighbouring mount, according to a promise they had given his Lordship, that it should be exposed to the first cold ray of the moon that rose after his death. Aubrey was astonished, and taking several of the men, determined to go and bury it upon the spot where it lay. But, when he had mounted to the summit he found no trace of either the corpse or the clothes, though the robbers swore they pointed out the identical rock on which they had laid the body. For a time his mind was bewildered in conjectures, but he at last returned, convinced that they had buried the corpse for the sake of the clothes.

Weary of a country in which he had met with such terrible misfortunes, and in which all apparently conspired to heighten that superstitious melancholy that had seized upon his mind, he resolved to leave it, and soon arrived at Smyrna. While waiting for a vessel to convey him to Otranto, or to Naples, he occupied himself in arranging those effects he had with him belonging to Lord Ruthven. Amongst other things there was a case containing several weapons of offence, more or less adapted to ensure the death of the victim. There were several daggers and yagatans. Whilst turning them over, and examining their curious forms, what was his surprise at finding a sheath apparently ornamented in the same style as the dagger discovered in the fatal hut; he shuddered; hastening to gain further proof, he found the weapon, and his horror may be imagined when he discovered that it fitted, though peculiarly shaped, the sheath he held in his hand. His eyes seemed to need no further certainty—they seemed gazing to be bound to the dagger; yet still he wished to disbelieve; but the particular form, the same varying tints upon the haft and sheath were alike in splendour on both, and left no room for doubt; there were also drops of blood on each.

He left Smyrna, and on his way home, at Rome, his first inquiries were concerning the lady he had attempted to snatch from Lord Ruthven's seductive arts. Her parents were in distress, their fortune ruined, and she had not been heard of since the departure of his Lordship. Aubrey's mind became almost broken under so many repeated horrors; he was afraid that this lady had fallen a victim to the destroyer of Ianthe. He became morose and silent; and his only occupation consisted in urging the speed of the postilions, as if he were going to save the life of some one he held dear. He arrived at Calais; a breeze, which seemed obedient to his will, soon wafted him to the English shores; and he hastened to the mansion of his fathers, and there, for a moment, appeared to lose, in the embraces and caresses of his sister, all memory of the past. If she before, by her infantine caresses, had gained his affection, now that the woman began to appear, she was still more attaching as a companion.

Miss Aubrey had not that winning grace which gains the gaze and applause of the drawing-room assemblies. There was none of that light brilliancy which only exists in the heated atmosphere of a crowded apartment. Her blue eye was never lit up by the levity of the mind beneath. There was a melancholy charm about it which did not seem to arise from misfortune, but from some feeling within, that appeared to indicate a soul conscious of a brighter realm. Her step was not that light footing, which strays where'ere a butterfly or a colour may attract—it was sedate and pensive. When alone, her face was never brightened by the smile of joy; but when her brother breathed to her his affection, and would in her presence forget those griefs she knew destroyed his rest, who would have exchanged her smile for that of the voluptuary? It seemed as if those eyes, that face were then playing in the light of their own native sphere. She was yet only eighteen, and had not been presented to the world, it having been thought by her guardians more fit that her presentation should be delayed until her brother's return from the continent, when he might be her protector. It was now, therefore, resolved that the next drawing-room, which was fast approaching, should be the epoch of her entry into the "busy scene." Aubrey would rather have remained in the mansion of his fathers, and fed upon the melancholy which overpowered him. He could not feel interest about the frivolities of fashionable strangers, when his mind had been so torn by the events he had witnessed; but he determined to sacrifice his own comfort to the protection of his sister. They soon arrived in town, and prepared for the next day, which had been announced as a drawing-room.

The crowd was excessive—a drawing-room had not been held for a long time, and all who were anxious to bask in the smile of royalty, hastened thither. Aubrey was there with his sister. While he was standing in a corner by himself, heedless of all around him, engaged in the remembrance that the first time he had seen Lord Ruthven was in that very place—he felt himself suddenly seized by the arm, and a voice he recognised too well, sounded in his ear—"Remember your oath." He had hardly courage to turn, fearful of seeing a spectre that would blast him, when he perceived, at a little distance, the same figure which had attracted his notice on this spot upon his first entry into society. He gazed till his limbs almost refusing to bear their weight, he was obliged to take the arm of a friend, and forcing a passage through the crowd, he threw himself into his carriage, and was driven home. He paced the room with hurried steps, and fixed his hands upon his head, as if he were afraid his thoughts were bursting from his brain. Lord Ruthven again before him—circumstances started up in dreadful array—the dagger—his oath.—He roused himself, he could not believe it possible—the dead rise again!—He thought his imagination had conjured up the image his mind was resting upon. It was impossible that it could be real—he determined, therefore, to go again into society; for though he attempted to ask concerning Lord Ruthven, the name hung upon his lips, and he could not succeed in gaining information. He went a few nights after with his sister to the assembly of a near relation. Leaving her under the protection of a matron, he retired into a recess, and there gave himself up to his own devouring thoughts. Perceiving, at last, that many were leaving, he roused himself, and entering another room, found his sister surrounded by several, apparently in earnest conversation; he attempted to pass and get near her, when one, whom he requested to move, turned round, and revealed to him those features he most abhorred. He sprang forward, seized his sister's arm, and, with hurried step, forced her towards the street: at the door he found himself impeded by the crowd of servants who were waiting for their lords; and while he was engaged in passing them, he again heard that voice whisper close to him—"Remember your oath!"—He did not dare to turn, but, hurrying his sister, soon reached home.

Aubrey became almost distracted. If before his mind had been absorbed by one subject, how much more completely was it engrossed, now that the certainty of the monster's living again pressed up his thoughts. His sister's attentions were now unheeded, and it was in vain that she entreated him to explain to her what had caused his abrupt conduct. He only uttered a few words, and those terrified her. The more he thought, the more he was bewildered. His oath startled him;—was he then to allow this monster to roam, bearing ruin upon his breath, amidst all he held dear, and not avert its progress? His very sister might have been touched by him. But even if he were to break his oath, and disclose his suspicions, who would believe him? He thought of employing his own hand to free the world from such a wretch; but death, he remembered, had been already mocked. For days he remained in this state; shut up in his room, he saw no one, and ate only when his sister came, who, with eyes streaming with tears, besought him, for her sake, to support nature. At last, no longer capable of bearing stillness and solitude, he left his house, roamed from street to street, anxious to fly that image which haunted him. His dress became neglected, and he wandered, as often exposed to the noon-day sun as to the midnight damps. He was no longer to be recognised; at first he returned with the evening to the house; but at last he laid him down to rest wherever fatigue overtook him. His sister, anxious for his safety, employed people to follow him; but they were soon distanced by him who fled from a pursuer swifter than any—from thought. His conduct, however, suddenly changed. Struck with the idea that he left by his absence the whole of his friends, with a fiend amongst them, of whose presence they were unconscious, he determined to enter again into society, and watch him closely, anxious to forewarn, in spite of his oath, all whom Lord Ruthven approached with intimacy. But when he entered into a room, his haggard and suspicious looks were so striking, his inward shudderings so visible, that his sister was at last obliged to beg of him to abstain from seeking, for her sake, a society which affected him so strongly. When, however, remonstrance proved unavailing, the guardians thought proper to interpose, and, fearing that his mind was becoming alienated, they thought it high time to resume again that trust which had been before imposed upon them by Aubrey's parents.

Desirous of saving him from the injuries and sufferings he had daily encountered in his wanderings, and of preventing him from exposing to the general eye those marks of what they considered folly, they engaged a physician to reside in the house, and take constant care of him. He hardly appeared to notice it, so completely was his mind absorbed by one terrible subject. His incoherence became at last so great, that he was confined to his chamber. There he would often lie for days, incapable of being roused. He had become emaciated, his eyes had attained a glassy lustre;—the only sign of affection and recollection remaining displayed itself upon the entry of his sister; then he would sometimes start, and seizing her hands, with looks that severely afflicted her, he would desire her not to touch him. "Oh, do not touch him—if your love for me is aught, do not go near him!" When, however, she inquired to whom he referred, his only answer was "True! true!" and again he sank into a state, whence not even she could rouse him. This lasted many months: gradually, however, as the year was passing, his incoherences became less frequent, and his mind threw off a portion of its gloom, whilst his guardians observed, that several times in the day he would count upon his fingers a definite number, and then smile.

The time had nearly elapsed, when, upon the last day of the year, one of his guardians entering his room, began to converse with his physician upon the melancholy circumstance of Aubrey's being in so awful a situation, when his sister was going next day to be married. Instantly Aubrey's attention was attracted; he asked anxiously to whom. Glad of this mark of returning intellect, of which they feared he had been deprived, they mentioned the name of the Earl of Marsden. Thinking this was a young Earl whom he had met with in society, Aubrey seemed pleased, and astonished them still more by his expressing his intention to be present at the nuptials, and desiring to see his sister. They answered not, but in a few minutes his sister was with him. He was apparently again capable of being affected by the influence of her lovely smile; for he pressed her to his breast, and kissed her cheek, wet with tears, flowing at the thought of her brother's being once more alive to the feelings of affection. He began to speak with all his wonted warmth, and to congratulate her upon her marriage with a person so distinguished for rank and every accomplishment; when he suddenly perceived a locket upon her breast; opening it, what was his surprise at beholding the features of the monster who had so long influenced his life. He seized the portrait in a paroxysm of rage, and trampled it under foot. Upon her asking him why he thus destroyed the resemblance of her future husband, he looked as if he did not understand her;—then seizing her hands, and gazing on her with a frantic expression of countenance, he bade her swear that she would never wed this monster, for he—But he could not advance—it seemed as if that voice again bade him remember his oath—he turned suddenly round, thinking

Lord Ruthven was near him but saw no one. In the meantime the guardians and physician, who had heard the whole, and thought this was but a return of his disorder, entered, and forcing him from Miss Aubrey, desired her to leave him. He fell upon his knees to them, he implored, he begged of them to delay but for one day. They, attributing this to the insanity they imagined had taken possession of his mind, endeavoured to pacify him, and retired.

Lord Ruthven had called the morning after the drawing-room, and had been refused with every one else. When he heard of Aubrey's ill health, he readily understood himself to be the cause of it; but when he learned that he was deemed insane, his exultation and pleasure could hardly be concealed from those among whom he had gained this information. He hastened to the house of his former companion, and, by constant attendance, and the pretence of great affection for the brother and interest in his fate, he gradually won the ear of Miss Aubrey. Who could resist his power? His tongue had dangers and toils to recount—could speak of himself as of an individual having no sympathy with any being on the crowded earth, save with her to whom he addressed himself;—could tell how, since he knew her, his existence had begun to seem worthy of preservation, if it were merely that he might listen to her soothing accents;—in fine, he knew so well how to use the serpent's art, or such was the will of fate, that he gained her affections. The title of the elder branch falling at length to him, he obtained an important embassy, which served as an excuse for hastening the marriage (in spite of her brother's deranged state), which was to take place the very day before his departure for the continent.

Aubrey, when he was left by the physician and his guardians, attempted to bribe the servants, but in vain. He asked for pen and paper; it was given him; he wrote a letter to his sister, conjuring her, as she valued her own happiness, her own honour, and the honour of those now in the grave, who once held her in their arms as their hope and the hope of their house, to delay but for a few hours that marriage, on which he denounced the most heavy curses. The servants promised they would deliver it; but giving it to the physician, he thought it better not to harass any more the mind of Miss Aubrey by, what he considered, the ravings of a maniac. Night passed on without rest to the busy inmates of the house; and Aubrey heard, with a horror that may more easily be conceived than described, the notes of busy preparation. Morning came, and the sound of carriages broke upon his ear. Aubrey grew almost frantic. The curiosity of the servants at last overcame their vigilance, they gradually stole away, leaving him in the custody of an helpless old woman. He seized the opportunity, with one bound was out of the room, and in a moment found himself in the apartment where all were nearly assembled. Lord Ruthven was the first to perceive him: he immediately approached, and, taking his arm by force, hurried him from the room, speechless with rage. When on the staircase, Lord Ruthven whispered in his ear—"Remember your oath, and know, if not my bride today, your sister is dishonoured. Women are frail!" So saying, he pushed him towards his attendants, who, roused by the old woman, had come in search of him. Aubrey could no longer support himself; his rage not finding vent, had broken a blood-vessel, and he was conveyed to bed. This was not mentioned to his sister, who was not present when he entered, as the physician was afraid of agitating her. The marriage was solemnised, and the bride and bridegroom left London.

Aubrey's weakness increased; the effusion of blood produced symptoms of the near approach of death. He desired his sister's guardians might be called, and when the midnight hour had struck, he related composedly what the reader has perused—he died immediately after.

The guardians hastened to protect Miss Aubrey; but when they arrived, it was too late. Lord Ruthven had disappeared, and Aubrey's sister had glutted the thirst of a VAMPYRE!

1823

WAKE NOT THE DEAD!

Ernst Raupach

"WILT thou for ever sleep? Wilt thou never more awake, my beloved, but henceforth repose for ever from thy short pilgrimage on earth? O yet once again return! and bring back with thee the vivifying dawn of hope to one whose existence hath, since thy departure, been obscured by the dunnest shades. What! dumb? for ever dumb? Thy friend lamenteth, and thou heedest him not? He sheds bitter, scalding tears, and thou reposest unregarding his affliction? He is in despair, and thou no longer openest thy arms to him as an asylum from his grief? Say then, doth the paly shroud become thee better than the bridal veil? Is the chamber of the grave a warmer bed than the couch of love? Is the spectre death more welcome to thy arms than thy enamoured consort? Oh! return, my beloved, return once again to this anxious disconsolate bosom." Such were the lamentations which Walter poured forth for his Brunhilda, the partner of his youthful passionate love: thus did he bewail over her grave at the midnight hour, what time the spirit that presides in the troublous atmosphere, sends his legions of monsters through mid-air; so that their shadows, as they flit beneath the moon and across the earth, dart as wild, agitating thoughts that chase each other o'er the sinner's bosom: thus did he lament under the tall linden trees by her grave, while his head reclined on the cold stone.

Walter was a powerful lord in Burgundy, who, in his earliest youth, had been smitten with the charms of the fair Brunhilda, a beauty far surpassing in loveliness all her rivals; for her tresses, dark as the raven face of night, streaming over her shoulders, set off to the utmost advantage the beaming lustre of her slender form, and the rich dye of a cheek whose tint was deep and brilliant as that of the western heaven: her eyes did not resemble those burning orbs whose pale glow gems the vault of night, and whose immeasurable distance fills the soul with deep thoughts of eternity, but rather as the sober beams which cheer this nether world, and which, while they enlighten, kindle the sons of earth to joy and love. Brunhilda became the wife of Walter, and both being equally enamoured and devoted, they abandoned themselves to the enjoyment of a passion that rendered them reckless of aught besides, while it lulled them in a fascinating dream. Their sole apprehension was lest aught should awaken them from a delirium which they prayed might continue for ever. Yet how vain is the wish that would arrest the decrees of destiny! as well might it seek to divert the circling planets from their eternal course. Short was the duration of this phrenzied passion; not that it gradually decayed and subsided into apathy, but death snatched away his blooming victim, and left Walter to a widowed couch. Impetuous, however, as was his first burst of grief, he was not inconsolable, for ere long another bride became the partner of the youthful nobleman.

Swanhilda also was beautiful; although nature had formed her charms on a very different model from those of Brunhilda. Her golden locks waved bright as the beams of morn: only when excited by some emotion of her soul did a rosy hue tinge the lily paleness of her cheek: her limbs were proportioned in the nicest symmetry, yet did they not possess that luxuriant fullness of animal life: her eye beamed eloquently, but it was with the milder radiance of a star, tranquillising to tenderness rather than exciting to warmth. Thus formed, it was not possible that she should steep him in his former delirium, although she rendered happy his waking hours—tranquil and serious, yet cheerful, studying in all things her husband's pleasure, she restored order and comfort in his family, where her presence shed a general influence all around. Her mild benevolence tended to restrain the fiery, impetuous disposition of Walter: while at the same time her prudence recalled him in some degree

WAKE NOT THE DEAD!

from his vain, turbulent wishes, and his aspirings after unattainable enjoyments, to the duties and pleasures of actual life. Swanhilda bore her husband two children, a son and a daughter; the latter was mild and patient as her mother, well contented with her solitary sports, and even in these recreations displayed the serious turn of her character. The boy possessed his father's fiery, restless disposition, tempered, however, with the solidity of his mother. Attached by his offspring more tenderly towards their mother, Walter now lived for several years very happily: his thoughts would frequently, indeed, recur to Brunhilda, but without their former violence, merely as we dwell upon the memory of a friend of our earlier days, borne from us on the rapid current of time to a region where we know that he is happy.

But clouds dissolve into air, flowers fade, the sands of the hour-glass run imperceptibly away, and even so, do human feelings dissolve, fade, and pass away, and with them too, human happiness. Walter's inconstant breast again sighed for the ecstatic dreams of those days which he had spent with his equally romantic, enamoured Brunhilda—again did she present herself to his ardent fancy in all the glow of her bridal charms, and he began to draw a parallel between the past and the present; nor did imagination, as it is wont, fail to array the former in her brightest hues, while it proportionably obscured the latter; so that he pictured to himself, the one much more rich in enjoyment, and the other, much less so than they really were. This change in her husband did not escape Swanhilda; whereupon, redoubling her attentions towards him, and her cares towards their children, she expected, by this means, to re-unite the knot that was slackened; yet the more she endeavoured to regain his affections, the colder did he grow—the more intolerable did her caresses seem, and the more continually did the image of Brunhilda haunt his thoughts. The children, whose endearments were now become indispensable to him, alone stood between the parents as genii eager to affect a reconciliation; and, beloved by them both, formed a uniting link between them. Yet, as evil can be plucked from the heart of man, only ere its root has yet struck deep, its fangs being afterwards too firm to be eradicated; so was

Walter's diseased fancy too far affected to have its disorder stopped, for, in a short time, it completely tyrannised over him. Frequently of a night, instead of retiring to his consort's chamber, he repaired to Brunhilda's grave, where he murmured forth his discontent, saying: "Wilt thou sleep for ever?"

One night as he was reclining on the turf, indulging in his wonted sorrow, a sorcerer from the neighbouring mountains, entered into this field of death for the purpose of gathering, for his mystic spells, such herbs as grow only from the earth wherein the dead repose, and which, as if the last production of mortality, are gifted with a powerful and supernatural influence. The sorcerer perceived the mourner, and approached the spot where he was lying.

"Wherefore, fond wretch, dost thou grieve thus, for what is now a hideous mass of mortality—mere bones, and nerves, and veins? Nations have fallen unlamented; even worlds themselves, long ere this globe of ours was created, have mouldered into nothing; nor hath any one wept over them; why then should'st thou indulge this vain affliction for a child of the dust—a being as frail as thyself, and like thee the creature but of a moment?"

Walter raised himself up:—"Let yon worlds that shine in the firmament" replied he, "lament for each other as they perish. It is true, that I who am myself clay, lament for my fellow-clay: yet is this clay impregnated with a fire,—with an essence, that none of the elements of creation possess—with love: and this divine passion, I felt for her who now sleepeth beneath this sod."

"Will thy complaints awaken her: or could they do so, would she not soon upbraid thee for having disturbed that repose in which she is now hushed?"

"Avaunt, cold-hearted being: thou knowest not what is love. Oh! that my tears could wash away the earthy covering that conceals her from these eyes; that my groan of anguish could rouse her from her slumber of death! No, she would not again seek her earthy couch."

"Insensate that thou art, and couldst thou endure to gaze without shuddering on one disgorged from the jaws of the grave? Art thou too thyself the same from whom she parted; or hath time passed o'er thy brow and left no traces there? Would not thy love rather be converted into hate and disgust?"

"Say rather that the stars would leave yon firmament, that the sun will henceforth refuse to shed his beams through the heavens. Oh! that she stood once more before me; that once again she reposed on this bosom!—how quickly should we then forget that death or time had ever stepped between us."

"Delusion! mere delusion of the brain, from heated blood, like to that which arises from the fumes of wine. It is not my wish to tempt thee; to restore to thee thy dead; else wouldst thou soon feel that I have spoken truth."

"How! restore her to me," exclaimed Walter casting himself at the sorcerer's feet. "Oh! if thou art indeed able to effect that, grant it to my earnest supplication; if one throb of human feeling vibrates in thy bosom, let my tears prevail with thee: restore to me my beloved; so shalt thou hereafter bless the deed, and see that it was a good work."

"A good work! a blessed deed!"—returned the sorcerer with a smile of scorn; "for me there exists nor good nor evil; since my will is always the same. Ye alone know evil, who will that which ye would not. It is indeed in my power to restore her to thee: yet, bethink thee well, whether it will prove thy weal. Consider too, how deep the abyss between life and death; across this, my power can build a bridge, but it can never fill up the frightful chasm."

Walter would have spoken, and have sought to prevail on this powerful being by fresh entreaties, but the latter prevented him, saying: "Peace! bethink thee well! and return hither to me tomorrow at midnight. Yet once more do I warn thee, 'Wake not the dead.'"

Having uttered these words, the mysterious being disappeared. Intoxicated with fresh hope, Walter found no sleep on his couch; for fancy, prodigal of her richest stores, expanded before him the glittering web of futurity; and his eye, moistened with the dew of rapture, glanced from one vision of happiness to another. During the next day he wandered through the woods, lest wonted objects by recalling the memory of later and less happier times, might disturb the blissful idea, that he should again behold her—again fold her in his arms, gaze on her beaming brow by day, repose on her bosom at night: and, as this sole idea filled his imagination, how was it possible that the least doubt should arise: or that the warning of the mysterious old man should recur to his thoughts.

No sooner did the midnight hour approach, than he hastened before the grave-field where the sorcerer was already standing by that of Brunhilda. "Hast thou maturely considered?" inquired he.

"Oh! restore to me the object of my ardent passion," exclaimed Walter with impetuous eagerness. "Delay not thy generous action, lest I die even this night, consumed with disappointed desire; and behold her face no more."

"Well then," answered the old man, "return hither again tomorrow at the same hour. But once more do I give thee this friendly warning, 'Wake not the dead.'"

All in the despair of impatience, Walter would have prostrated himself at his feet, and supplicated him to fulfil at once a desire now increased to agony; but the sorcerer had already disappeared. Pouring forth his lamentations more wildly and impetuously than ever, he lay upon the grave of his adored one, until the grey dawn streaked the east. During the day, which seemed to him longer than any he had ever experienced, he wandered to and fro, restless and impatient, seemingly without any object, and deeply buried in his own reflections, unquiet as the murderer who meditates his first deed of blood: and the stars of evening found him once more at the appointed spot. At midnight the sorcerer was there also.

"Hast thou yet maturely deliberated?" inquired he, "as on the preceding night?"

"Oh what should I deliberate?" returned Walter impatiently. "I need not to deliberate: what I demand of thee, is that which thou hast promised me—that which will prove my bliss. Or dost thou but mock me? if so, hence from my sight, lest I be tempted to lay my hands on thee."

"Once more do I warn thee," answered the old man with undisturbed composure, 'Wake not the dead'—let her rest."

"Aye, but not in the cold grave: she shall rather rest on this bosom which burns with eagerness to clasp her."

"Reflect, thou mayst not quit her until death, even though aversion and horror should seize thy heart. There would then remain only one horrible means."

"Dotard!" cried Walter, interrupting him, "how may I hate that which I love with such intensity of passion? how should I abhor that for which my every drop of blood is boiling?"

"Then be it even as thou wishest," answered the sorcerer; "step back."

The old man now drew a circle round the grave, all the while muttering words of enchantment. Immediately the storm began to bowl among the tops of the trees; owls flapped their wings, and uttered their low voice of omen; the stars hid their mild, beaming aspect, that they might not behold so unholy and impious a spectacle; the stone then rolled from the grave with a hollow sound, leaving a free passage for the inhabitant of that dreadful tenement. The sorcerer scattered into the yawning earth, roots and herbs of most magic power, and of most penetrating odour, so that the worms crawling forth from the earth congregated together, and raised themselves in a fiery column over the grave: while rushing wind burst from the earth, scattering the mould before it, until at length the coffin lay uncovered. The moonbeams fell on it, and the lid burst open with a tremendous sound. Upon this the sorcerer poured upon it some blood from out of a human skull, exclaiming at the same time: "Drink, sleeper, of this warm stream, that thy heart may again beat within thy bosom." And, after a short pause, shedding on her some other mystic liquid, he cried aloud with the voice of one inspired: "Yes, thy heart beats once more with the flood of life: thine eye is again opened to sight. Arise, therefore, from the tomb."

As an island suddenly springs forth from the dark waves of the ocean, raised upwards from the deep by the force of subterraneous fires, so did Brunhilda start from her earthy couch, borne forward by some invisible power. Taking her by the hand, the sorcerer led her towards Walter, who stood at some little distance, rooted to the ground with amazement.

"Receive again," said he, "the object of thy passionate sighs: mayest thou never more require my aid; should that, however, happen, so wilt thou find me, during the full of the moon, upon the mountains in that spot and where the three roads meet."

Instantly did Walter recognise in the form that stood before him, her whom he so ardently loved; and a sudden glow shot through his frame at finding her thus restored to him: yet the night-frost had chilled his limbs and palsied his tongue. For a while he gazed upon her without either motion or speech, and during his pause, all was again become hushed and serene; and the stars shone brightly in the clear heavens.

"Walter!" exclaimed the figure; and at once the well-known sound, thrilling to his heart, broke the spell by which he was bound.

"Is it reality? Is it truth?" cried he, "or a cheating delusion?"

"No, it is no imposture: I am really living:—conduct me quickly to thy castle in the mountains."

Walter looked around: the old man had disappeared, but he perceived close by his side, a coal-black steed of fiery eye, ready equipped to conduct him thence; and on his back lay all proper attire for Brunhilda, who lost no time in arraying herself. This being done, she cried; "Haste, let us away ere the dawn breaks, for my eye is yet too weak to endure the light of day." Fully recovered from his stupor, Walter leaped into his saddle, and catching up, with a mingled feeling of delight and awe, the beloved being thus mysteriously restored from the power of the grave, he spurred on across the wild, towards the mountains, as furiously as if pursued by the shadows of the dead, hastening to recover from him their sister.

The castle to which Walter conducted his Brunhilda, was situated on a rock between other rocks rising up above it. Here they arrived, unseen by any save one àged domestic, on whom Walter imposed secrecy by the severest threats.

"Here will we tarry," said Brunhilda, "until I can endure the light, and until thou canst look upon me without trembling: as if struck with a cold chill." They accordingly continued to make that place their abode: yet no one knew that Brunhilda existed, save only that aged attendant, who provided their meals. During seven entire days they had no light except that of tapers; during the next seven, the light was admitted through the lofty casements only while the rising or setting-sun faintly illumined the mountain-tops, the valley being still enveloped in shade.

Seldom did Walter quit Brunhilda's side: a nameless spell seemed to attach him to her; even the shudder which he felt in her presence, and which would not permit him to touch her, was not unmixed with pleasure, like that thrilling awful emotion felt when strains of sacred music float under the vault of some temple; he rather sought, therefore, than avoided this feeling. Often too as he had indulged in calling to mind the beauties of Brunhilda, she had never appeared so fair, so fascinating, so admirable when depicted by his imagination, as when now beheld in reality. Never till now had her voice sounded with such tones of sweetness; never before did her language possess such eloquence as it now did, when she conversed with him on the subject of the past. And this was the magic fairy-land towards which her words constantly conducted him. Ever did she dwell upon the days of their first love, those hours of delight which they had participated together when the one derived all enjoyment from the other: and so rapturous, so enchanting, so full of life did she recall to his imagination that blissful season, that he even doubted whether he had ever experienced with her so much felicity, or had been so truly happy. And, while she thus vividly portrayed their hours of past delight, she delineated in still more glowing, more enchanting colours, those hours of approaching bliss which now awaited them, richer in enjoyment than any preceding ones. In this manner did she charm her attentive auditor with enrapturing hopes for the future, and lull him into dreams of more than mortal ecstasy; so that while he listened to her siren strain, he entirely forgot how little blissful was the latter period of their union, when he had often sighed at her imperiousness, and at her harshness both to himself and all his household. Yet even had he recalled this to mind would it have disturbed him in his present delirious trance? Had she not now left behind in the grave all the frailty of mortality? Was not her whole being refined and purified by that long sleep in which neither passion nor sin had approached her even in dreams? How different now was the subject of her discourse! Only when speaking of her affection for him, did she betray anything of earthly feeling: at other times, she uniformly dwelt upon themes relating to the invisible and future world; when in descanting and declaring the mysteries of eternity, a stream of prophetic eloquence would burst from her lips.

In this manner had twice seven days elapsed, and, for the first time, Walter beheld the being now dearer to him than ever, in the full light of day. Every trace of the grave had disappeared from her countenance; a roseate tinge like the ruddy streaks of dawn again beamed on her pallid cheek; the faint, mouldering taint of the grave was changed into a delightful violet scent; the only sign of earth that never disappeared. He no longer felt either apprehension or awe, as he gazed upon her in the sunny light of day: it is not until now, that he seemed to have recovered her completely; and, glowing with all his former passion towards her, he would have pressed her to his bosom, but she gently repulsed him, saying:—"Not yet—spare your caresses until the moon has again filled her horn."

Spite of his impatience, Walter was obliged to await the lapse of another period of seven days: but, on the night when the moon was arrived at the full, he hastened to Brunhilda, whom he found more lovely than she had ever appeared before. Fearing no obstacles to his transports, he embraced her with all the fervour of a deeply enamoured and successful lover. Brunhilda, however, still refused to yield to his passion. "What!" exclaimed she, "is it fitting that I who have been purified by death from the frailty of mortality, should become thy concubine, while a mere daughter of the earth bears the title of thy wife: never shall it be. No, it must be within the walls of thy palace, within that chamber where I once reigned as queen, that thou obtainest the end of thy wishes—and of mine also," added she, imprinting a glowing kiss on the lips, and immediately disappeared.

Heated with passion, and determined to sacrifice everything to the accomplishment of his desires, Walter hastily quitted the apartment, and shortly after the castle itself. He travelled over mountain and across heath, with the rapidity of a storm, so that the turf was flung up by his horse's hoofs; nor once stopped until he arrived home.

Here, however, neither the affectionate caresses of Swanhilda, or those of his children could touch his heart, or induce him to restrain his furious desires. Alas! is the impetuous torrent to be checked in its devastating course by the beauteous flowers over which it rushes, when they exclaim:—"Destroyer, commiserate our helpless innocence and beauty, nor lay us waste?"— the stream sweeps over them unregarding, and a single moment annihilates the pride of a whole summer.

Shortly afterwards, did Walter begin to hint to Swanhilda, that they were ill-suited to each other; that he was anxious to taste that wild, tumultuous life, so well according with the spirit of his sex, while she, on the contrary, was satisfied with the monotonous circle of household enjoyments:—that he was eager for whatever promised novelty, while she felt most attached to what was familiarised to her by habit: and lastly, that her cold disposition, bordering upon indifference, but ill assorted with his ardent temperament: it was therefore more prudent that they should seek apart from each other, that happiness which they could not find together. A sigh, and a brief acquiescence in his wishes was all the reply that Swanhilda made: and, on the following morning, upon his presenting her with a paper of separation, informing her that she was at liberty to return home to her father, she received it most submissively: yet, ere she departed, she gave him the following warning: "Too well do I conjecture to whom I am indebted for this our separation. Often have I seen thee at Brunhilda's grave, and beheld thee there even on that night when the face of the heavens was suddenly enveloped in a veil of clouds. Hast thou rashly dared to tear aside the awful veil that separates the mortality that dreams, from that which dreameth not? Oh! then woe to thee, thou wretched man, for thou hast attached to thyself that which will prove thy destruction." She ceased: nor did Walter attempt any reply, for the similar admonition uttered by the sorcerer flashed upon his mind, all obscured as it was by passion, just as the lightning glares momentarily through the gloom of night without dispersing the obscurity.

Swanhilda then departed, in order to pronounce to her children, a bitter farewell, for they, according to national custom, belonged to the father; and, having bathed them in her tears, and consecrated them with the holy water of maternal love, she quitted her husband's residence, and departed to the home of her father's.

Thus was the kind and benevolent Swanhilda, driven an exile from those halls, where she had presided with such graces—from halls which were now newly decorated to receive another mistress. The day at length arrived, on which Walter, for the second time, conducted Brunhilda home, as a newly made bride. And he caused it to be reported amongst his domestics, that his new consort had gained his affections by her extraordinary likeness to Brunhilda, their former mistress. How ineffably happy did he deem himself, as he conducted his beloved once more into the chamber which had often witnessed their former joys, and which was now newly gilded and adorned in a most costly style: among the other decorations were figures of angels scattering roses, which served to support the purple draperies, whose ample folds o'ershadowed the nuptial couch. With what impatience did he await the hour that was to put him in possession of those beauties, for which he had already paid so high a price, but, whose enjoyment was to cost him most dearly yet! Unfortunate Walter! revelling in bliss, thou beholdest not the abyss that yawns beneath thy feet, intoxicated with the luscious perfume of the flower thou hast plucked, thou little deemest how deadly is the venom with which it is fraught, although, for a short season, its potent fragrance bestows new energy on all thy feelings.

Happy, however, as Walter now was, his household were far from being equally so. The strange resemblance between their new lady and the deceased Brunhilda, filled them with a secret dismay—an undefinable horror; for there was not a single difference of feature, of tone of voice, or of gesture. To add too to these mysterious circumstances, her female attendants discovered a particular mark on her back, exactly like one which Brunhilda had. A report was now soon circulated, that their lady was no other than Brunhilda herself, who had been recalled to life by the power of necromancy. How truly horrible was the idea of living under the same roof with one who had been an inhabitant of the tomb, and of being obliged to attend upon her, and acknowledge her as mistress! There was also in Brunhilda, much to increase this aversion, and favour their superstition: no ornaments of gold ever decked her person; all that others were wont to wear of this metal, she had formed of silver: no richly coloured and sparkling jewels glittered upon her; pearls alone, lent their pale lustre to adorn her bosom. Most carefully did she always avoid the cheerful light of the sun, and was wont to spend the brightest days in the most retired and gloomy apartments: only during the twilight of the commencing, or declining day did she ever walk abroad, but her favourite hour was, when the phantom light of the moon bestowed on all objects a shadowy appearance, and a sombre hue; always too at the crowing of the cock, an involuntary shudder was observed to seize her limbs. Imperious as before her death, she quickly imposed her iron yoke on every one around her, while she seemed even far more terrible than ever, since a dread of some supernatural power attached to her, appalled all who approached her. A malignant withering glance seemed to shoot from her eye on the unhappy object of her wrath, as if it would annihilate its victim. In short, those halls which, in the time of Swanhilda were the residence of cheerfulness and mirth, now resembled an extensive desert tomb. With fear imprinted on their pale countenances, the domestics glided through the apartments of the castle; and, in this abode of terror, the crowing of the cock caused the living to tremble, as if they were the spirits of the departed; for the sound always reminded them of their mysterious mistress. There was no one but who shuddered at meeting her in a lonely place, in the dusk of evening, or by the light of the moon, a circumstance that was deemed to be ominous of some evil: so great was the apprehension of her female attendants, they pined in continual disquietude, and, by degrees, all quitted her. In the course of time even others of the domestics fled, for an insupportable horror had seized them.

The art of the sorcerer had indeed bestowed upon Brunhilda an artificial life, and due nourishment had continued to support the restored body; yet, this body was not able of itself to keep up the genial glow of vitality, and to nourish the flame whence springs all the affections and passions, whether of love or hate; for death had for ever destroyed and withered it: all that Brunhilda now possessed was a chilled existence, colder than that of the snake. It was nevertheless necessary that she should love, and return with equal ardour the warm caresses of her spell-enthralled husband, to whose passion alone she was indebted for her renewed existence. It was necessary that a magic draught should animate the dull current in her veins, and awaken her to the glow of life and the flame of love—a potion of abomination—one not even to be named without a curse—human blood, imbibed whilst yet warm, from the veins of youth. This was the hellish drink for which she thirsted: possessing no sympathy with the purer feelings of humanity; deriving no enjoyment from aught that interests in life, and occupies its varied hours; her existence was a mere blank, unless when in the arms of her paramour husband, and therefore was it that she craved incessantly after the horrible draught. It was even with the utmost effort that she could forbear sucking even the blood of Walter himself, as he reclined beside her. Whenever she beheld some innocent child, whose lovely face denoted the exuberance of infantine health and vigour, she would entice it by soothing words and fond caresses into her most secret apartment, where, lulling it to sleep in her arms, she would suck from its bosom the warm, purple tide of life. Nor were youths of either sex safe from her horrid attack: having first breathed upon her unhappy victim, who never failed immediately to sink into a lengthened sleep, she would then in a similar manner drain his veins of the vital juice. Thus children, youths, and maidens quickly faded away, as flowers gnawn by the cankering worm: the fullness of their limbs disappeared; a sallow line succeeded to the rosy freshness of their cheeks, the liquid lustre of the eye was deadened, even as the sparkling stream when arrested by the touch of frost; and their locks became thin and grey, as if already ravaged by the storm of life. Parents beheld with horror this desolating pestilence, devouring their offspring; nor could simple charm, potion or amulet avail aught against it. The grave swallowed up one after the other; or did the miserable victim survive, he became cadaverous and wrinkled even in the very morn of existence. Parents observed with horror, this devastating pestilence snatch away their offspring—a pestilence which, nor herb however potent, nor charm, nor holy taper, nor exorcism could avert. They either beheld their children sink one after the other into the grave, or their youthful forms, withered by the unholy, vampire embrace of Brunhilda, assume the decrepitude of sudden age.

At length strange surmises and reports began to prevail; it was whispered the Brunhilda herself was the cause of all these horrors; although no one could pretend to tell in what manner she destroyed her victims, since no marks of violence were discernible. Yet when young children confessed that she had frequently lulled them asleep in her arms, and elder ones said that a sudden slumber had come upon them whenever she began to converse with them, suspicion became converted into certainty, and those whose offspring had hitherto escaped unharmed, quitted their hearths and home—all their little possessions—the dwellings of their fathers and the inheritance of their children, in order to rescue from so horrible a fate those who were dearer to their simple affections than aught else the world could give.

Thus daily did the castle assume a more desolate appearance; daily did its environs become more deserted; none but a few aged decrepit old women and grey-headed menials were to be seen remaining of the once numerous retinue. Such will in the latter days of the earth, be the last generation of mortals, when child-bearing shall have ceased, when youth shall no more be seen, nor any arise to replace those who shall await their fate in silence.

Walter alone noticed not, or heeded not, the desolation around him; he apprehended not death, lapped as he was in a glowing elysium of love. Far more happy than formerly did he now seem in the possession of Brunhilda. All those caprices and frowns which had been wont to overcloud their former union had now entirely disappeared. She even seemed to doat on him with a warmth of passion that she had never exhibited even during the happy season of bridal love; for the flame of that youthful blood, of which she drained the veins of others, rioted in her own. At night, as soon as he closed his eyes, she would breathe on him till he sank into delicious dreams, from which he awoke only to experience more rapturous enjoyments. By day she would continually discourse with him on the bliss experienced by happy spirits beyond the grave, assuring him that, as his affection had recalled her from the tomb, they were now irrevocably united. Thus fascinated by a continual spell, it was not possible that he should perceive what was taking place around him. Brunhilda, however, foresaw with savage grief that the source of her youthful ardour was daily decreasing, for, in a short time, there remained nothing gifted with youth, save Walter and his children, and these latter she resolved should be her next victims.

On her first return to the castle, she had felt an aversion towards the off-spring of another, and therefore abandoned them entirely to the attendants appointed by Swanhilda. Now, however, she began to pay considerable atten-tion to them, and caused them to be frequently admitted into her presence. The aged nurses were filled with dread at perceiving these marks of regard from her towards their young charges, yet dared they not to oppose the will of their terrible and imperious mistress. Soon did Brunhilda gain the affec-tion of the children, who were too unsuspecting of guile to apprehend any danger from her; on the contrary, her caresses won them completely to her. Instead of ever checking their mirthful gambols, she would rather instruct them in new sports; often too did she recite to them tales of such strange and wild interest as to exceed all the stories of their nurses. Were they wearied either with play or with listening to her narratives, she would take them on her knees and lull them to slumber. Then did visions of the most surpassing magnificence attend their dreams: they would fancy themselves in some garden where flowers of every hue rose in rows one above the other, from the humble violet to the tall sun-flower, forming a party-coloured broidery of every hue, sloping upwards towards the golden clouds, where little angels, whose wings sparkled with azure and gold, descended to bring them delicious foods, or splendid jewels; or sung to them soothing melodious hymns. So delightful did these dreams in short time become to the children, that they longed for nothing so eagerly as to slumber on Brunhilda's lap, for never did they else enjoy such visions of heavenly forms. Thus were they most anxious for that which was to prove their destruction:—yet do we not all aspire after that which conducts us to the grave—after the enjoyment of life? These innocents stretched out their arms to approaching death, because it assumed the mask of pleasure; for, while they were lapped in these ecstatic slumbers, Brunhilda sucked the life-stream from their bosoms. On waking, indeed, they felt themselves faint and exhausted, yet did no pain, nor any mark betray the cause. Shortly, however, did their strength entirely fail, even as the summer brook is gradually dried up; their sports became less and less noisy; their loud, frolicsome laughter was converted into a faint smile; the full tones of their voices died away into a mere whisper. Their attendants were filled with horror and despair; too well did they conjecture the horrible truth, yet dared not to impart their suspicions to Walter, who was so devotedly attached to his horrible partner. Death had already smote his prey: the children were but the mere shadows of their former selves, and even this shadow quickly disappeared.

The anguished father deeply bemoaned their loss, for, notwithstanding his apparent neglect, he was strongly attached to them, nor until he had experienced their loss, was he aware that his love was so great. His affliction could not fail to excite the displeasure of Brunhilda: "Why dost thou lament so fondly," said she, "for these little ones? What satisfaction could such unformed beings yield to thee, unless thou wert still attached to their mother? Thy heart then is still hers? Or dost thou now regret her and them, because thou art satiated with my fondness, and weary of my endearments? Had these young ones grown up, would they not have attached thee, thy spirit and thy affections more closely to this earth of clay—to this dust, and have alienated thee from that sphere to which I, who have already passed the grave, endeavour to raise thee? Say is thy spirit so heavy, or thy love so weak, or thy faith so hollow, that the hope of being mine for ever is unable to touch thee?" Thus did Brunhilda express her indignation at her consort's grief, and forbade him her presence. The fear of offending her beyond forgiveness, and his anxiety to appease her soon dried up his tears; and he again abandoned himself to his fatal passion, until approaching destruction at length awakened him from his delusion.

Neither maiden, nor youth, was any longer to be seen, either within the dreary walls of the castle, or the adjoining territory:—all had disappeared; for those whom the grave had not swallowed up, had fled from the region of death. Who, therefore, now remained to quench the horrible thirst of the female vampire, save Walter himself? and his death she dared to contemplate unmoved; for that divine sentiment that unites two beings in one joy and one sorrow was unknown to her bosom. Was he in his tomb, so was she free to search out other victims, and glut herself with destruction, until she herself should, at the last day, be consumed with the earth itself, such is the fatal law, to which the dead are subject, when awoke by the arts of necromancy from the sleep of the grave.

She now began to fix her blood-thirsty lips on Walter's breast, when cast into a profound sleep by the odour of her violet breath, he reclined beside her quite unconscious of his impending fate: yet soon did his vital powers begin to decay; and many a grey hair peeped through his raven locks. With his strength, his passion also declined; and he now frequently left her in order to pass the whole day in the sports of the chase, hoping thereby, to regain his wonted vigour. As he was reposing one day in a wood beneath the shade of an oak, he perceived, on the summit of a tree, a bird of strange appearance, and quite unknown to him; but, before he could take aim at it with his bow, it flew away into the clouds; at the same time, letting fall a rose-coloured root which dropped at Walter's feet, who immediately took it up, and, although he was well acquainted with almost every plant, he could not remember to have seen any at all resembling this. Its delightfully odoriferous scent induced him to try its flavour, but ten times more bitter than wormwood, it was even as gall in his mouth; upon which, impatient of the disappointment, he flung it away with violence. Had he, however, been aware of its miraculous quality, and that it acted as a counter charm against the opiate perfume of Brunhilda's breath, he would have blessed it in spite of its bitterness: thus do mortals often blindly cast away in displeasure, the unsavoury remedy that would otherwise work their weal.

When Walter returned home in the evening, and laid him down to repose as usual by Brunhilda's side, the magic power of her breath produced no effect upon him; and for the first time during many months did he close his eyes in a natural slumber. Yet hardly had he fallen asleep, ere a pungent smarting pain disturbed him from his dreams; and, opening his eyes, he discerned, by the gloomy rays of a lamp, that glimmered in the apartment, what for some moments transfixed him quite aghast, for it was Brunhilda, drawing with her lips, the warm blood from his bosom. The wild cry of horror which at length escaped him, terrified Brunhilda, whose mouth was besmeared with the warm blood. "Monster!" exclaimed he, springing from the couch, "is it thus that you love me?"

"Aye, even as the dead love," replied she, with a malignant coldness.

"Creature of blood!" continued Walter, "the delusion which has so long blinded me is at an end: thou art the fiend who hast destroyed my children—who hast murdered the offspring of my vassals." Raising herself upwards and, at the same time, casting on him a glance that froze him to the spot with dread, she replied. "It is not I who have murdered them;—I was obliged to pamper myself with warm youthful blood, in order that I might satisfy thy furious desires—thou art the murderer!"—These dreadful words summoned, before Walter's terrified conscience, the threatening shades of all those who had thus perished; while despair choked his voice. "Why," continued she, in a tone that increased his horror, "why dost thou make mouths at me like a puppet? Thou who hadst the courage to love the dead—to take into thy bed, one who had been sleeping in the grave, the bed-fellow of the worm—who hast clasped in thy lustful arms, the corruption of the tomb—dost thou, unhallowed as thou art, now raise this hideous cry for the sacrifice of a few lives?—They are but leaves swept from their branches by a storm.—Come, chase these idiot fancies, and taste the bliss thou hast so dearly purchased." So saying, she extended her arms towards him; but this motion served only to increase his terror, and exclaiming: "Accursed Being,"—he rushed out of the apartment.

All the horrors of a guilty, upbraiding conscience became his companions, now that he was awakened from the delirium of his unholy pleasures. Frequently did he curse his own obstinate blindness, for having given no heed to the hints and admonitions of his children's nurses, but treating them as vile calumnies. But his sorrow was now too late, for, although repentance may gain pardon for the sinner, it cannot alter the immutable decrees of fate—it cannot recall the murdered from the tomb. No sooner did the first break of dawn appear, than he set out for his lonely castle in the mountains, determined no longer to abide under the same roof with so terrific a being; yet vain was his flight, for, on waking the following morning, he perceived himself in Brunhilda's arms, and quite entangled in her long raven tresses, which seemed to involve him, and bind him in the fetters of his fate; the powerful fascination of her breath held him still more captivated, so that, forgetting all that had passed, he returned her caresses, until awakening as if from a dream he recoiled in unmixed horror from her embrace. During the day he wandered through the solitary wilds of the mountains, as a culprit seeking an asylum from his pursuers; and, at night, retired to the shelter of a cave; fearing less to couch himself within such a dreary place, than to expose himself to the horror of again meeting Brunhilda; but alas! it was in vain that he endeavoured to flee her. Again, when he awoke, he found her the partner of his miserable bed. Nay, had he sought the centre of the earth as his hiding place; had he even imbedded himself beneath rocks, or formed his chamber in the recesses of the ocean, still had he found her his constant companion; for, by calling her again into existence, he had rendered himself inseparably hers; so fatal were the links that united them.

Struggling with the madness that was beginning to seize him, and brooding incessantly on the ghastly visions that presented themselves to his horror-stricken mind, he lay motionless in the gloomiest recesses of the woods, even from the rise of sun till the shades of eve. But, no sooner was the light of day extinguished in the west, and the woods buried in impenetrable darkness, than the apprehension of resigning himself to sleep drove him forth among the mountains. The storm played wildly with the fantastic clouds, and with the rattling leaves, as they were caught up into the air, as if some dread spirit was sporting with these images of transitoriness and decay: it roared among the summits of the oaks as if uttering a voice of fury, while its hollow sound rebounding among the distant hills, seemed as the moans of a departing sinner, or as the faint cry of some wretch expiring under the murderer's hand: the owl too, uttered its ghastly cry as if foreboding the wreck of nature. Walter's hair flew disorderly in the wind, like black snakes wreathing around his temples and shoulders; while each sense was awake to catch fresh horror. In the clouds he seemed to behold the forms of the murdered; in the howling wind to hear their laments and groans; in the chilling blast itself he felt the dire kiss of Brunhilda; in the cry of the screeching bird he heard her voice; in the mouldering leaves he scented the charnel-bed out of which he had awakened her. "Murderer of thy own offspring," exclaimed he in a voice making night, and the conflict of the element still more hideous, "paramour of a blood-thirsty vampire, reveller with the corruption of the tomb!" while in his despair he rent the wild locks from his head. Just then the full moon darted from beneath the bursting clouds; and the sight recalled to his remembrance the advice of the sorcerer, when he trembled at the first apparition of Brunhilda rising from her sleep of death;—namely, to seek him, at the season of the full moon, in the mountains, where three roads met. Scarcely had this gleam of hope broke in on his bewildered mind, than he flew to the appointed spot.

On his arrival, Walter found the old man seated there upon a stone, as calmly as though it had been a bright sunny day, and completely regardless of the uproar around. "Art thou come then?" exclaimed he to the breathless wretch, who, flinging himself at his feet, cried in a tone of anguish:—"Oh save me—succour me—rescue me from the monster that scattereth death and desolation around her."

"And wherefore a mysterious warning? why didst thou not perceive how wholesome was the advice—'Wake not the dead.'"

"And wherefore a mysterious warning? why didst thou not rather disclose to me, at once, all the horrors that awaited my sacrilegious profanation of the grave?"

"Wert thou able to listen to any other voice than that of thy impetuous passions? Did not thy eager impatience shut my mouth at the very moment I would have cautioned thee?"

"True, true:—thy reproof is just: but what does it avail now;—I need the promptest aid."

"Well," replied the old man, "there remains even yet a means of rescuing thyself, but it is fraught with horror, and demands all thy resolution."

"Utter it then, utter it; for what can be more appalling, more hideous than the misery I now endure?"

"Know then," continued the sorcerer, "that only on the night of the new moon, does she sleep the sleep of mortals; and then all the supernatural power which she inherits from the grave totally fails her. 'Tis then that thou must murder her."

"How! murder her!" echoed Walter.

"Aye," returned the old man calmly, "pierce her bosom with a sharpened dagger, which I will furnish thee with; at the same time renounce her memory for ever, swearing never to think of her intentionally, and that, if thou dost involuntarily, thou wilt repeat the curse."

"Most horrible! yet what can be more horrible than she herself is?—I'll do it."

"Keep then this resolution until the next new moon."

"What, must I wait until then?" cried Walter, "alas ere then, either her savage thirst for blood will have forced me into the night of the tomb, or horror will have driven me into the night of madness."

"Nay," replied the sorcerer, "that I can prevent;" and, so saying he conducted him to a cavern further among the mountains. "Abide here twice seven days," said he; "so long can I protect thee against her deadly caresses. Here wilt thou find all due provision for thy wants; but take heed that nothing tempt thee to quit this place. Farewell, when the moon renews itself, then do I repair hither again." So saying, the sorcerer drew a magic circle around the cave, and then immediately disappeared.

Twice seven days did Walter continue in this solitude, where his companions were his own terrifying thoughts, and his bitter repentance. The present was all desolation and dread; the future presented the image of a horrible deed, which he must perforce commit; while the past was empoisoned by the memory of his guilt. Did he think on his former happy union with Brunhilda, her horrible image presented itself to his imagination with her lips defiled with dripping blood: or, did he call to mind the peaceful days he had passed with Swanhilda, he beheld her sorrowful spirit, with the shadows of her murdered children. Such were the horrors that attended him by day: those of night were still more dreadful, for then he beheld Brunhilda herself, who, wandering round the magic circle which she could not pass, called upon his name, till the cavern re-echoed the horrible sound. "Walter, my beloved," cried she, "wherefore dost thou avoid me? art thou not mine? for ever mine—mine here, and mine hereafter? And dost thou seek to murder me?—ah! commit not a deed which hurls us both to perdition—thyself as well as me." In this manner did the horrible visitant torment him each night, and, even when she departed, robbed him of all repose.

The night of the new moon at length arrived, dark as the deed it was doomed to bring forth. The sorcerer entered the cavern; "Come," said he to Walter, "let us depart hence, the hour is now arrived:" and he forthwith conducted him in silence from the cave to a coal-black steed, the sight of which recalled to Walter's remembrance the fatal night. He then related to the old man Brunhilda's nocturnal visits, and anxiously inquired whether her apprehensions of eternal perdition would be fulfilled or not. "Mortal eye," exclaimed the sorcerer, "may not pierce the dark secrets of another world, or penetrate the deep abyss that separates earth from heaven." Walter hesitated to mount the steed. "Be resolute," exclaimed his companion, "but this once is it granted to thee to make the trial, and, should thou fail now, nought can rescue thee from her power."

"What can be more horrible than she herself?—I am determined:" and he leaped on the horse, the sorcerer mounting also behind him.

Carried with a rapidity equal to that of the storm that sweeps across the plain, they in brief space arrived at Walter's castle. All the doors flew open at the bidding of his companion, and they speedily reached Brunhilda's chamber, and stood beside her couch. Reclining in a tranquil slumber; she reposed in all her native loveliness, every trace of horror had disappeared from her countenance; she looked so pure, meek and innocent that all the sweet hours of their endearments rushed to Walter's memory, like interceding angels pleading in her behalf. His unnerved hand could not take the dagger which the sorcerer presented to him. "The blow must be struck even now:" said the latter, "shouldst thou delay but an hour, she will lie at day-break on thy bosom, sucking the warm life drops from thy heart."

"Horrible! most horrible!" faltered the trembling Walter, and turning away his face, he thrust the dagger into her bosom, exclaiming—"I curse thee for ever!"—and the cold blood gushed upon his hand. Opening her eyes once more, she cast a look of ghastly horror on her husband, and, in a hollow dying accent said—"Thou too art doomed to perdition."

"Lay now thy hand upon her corse," said the sorcerer, "and swear the oath."—Walter did as commanded, saying—"Never will I think of her with love, never recall her to mind intentionally, and, should her image recur to my mind involuntarily, so will I exclaim to it: be thou accursed."

"Thou hast now done everything," returned the sorcerer;—"restore her therefore to the earth, from which thou didst so foolishly recall her; and be sure to recollect thy oath: for, shouldst thou forget it but once, she would return, and thou wouldst be inevitably lost. Adieu—we see each other no more." Having uttered these words he quitted the apartment, and Walter also fled from this abode of horror, having first given direction that the corse should be speedily interred.

Again did the terrific Brunhilda repose within her grave; but her image continually haunted Walter's imagination, so that his existence was one continued martyrdom, in which he continually struggled, to dismiss from his recollection the hideous phantoms of the past; yet, the stronger his effort to banish them, so much the more frequently and the more vividly did they return; as the nightwanderer, who is enticed by a fire-wisp into quagmire or bog, sinks the deeper into his damp grave the more he struggles to escape. His imagination seemed incapable of admitting any other image than that of Brunhilda: now he fancied he beheld her expiring, the blood streaming from her beautiful bosom: at others he saw the lovely bride of his youth, who reproached him with having disturbed the slumbers of the tomb: and to both he was compelled to utter the dreadful words, "I curse thee for ever." The terrible imprecation was constantly passing his lips; yet was he in incessant terror lest he should forget it, or dream of her without being able to repeat it, and then, on awaking, find himself in her arms. Else would he recall her expiring words, and, appalled at their terrific import, imagine that the doom of his perdition was irrecoverably passed. Whence should he fly from himself? or how erase from his brain these images and forms of horror? In the din of combat, in the tumult of war and its incessant pour of victory to defeat; from the cry of anguish to the exultation of victory—in these he hoped to find at least relief of distraction: but here too he was disappointed. The giant fang of apprehension now seized him who had never before known fear; each drop of blood that sprayed upon him seemed the cold blood that had gushed from Brunhilda's wound; each dying wretch that fell beside him looked like her, when expiring, she exclaimed:—"Thou too art doomed to perdition;" so that the aspect of death seemed more full of dread to him than aught beside, and this unconquerable terror compelled him to abandon the battle-field. At length, after many a weary and fruitless wandering, he returned to his castle. Here all was deserted and silent, as if the sword, or a still more deadly pestilence had laid everything waste: for the few inhabitants that still remained, and even those servants who had once shewn themselves the most attached, now fled from him, as though he had been branded with the mark of Cain. With horror he perceived that, by uniting himself as he had done with the dead, he had cut himself off from the living, who refused to hold any intercourse with him. Often, when he stood on the battlements of his castle, and looked down upon desolate fields, he compared their present solitude with the lively activity they were wont to exhibit, under the strict but benevolent discipline of Swanhilda. He now felt that she alone could reconcile him to life, but durst he hope that one, whom he so deeply aggrieved, could pardon him, and receive him again? Impatience at length got the better of fear; he sought Swanhilda, and, with the deepest contrition, acknowledged his complicated guilt; embracing her knees he beseeched her to pardon him, and to return to his desolate castle, in order that it might again become the abode of contentment and peace. The pale form which she beheld at her feet, the shadow of the lately blooming youth, touched Swanhilda. "The folly," said she gently, "though it has caused me much sorrow, has never excited my resentment or my anger. But say, where are my children?" To this dreadful interrogation the agonised father could for a while frame no reply: at length he was obliged to confess the dreadful truth. "Then we are sundered for ever," returned Swanhilda; nor could all his tears or supplications prevail upon her to revoke the sentence she had given.

Stripped of his last earthly hope, bereft of his last consolation, and thereby rendered as poor as mortal can possibly be on this side of the grave, Walter returned homewards; when, as he was riding through the forest in the neighbourhood of his castle, absorbed in his gloomy meditations, the sudden sound of a horn roused him from his reverie. Shortly after he saw appear a female figure clad in black, and mounted on a steed of the same colour: her attire was like that of a huntress, but, instead of a falcon, she bore a raven in her hand; and she was attended by a gay troop of cavaliers and dames. The first salutations being passed, he found that she was proceeding the same road as himself; and, when she found that Walter's castle was close at hand, she requested that he would lodge her for that night, the evening being far advanced. Most willingly did he comply with this request, since the appearance of the beautiful stranger had struck him greatly; so wonderfully did she resemble Swanhilda, except that her locks were brown, and her eye dark and full of fire. With a sumptuous banquet did he entertain his guests, whose mirth and songs enlivened the lately silent halls. Three days did this revelry continue, and so exhilarating did it prove to Walter, that he seemed to have forgotten his sorrows and his fears; nor could he prevail upon himself to dismiss his visitors, dreading lest, on their departure, the castle would seem a hundred times more desolate than before, and his grief be proportionately increased. At his earnest request, the stranger consented to stay seven days, and again another seven days. Without being requested, she took upon herself the superintendence of the household, which she regulated as discreetly and cheerfully as Swanhilda had been wont to do, so that the castle, which had so lately been the abode of melancholy and horror, became the residence of pleasure and festivity, and Walter's grief disappeared altogether in the midst of so much gaiety. Daily did his attachment to the fair unknown increase; he even made her his confidant; and, one evening as they were walking together apart from any of her train, he related to her his melancholy and frightful history. "My dear friend," returned she, as soon as he had finished his tale, "it ill beseems a man of thy discretion to afflict thyself, on account of all this. Thou hast awakened the dead from the sleep of the grave, and afterwards found—what might have been anticipated, that the dead possess no sympathy with life. What then? thou wilt not commit this error a second time. Thou hast however murdered the being whom thou hadst thus recalled again to existence—but it was only in appearance, for thou couldst not deprive that of life, which properly had none. Thou hast, too, lost a wife and two children: but, at thy years, such a loss is most easily repaired. There are beauties who will gladly share thy couch, and make thee again a father. But thou dreadst the reckoning of hereafter:—go, open the graves and ask the sleepers there whether that hereafter disturbs them." In such manner would she frequently exhort and cheer him, so that, in a short time, his melancholy entirely disappeared. He now ventured to declare to the unknown the passion with which she had inspired him, nor did she refuse him her hand. Within seven days afterwards the nuptials were celebrated, and the very foundations of the castle seemed to rock from the wild tumultuous uproar of unrestrained riot. The wine streamed in abundance; the goblets circled incessantly: intemperance reached its utmost bounds, while shouts of laughter, almost resembling madness, burst from the numerous train belonging to the unknown. At length Walter, heated with wine and love, conducted his bride into the nuptial chamber: but, oh horror! scarcely had he clasped her in his arms, ere she transformed herself into a monstrous serpent, which entwining him in its horrid folds, crushed him to death. Flames crackled on every side of the apartment; in a few minutes after, the whole castle was enveloped in a blaze that consumed it entirely: while, as the walls fell in with a tremendous crash, a voice exclaimed aloud—"Wake not the dead!"

THE WHITE MANIAC

Waif Wander

I N the year 1858 I had established a flourishing practice in London; a practice which I owed a considerable portion of, not to my ability, I am afraid, but to the fact that I occupied the singular position of a man professional, who was entirely independent of his profession. Doubtless, had I been a poor man, struggling to earn a bare existence for wife and family, I might have been the cleverest physician that ever administered a bolus, yet have remained in my poverty to the end of time. But it was not so, you see. I was the second son of a nobleman, and had Honourable attached to my name; and I practised the profession solely and entirely because I had become enamoured of it, and because I was disgusted at the useless existence of a fashionable and idle young man, and determined that I, at least, would not add another to their ranks.

And so I had a handsome establishment in a fashionable portion of the city, and my door was besieged with carriages, from one end of the week to the other. Many of the occupants were disappointed, however, for I would not demean myself by taking fees from some vapourish Miss or dissipated Dowager. Gout in vain came rolling to my door, even though it excruciated the leg of a Duke; I undertook none but oases that enlisted my sympathy, and after a time the fact became known, and my levees were not so well attended.

One day I was returning on horseback toward the city. I had been paying a visit to a patient in whom I was deeply interested, and for whom I had ordered the quiet and purer air of a suburban residence. I had reached a spot, in the neighbourhood of Kensington, where the villas were enclosed in large gardens, and the road was marked for a considerable distance by the brick and stone walls that enclosed several of the gardens belonging to these mansions. On the opposite side of the road stood a small country-looking inn, which I had patronised before, and I pulled up my horse and alighted, for the purpose of having some rest and refreshment after my ride.

As I sat in a front room sipping my wine and water, my thoughts were fully occupied with a variety of personal concerns. I had received a letter from my mother that morning, and the condition of the patient I had recently left was precarious in the extreme.

It was fortunate that I was thought-occupied and not dependent upon outward objects to amuse them, for although the window at which I sat was open, it presented no view whatever, save the bare, blank, high brick wall belonging to a house at the opposite side of the road. That is to say, I presume, it enclosed some residence, for from where I sat not even the top of a chimney was visible.

Presently, however, the sound of wheels attracted my eyes from the pattern of the wall-paper at which I had been unconsciously gazing, and looked out to see a handsome, but very plain carriage drawn up at a small door that pierced the brick wall I have alluded to; and almost at the same moment the door opened and closed again behind two figures in a most singular attire. They were both of the male sex, and one of them was evidently a gentleman, while the other waited on him as if he was the servant; but it was the dress of these persons that most strangely interested me. They were attired in white from head to heel; coats, vests, trousers, hats, shoes, not to speak of shirts at all, all were white as white could be.

While I stared at this strange spectacle, the gentleman stepped into the vehicle; but although he did so the coachman made no movement toward driving onward, nor did the attendant leave his post at the carriage door. At the expiration, however, of about a quarter of an hour, the servant closed the door and re-entered through the little gate, closing it, likewise, carefully behind him. Then the driver leisurely made a start, only, however, to stop suddenly again, when the door of the vehicle was burst open and a gentleman jumped out and rapped loudly at the gate.

He turned his face hurriedly around as he did so, hiding, it seemed to me, meanwhile, behind the wall so as not to be seen when it opened. Judge of my astonishment when I recognised in this gentleman the one who had but a few minutes before entered the carriage dressed in white, for he was now in garments of the hue of Erebus. While I wondered at this strange metamorphosis the door in the wall opened, and the gentleman, now attired in black, after giving some hasty instructions to the servant, sprang once more into the carriage and was driven rapidly toward London.

My curiosity was strangely excited; and as I stood at the door before mounting my horse, I asked the landlord who and what were the people who occupied the opposite dwelling.

"Well, sir," he replied, looking curiously at the dead wall over against him, "They've been there now a matter of six months, I dare say, and you've seen as much of them as I have. I believe the whole crew of them, servants and all, is foreigners, and we, that is the neighbours around, sir, calls them the 'white mad people.'"

"What! do they always wear that singular dress?"

"Always, sir, saving as soon as ever the old gentleman goes outside the gate he puts black on in the carriage, and as soon as he comes back takes it off again, and leaves it in the carriage."

"And why in the name of gracious does he not dress himself inside?"

"Oh, that I can't tell you, sir! only it's just as you see, always. The driver or coachman never even goes inside the walls, or the horses or any one thing that isn't white in colour, sir; and if the people aren't mad after that, what else can it be?"

"It seems very like it, indeed; but do you mean to say that everything inside the garden wall is white? Surely you must be exaggerating a little?"

"Not a bit on it, sir! The coachman, who can't speak much English, sir, comes here for a drink now and then. He don't live in the house, you see, and is idle most of his time. Well, he told me himself, one day, that every article in the house was white, from the garret to the drawing-room, and that everything *outside* it is white I can swear, for I saw it myself, and a stranger sight surely no eye ever saw."

"How did you manage to get into the enchanted castle, then?"

"I didn't get in sir, I only saw it outside, and from a place where you can see for yourself too, if you have a mind. When first the people came to the place over there, you see, sir, old Mat the sexton and bell-ringer of the church there, began to talk of the strange goings on he had seen from the belfry; and so my curiosity took me there one day to look for myself. Blest if I ever heard of such a strange sight! no wonder they call them the white mad folk."

"Well, you've roused my curiosity," I said, as I got on my horse, "and I'll certainly pay old Mat's belfry a visit the very next time I pass this way, if I'm not hurried."

It appeared unaccountable to even myself that these mysterious people should make such a singular impression on me; I thought of little else during the next two days. I attended to my duties in an absent manner, and my mind was ever recurring to the one subject—viz. an attempt to account for the strange employment of one hue only in the household of this foreign gentleman. Of whom did the household consist? Had he any family? and could one account for the eccentricity in any other way save by ascribing it to lunacy, as mine host of the inn had already done. As it happened, the study of brain diseases had been my hobby during my noviciate, and I was peculiarly interested in observing a new symptom of madness, if this was really one.

At length I escaped to pay my country patient his usual visit, and on my return alighted at the inn, and desired the landlord to have my horse put in the stable for a bit.

"I'm going to have a peep at your madhouse," I said, "do you think I shall find old Mat about?"

"Yes, doctor; I saw him at work in the churchyard not half an hour ago, but at any rate he won't be farther off than his cottage, and it lies just against the yard wall."

The church was an old, ivy-wreathed structure, with a square Norman belfry, and a large surrounding of grey and grass-grown old headstones. It was essentially a country church, and a country churchyard; and one wondered to find it so close to the borders of a mighty city, until they remembered that the mighty city had crept into the country, year by year, until it had covered with stone and mortar the lowly site of many a cottage home, and swallowed up many an acre of green meadow and golden corn. Old Mat was sitting in the middle of the graves; one tombstone forming his seat, and he was engaged in scraping the moss from a headstone that seemed inclined to tumble over, the inscription on which was all but obliterated by a growth of green slimy-looking moss.

"Good-day, friend, you are busy," I said. "One would fancy that stone so old now, that the living had entirely forgotten their loss. But I suppose they have not, or you would not be cleaning it."

"It's only a notion of my own, sir; I'm idle, and when I was a lad I had a sort o' likin' for this stone, Lord only knows why. But you see I've clean forgotten what name was on it, and I thought I'd like to see."

"Well, I want to have a look at these 'white mad folk' of yours, Mat, will you let me into the belfry? Mr Tanning tells me you can see something queer up there."

"By jove you can, sir!" he replied, rising with alacrity, "I often spend an hour watching the mad folk; faith if they had my old church and yard they'd whitewash 'em, belfry and all!" and the old man led the way into the tower.

Of course my first look on reaching the summit was in the direction of the strange house, and I must confess to an ejaculation of astonishment as I peeped through one of the crevices. The belfry was elevated considerably

55

above the premises in which I was interested, and not at a very great distance, so that grounds and house lay spread beneath me like a map.

I scarcely know how to commence describing it to you, it was something I had never seen or imagined. The mansion itself was a square and handsome building of two stories, built in the Corinthian style, with pillared portico, and pointed windows. But the style attracted my attention but little, it was the universal white, white everywhere, that drew from me the ejaculation to which I have alluded.

From the extreme top of the chimneys to the basement, roof, windows, everything was pure white; not a shade lurked even inside a window; the windows themselves were painted white, and the curtains were of white muslin that fell over every one of them. Every yard of the broad space that one might reasonably have expected to see decorated with flowers and grass and shrubberies, was covered with a glaring and sparkling white gravel, the effect of which, even in the hot brilliant sun of a London afternoon, was to dazzle, and blind, and aggravate. And as if this was not enough, the inside of the very brick walls was whitewashed like snow, and at intervals, here and there, were placed a host of white marble statues and urns that only increased the, to me, horrible aspect of the place.

"I don't wonder they are mad!" I exclaimed, "I should soon become mad in such a place myself."

"Like enough, sir," replied old Mat, stolidly, "but you see it *didn't* make they mad, for they did it theirselves, so they must 'a been mad afore."

An incontrovertible fact, according to the old man's way of putting it; and as I had no answer for it, I went down the old stone stairs, and having given my guide his donation, left the churchyard as bewildered as I had entered it. Nay, more so, for then I had not seen the extraordinary house that had made so painful an impression upon me.

I was in no humour for a gossip with mine host, but just as I was about to mount my horse, which had been brought round, the same carriage drove round to the mysterious gate, and the same scene was enacted to which I had before been a witness. I drew back until the old gentleman had stepped inside and performed his toilet, and when the carriage drove rapidly toward the city, I rode thoughtfully onward toward home.

I was young, you see, and although steady, and, unlike most young gentlemen of my age and position in society, had a strong vein of romance in my character. That hard study and a sense of its inutility had kept it under, had not rendered it one whit less ready to be at a moment's call; and, in addition to all this, I had never yet, in the seclusion of my student life, met with an opportunity of falling in love, so that you will see I was in the very best mood for making the most of the adventure which was about to befall me, and which had so tragic a termination.

My thoughts were full of the "White mad folk," as I reached my own door; and there, to my utter astonishment, I saw drawn up the very carriage of the white house, which had preceded me. Hastily giving my horse to the groom I passed through the hall and was informed by a servant that a gentleman waited in my private consulting-room.

Very rarely indeed had my well-strung nerves been so troublesome as upon that occasion; I was so anxious to see this gentleman, and yet so fearful of exposing the interest I had already conceived in his affairs, that my hand absolutely trembled as I turned the handle of the door of the room in which he was seated. The first glance, however, at the aristocratic old gentleman who rose on my entrance, restored all my self-possession, and I was myself once more. In the calm, sweet face of the perfectly dressed gentleman before me there was no trace of the lunacy that had created that strange abode near Kensington; the principal expression in his face was that of ingrained melancholy, and his deep mourning attire might have suggested to a stranger the reason of that melancholy. He addressed me in perfect English, the entire absence of idiom alone declaring him to be a foreigner.

"I have the pleasure of addressing Doctor Elveston?" he said.

I bowed, and placed a chair in which he re-seated himself, while I myself took possession of another.

"And Doctor Elveston is a clever physician and a man of honour?"

"I hope to be worthy of the former title, sir, while my position ought at least to guarantee the latter."

"Your public character does, sir," said the old gentleman, emphatically, "and it is because I believe that you will preserve the secret of an unfortunate family that I have chosen you to assist me with your advice."

My heart was beating rapidly by this time. There *was* a secret then, and I was about to become the possessor of it. Had it anything to do with the mania for white?

"Anything in my power," I hastened to reply, "you may depend on; my advice, I fear, may be of little worth, but such as it is—"

"I beg your pardon, Doctor," interrupted he, "it is your medical advice that I allude to, and I require it for a young lady—a relative."

"My dear sir, that is, of course, an every day affair, my professional advice and services belong to the public, and as the public's they are of course yours."

"Oh, my dear young friend, but mine is not an every day affair, and because it is not is the reason that I have applied to you in particular. It is a grievous case, sir, and one which fills many hearts with a bitterness they are obliged to smother from a world whose sneers are poison."

The old gentleman spoke in tones of deep feeling, and I could not help feeling sorry for him at the bottom of my very heart.

"If you will confide in me, my dear sir," I said, "believe that I will prove a friend as faithful and discreet as you could wish."

He pressed my hand, turned away for a moment to collect his agitated feelings and then he spoke again.

"I shall not attempt to hide my name from you, sir, though I have hitherto carefully concealed it. I am the Duke de Rohan, and circumstances, which it is impossible for me to relate to you, have driven me to England to keep watch and ward over my sister's daughter, the Princess d'Alberville. It is for this young lady I wish your attendance, her health is rapidly failing within the last week."

"Nothing can be more simple," I observed, eagerly, "I can go with you at once—this very moment."

"Dear Doctor, it is unfortunately far from being as simple a matter as you think," he replied, solemnly, "for my wretched niece is mad."

"Mad!"

"Alas! yes, frightfully—horribly mad!" and he shuddered as if a cold wind had penetrated his bones.

"Has this unhappy state of mind been of long duration?" I questioned.

"God knows; the first intimation her friends had of it was about two years ago, when it culminated in such a fearful event that horrified them. I cannot explain it to you, however, for the honour of a noble house deeply concerned; and even the very existence of the unfortunate being I beg of you to keep a secret for ever."

"You must at any rate tell me what you wish me to do," I observed, "and give me as much information as you can to guide me, or I shall be powerless."

"The sight of one colour has such an effect on the miserable girl that we have found out, by bitter experience, the only way to avoid a repetition of the most fearful tragedies, is to keep every hue or shade away from her vision; for, although it is only one colour that affects her, any of the others seems to suggest that *one* to her mind and produce uncontrollable agitation. In consequence of this she is virtually imprisoned within the grounds of the house I have provided for her, and every object that meets her eye is white, even the ground, and the very roof of the mansion."

"How very strange!"

"It will be necessary for you, my dear sir," the Duke continued, "to attire yourself in a suit of white. I have brought one in the carriage for your use, and if you will now accompany me I shall be grateful."

Of course I was only too glad to avail myself of the unexpected opportunity of getting into the singular household, and becoming acquainted with the lunatic princess; and in a few moments we were being whirled on our way toward Kensington.

On stopping at the gate of the Duke's residence, I myself became an actor in the scene which had so puzzled me on two previous occasions. My companion produced two suits of white, and proceeded to turn the vehicle into a dressing-room, though not without many apologies for the necessity. I followed his example, and in a few moments we stood inside the gate, and I had an opportunity of more closely surveying the disagreeable enclosure I had seen from the church belfry. And a most disagreeable survey it was; the sun shining brilliantly, rendered the unavoidable contact with the white glare, absolutely painful to the eye; nor was it any escape to stand in the lofty vestibule, save that there the absence of sunshine made the uniformity more bearable.

My companion led the way up a broad staircase covered with white cloth, and balustraded with carved rails, the effect of which was totally destroyed by their covering of white paint. The very stair-rods were of white enamel, and the corners and landing places served as room for more marble statues, that held enamelled white lamps in their hands, lamps that were shaded by globes of ground glass. At the door of an apartment pertaining, as he informed me, to the Princess d'Alberville, the Duke stopped, and shook my hand. "I leave you to make your own way," he said, pointing to the door. "She has never showed any symptoms of violence while under the calm influence of white; but, nevertheless, we shall be at hand, the least sound will bring you assistance," and he turned away.

I opened the door without a word, and entered the room, full of curiosity as to what I should see and hear of this mysterious princess. It was a room of vast and magnificent proportions, and, without having beheld such a scene, one can hardly conceive the strange cold look the utter absence of colour gave it. A Turkey carpet that looked like a woven fall of snow; white satin damask on chair, couch, and ottoman; draped satin and snowy lace around the windows, with rod, rings, and bracelets of white enamel. Tables with pedestals of enamel and tops of snowy marble, and paper on the walls of purest white; altogether it was a weird-looking room, and I shook with cold as I entered it.

The principal object of my curiosity was seated in a deep chair with her side toward me, and I had an opportunity of examining her leisurely, as she neither moved or took the slightest notice of my entrance; most probably she was quite unaware of it. She was the most lovely being I had ever beheld, a fair and perfect piece of statuary one might have thought, so immobile and abstracted, nay, so entirely expressionless were her beautiful features. Her dress was pure white, her hair of a pale golden hue, and her eyes dark as midnight. Her hands rested idly on her lap, her gaze seemed intent on the high white wall that shot up outside the window near her; and in the whole room there was neither book, flower, work, or one single *loose* article of ornament, nothing but the heavy, white-covered furniture, and the draping curtains. I advanced directly before her and bowed deeply, and then I calmly drew forward a chair and seated myself. As I did so she moved her eyes from the window and rested them on me, but, for all the interest they evinced, I might as well have been the white-washed wall outside. She was once more returning her eyes to the blank window, when I took her hand and laid my fingers on her blue-veined wrist. The action seemed to arouse her, for she looked keenly into my face, and then she laughed softly.

"One may guess you are a physician," she said, in a musical, low voice, and with a slightly foreign accent, that was in my opinion, a great improvement to our harsh language.

"I am," I replied, with a smile, "your uncle has sent me to see about your health, which alarms him."

"Poor man!" she said, with a shade of commiseration clouding her beautiful face, "poor uncle! But I assure you there is nothing the matter with me; nothing but what must be the natural consequence of the life I am leading."

"Why do you lead one which you know to be injurious then?" I asked, still keeping my fingers on the pulse, that beat as calmly as a sleeping infant's, and was not increased by a single throb though a stranger sat beside her.

"How can I help it?" she asked, calmly meeting my inquisitorial gaze, "Do you think a sane person would choose to be imprisoned thus and to be surrounded by the colour of death ever? Had mine not been a strong mind I should have been mad long ago."

"Mad!" I could not help ejaculating, in a puzzled tone.

"Yes, mad," she replied, "could *you* live here, month after month, in a hueless atmosphere and with nothing but *that* to look at," and she pointed her slender finger toward the white wall, "could you, I ask, and retain your reason?"

"I do not believe I could!" I answered, with sudden vehemence, "then, again I repeat why do it?"

"And again I reply, how can I help it?"

I was silent. I was looking in the eyes of the beautiful being before me for a single trace of the madness I had been told of, but I could not find it. It was a lovely girl, pale and delicate from confinement, and with a manner that told of a weariness endured at least patiently. She was about twenty years old, perhaps, and the most perfect creature, I have already said, that I had ever beheld; and so we sat looking into each other's eyes; what mine expressed I cannot say, but her's were purity, and sweetness itself.

"Who are you?" she asked, suddenly, "tell me something of yourself. It will be at least a change from this white solitude."

"I am a doctor, as you have guessed; and a rich and fashionable doctor," I added smilingly.

"To be either is to be also the other," she remarked, "you need not have used the repetition."

"Come," I thought to myself, "there is little appearance of lunacy in that observation."

"But you doubtless have a name, what is it?"

"My name is Elveston—Doctor Elveston."

"Your christian name?"

"No, my christian name is Charles."

"Charles," she repeated dreamily.

"I think it is your turn now," I remarked, "it is but fair that you should make me acquainted with your name, since I have told you mine."

"Oh! my name is d'Alberville—Blanche d'Alberville. Perhaps it was in consequence of my christian name that my poor uncle decided upon burying me in white," she added, with a look round the cold room, "poor old man!"

"Why do you pity him so?" I asked, "he seems to me little to require it. He is strong and rich, and the uncle of Blanche," I added, with a bow; but the compliment seemed to glide off her as if it had been a liquid, and she were made of glassy marble like one of the statues that stood behind her.

"And you are a physician," she said, looking wonderingly at me, "and have been in the Duke's company, without discovering it?"

"Discovering what, my dear young lady?"

"That he is mad."

"Mad!" How often had I already ejaculated that word since I had become interested in this singular household; but this time it must assuredly have expressed the utmost astonishment, for I was never more confounded in my life; and yet a light seemed to be breaking in upon my bewilderment, as I stared in wondering silence at the calm face of the lovely maiden before me.

"Alas, yes!" she replied, sadly, to my look, "my poor uncle is a maniac, but a harmless one to all but me; it is I who suffer all."

"And why you?" I gasped.

"Because it is his mania to believe *me* mad," she replied, "and so he treats me."

"But in the name of justice why should you endure this?" I cried, angrily starting to my feet, "you are in a free land at least, and doors will open!"

"Calm yourself, my friend," she said, laying her white hand on my arm, and the contact, I confess, thrilled through every nerve of my system, "compose yourself, and see things as they are; what could a young, frail girl like me do out in the world alone? and I have not a living relative but my uncle. Besides, would it be charitable to desert him and leave him to his own madness thus! Poor old man!"

"You are an angel!" I ejaculated, "and I would die for you!"

The reader need not be told that my enthusiastic youth was at last beginning to make its way through the crust of worldly wisdom that had hitherto subdued it.

"It is not necessary that anyone should die for me; I can do that for myself, and no doubt shall ere long, die of the want of colour and air," she said, with a sad smile.

There is little use following our conversation to the end. I satisfied myself that there was really nothing wrong with her constitution, save the effects of the life she was obliged to lead; and I determined, instead of interfering with her at present, to devote myself to the poor Duke, with a hope that I might be of service to him, and succeed in gaining the liberation of poor Blanche. We parted, I might almost say as lovers, although no words of affection were spoken; but I carried away her image entwined with every fibre of my heart, and in the deep sweetness of her lingering eyes I fancied I read hope and love.

The Duke was waiting impatiently in the corridor as I left the lovely girl, and he led me into another apartment to question me eagerly. What did I think of the princess's state of health? Had she shown any symptoms of uneasiness during my visit? As the old gentleman asked questions he watched my countenance keenly; while on my part I observed him with deep interest to discover traces of his unfortunate mental derangement.

"My dear sir, I perceive nothing alarming whatever in the state of your niece; she is simply suffering from confinement and monotony of existence, and wants nothing whatever but fresh air and amusement, and exercise; in short, life."

"Alas! you know that is impossible; have I not told you that her state precludes everything of the sort?"

"You must excuse me, my friend," I said, firmly, "I have conversed for a considerable time with the Princess d'Alberville, and I am a medical man accustomed to dealing with, and the observation of, lunacy, and I give you my word of honour there is no weakness whatever in the brain of this fair girl; you are simply killing her, it is my duty to tell you so, killing her under the influence of some, to me, most unaccountable whim."

The duke wrung his hands in silence, but his excited eye fell under my steady gaze. It was apparently with a strong effort that he composed himself sufficiently to speak, and when he did his words had a solemnity in their tone that ought to have made a deep impression upon me; but it did not, for the sweetness of the imprisoned Blanche's voice was still lingering in my ears.

"You are a young man, Doctor Elveston; it is one of the happy provisions of youth, no doubt, to be convinced of its own infallibility. But you must believe that one of my race does not lie, and I swear to you that my niece is the victim of a most fearful insanity, which but to name makes humanity shudder with horror."

"I do not doubt that you believe such to be the case, my dear sir," I said, soothingly, for I fancied I saw the fearful light of insanity in his glaring eye at that moment, "but to my vision everything seems different."

"Well, my young friend, do not decide yet too hastily. Visit us again, but God in mercy grant that you may never see the reality as I have seen it!"

And so I did repeat my visits, and repeat them so often and that without changing my opinion, that the Duke, in spite of his mania, began to see that they were no longer necessary. One day on my leaving Blanche he requested a few moments of my time, and drawing me into his study, locked the door. I began to be a little alarmed, and more particularly as he seemed to be in a state of great agitation; but, as it appeared, my alarm of personal violence was entirely without foundation.

He placed a chair for me, and I seated myself with all the calmness I could muster, while I kept my eyes firmly fixed upon his as he addressed me.

"My dear young friend; I hope it is unnecessary for me to say that these are no idle words, for I have truly conceived an ardent appreciation of your character; yet it is absolutely necessary that I should put a stop to your visits to my niece. Good Heavens, what could I say—how could I ever forgive myself if any—any—"

"I beg of you to go no farther, Duke," I said, interrupting him. "You have only by a short time anticipated what I was about to communicate myself. If your words allude to an attachment between Blanche and myself, your care is now too late. We love each other, and intend, subject to your approval, to be united immediately."

Had a sudden clap of thunder reverberated in the quiet room the poor man could not have been more affected. He started to his feet, and *glared* into my eyes with terror.

"Married!" he gasped, "Married! Blanche d'Alberville wedded! Oh God!" and then he fell back into his chair as powerless as a child.

"And why should this alarm you?" I asked. "She is youthful and lovely, and as sane, I believe in my soul, as I am myself. I am rich, and of a family which may aspire to mate with the best. You are her only relative and guardian, and you say that you esteem me; whence then this great distaste to hear even a mention of your fair ward's marriage?"

"She is not my ward!" he cried, hoarsely, and it seemed to me angrily, "her father and mother are both in existence, and destroyed for all time by the horror she has brought around them! But, my God, what is the use of speaking—I talk to a madman!" and he turned to his desk and began to write rapidly.

There I sat in bewilderment. I had not now the slightest doubt but that my poor friend was the victim of monomania; his one idea was uppermost, and that idea was that his unfortunate niece WAS mad. I was fully determined now to carry her away and make her my wife at once, so as to relieve the poor girl from an imprisonment, to which there seemed no other prospect of an end. And my hopes went still farther; who could tell but that the sight of Blanche living and enjoying life as did others of her sex, might have a beneficial effect upon the poor duke's brain, and help to eradicate his fixed idea.

As I was thus cogitating, the old gentleman rose from his desk, and handed me a letter addressed, but unsealed. His manner was now almost unearthly calm, as if he had come to some great determination, to which he had only been driven by the most dreadful necessity.

"My words are wasted, Charles," he said, "and I cannot tell the truth; but if you ever prized home and name, friends or family, mother or wife, send that letter to its address after you have perused it, and await its reply."

I took the letter and put it into my pocket, and then I took his hand and pressed it warmly. I was truly sorry for the poor old gentleman, who suffered, no doubt, as much from his fancied trouble as if it were the most terrible of realities.

"I hope you will forgive me for grieving you, my dear sir; believe me it pains me much to see you thus. I will do as you wish about the letter. But oh, how I wish you could see Blanche with my eyes! To me she is the most perfect of women!"

"You have *never* seen her yet!"—he responded, bitterly, "could you—*dare* you only once witness but a part of her actions under one influence, you would shudder to your very marrow!"

"To what influence do you allude, dear sir!"

"To that of colour—one colour."

"And that colour? have you any objection to name it?"

"It is red!" and as the duke answered he turned away abruptly, and left me standing bewildered, but still unbelieving.

I hastened home that day, anxious to peruse the letter given me by the duke, and as soon as I had reached my own study drew it from my pocket and spread it before me. It was addressed to the Prince d'Alberville, Chateau Gris, Melun, France; and the following were its singular contents:—

"DEAR BROTHER.—A terrible necessity for letting another into our fearful secret has arisen. A young gentleman of birth and fortune has, in spite of my assurances that she is insane, determined to wed Blanche. Such a sacrifice cannot be permitted, even were such a thing not morally impossible. You are her parent, it is then your place to inform this unhappy young man of the unspoken curse that rests on our wretched name. I enclose his address. Write to him at once.

"Your afflicted brother,
"De Rohan."

I folded up this strange epistle and despatched it; and then I devoted nearly an hour to pondering over the strange contradictions of human nature, and more particularly diseased human nature. Of course I carried the key to this poor man's strangeness in my firm conviction of his insanity, and my entire belief in the martyrdom of Blanche; yet I could not divest myself of an anxiety to receive a reply to this letter, a reply which I was certain would explain the duke's lunacy, and beg of me to pardon it. That is to say if such a party as the Prince d'Alberville existed at all, and I did not quite lose sight of the fact that Blanche had assured me that, with the exception of her uncle, she had not a living relative.

It seemed a long week to me ere the French reply, that made my hand tremble as I received it, was put into it. I had abstained from visiting my beloved Blanche, under a determination that I would not do so until armed with such a letter as I anticipated receiving; or until I should be able to say, "ample time for a reply to your communication has elapsed; none has come, give me then my betrothed." Here then at last was the letter, and I shut myself into my own room and opened it; the words are engraven on my memory and will never become less vivid.

"SIR,—You wish to wed my daughter, the Princess Blanche d'Alberville. Words would vainly try to express the pain with which I expose our disgrace—our horrible secret—to a stranger, but it is to save from a fate worse than death. Blanche d'Alberville is an *anthropophagus*, already has one of her own family fallen a victim to her thirst for human blood. Spare us if you can, and pray for us.

"d'Alberville."

I sat like one turned to stone, and stared at the fearful paper! An anthropophagus! a cannibal! Good heavens, the subject was just now engaging the attention of the medical world in a remarkable degree, in consequence of two frightful and well authenticated cases that had lately occurred in France! All the particulars of these cases, in which I had taken a deep interest, flashed before me, but not for one moment did I credit the frightful story of my beloved. Some detestable plot had been formed against her, for what vile purpose, or with what end in view I was ignorant; and I cast the whole subject from my mind with an effort, and went to attend to my daily round of duties. During the two or three hours that followed, and under the influence of the human suffering I had witnessed, a revolution took place in my feelings, God only knows by what means induced; but when I returned home, to prepare for my eventful visit to the "white house," a dreadful doubt had stolen into my heart, and filled it with a fearful determination.

Having ordered my carriage and prepared the white suit, which I was now possessor of, I went directly to the conservatory, and looked around among the brilliant array of blossoms for the most suitable to my purpose. I chose the flaring scarlet verbena to form my bouquet; a tasteless one it is true, but one decidedly distinctive in colour. I collected quite a large nosegay of this flower, without a single spray of green to relieve its bright hue. Then I went to my carriage, and gave directions to be driven to Kensington.

At the gate of the Duke's residence I dressed myself in the white suit mechanically, and followed the usual servant into the house, carefully holding my flowers, which I had enveloped in a newspaper. I was received as usual, also by the Duke, and in a few seconds we stood, face to face in his study. In answer to his look of fearful inquiry I handed him my French epistle, and stood silently by as he read it tremblingly.

"Well, are you satisfied now?" he asked, looking me pitifully in the face, "has this dreadful exposure convinced you?"

"No!" I answered, recklessly, "I am neither satisfied nor convinced of anything save that you are either a lunatic yourself, or in collusion with the writer of that abominable letter!" and as I spoke I uncovered my scarlet bouquet and shook out its blossoms. The sight of it made a terrible impression upon my companion; his knees trembled as if he were about to fall, and his face grew whiter than his garments.

"In the name of heaven what are you going to do?" he gasped.

"I am simply going to present my bride with a bouquet," I said, and as I said so I laughed an empty, hollow laugh. I cannot describe my strange state of mind at that moment; I felt as if myself under the influence of some fearful mania.

"By all you hold sacred, Charles Elveston, I charge you to desist! who or what are *you* that you should set your youth, and ignorance of this woman against my age and bitter experience?"

"Ha, ha!" was my only response, as I made toward the door.

"By heavens, he is mad!" cried the excited nobleman, "young man, I tell you that you carry in your hand a colour which had better be shaken in the eyes of a mad bull than be placed in sight of my miserable niece! Fool! I tell you it will arouse in her an unquenchable thirst for blood, and the blood may be yours!"

"Let it!" I cried, and passed on my way to Blanche.

I was conscious of the Duke's cries to the servants as I hurried up the broad staircase, and guessed that they were about to follow me; but to describe my feelings is utterly impossible.

I was beginning now to believe that my betrothed was something terrible, and I faced her desperately, as one who had lost everything, worth living for, or placed his last stake upon the cast of a die.

I opened the well-known door of the white room, that seemed to me colder, and more death-like than ever; and I saw the figure of Blanche seated in her old way, and in her old seat, looking out of the window. I did not wait to scan her appearance just then, however, for I caught a glimpse of myself in a large mirror opposite, and was fascinated, as it were by the strange sight.

The mirror reflected, in unbroken stillness, the cold whiteness of the large apartment, but it also reflected my face and form, wearing an expression that half awoke me to a consciousness of physical indisposition. There was a wild look in my pallid countenance, and a reckless air in my figure which the very garments seemed to have imbibed, and which was strangely unlike my usual calm propriety of demeanour. My coat seemed awry; the collar of my shirt was unbuttoned, and I had even neglected to put on my neck-tie; but it was upon the blood-red bouquet that my momentary gaze became riveted.

It was such a contrast; the cold, pure white of all the surroundings, and that circled patch of blood-colour that I held in my hand was so suggestive! "Of what?" I asked myself, "am I really mad?" and then I laughed loudly and turned toward Blanche.

Possibly the noise of the opening door had attracted her, for when I turned she was standing on her feet, directly confronting me. Her eyes were distended with astonishment at my peculiar examination of myself in the mirror, no doubt, but they flashed into madness at the sight of the flowers as I turned. Her face grew scarlet, her hands clenched, and her regards *devoured* the scarlet bouquet, as I madly held it towards her. At this moment my eye caught a side glimpse of half-a-dozen terrified faces peeping in the doorway, and conspicuous and foremost that of the poor terrified Duke; but my fate must be accomplished, and I still held the bouquet tauntingly toward the transfixed girl. She gave one wild look into my face, and recognised the sarcasm which I *felt* in my eyes, and then she snatched the flowers from my hand, and scattered them in a thousand pieces at her feet.

How well I remember that picture today. The white room—the torn and brilliant flowers—and the mad fury of that lovely being. A laugh echoed again upon my lips, an involuntary laugh it was, for I knew not that I had laughed; and then there was a rush and white teeth were at my throat, tearing flesh, and sinews, and veins; and a horrible sound was in my ears, as if some wild animal was tearing at my body! I dreamt that I was in a jungle of Africa, and that a tiger, with a tawney coat, was devouring my still living flesh, and then I became insensible!

When I opened my eyes faintly, I lay in my own bed, and the form of the Duke was bending over me. One of my medical *confreres* held my wrist between his fingers, and the room was still and dark.

"How is this, Bernard?" I asked, with difficulty, for my voice seemed lost, and the weakness of death hanging around my tongue, "what has happened?"

"Hush! my dear fellow, you must not speak. You have been nearly worried to death by a maniac, and you have lost a fearful quantity of blood."

"Oh!" I recollected it all, and turned to the Duke, "and Blanche?"

"She is dead, thank God!" he whispered, calmly.

I shuddered through every nerve and was silent.

It was many long weeks ere I was able to listen to the Duke as he told the fearful tale of the dead girl's disease. The first intimation her wretched relatives had of the horrible thing was upon the morning of her eighteenth year. They went to her room to congratulate her, and found her lying upon the dead body of her younger sister, who occupied the same chamber; she had literally torn her throat with her teeth, and was sucking the hot blood as she was discovered. No words could describe the horror of the wretched parents. The end we have seen.

I never asked how Blanche had died, I did not wish to know; but I guessed that force had been obliged to be used in dragging her teeth from my throat, and that the necessary force was sufficient to destroy her. I have never since met with a case of anthropophagy, but I never even read of the rare discovery of the fearful disease, but I fancy I feel Blanche's teeth at my throat.

1884

THE FAMILY OF THE VOURDALAK

Aleksey Konstantinovich Tolstoy

1815. Vienna. While the Congress had been in session, the city had attracted all the most distinguished European intellectuals, the fashion leaders of the day, and, of course, members of the highest diplomatic élite. But the Congress of Vienna was no longer in session.

Royalist émigrés were preparing to return to their country chateaux (hoping to stay there this time); Russian soldiers were anxiously awaiting the time when they could return to their abandoned homes; and discontented Poles—still dreaming of liberty—were wondering whether their dreams would come true, back in Cracow, under the protection of the precarious 'independence' that had been arranged for them by the trio of Prince Metternich, Prince Hardenberg and Count Nesselrode.

It was as if a masked ball was coming to an end. Of the assembled 'guests', only a select few had stayed behind and delayed packing their bags in the hope of still finding some amusement, preferably in the company of the charming and glamorous Austrian ladies.

This delightful group of people (of which I was a member) met twice a week in a chateau belonging to Madame the dowager Princess of Schwarzenberg. It was a few miles from the city centre, just beyond a little hamlet called Hitzing. The splendid hospitality of our hostess, as well as her amiability and intellectual brilliance, made any stay at her chateau extremely agreeable.

Our mornings were spent *à la promenade*; we lunched all together either at the chateau or somewhere in the grounds; and in the evenings, seated around a welcoming fireside, we amused ourselves by gossiping and telling each other stories. A rule of the house was that we should not talk about anything to do with politics. Everyone had had enough of *that* subject. So our tales were based either on legends from our own countries or else on our own experiences.

One evening, when each of us had told a tale and when our spirits were in that tense state which darkness and silence usually create, the Marquis d'Urfé, an elderly émigré we all loved dearly for his childish gaiety and for the piquant way in which he reminisced about his past life and good fortunes, broke the ominous silence by saying, "Your stories, gentlemen, are all out of the ordinary of course, but it seems to me that each one lacks an essential ingredient—I mean *authenticity*; for I am pretty sure that none of you has seen with his own eyes the fantastic incidents that he has just narrated, nor can he vouch for the truth of his story on his word of honour as a gentleman."

We all had to agree with this, so the elderly gentleman continued, after smoothing down his jabot: "As for me, gentlemen, I know only one story of this kind, but it is at once so strange, so horrible and so *authentic* that it will suffice to strike even the most jaded of imaginations with terror. Having unhappily been both a witness to these strange events and a participant in them, I do not, as a rule, like to remind myself of them—but just this once I will tell the tale, provided, of course, the ladies present will permit me."

Everyone agreed instantly. I must admit that a few of us glanced furtively at the long shadows which the moonlight was beginning to sketch out on the parquet floor. But soon our little circle huddled closer together and each of us kept silent to hear the Marquis's story. M. d'Urfé took a pinch of snuff, slowly inhaled it and began as follows:

Before I start mesdames (said d'Urfé), I ask you to forgive me if, in the course of my story, I should find occasion to talk of my *affaires de coeur* more often than might be deemed appropriate for a man of my advanced years. But I assure that they must be mentioned if you are to make full sense of my story. In any case, one can forgive an elderly man for certain lapses of this kind—surrounded as I am by such attractive young ladies, it is no fault of mine that I am tempted to imagine myself a young man again. So, without further apology, I will commence by telling you that in the year 1759 I was madly in love with the beautiful Duchesse de Gramont. This passion, which I then believed was deep and lasting, gave me no respite either by day or by night and the Duchesse, as young girls often do, enjoyed adding to my torment by her *coquetterie*. So much so that in a moment of spite I determined to solicit and be granted a diplomatic mission to the hospodar of Moldavia, who was then involved in negotiations with Versailles over matters that it would be as tedious as it would be pointless to tell you about.

The day before my departure I called in on the Duchesse. She received me with less mockery than usual and could not hide her emotions as she said, "D'Urfé—you are behaving like a madman, but I know you well enough to be sure that you will never go back on a decision, once taken. So I will only ask one thing of you. Accept this little cross as a token of my affection and wear it until you return. It is a family relic which we treasure a great deal."

With *galanterie* that was perhaps misplaced at such a moment I kissed not the relic but the delightful hand which proffered it to me, and I fastened the cross around my neck—you can see it now. Since then, I have never been parted from it.

I will not bore you, mesdames, with the details of my journey nor with the observations that I made on the Hungarians and the Serbians, those poor and ignorant people who, enslaved as they were by the Turks, were brave and honest enough not to have forgotten either their dignity or their time-honoured independence. It's enough for me to tell you that having learned to speak a little Polish during my stay in Warsaw, I soon had a working knowledge of Serbian as well—for these two languages, like Russian and Bohemian are, as you no doubt know very well, only branches of one and the same root, which is known as Slovonian.

Anyway, I knew enough to make myself understood. One day I arrived in a small village. The name would not interest you very much. I found those who lived in the house where I intended to stay in a state of confusion, which seemed to me all the more strange because it was a Sunday, a day when the Serbian people customarily devote themselves to different pleasures, such as dancing, arquebus shooting, wrestling and so on. I attributed the confusion of my hosts to some very recent misfortune and was about to withdraw when a man of about thirty, tall and impressive to look at, came up to me and shook me by the hand.

"Come in, come in stranger," he said. "Don't let yourself be put off by our sadness; you will understand it well enough when you know the cause."

He then told me about how his old father (whose name was Gorcha), a man of wild and unmanageable temperament, had got up one morning and had taken down his long Turkish arquebus from a rack on a wall.

"My children," he had said to his two sons Georges and Pierre, "I am going to the mountains to join a band of brave fellows who are hunting that dog Ali Bek." (That was the name of a Turkish brigand who had been ravaging the countryside for some time.) "Wait for me patiently for ten days and if I do not return on the tenth, arrange for a funeral mass to be said—for by then I will have been killed. But," old Gorcha had added, looking very serious indeed, "if, may God protect you, I should return after the ten days have passed, do not under any circumstances let me come in. I command you, if this should happen, to forget that I was once your father and to pierce me through the heart with an aspen stake, whatever I might say or do, for then I would no longer be human. I would be a cursed *vourdalak*, come to suck your blood."

It is important at this stage to tell you, mesdames, that the *vourdalaks* (the name given to vampires by Slavic peoples) are, according to local folklore, dead bodies who rise from their graves to suck the blood of the living. In this respect they behave like all types of vampire, but they have one other characteristic which makes them even more terrifying. The *vourdalaks*, mesdames, prefer to suck the blood of their closest relatives and their most intimate friends; once dead, the victims become vampires themselves. People have claimed that entire villages in Bosnia and Hungary have been transformed into *vourdalaks* in this way. The Abbé Augustin Calmet in his strange book on apparitions cites many horrible examples.

Apparently, commissions have been appointed many times by German emperors to study alleged epidemics of vampirism. These commissions collected many eye-witness accounts. They exhumed bodies, which they found to be sated with blood, and ordered them to be burned in the public square after staking them through the heart. Magistrates who witnessed these executions have stated on oath that they heard blood-curdling shrieks coming from these corpses at the moment the executioner hammered his sharpened stake into their hearts. They have formal depositions to this effect and have corroborated them with signatures and with oaths on the Holy Book.

With this information as background, it should be easier for you to understand, mesdames, the effect that old Gorcha's words had on his sons. Both of them went down on their bended knees and begged him to let them go in his place. But instead of replying he had turned his back on them and had set out for the mountains, singing the refrain of an old ballad. The day I arrived in the village was the very day that Gorcha had fixed for his return, so I had no difficulty understanding why his children were so anxious.

This was a good and honest family. Georges, the older of the two sons, was rugged and weatherbeaten. He seemed to me a serious and decisive man. He was married with two children. His brother Pierre, a handsome youth of about eighteen, looked rather less tough and appeared to be the favourite of a younger sister called Sdenka, who was a genuine Slavic beauty. In addition to the striking beauty of her features, a distant resemblance to the Duchesse de Gramont struck me especially. She had a distinctive line on her forehead which in all my experience I have found only on these two people. This line did not seem particularly attractive at first glance, but became irresistible when you had seen it a few times.

77

Perhaps I was still very naive. Perhaps this resemblance, combined with a lively and charmingly simple disposition, was really irresistible. I do not know. But I had not been talking with Sdenka for more than two minutes when I already felt for her an affection so tender that it threatened to become something deeper still if I stayed in the village much longer.

We were all sitting together in front of the house, around a table laden with cheeses and dishes of milk. Sdenka was sewing; her sister-in-law was preparing supper for her children, who were playing in the sand; Pierre, who was doing his best to appear at ease, was whistling as he cleaned a yagatan, or long Turkish knife. Georges was leaning on the table with his head in his hands and looking for signs of movement on the great highway. He was silent.

For my part, I was profoundly affected by the general atmosphere of sadness and, in a fit of melancholy, looked up at the evening clouds which shrouded the dying sun and at the silhouette of a monastery, which was half hidden from my view by a black pine forest.

This monastery, as I subsequently discovered, had been very famous in former times on account of a miraculous icon of the Virgin Mary which, according to legend, had been carried away by the angels and set down on an old oak tree. But at the beginning of the previous century the Turks had invaded this part of the country; they had butchered the monks and pillaged the monastery. Only the walls and a small chapel had survived; an old hermit continued to say Mass there. This hermit showed travellers around the ruins and gave hospitality to pilgrims who, as they walked from one place of devotion to another, liked to rest a while at the Monastery of Our Lady of the Oak. As I have said, I didn't learn all this until much later, for on this particular evening my thoughts were very far from the archaeology of Serbia. As often happens when one allows one's imagination free rein, I was musing on past times—on the good old days of my childhood; on the beauties of France that I had left for a wild and faraway country. I was thinking about the Duchesse de Gramont and—why not admit it?—I was also thinking about several other ladies who lived at the same time as your grandmothers, the memory of whose beauty had quietly entered my thoughts in the train of the beautiful Duchesse. I had soon forgotten all about my hosts and their terrible anxiety.

Suddenly Georges broke the silence. "Wife," he said, "at exactly what time did the old man set out?"

"At eight o'clock. I can clearly remember hearing the monastery bell."

"Well, that's all right then," said Georges. "It cannot be more than half past seven." And he again looked for signs of movement on the great highway which led to the dark forest.

I have forgotten to tell you mesdames, that when the Serbians suspect that someone has become a vampire, they avoid mentioning him by name or speaking of him directly, for they think that this would be an invitation for him to leave his tomb. So Georges, when he spoke of his father, now referred to him simply as 'the old man'.

There was a brief silence. Suddenly one of the children started tugging at Sdenka's apron and crying, "Auntie, when will grandpapa be coming back?"

The only reply he got to this untimely question was a hard slap from Georges. The child began to cry, but his little brother, who by now was surprised and frightened, wanted to know more. "Father, why are we not allowed to talk about grandpapa?"

Another slap shut him up firmly. Both children now began to howl and the whole family made a sign of the cross. Just at that moment, I heard the sound of the monastery bell. As the first chime of the eight was ringing in our ears, we saw a human figure coming out of the darkness of the forest and approaching us.

"It is he, God be praised," cried Sdenka, her sister-in-law and Pierre all at once.

"May the good God protect us," said Georges solemnly. "How are we to know if the ten days have passed or not?"

Everyone looked at him, terror struck. But the human form came closer and closer. It was a tall old man with a silver moustache and a pale, stern face; he was dragging himself along with the aid of a stick. The closer he got, the more shocked Georges looked. When the new arrival was a short distance from us, he stopped and stared at his family with eyes that seemed not to see—they were dull, glazed, deep sunk in their sockets.

"Well, well," he said in a dead voice, "will no one get up to welcome me? What is the meaning of this silence, can't you see I am wounded?"

I saw that the old man's left side was dripping with blood.

"Go and help your father," I said to Georges. "And you, Sdenka, offer him some refreshment. Look at him—he is almost collapsing from exhaustion!"

"Father," said Georges, going up to Gorcha, "show me your wound. I know all about such things and I can take care of it..."

He was just about to take off the old man's coat when Gorcha pushed his son aside roughly and clutched at his body with both hands. "You are too clumsy," he said, "leave me alone... Now you have hurt me."

"You must be wounded in the heart," cried Georges, turning pale. "Take off your coat, take it off. You must, I insist."

The old man pulled himself up to his full height. "Take care," he said in a sepulchral voice. "If you so much as touch me, I shall curse you."

Pierre rushed between Georges and his father. "Leave him alone," he said. "Can't you see that he's suffering?"

"Do not cross him," Georges's wife added. "You know he has never tolerated that."

At that precise moment we saw a flock of sheep returning from pasture raising a cloud of dust as it made its way towards the house. Whether the dog which was escorting the flock did not recognise its own master, or whether it had some other reason for acting as it did, as soon as it caught sight of Gorcha it stopped dead, hackles raised, and began to howl as if it had seen a ghost.

"What is wrong with that dog?" said the old man, looking more and more furious. "What is going on here? Have I become a stranger in my own house? Have ten days spent in the mountains changed me so much that even my own dogs do not recognise me?"

"Did you hear that?" said Georges to his wife.

"What of it?"

"He admits that the ten days *have been spent.*"

"Surely not, for he has come back to us within the appointed time."

"I know what has to be done."

The dog continued to howl. "I want that dog destroyed!" cried Gorcha. "Well, did you hear me?"

Georges made no move, but Pierre got up with tears in his eyes, and grabbed his father's arquebus; he aimed at the dog, fired, and the creature rolled over in the dust.

"That was my favourite dog," he said sulkily. "I don't know why father wanted it to be destroyed."

"Because it deserved to be," bellowed Gorcha. "Come on now, it's cold and I want to go inside." While all this was going on outside, Sdenka had been preparing a cordial for the old man consisting of pears, honey and raisins, laced with *eau de vie*, but her father pushed it aside with disgust. He seemed equally disgusted by the plate of mutton with rice that Georges offered him. Gorcha shuffled over to the fireplace, muttering gibberish from behind clenched teeth.

A pine-log fire crackled in the grate and its flickering light seemed to give life to the pale, emaciated features of the old man. Without the fire's glow, his features could have been taken for those of a corpse.

Sdenka sat down beside him. "Father," she said, "you do not wish to eat anything, you do not wish to rest; perhaps you feel up to telling us about your adventures in the mountains."

By suggesting that, the young girl knew that she was touching her father's most sensitive spot, for the old man loved to talk of wars and adventures.

The trace of a smile creased his colourless lips, although his eyes showed no animation, and as he began to stroke his daughter's beautiful blonde hair, he said: "Yes, my daughter, yes, Sdenka, I would like to tell you all about my adventures in the mountains—but that must wait for another time, for I am too tired today. I can tell you, though, that Ali Bek is dead and that he perished by my hand. If anyone doubts my word," continued the old man, looking hard at his two sons, "here is the proof."

He undid a kind of sack which was slung behind his back, and pulled out a foul, bloody head which looked about as pale as his own! We all recoiled in horror, but Gorcha gave it to Pierre.

"Take it," he said, "and nail it above the door, to show all who pass by that Ali Bek is dead and that the roads are free of brigands—except, of course, for the Sultan's janissaries!"

Pierre was disgusted. But he obeyed. "Now I understand why that poor dog was howling," he said. "He could smell dead flesh!"

"Yes, he could smell dead flesh," murmured Georges; he had gone out of the room without anyone noticing him and had returned at that moment with something in his hand which he placed carefully against a wall. It looked to me like a sharpened stake.

"Georges," said his wife, almost in a whisper, "I hope you do not intend to…"

"My brother," Sdenka added anxiously, "what do you mean to do? No, no—surely you're not going to…"

"Leave me alone," replied Georges, "I know what I have to do and I will only do what is absolutely necessary."

While all this had been going on, night had fallen, and the family went to bed in a part of the house which was separated from my room only by a narrow partition. I must admit that what I had seen that evening had made an impression on my imagination. My candle was out; the moonlight shone through a little window near my bed and cast blurred shadows on the floor and walls, rather like those we see now, mesdames, in this room. I wanted to go to sleep but I could not. I thought this was because the moonlight was so clear; but when I looked for something to curtain the window, I could find nothing suitable. Then I overheard confused voices from the other side of the partition. I tried to make out what was being said.

"Go to sleep, wife," said Georges. "And you Pierre, and you Sdenka. Do not worry, I will watch over you."

"But Georges," replied his wife, "it is I who should keep watch over you— you worked all last night and you must be tired. In any case, I ought to be staying awake to watch over our eldest boy. You know he has not been well since yesterday!"

"Be quiet and go to sleep," said Georges. "I will keep watch for both of us."

"Brother," put in Sdenka in her sweetest voice, "there is no need to keep watch at all. Father is already asleep—he seems calm and peaceful enough."

"Neither of you understands what is going on," said Georges in a voice which allowed for no argument. "Go to sleep I tell you, and let me keep watch."

There followed a long silence. Soon my eyelids grew heavy and sleep began to take possession of my senses.

I thought I saw the door of my room opening slowly, and old Gorcha standing in the doorway. Actually, I did not so much see as *feel* his presence, as there was only darkness behind him. I felt his dead eyes trying to penetrate my deepest thoughts as they watched the movement of my breathing. One step forward, then another, Then, with extreme care, he began to walk towards me, with a wolflike motion. Finally he leaped forward. Now he was right beside my bed. I was absolutely terrified, but somehow managed not to move. The old man leaned over me and his waxen face was so close to mine that I could feel his corpselike breath. Then, with a superhuman effort, I managed to wake up, soaked in perspiration.

There was nobody in my room, but as I looked towards the window I could distinctly see old Gorcha's face pressed against the glass from outside, staring at me with his sunken eyes. By sheer willpower I stopped myself from crying out and I had the presence of mind to stay lying down, just as if I had seen nothing out of the ordinary. Luckily, the old man was only making sure that I was asleep, for he made no attempt to come in, and after staring at me long enough to satisfy himself, he moved away from the window and I could hear his footsteps in the neighbouring room. Georges was sound asleep and snoring loudly enough to wake the dead.

At that moment the child coughed, and I could make out Gorcha's voice. "You are not asleep little one?"

"No, grandpapa," replied the child, "And I would so like to talk with you."

"So, you would like to talk with me, would you? And what would we talk about?"

"We would talk with how you fought the Turks. I would love to fight the Turks!"

"I thought you might, child, and I brought back a little yagatan for you. I'll give it to you tomorrow."

"Grandpapa, grandpapa, give it to me now."

"But little one, why didn't you talk to me about this when it was daytime?"

"Because papa would not let me."

"He is careful, your papa... So you really would like to have your little yagatan?"

"Oh yes, I would love that, but not here, for papa might wake up."

"Where then?"

"If we go outside, I promise to be good and not to make any noise at all."

I thought I could hear Gorcha chuckle as the child got out of bed. I didn't believe in vampires, but the nightmare had preyed on my nerves, and just in case I should have to reproach myself in the morning I got up and banged my fist against the partition. It was enough to wake up the 'seven sleepers', but there was no sign of life from the family. I threw myself against the door, determined to save the child—but it was locked from the outside and I couldn't shift the bolts. While I was trying to force it open, I saw the old man pass by my window with the little child in his arms.

"Wake up! Wake up!" I cried at the top of my voice, as I shook the partition. Even then only Georges showed any sign of movement.

"Where is the old man?" he murmured blearily.

"Quick," I yelled, "he's just taken away your child."

With one kick, Georges broke down the door of his room—which like mine had been locked from the outside—and he sprinted in the direction of the dark forest. At last I succeeded in waking Pierre, his sister-in-law and Sdenka. We all assembled in front of the house and after a few minutes anxious waiting we saw Georges return from the dark forest with his son. The child had apparently passed out on the highway, but he was soon revived and didn't seem to be any more ill than before. After questioning him we discovered that his grandpapa had not, in fact, done him any harm; they had apparently gone out together to talk undisturbed, but once outside the child had lost consciousness without remembering why. Gorcha himself had disappeared.

As you can imagine, no one could sleep for the rest of that night. The next day, I learned that the river Danube, which cut across the highway about a quarter of a league from the village, had begun to freeze over; drift ice now blocked my route. This often happens in these parts some time between the end of autumn and the beginning of spring. Since the highway was expected to be blocked for some days, I could not think of leaving. In any case, even if I could have left, curiosity—as well as a more powerful emotion—would have held me back. The more I saw Sdenka, the more I felt I was falling in love with her.

I am not among those, mesdames, who believe in love at first sight of the kind which novelists so often write about; but I do believe that there are occasions when love develops more quickly than is usual. Sdenka's strange beauty, her singular resemblance to the Duchesse de Gramont—the lady from whom I had fled in Paris, and who I saw again in this remote setting, dressed in a rustic costume and speaking in a musical foreign tongue—the fascinating line on her forehead, like that for which I had been prepared to kill myself at least twenty times in France: all this, combined with the incredible, mysterious situation in which I found myself... everything helped to nurture in me a passion which, in other circumstances, would perhaps have proved itself to be more vague and passing.

During the course of the day I overheard Sdenka talking to her younger brother. "What do you think of all this?" she asked. "Do you also suspect our father?"

"I dare not suspect him," replied Pierre, "especially since the child insists that he came to no harm. And as for father's disappearance, you know that he never used to explain his comings and goings."

"I know," said Sdenka. "All the more reason why we must think about saving him, for you know that Georges..."

"Yes, yes, I know. It would be useless to talk him out of it. We can at least hide the stake. He certainly won't go out looking for another one, since there is not a single aspen tree this side of the mountains."

"Yes, let's hide the stake—but don't mention it to the children, for they might chatter about it with Georges listening."

"We must take care not to let that happen," said Pierre. And they went their separate ways.

At nightfall we had still discovered nothing about old Gorcha. As on the previous night I was lying on my bed, and the moonlight again stopped me from going to sleep. When at last sleep began to confuse my thoughts, I again felt, as if by instinct, that the old man was coming towards me. I opened my eyes and saw his waxen face pressed against my window.

This time I wanted to get up but could not. All my limbs seemed to be paralysed. After taking a good long look at me, the old man disappeared. I heard him wandering around the house and tapping gently on the window of Georges's room. The child turned over on his bed and moaned as he dreamed. After several minutes silence the tapping on the window resumed.

86

Then the child groaned once again and woke up. "Is that you grandpapa?" he asked.

"It is me," replied a dead voice, "and I have brought you your little yagatan."

"But I dare not go outside. Papa has forbidden it."

"There is no need to go outside; just open the window and embrace me!"

The child got up and I could hear him opening the window. Then somehow finding the strength, I leaped to the foot of my bed and ran over to the partition. I struck it hard with my fist. In a few seconds Georges was on his feet. I heard him mutter an oath. His wife screamed. In no time at all the whole household had gathered around the lifeless child. Just as on the previous occasion, there was no sign of Gorcha. We tried carefully to revive the child, but he was very weak and breathed with difficulty. The poor little chap had no idea why he had passed out. His mother and Sdenka thought it was because of the shock of being caught talking with his grandpapa. I said nothing. However, by now the child seemed to be more calm and everybody except Georges went back to bed.

At daybreak, I overheard Georges waking his wife and whispering with her. Sdenka joined them and I could hear both the women sobbing. The child was dead.

Of the family's despair, the less said the better. Strangely enough no one blamed the child's death on old Gorcha—at least, not openly. Georges sat in silence, but his expression, always gloomy, now became terrible to behold. Two days passed and there was still no sign of the old man. On the night of the third day (the day of the child's burial) I thought I heard footsteps all around the house and an old man's voice which called out the name of the dead child's brother. For a split second I also thought I saw Gorcha's face pressed against my window, but I couldn't be sure if I was imagining it or not, for the moon was veiled by cloud that night. Nevertheless I considered it my duty to mention this apparition to Georges. He questioned the child, who replied that he *had* in fact heard grandpapa calling and had also seen him looking in through the window. Georges strictly charged his son to wake him up if the old man should appear again.

All these happenings did not prevent my passion for Sdenka from developing more and more each day. In the daytime, I couldn't talk to her alone. At night, the mere thought that I would shortly have to leave broke my heart. Sdenka's room was only separated from mine by a kind of corridor which led to the road on one side and a courtyard on the other. When the whole family had gone to bed, I decided to go for a short walk in the fields to ease my mind. As I walked along the corridor I saw that Sdenka's door was slightly open. Instinctively, I stopped and listened. The rustling of her dress, a sound I knew well, made my heart pound against my chest. Then I heard her singing softly. She was singing about a Serbian king who was saying farewell to his lady before going to the war.

"Oh my young Poplar," said the old king, "I am going to the war and you will forget me.

"The trees which grow beneath the mountain are slender and pliant, but they are nothing beside your young body!

"The berries of the rowan tree which sway in the wind are red, but your lips are more red than the berries of the rowan tree!

"And I am like an old oak stripped of leaves, and my beard is whiter than the foam of the Danube!

"And you will forget me, oh my soul, and I will die of grief, for the enemy will not dare to kill the old King!"

The beautiful lady replied: "I swear to be faithful to you and never to forget you. If I should break my oath, come to me after your death and drink all my heart's blood!"

And the old king said: "So be it!"

And he set off for the war. Soon the beautiful lady forgot him...!

At this point Sdenka paused, as if she was frightened to finish the ballad. I could restrain myself no longer. That voice—so sweet, so expressive—was the voice of the Duchesse de Gramont... Without pausing to think, I pushed open the door and went in. Sdenka had just taken off her knitted jacket (of a kind often worn by women in those regions). All she was wearing was a nightgown of red silk, embroidered with gold, held tight against her body by a simple, brightly coloured belt. Her fine blonde hair hung loose over her shoulders. She looked more beautiful than ever. She did not seem upset by my sudden entry, but she was confused and blushed slightly.

"Oh," she said, "why have you come? What will the family think of me if we are discovered?"

"Sdenka, my soul, do not be frightened! Everyone is asleep. Only the cricket in the grass and the mayfly in the air can hear what I have to say to you."

"Oh my friend, leave me, leave me! If my brother should discover us I am lost!"

"Sdenka, I will not leave you until you have promised to love me for ever, as the beautiful lady promised the king in your ballad. Soon I will have to leave… Who knows when we will see each other again? Sdenka, I love you more than my soul, more than my salvation… my life's blood is yours… may I not be granted one hour with you in return?"

"Many things can happen in an hour," said Sdenka calmly. But she did let her hand slip into mine.

"You do not know my brother," she continued, beginning to tremble. "I fear he will discover us."

"Calm yourself, my darling Sdenka. Your brother is exhausted from watching late into the night; he has been lulled to sleep by the wind rustling in the trees; heavy is his sleep, long is the night and I only ask to be granted one hour—then, farewell, perhaps for ever!"

"Oh no, no, not for ever!" cried Sdenka; then she recoiled, as if frightened by the sound of her own voice.

"Oh Sdenka, I see only you, I hear only you; I am no longer master of my own destiny; a superior strength commands my obedience. Forgive me, Sdenka!" Like a madman I clutched her to my heart.

"You are no friend to me," she cried, tearing herself from my embrace and rushing to another part of the room. I do not know what I said to her then, for I was as alarmed as she was by my own forwardness, not because such boldness had failed me in the past—far from it—but because in spite of my passion, I could not help having a sincere respect for Sdenka's innocence. It is true that I had used the language of *galanterie* with this girl at first (a language which did not seem to displease the society ladies of the time) but I was now ashamed of these empty phrases and renounced them when I saw that the young girl was too naive to comprehend fully what I meant by them—what you, mesdames, to judge by your suggestive smiles, have understood immediately. I stood before her, at a loss as to what to say, when suddenly she began to tremble and look towards the window, terror struck. I followed her gaze and clearly saw the corpse-like face of Gorcha, staring at us from outside.

At precisely that moment, I felt a heavy hand on my shoulder.

I froze. It was Georges. "What are you doing here?" he snapped.

Embarrassed by his tone of voice, I simply pointed towards his father, who was still staring at us through the window—but he disappeared the moment Georges turned to look at him.

"I heard the old man and came to warn your sister," I stammered.

Georges looked me straight in the eye, as if trying to read my innermost thoughts. Then he took me by the arm, led me to my room and left, without a single word.

The next day the family had gathered in front of the house, around a table laden with jugs of milk and cakes.

"Where is the child?" said Georges.

"In the courtyard," replied his wife. "He is playing his favourite game, imagining that he is fighting the Turks single-handed."

No sooner had she said these words, than to our amazement we saw the tall figure of Gorcha walking slowly towards us from out of the dark forest. He sat at the table just as he had done the day I arrived.

"Father, we welcome you," murmured Georges's wife in a hoarse voice.

"We welcome you, father," whispered Sdenka and Pierre in unison.

"My father," said Georges firmly, turning pale, "we are waiting for you to say Grace!"

The old man glared at him and turned away.

"Yes… Grace—say it now!" repeated Georges, crossing himself. "Say it this instant, or by St George…"

Sdenka and her sister-in-law threw themselves at the old man's feet and begged him to say Grace.

"No, no, no," said the old man. "He has no right to speak to me in that way, and if he continues, I will curse him!"

Georges got up and rushed into the house. He returned almost immediately, looking furious. "Where is that stake?" he yelled. "Where have you hidden it?"

Sdenka and Pierre looked at each other.

"Corpse!" Georges shouted at the old man. "What have you done with my elder boy? Why have you killed my little child? Give me back my son, you creature of the grave!"

As he said this, he became more and more pale and his eyes began to burn with fury. The old man simply glared at him.

"The stake, the stake," yelled Georges. "Whoever has hidden it must answer for all the evils which will befall us!"

At this moment we heard the excited laughter of the younger child. We saw him galloping towards us on a wooden horse, or rather on a long aspen stake, shrieking the Serbian battle cry at the top of his voice. Georges's eyes lit up, as he realised what was happening. He grabbed the stake from the child and threw himself at his father. The old man let out a fearful groan and began to sprint towards the dark forest as if possessed by demons. Georges raced after him across the fields, and soon they were both out of sight.

It was after sunset when Georges returned to the house. He was as pale as death; his hair stood on end. He sat down by the fireside, and I could hear his teeth chattering. No one could pluck up the courage to question him. By about the time the family normally went to bed he seemed to be more his usual self and, taking me to one side, said to me quite calmly: "My dear guest, I have been to the river. The ice has gone, the road is clear—nothing now prevents you from leaving. There is no need," he added, glancing at Sdenka, "to take your leave of my family. Through me, the family wishes you all the happiness you could desire and I hope that you will have some happy memories of the time you have spent with us. Tomorrow at daybreak, you will find your horse saddled and your guide ready to escort you. Farewell. Think about your host from time to time, and forgive him if your stay here has not been as carefree as he would have liked."

As he said this, even Georges's rough features looked almost friendly. He led me to my room and shook my hand for one last time. Then he began to tremble and his teeth chattered as if he were suffering from the cold.

Now I was alone, I had no thoughts of going to sleep—as you can imagine. Other things were on my mind. I had loved many times in my life, and had experienced the whole range of passions—tenderness, jealousy, fury—but never, not even when I left the Duchesse de Gramont, had I felt anything like the sadness that I felt in my heart at that moment. Before sunrise, I changed into my travelling clothes, hoping to have a few words with Sdenka before I departed. But Georges was waiting for me in the hall. There was no chance of my seeing her again.

I leaped into the saddle and spurred on my horse. I made a resolution to return from Jassy via this village, and although that might be some time hence, the thought made me feel easier in my mind. It was some consolation for me to imagine in advance all the details of my return. But this pleasant reverie was soon shattered. My horse shied away from something and nearly had me out of the saddle. The animal stopped dead, dug in its forelegs and began to snort wildly as if some danger was nearby. I looked around anxiously and saw something moving about a hundred paces away. It was a wolf digging in the ground. Sensing my presence, the wolf ran away; digging my spurs into the horse's flanks, I managed with difficulty to get him to move forward. It was then that I realised that on the spot where the wolf had been standing, there was a freshly dug grave. I seem to remember also that the end of a stake protruded a few inches out of the ground where the wolf had been digging. However, I do not swear to this, for I rode away from that place as fast as I could.

At this point the Marquis paused and took a pinch of snuff.

"Is that the end of the story?" the ladies asked.

"I'm afraid not," replied M. d'Urfé. "What remains to be told is a very unhappy memory for me, and I would give much to cast it from my mind."

My reasons for going to Jassy (he continued) kept me there for much longer than I had expected—well over six months, in fact. What can I say to justify my conduct during that time? It is a sad fact, but a fact nonetheless, that there are very few emotions in this life which can stand the test of time. The success of my negotiations, which were very well received in Versailles—politics, in a word, vile politics, a subject which has become so boring to us in recent times—preoccupied my thoughts and dimmed the memory of Sdenka. In addition, from the moment I arrived, the wife of the hospodar, a very beautiful lady who spoke fluent French, did me the honour of receiving my attentions, singling me out from among all the other young foreigners who were staying in Jassy. Like me, she had been brought up to believe in the principles of French *galanterie*; the mere thought that I should rebuff the advances of such a beautiful lady stirred up my Gallic blood. So I received her advances with courtesy, and since I was there to represent the interests and rights of France, I made a start by representing those of her husband the hospodar as well.

When I was recalled home, I left by the same road I had ridden to Jassy. I no longer even thought about Sdenka or her family, but one evening when I was riding in the countryside, I heard a bell ringing the eight o'clock chime.

I seemed to recognise that sound and my guide told me that it came from a nearby monastery. I asked him the name: it was the monastery of Our Lady of the Oak. I galloped ahead and in no time at all we had reached the monastery gate. The old hermit welcomed us and led us to his hostel.

The number of pilgrims staying there put me off the idea of spending the night at the hostel, and I asked if there was any accommodation available in the village.

"You can stay where you like in the village," replied the old hermit with a gloomy sigh. "Thanks to that devil Gorcha, there are plenty of empty houses!"

"What on earth do you mean?" I asked. "Is old Gorcha still alive?"

"Oh no, he's well and truly buried with a stake through his heart! But he rose from the grave to suck the blood of Georges's little son. The child returned one night and knocked on the door, crying that he was cold and wanted to come home. His foolish mother, although she herself had been present at his burial, did not have the strength of mind to send him back to the cemetery, so she opened the door. He threw himself at her throat and sucked away her life's blood. After she had been buried, she in turn rose from the grave to suck the blood of her second son, then the blood of her husband, then the blood of her brother-in-law. They all went the same way."

"And Sdenka?"

"Oh, she went mad with grief; poor, poor child, do not speak to me of her!"

The old hermit had not really answered my question, but I did not have the heart to repeat it. He crossed himself. "Vampirism is contagious," he said after a pause. "Many families in the village have been afflicted by it, many families have been completely destroyed, and if you take my advice you will stay in my hostel tonight; for even if the *vourdalaks* of the village do not attack you, they will terrify you so much that your hair will have turned white before I ring the bells for morning mass.

"I am only a poor and simple monk," he continued, "but the generosity of passing travellers gives me enough to provide for their needs. I can offer you fresh country cheese and sweet plums which will make your mouth water; I also have some flagons of Tokay wine which are every bit as good as those which grace the cellars of His Holiness the Patriarch!"

The old hermit seemed to be behaving more like an innkeeper than a poor and simple monk. I reckoned he had told me some old wives' tales about the village in order to make me feel grateful enough for his hospitality to show my appreciation in the usual way, by giving the holy man enough to provide for the needs of passing travellers. In any case, the word terror has always had the effect on me that a battle cry has on a war horse. I would have been thoroughly ashamed of myself if I had not set out immediately to see for myself. But my guide, who was less enthusiastic about the idea, asked my permission to stay in the hostel. This I willingly granted.

It took me about half an hour to reach the village. Deserted. No lights shone through the windows, no songs were being sung. I rode past many houses that I knew, all as silent as the grave. Finally I reached Georges's. Whether I was being sentimental or just rash, I don't know, but it was there I decided to spend the night. I got off my horse, and banged on the gate. Still no sign of life. I pushed the gate and the hinges creaked eerily as it slowly opened. Then I crept into the courtyard. In one of the outhouses I found enough oats to last the night, so I left my horse tethered there, still saddled, and strode towards the main house. Although all the rooms were deserted, no doors were locked. Sdenka's room had been occupied only a few hours before. Some of her clothes were draped carelessly over the bed. A few pieces of jewellery that I had given her, including a small enamel cross from Budapest, lay on her table sparkling in the moonlight. Even though my love for her was a thing of the past, I must admit that my heart was heavy. Nevertheless, I wrapped myself up in my cloak and stretched out on her bed. Soon I was asleep. I cannot recall everything, but I do remember that I dreamed of Sdenka, as beautiful, as simple and as loving as she had been when first I met her. I remember also feeling ashamed of my selfishness and my inconstancy. How could I have abandoned that poor child who loved me; how could I have forgotten her? Then her image became confused with that of the Duchesse de Gramont and I saw only one person. I threw myself at Sdenka's feet and begged her forgiveness. From the depths of my being, from the depths of my soul came an indescribable feeling of melancholy and of joy.

I lay there dreaming, until I was almost awakened by a gentle musical sound, like the rustling of a cornfield in a light breeze. I heard the sweet rustling of the corn and the music of singing birds, the rushing of a waterfall and the whispering of trees. Then I realised that all these sounds were merely the swishing of a woman's dress and I opened my eyes. There was Sdenka standing beside my bed. The moon was shining so brightly that I could distinguish every single feature which had been so dear to me and which my dream made me love again as if for the first time. Sdenka seemed more beautiful, and somehow more mature. She was dressed as she had been when last I saw her alone: a simple nightgown of red silk, gold embroidered, and a coloured belt, clinging tightly above her hips.

"Sdenka!" I cried, sitting up. "Is it really you, Sdenka?"

"Yes, it is me," she replied in a sweet, sad voice. "It is that same Sdenka you have forgotten. Why did you not return sooner? Everything is finished now; you must leave; a moment longer and you are lost! Farewell my friend, farewell for ever!"

"Sdenka: you have seen so much unhappiness they say! Come, let us talk, let us ease your pain!"

"Oh, my friend, you must not believe everything they say about us; but leave me, leave me now, for if you stay a moment longer you are doomed."

"Sdenka, what are you afraid of? Can you not grant me an hour, just one hour to talk with you?"

Sdenka began to tremble and her whole being seemed to undergo a strange transformation. "Yes," she said, "one hour, just one hour, the same hour you begged of me when you came into this room and heard me singing the ballad of the old king. Is that what you mean? So be it, I will grant you one hour! But no, no!" she cried, as if fighting her inclinations, "leave me, go away!—leave now, I tell you, fly! Fly, while you still have the chance!"

Her features were possessed with a savage strength. I could not understand why she should be saying these things, but she was so beautiful that I determined to stay, whatever she said. At last she surrendered, sat down beside me, and spoke to me of the past; she blushed as she admitted that she had fallen in love with me the moment she set eyes on me. But little by little I began to notice that Sdenka was not as I had remembered her. Her former timidity had given way to a strange wantonness of manner. She seemed more forward, more knowing. It dawned on me that her behaviour was no longer that of the naive young girl I recalled in my dream. Is it possible, I mused, that Sdenka was never the pure and innocent maiden that I imagined her to be? Did she simply put on an act to please her brother? Was I gulled by an affected virtue? If so, why insist that I leave? Was this perhaps a refinement of *coquetterie*? And I thought I knew her! What did it matter? If Sdenka was not a Diana, as I thought, she began to resemble another goddess at least as attractive—perhaps more so. By God! I preferred the role of Adonis to that of Actaeon.

If this classical style that I adopted seems a little out of place, mesdames, remember that I have the honour to be telling you of incidents which occurred in the year of grace 1758. At that time mythology was *very* fashionable, and I am trying to keep my story in period. Things have changed a lot since then, and it was not so long ago that the Revolution, having overthrown both the traces of paganism and the Christian religion, erected the goddess Reason in their place. This goddess, mesdames, has never been my patron saint, least of all when I am in the presence of other goddesses, and, at the time I am referring to, I was less disposed than ever to worship at her shrine.

I abandoned myself passionately to Sdenka, and willingly outdid even her in the provocative game she was playing. Some time passed in sweet intimacy, until, as Sdenka was amusing me by trying on various pieces of jewellery, I thought it would be a good idea to place the little enamel cross around her neck. But as I tried to do this, Sdenka recoiled sharply.

"Enough of these childish games, my dearest," she said. "Let us talk about you and what is on your mind!"

This sudden change in Sdenka's behaviour made me pause a moment and think. Looking at her more closely I noticed that she no longer wore around her neck the cluster of tiny icons, holy relics and charms filled with incense which Serbians are usually given as children, to wear for the rest of their lives.

"Sdenka," I asked, "where are those things you used to wear around your neck?"

"I have lost them," she replied impatiently, and hastily changed the subject.

I do not know exactly why, but at that moment I began to feel a strong sense of foreboding. I wanted to leave, but Sdenka held me back. "What is this?" she said. "You asked to be granted an hour, and here you are trying to leave after only a few minutes!"

"Sdenka, you were right when you tried to persuade me to leave; I think I hear a noise and I fear we will be discovered!"

"Calm yourself my love, everyone is asleep; only the cricket in the grass and the mayfly in the air can hear what I have to say!"

"No, no, Sdenka, I must leave now...!"

"Stay, stay," she implored, "I love you more than my soul, more than my salvation. You once told me that your life's blood belonged to me...!"

"But your brother—your brother, Sdenka—I have a feeling he will discover us!"

"Calm yourself my soul; my brother has been lulled to sleep by the wind rustling in the trees; heavy is his sleep, long is the night and I only ask to be granted one hour!"

As she said this, Sdenka looked so ravishing that my vague sense of foreboding turned into a strong desire to remain near her. A strange, almost sensual feeling, part fear, part excitement, filled my whole being. As I began to weaken, Sdenka became more tender, and I resolved to surrender, hoping to keep up my guard. However, as I told you at the beginning, I have always overestimated my own strength of mind, and when Sdenka, who had noticed that I was holding back, suggested that we chase away the chill of the night by drinking a few glasses of the good hermit's full-blooded wine, I agreed with a readiness which made her smile. The wine had its desired effect. By the second glass, I had forgotten all about the incident of the cross and the holy relics; Sdenka, with her beautiful blonde hair falling loose over her shoulders, with her jewels sparkling in the moonlight, was quite irresistible. Abandoning all restraint, I held her tight in my arms.

Then, mesdames, a strange thing happened. One of those mysterious revelations that I can never hope to explain. If you had asked me then, I would have denied that such things could happen, but now I know better. As I held Sdenka tightly against my body, one of the points of the cross which the Duchesse de Gramont gave me before I left stuck sharply into my chest. The stab of pain that I felt affected me like a ray of light passing right through my body. Looking up at Sdenka I saw for the first time that her features, though still beautiful, were those of a corpse; that her eyes did not see; and that her smile was the distorted grimace of a decaying skull. At the same time, I sensed in that room the putrid smell of the charnel-house. The fearful truth was revealed to me in all its ugliness, and I remembered too late what the old hermit had said to me. I realised what a fearsome predicament I was in. Everything depended on my courage and my self control.

I turned away from Sdenka to hide the horror which was written on my face. It is then that I looked out of the window and saw the satanic figure of Gorcha, leaning on a bloody stake and staring at me with the eyes of a hyena. Pressed against the other window were the waxen features of Georges, who at that moment looked as terrifying as his father. Both were watching my every movement, and I knew that they would pounce on me the moment I tried to escape. So I pretended not to know they were there, and, with incredible self control, continued—yes, mesdames, I actually continued—passionately to embrace Sdenka, just as I had done before my horrifying discovery. Meanwhile, I desperately racked my brains for some means of escape. I noticed that Gorcha and Georges were exchanging knowing glances with Sdenka and that they were showing signs of losing patience. Then, from somewhere outside, I heard a woman's shriek and the sound of children crying, like the howling of wild cats; these noises set my nerves on edge.

Time to make for home, I said to myself, *and the sooner the better!*

Turning to Sdenka, I raised my voice so that her hideous family would be sure to hear me: "I am tired, my dear child; I must go to bed and sleep for a few hours. But first I must go and see whether my horse needs feeding. I beg you to stay where you are and to wait for me to come back." I then pressed my mouth against her cold, dead lips and left the room.

I found my horse in a panic, covered with lather and crashing his hooves against the outhouse wall. He had not touched the oats, and the fearful noise he made when he saw me coming gave me gooseflesh, for I feared he would give the game away. But the vampires, who had almost certainly overheard my conversion with Sdenka, did not appear to think that anything suspicious was happening. After making sure that the main gate was open, I vaulted into the saddle and dug my spurs into the horse's flanks.

As I rode out of the gates I just had time to glimpse a whole crowd gathered around the house, many of them with their faces pressed against the windows. I think it was my sudden departure which first confused them, but I cannot be sure: the only sound I could hear at that moment was the regular beat of my horse's hooves which echoed in the night. I was just about to congratulate myself on my cunning, when all of a sudden I heard a fearful noise behind me, like the sound of a hurricane roaring through the mountains. A thousand discordant voices shrieked, moaned and contended with one another. Then complete silence, as if by common assent. And I heard a rhythmic stamping, like a troop of foot soldiers advancing in double-quick time.

I spurred on my horse until I tore into his flanks. A burning fever coursed through my veins. I was making one last effort to preserve my sanity, when I heard a voice behind me which cried out: "Stop, don't leave me, my dearest! I love you more than my soul, I love you more than my salvation! Turn back, turn back, your life's blood is mine!"

A cold breath brushed my ear and I sensed that Sdenka had leaped on to my horse from behind. "My heart, my soul!" she cried, "I see only you, hear only you! I am not mistress of my own destiny—a superior force commands my obedience. Forgive me, my dearest, forgive me!"

Twisting her arms around me she tried to sink her teeth into my neck and to wrench me from my horse. There was a terrible struggle. For some time I had difficulty even defending myself, but eventually I managed to grab hold of Sdenka by curling one arm around her waist and knotting the other hand in her hair. Standing bolt upright in my stirrups, I threw her to the ground!

Then my strength gave out completely and I became delirious. Frenzied shapes pursued me—mad, grimacing faces. Georges and his brother Pierre ran beside the road and tried to block my way. They did not succeed, but just as I was about to give thanks, I looked over my shoulder and caught sight of old Gorcha, who was using his stake to propel himself forward as the Tyrolean mountain men do when they leap over Alpine chasms. But Gorcha did not manage to catch up with me. Then his daughter-in-law, dragging her children behind her, threw one of them to him; he caught the child on the sharpened point of his stake. Using the stake as a catapult he slung the creature towards me with all his might. I fended off the blow, but with the true terrier instinct the little brat sunk his teeth into my horse's neck, and I had some difficulty tearing him away. The other child was propelled towards me in the same way, but he landed beyond the horse and was crushed to pulp. I do not know what happened after that, but when I regained consciousness it was daylight, and I found myself lying near the road next to my dying horse.

So ended, mesdames, a love affair which should perhaps have cured me for ever of the desire to become involved in any others. Some contemporaries of your grandmothers could tell you whether I had learned my lesson or not. But, joking aside, I still shudder at the thought that if I had given in to my enemies, I would myself have become a vampire. As it was, Heaven did not allow things to come to that, and so far from wishing to suck your blood, mesdames, I only ask—old as I am—to be granted the privilege of shedding my own blood in your service!

1869

GOOD LADY DUCAYNE

Mary Elizabeth Braddon

BELLA Rolleston had made up her mind that her only chance of earning her bread and helping her mother to an occasional crust was by going out into the great unknown world as companion to a lady. She was willing to go to any lady rich enough to pay her a salary and so eccentric as to wish for a hired companion. Five shillings told off reluctantly from one of those sovereigns which were so rare with the mother and daughter, and which melted away so quickly, five solid shillings, had been handed to a smartly dressed lady in an office in Harbeck Street, W., in the hope that this very Superior Person would find a situation and a salary for Miss Rolleston.

The Superior Person glanced at the two half-crowns as they lay on the table where Bella's hand had placed them, to make sure they were neither of them florins, before she wrote a description of Bella's qualifications and requirements in a formidable-looking ledger.

"Age?" she asked curtly.

"Eighteen, last July."

"Any accomplishments?"

"No; I am not at all accomplished. If I were I should want to be a governess—a companion seems the lowest stage."

"We have some highly accomplished ladies on our books as companions, or chaperone companions."

"Oh, I know!" babbled Bella, loquacious in her youthful candour. "But that is quite a different thing. Mother hasn't been able to afford a piano since I was twelve years old, so I'm afraid I've forgotten how to play. And I have had to help mother with her needlework, so there hasn't been much time to study."

"Please don't waste time upon explaining what you can't do, but kindly tell me anything you can do," said the Superior Person crushingly, with her pen poised between delicate fingers waiting to write. "Can you read aloud for two or three hours at a stretch? Are you active and handy, an early riser, a good walker, sweet-tempered, and obliging?"

"I can say yes to all those questions except about the sweetness. I think I have a pretty good temper, and I should be anxious to oblige anybody who paid for my services. I should want them to feel that I was really earning my salary."

"The kind of ladies who come to me would not care for a talkative companion," said the Person severely, having finished writing in her book. "My connection lies chiefly among the aristocracy, and in that class considerable deference is expected."

"Oh, of course," said Bella; "but it's quite different when I'm talking to you. I want to tell you all about myself once and for ever."

"I am glad it is to be only once!" said the Person, with the edges of her lips.

The Person was of uncertain age, tightly laced in a black silk gown. She had a powdery complexion and a handsome clump of somebody else's hair on the top of her head. It may be that Bella's girlish freshness and vivacity had an irritating effect upon nerves weakened by an eight hours' day in that over-heated second floor in Harbeck Street. To Bella the official apartment, with its Brussels carpet, velvet curtains and velvet chairs, and French clock, ticking loud on the marble chimney-piece, suggested the luxury of a palace, as compared with another second floor in Walworth where Mrs Rolleston and her daughter had managed to exist for the last six years.

"Do you think you have anything on your books that would suit me?" faltered Bella, after a pause.

"Oh, dear, no; I have nothing in view at present," answered the Person, who had swept Bella's half-crowns into a drawer, absent-mindedly, with the tips of her fingers. "You see, you are so very unformed—so much too young to be companion to a lady of position. It is a pity you have not enough education for a nursery governess; that would be more in your line."

"And do you think it will be very long before you can get me a situation?" asked Bella doubtfully.

"I really cannot say. Have you any particular reason for being so impatient—not a love affair, I hope?"

"A love affair!" cried Bella, with flaming cheeks. "What utter nonsense. I want a situation because mother is poor, and I hate being a burden to her. I want a salary that I can share with her."

"There won't be much margin for sharing in the salary you are likely to get at your age—and with your—very—unformed manners," said the Person, who found Bella's peony cheeks, bright eyes, and unbridled vivacity more and more oppressive.

"Perhaps if you'd be kind enough to give me back the fee, I could take it to an agency where the connection isn't quite so aristocratic," said Bella, who—as she told her mother in her recital of the interview—was determined not to be sat upon.

"You will find no agency that can do more for you than mine," replied the Person, whose harpy fingers never relinquished coin. "You will have to wait for your opportunity. Yours is an exceptional case: but I will bear you in mind, and if anything suitable offers I will write to you. I cannot say more than that."

The half-contemptuous bend of the stately head, weighted with borrowed hair, indicated the end of the interview. Bella went back to Walworth—tramped sturdily every inch of the way in the September afternoon—and "took off" the Superior Person for the amusement of her mother and the landlady, who lingered in the shabby little sitting-room after bringing in the tea-tray, to applaud Miss Rolleston's "taking off".

"Dear, dear, what a mimic she is!" said the landlady. "You ought to have let her go on the stage, mum. She might have made her fortune as a h'actress."

11

Bella waited and hoped, and listened for the postman's knocks which brought such store of letters for the parlours and the first floor, and so few for that humble second floor, where mother and daughter sat sewing with hand and with wheel and treadle, for the greater part of the day. Mrs Rolleston was a lady by birth and education; but it had been her bad fortune to marry a scoundrel; for the last half-dozen years she had been that worst of widows, a wife whose husband had deserted her. Happily, she was courageous, industrious, and a clever needle-woman; and she had been able just to earn a living for herself and her only child, by making mantles and cloaks for a West End house. It was not a luxurious living. Cheap lodgings in a shabby street off the Walworth Road, scanty dinners, homely food, well-worn raiment, had been the portion of mother and daughter; but they loved each other so dearly, and Nature had made them both so light-hearted, that they had contrived somehow to be happy.

But now this idea of going out into the world as companion to some fine lady had rooted itself into Bella's mind, and although she idolised her mother, and although the parting of mother and daughter must needs tear two loving hearts into shreds, the girl longed for enterprise and change and excitement, as the pages of old longed to be knights, and to start for the Holy Land to break a lance with the infidel.

She grew tired of racing downstairs every time the postman knocked, only to be told "nothing for you, miss," by the smudgy-faced drudge who picked up the letters from the passage floor. "Nothing for you, miss," grinned the lodging-house drudge, till at last Bella took heart of grace and walked up to Harbeck Street, and asked the Superior Person how it was that no situation had been found for her.

"You are too young," said the Person, "and you want a salary."

"Of course I do," answered Bella; "don't other people want salaries?"

"Young ladies of your age generally want a comfortable home."

"I don't," snapped Bella; "I want to help mother."

"You can call again this day week," said the Person; "or, if I hear of anything in the meantime, I will write to you."

No letter came from the Person, and in exactly a week Bella put on her neatest hat, the one that had been seldomest caught in the rain, and trudged off to Harbeck Street.

It was a dull October afternoon, and there was a greyness in the air which might turn to fog before night. The Walworth Road shops gleamed brightly through that grey atmosphere, and though to a young lady reared in Mayfair or Belgravia such shop-windows would have been unworthy of a glance, they were a snare and temptation for Bella. There were so many things that she longed for, and would never be able to buy.

Harbeck Street is apt to be empty at this dead season of the year, a long, long street, an endless perspective of eminently respectable houses. The Person's office was at the farther end, and Bella looked down that long grey vista almost despairingly, more tired than usual with the trudge from Walworth. As she looked, a carriage passed her, an old-fashioned yellow chariot, on Cee-springs, drawn by a pair of high grey horses, with the stateliest of coachmen driving them, and a tall footman sitting by his side.

"It looks like the fairy godmother's coach," thought Bella. "I shouldn't wonder if it began by being a pumpkin."

It was a surprise when she reached the Person's door to find the yellow chariot standing before it, and the tall footman waiting near the doorstep. She was almost afraid to go in and meet the owner of that splendid carriage. She had caught only a glimpse of its occupant as the chariot rolled by, a plumed bonnet, a patch of ermine.

The Person's smart page ushered her upstairs and knocked at the official door. "Miss Rolleston," he announced apologetically, while Bella waited outside.

"Show her in," said the Person quickly; and then Bella heard her murmuring something in a low voice to her client.

Bella went in fresh, blooming, a living image of youth and hope, and before she looked at the Person her gaze was riveted by the owner of the chariot.

Never had she seen anyone as old as the old lady sitting by the Person's fire: a little old figure, wrapped from chin to feet in an ermine mantle; a withered old face under a plumed bonnet—a face so wasted by age that it seemed only a pair of eyes and a peaked chin. The nose was peaked, too, but between the sharply pointed chin and the great, shining eyes, the small, aquiline nose was hardly visible.

"This is Miss Rolleston, Lady Ducayne."

Claw-like fingers, flashing with jewels, lifted a double eye-glass to Lady Ducayne's shining black eyes, and through the glasses Bella saw those unnaturally bright eyes magnified to a gigantic size, and glaring at her awfully.

"Miss Torpinter has told me all about you," said the old voice that belonged to the eyes. "Have you good health? Are you strong and active, able to eat well, sleep well, walk well, able to enjoy all that there is good in life?"

"I have never known what is to be ill, or idle," answered Bella.

"Then I think you will do for me."

"Of course, in the event of references being perfectly satisfactory," put in the Person.

"I don't want references. The young woman looks frank and innocent. I'll take her on trust."

"So like you, dear Lady Ducayne," murmuring Miss Torpinter.

"I want a strong young woman whose health will give me no trouble."

"You have been so unfortunate in that respect," cooed the Person, whose voice and manner were subdued to a melting sweetness by the old woman's presence.

"Yes, I've been rather unlucky," grunted Lady Ducayne.

"But I am sure Miss Rolleston will not disappoint you, though certainly after your unpleasant experience with Miss Tomson, who looked the picture of health—and Miss Blandy, who said she had never seen a doctor since she was vaccinated—"

"Lies, no doubt," muttered Lady Ducayne, and then turning to Bella, she asked curtly, "You don't mind spending the winter in Italy, I suppose?"

In Italy! The very word was magical. Bella's fair young face flushed crimson.

"It has been the dream of my life to see Italy," she gasped.

From Walworth to Italy! How far, how impossible such a journey had seemed to that romantic dreamer.

"Well, your dream will be realised. Get yourself ready to leave Charing Cross by the train de luxe this day week at eleven. Be sure you are at the station a quarter before the hour. My people will look after you and your luggage."

Lady Ducayne rose from her chair, assisted by her crutch-stick, and Miss Torpinter escorted her to the door.

"And with regard to salary?" questioned the Person on the way.

"Salary, oh, the same as usual—and if the young woman wants a quarter's pay in advance you can write to me for a cheque," Lady Ducayne answered carelessly.

Miss Torpinter went all the way downstairs with her client, and waited to see her seated in the yellow chariot. When she came upstairs again she was slightly out of breath, and she had resumed that superior manner which Bella had found so crushing.

"You may think yourself uncommonly lucky, Miss Rolleston," she said. "I have dozens of young ladies on my books whom I might have recommended for this situation—but I remembered having told you to call this afternoon—and I thought I would give you a chance. Old Lady Ducayne is one of the best people on my books. She gives her companion a hundred a year, and pays all travelling expenses. You will live in the lap of luxury."

"A hundred a year! How too lovely! Shall I have to dress very grandly? Does Lady Ducayne keep much company?"

"At her age! No, she lives in seclusion—in her own apartments—her French maid, her footman, her medical attendant, her courier."

"Why did those other companions leave her?" asked Bella.

"Their health broke down!"

"Poor things, and so they had to leave?"

"Yes, they had to leave. I suppose you would like a quarter's salary in advance?"

"Oh, yes, please. I shall have things to buy."

"Very well, I will write for Lady Ducayne's cheque, and I will send you the balance—after deducting my commission for the year."

"To be sure, I had forgotten the commission."

"You don't suppose I keep this office for pleasure."

"Of course not," murmured Bella, remembering the five shillings entrance fee; but nobody could expect a hundred a year and a winter in Italy for five shillings.

III

"From Miss Rolleston, at Cap Ferrino, to Mrs Rolleston, in Beresford Street, Walworth.

"How I wish you could see this place, dearest; the blue sky, the olive woods, the orange and lemon orchards between the cliffs and the sea—sheltering in the hollow of the great hills—and with summer waves dancing up to the narrow ridge of pebbles and weeds which is the Italian idea of a beach! Oh, how I wish you could see it all, mother dear, and bask in this sunshine, that makes it so difficult to believe the date at the head of this paper. November! The air is like an English June—the sun is so hot that I can't walk a few yards without an umbrella. And to think of you at Walworth while I am here! I could cry at the thought that perhaps you will never see this lovely coast, this wonderful sea, these summer flowers that bloom in winter. There is a hedge of pink geraniums under my window, mother—a thick, rank hedge, as if the flowers grew wild—and there are Dijon roses climbing over arches and palisades all along the terrace—a rose garden full of bloom in November! Just picture it all! You could never imagine the luxury of this hotel. It is nearly new, and has been built and decorated regardless of expense. Our rooms are upholstered in pale blue satin, which shows up Lady Ducayne's parchment complexion; but as she sits all day in a corner of the balcony basking in the sun, except when she is in her carriage, and all the evening in her armchair close to the fire, and never sees anyone but her own people, her complexion matters very little.

"She has the handsomest suite of rooms in the hotel. My bedroom is inside hers, the sweetest room—all blue satin and white lace—white enamelled furniture, looking-glasses on every wall, till I know my pert little profile as I never knew it before. The room was really meant for Lady Ducayne's dressing-room, but she ordered one of the blue satin couches to be arranged as a bed for me—the prettiest little bed, which I can wheel near the window on sunny mornings, as it is on castors and easily moved about. I feel as if Lady Ducayne were a funny old grandmother, who had suddenly appeared in my life, very, very rich, and very, very kind.

"She is not all exacting. I read aloud to her a good deal, and she dozes and nods while I read. Sometimes I hear her moaning in her sleep—as if she had troublesome dreams. When she is tired of my reading she orders Francine, her maid, to read a French novel to her, and I hear her chuckle and groan now and then, as if she were more interested in those books than in Dickens or Scott. My French is not good enough to follow Francine, who reads very quickly. I have a great deal of liberty, for Lady Ducayne often tells me to run away and amuse myself; I roam about the hills for hours. Everything is so lovely. I lose myself in olive woods, always climbing up and up towards the pine woods above—and above the pines there are the snow mountains that just show their white peaks above the dark hills. Oh, you poor dear, how can I ever make you understand what this place is like—you, whose poor, tired eyes have only the opposite side of Beresford Street? Sometimes I go no farther than the terrace in front of the hotel, which is a favourite lounging-place with everybody. The gardens lie below, and the tennis courts where I sometimes play with a very nice girl, the only person in the hotel with whom I have made friends. She is a year older than I, and has come to Cap Ferrino with her brother, a doctor—or a medical student, who is going to be a doctor. He passed his M.B. exam at Edinburgh just before they left home, Lotta told me. He came to Italy entirely on his sister's account. She had a troublesome chest attack last summer and was ordered to winter abroad. They are orphans, quite alone in the world, and so fond of each other. It is very nice for me to have such a friend as Lotta. She is so thoroughly respectable. I can't help using that word, for some of the girls in this hotel go on in a way that I know you would shudder at. Lotta was brought up by an aunt, deep down in the country, and knows hardly anything about life. Her brother won't allow her to read a novel, French or English, that he has not read and approved.

"'He treats me like a child,' she told me, 'but I don't mind, for it's nice to know somebody loves me, and cares about what I do, and even about my thoughts.'

"Perhaps this is what makes some girls so eager to marry—the want of someone strong and brave and honest and true to care for them and order them about. I want no one, mother darling, for I have you, and you are all the world to me. No husband could ever come between us two. If I ever were to marry he would have only the second place in my heart. But I don't suppose I ever shall marry, or even know what it is like to have an offer of marriage. No young man can afford to marry a penniless girl nowadays. Life is too expensive.

"Mr Stafford, Lotta's brother, is very clever, and very kind. He thinks it is rather hard for me to have to live with such an old woman as Lady Ducayne, but then he does not know how poor we are—you and I—and what a wonderful life this seems to me in this lovely place. I feel a selfish wretch for enjoying all my luxuries, while you, who want them so much more than I, have none of them—hardly know what they are like—do you, dearest?—for my scamp of a father began to go to the dogs soon after you were married, and since then life has been all trouble and care and struggle for you."

This letter was written when Bella had been less than a month at Cap Ferrino, before the novelty had worn off the landscape, and before the pleasure of luxurious surroundings had begun to cloy. She wrote to her mother every week, such long letters as girls who have lived in closest companionship with a mother alone can write; letters that are like a diary of heart and mind. She wrote gaily always; but when the new year began Mrs Rolleston thought she detected a note of melancholy under all those lively details about the place and the people.

"My poor girl is getting homesick," she thought. "Her heart is in Beresford Street."

It might be that she missed her new friend and companion, Lotta Stafford, who had gone with her brother for a little tour to Genoa and Spezzia, and as far as Pisa. They were to return before February; but in the meantime Bella might naturally feel very solitary among all those strangers, whose manners and doings she described so well.

The mother's instinct had been true. Bella was not so happy as she had been in that first flush of wonder and delight which followed the change from Walworth to the Riviera. Somehow, she knew not how, lassitude had crept upon her. She no longer loved to climb the hills, no longer flourished her orange stick in sheer gladness of heart as her light feet skipped over the rough ground and the coarse grass on the mountain side. The odour of rosemary and thyme, the fresh breath of the sea, no longer filled her with rapture. She thought of Beresford Street and her mother's face with a sick longing. They were so far—so far away! And then she thought of Lady Ducayne, sitting by the heaped-up olive logs in the over-heated salon—thought of that wizened-nutcracker profile, and those gleaming eyes, with an invincible horror.

Visitors at the hotel had told her that the air of Cap Ferrino was relaxing—better suited to age than to youth, to sickness than to health. No doubt it was so. She was not so well as she had been at Walworth; but she told herself that she was suffering only from the pain of separation from the dear companion of her girlhood, the mother who had been nurse, sister, friend, flatterer, all things in this world to her. She had shed many tears over that parting, had spent many a melancholy hour on the marble terrace with yearning eyes looking westward, and with her heart's desire a thousand miles away.

She was sitting in her favourite spot, an angle at the eastern end of the terrace, a quiet little nook sheltered by orange trees, when she heard a couple of Riviera habitués talking in the garden below. They were sitting on a bench against the terrace wall.

She had no idea of listening to their talk, till the sound of Lady Ducayne's name attracted her, and then she listened without any thought of wrongdoing. They were talking no secrets—just casually discussing an hotel acquaintance.

They were two elderly people whom Bella only knew by sight. An English clergyman who had wintered abroad for half his lifetime; a stout, comfortable, well-to-do spinster, whose chronic bronchitis obliged her to migrate annually.

"I have met her about Italy for the last ten years," said the lady; "but have never found out her real age."

"I put her down at a hundred—not a year less," replied the parson. "Her reminiscences all go back to the Regency. She was evidently then in her zenith; and I have heard her say things that showed she was in Parisian society when the First Empire was at its best—before Josephine was divorced."

"She doesn't talk much now."

"No; there's not much life left in her. She is wise in keeping herself secluded. I only wonder that wicked old quack, her Italian doctor, didn't finish her off years ago."

"I should think it must be the other way, and that he keeps her alive."

"My dear Miss Manders, do you think foreign quackery ever kept anybody alive?"

"Well, there she is—and she never goes anywhere without him. He certainly has an unpleasant countenance."

"Unpleasant," echoed the parson. "I don't believe the foul fiend himself can beat him in ugliness. I pity that poor young woman who has to live between old Lady Ducayne and Dr Parravicini."

"But the old lady is very good to her companions."

"No doubt. She is very free with her cash; the servants call her good Lady Ducayne. She is a withered old female Croesus, and knows she'll never be able to get through her money, and doesn't relish the idea of other people enjoying it when she's in her coffin. People who live to be as old as she is become slavishly attached to life. I daresay she's generous to those poor girls—but she can't make them happy. They die in her service."

"Don't say they, Mr Carton; I know that one poor girl died at Mentone last spring."

"Yes, and another poor girl died in Rome three years ago. I was there at the time. Good Lady Ducayne left her there in an English family. The girl had every comfort. The old woman was very liberal to her—but she died. I tell you, Miss Manders, it is not good for any young woman to live with two such horrors as Lady Ducayne and Parravicini."

They talked of other things—but Bella hardly heard them. She sat motionless, and a cold wind seemed to come down upon her from the mountains and to creep up to her from the sea, till she shivered as she sat there in the sunshine, in the shelter of the orange trees in the midst of all that beauty and brightness.

Yes, they were uncanny, certainly, the pair of them—she so like an aristocratic witch in her withered old age; he of no particular age, with a face that was more like a waxen mask than any human countenance Bella had ever seen. What did it matter? Old age is venerable, and worthy of all reverence; and Lady Ducayne had been very kind to her. Dr Parravicini was a harmless, inoffensive student, who seldom looked up from the book he was reading. He had his private sitting-room, where he made experiments in chemistry and natural science—perhaps in alchemy. What could it matter to Bella? He had always been polite to her, in his far-off way. She could not be more happily placed than she was—in this palatial hotel, with this rich old lady.

No doubt she missed the young English girl who had been so friendly, and it might be that she missed the girl's brother, for Mr Stafford had talked to her a good deal—had interested himself in the books she was reading, and her manner of amusing herself when she was not on duty.

"You must come to our little salon when you are 'off', as the hospital nurses call it, and we can have some music. No doubt you play and sing?" upon which Bella had to own with a blush of shame that she had forgotten how to play the piano ages ago.

"Mother and I used to sing duets sometimes between the lights, without accompaniment," she said, and the tears came into her eyes as she thought of the humble room, the half-hour's respite from work, the sewing-machine standing where a piano ought to have been, and her mother's plaintive voice, so sweet, so true, so dear.

Sometimes she found herself wondering whether she would ever see that beloved mother again. Strange forebodings came into her mind. She was angry with herself for giving way to melancholy thoughts.

One day she questioned Lady Ducayne's French maid about those two companions who had died within three years.

"They were poor, feeble creatures," Francine told her. "They looked fresh and bright enough when they came to Miladi; but they ate too much and were lazy. They died of luxury and idleness. Miladi was too kind to them.

They had nothing to do; and so they took to fancying things; fancying the air didn't suit them, that they couldn't sleep."

"I sleep well enough, but I have had a strange dream several times since I have been in Italy."

"Ah, you had better not begin to think about dreams, or you will be like those other girls. They were dreamers—and they dreamt themselves into the cemetery."

The dream troubled her a little, not because it was a ghastly or frightening dream, but on account of sensations which she had never felt before in sleep—a whirring of wheels that went round in her brain, a great noise like a whirlwind, but rhythmical like the ticking of a gigantic clock: and then in the midst of this uproar as of winds and waves, she seemed to sink into a gulf of unconsciousness, out of sleep into far deeper sleep—total extinction. And then, after that blank interval, there had come the sound of voices, and then again the whirr of wheels, louder and louder—and again the blank—and then she knew no more till morning, when she awoke, feeling languid and oppressed.

She told Dr Parravicini of her dream one day, on the only occasion when she wanted his professional advice. She had suffered rather severely from the mosquitoes before Christmas—and had been almost frightened at finding a wound upon her arm which she could only attribute to the venomous sting of one of these torturers. Parravicini put on his glasses, and scrutinised the angry mark on the round white arm, as Bella stood before him and Lady Ducayne with her sleeve rolled up above her elbow.

"Yes, that's rather more than a joke," he said, "he has caught you on the top of a vein. What a vampire! But there's no harm done, Signorina, nothing that a little dressing of mine won't heal. You must always show me any bite of this nature. It might be dangerous if neglected. These creatures feed on poison and disseminate it."

"And to think that such tiny creatures can bite like this," said Bella; "my arm looks as if it had been cut by a knife."

"If I were to show you a mosquito's sting under my microscope, you wouldn't be surprised at that," replied Parravicini.

Bella had to put up with the mosquito bites, even when they came on the top of a vein, and produced that ugly wound. The wound recurred now and then at longish intervals, and Bella found Dr Parravicini's dressing a speedy cure. If he were the quack his enemies called him, he had at least a light hand and a delicate touch in performing this small operation.

"Bella Rolleston to Mrs Rolleston—April 14th.

"Ever Dearest: Behold the cheque for my second quarter's salary—five-and-twenty pounds. There is no one to pinch off a whole tenner for a year's commission as there was last time, so it is all for you, mother dear. I have plenty of pocket-money in hand from the cash I brought away with me, when you insisted on my keeping more than I wanted. It isn't possible to spend money here—except on occasional tips to servants, or sous to beggars and children—unless one had lots to spend, for everything one would like to buy—tortoise-shell, coral, lace—is so ridiculously dear that only a millionaire ought to look at it. Italy is a dream of beauty: but for shopping, give me Newington Causeway.

"You ask me so earnestly if I am quite well that I fear my letters must have been very dull lately. Yes, dear, I am well—but I am not quite so strong as I was when I used to trudge to the West End to buy half a pound of tea—just for a constitutional walk—or to Dulwich to look at the pictures. Italy is relaxing; and I feel what the people here call 'slack'. But I fancy I can see your dear face looking worried as you read this. Indeed, and indeed, I am not ill. I am only a little tired of this lovely scene—as I suppose one might get tired of looking at one of Turner's pictures if it hung on a wall that was always opposite one. I think of you every hour in every day—think of you and our homely little room—our dear little shabby parlour, with the armchairs from the wreck of your old home, and Dick singing in his cage over the sewing-machine. Dear, shrill, maddening Dick, who, we flattered ourselves, was so passionately fond of us. Do tell me in your next that he is well.

"My friend Lotta and her brother never came back after all. They went from Pisa to Rome. Happy mortals! And they are to be on the Italian lakes in May; which lake was not decided when Lotta last wrote to me. She has been a charming correspondent, and has confided all her little flirtations to me. We are all to go to Bellaggio next week—by Genoa and Milan. Isn't that lovely? Lady Ducayne travels by the easiest stages—except when she is bottled up in the train de luxe. We shall stop two days at Genoa and one at Milan. What a bore I shall be to you with my talk about Italy when I come home.

"Love and love—and ever more love from your adoring, Bella."

IV

Herbert Stafford and his sister had often talked of the pretty English girl with her fresh complexion, which made such a pleasant touch of rosy colour among all those sallow faces at the Grand Hotel. The young doctor thought of her with a compassionate tenderness—her utter loneliness in that great hotel where there were so many people, her bondage to that old, old woman, where everybody else was free to think of nothing but enjoying life. It was a hard fate; and the poor child was evidently devoted to her mother, and felt the pain of separation—"only two of them, and very poor, and all the world to each other," he thought.

Lotta told him one morning that they were to meet again at Bellaggio. "The old thing and her court are to be there before we are," she said. "I shall be charmed to have Bella again. She is so bright and gay—in spite of an occasional touch of homesickness. I never took to a girl on a short acquaintance as I did to her."

"I like her best when she is homesick," said Herbert; "for then I am sure she has a heart."

"What have you to do with hearts, except for dissection? Don't forget that Bella is an absolute pauper. She told me in confidence that her mother makes mantles for a West End shop. You can hardly have a lower depth than that."

"I shouldn't think any less of her if her mother made match-boxes."

"Not in the abstract—of course not. Match-boxes are honest labour. But you couldn't marry a girl whose mother makes mantles."

"We haven't come to the consideration of that question yet," answered Herbert, who liked to provoke his sister.

In two years' hospital practice he had seen too much of the grim realities of life to retain any prejudices about rank. Cancer, phthisis, gangrene, leave a man with little respect for the outward differences which vary the husk of humanity. The kernel is always the same—fearfully and wonderfully made—a subject for pity and terror.

Mr Stafford and his sister arrived at Bellaggio in a fair May evening. The sun was going down as the steamer approached the pier; and all that glory of purple bloom which curtains every wall at this season of the year flushed and deepened in the glowing light. A group of ladies were standing on the pier watching the arrivals, and among them Herbert saw a pale face that startled him out of his wonted composure.

"There she is," murmured Lotta, at his elbow, "but how dreadfully changed. She looks a wreck."

They were shaking hands with her a few minutes later, and a flush had lighted up her poor pinched face in the pleasure of meeting.

"I thought you might come this evening," she said. "We have been here a week."

She did not add that she had been there every evening to watch the boat in, and a good many times during the day. The Grand Bretagne was close by, and it had been easy for her to creep to the pier when the boat bell rang. She felt a joy in meeting these people again; a sense of being with friends; a confidence which Lady Ducayne's goodness had never inspired in her.

"Oh, you poor darling, how awfully ill you must have been," exclaimed Lotta, as the two girls embraced.

Bella tried to answer, but her voice was choked with tears.

"What has been the matter, dear? That horrid influenza, I suppose?"

"No, no, I have not been ill—I have only felt a little weaker than I used to be. I don't think the air of Cap Ferrino quite agreed with me."

"It must have disagreed with you abominably. I never saw such a change in anyone. Do let Herbert doctor you. He is fully qualified, you know. He prescribed for ever so many influenza patients at the Londres. They were glad to get advice from an English doctor in a friendly way."

"I am sure he must be very clever!" faltered Bella, "but there is really nothing the matter. I am not ill, and if I were ill, Lady Ducayne's physician—"

"That dreadful man with the yellow face? I would as soon one of the Borgias prescribed for me. I hope you haven't been taking any of his medicines."

"No, dear, I have taken nothing. I have never complained of being ill."

This was said while they were all three walking to the hotel. The Staffords' rooms had been secured in advance, pretty ground-floor rooms, opening into the garden. Lady Ducayne's statelier apartments were on the floor above.

"I believe these room are just under ours," said Bella.

"Then it will be all the easier for you to run down to us," replied Lotta, which was not really the case, as the grand staircase was in the centre of the hotel.

"Oh, I shall find it easy enough," said Bella. "I'm afraid you'll have too much of my society. Lady Ducayne sleeps away half the day in this warm weather, so I have a good deal of idle time; and I get awfully moped thinking of mother and home."

Her voice broke upon the last word. She could not have thought of that poor lodging which went by the name of home more tenderly had it been the most beautiful that art and wealth ever created. She moped and pined in this lovely garden, with the sunlit lake and the romantic hills spreading out their beauty before her. She was homesick and she had dreams: or, rather, an occasional recurrence of that one bad dream with all its strange sensations—it was more like a hallucination than dreaming—the whirring of wheels; the sinking into an abyss; the struggling back to consciousness. She had the dream shortly before she left Cap Ferrino, but not since she had come to Bellaggio, and she began to hope the air in this lake district suited her better, and that those strange sensations would never return.

Mr Stafford wrote a prescription and had it made up at the chemist's near the hotel. It was a powerful tonic, and after two bottles, and a row or two on the lake, and some rambling over the hills and in the meadows where the spring flowers made earth seem paradise, Bella's spirits and looks improved as if by magic.

"It is a wonderful tonic," she said, but perhaps in her heart of hearts she knew that the doctor's kind voice and the friendly hand that helped her in and out of the boat, and the watchful care that went with her by land and lake, had something to do with her cure.

"I hope you don't forget that her mother makes mantles," Lotta said warningly.

"Or match-boxes: it is just the same thing, so far as I am concerned."

"You mean that in no circumstances could you think of marrying her?"

"I mean that if ever I love a woman well enough to think of marrying her, riches or rank will count for nothing with me. But I fear—I fear your poor friend may not live to be any man's wife."

"Do you think her so very ill?"

He sighed, and left the question unanswered.

One day, while they were gathering wild hyacinths in an upland meadow, Bella told Mr Stafford about her bad dream.

"It is curious only because it is hardly like a dream," she said. "I daresay you could find some common-sense reason for it. The position of my head on my pillow, or the atmosphere, or something."

And then she described her sensations; how in the midst of sleep there came a sudden sense of suffocation; and then those whirring wheels, so loud, so terrible; and then a blank, and then a coming back to waking consciousness.

"Have you ever had chloroform given you—by a dentist, for instance?"

"Never—Dr Parravicini asked me that question one day."

"Lately?"

"No, long ago, when we were in the train de luxe."

"Has Dr Parravicini prescribed for you since you began to feel weak and ill?"

"Oh, he has given me a tonic from time to time, but I hate medicine, and took very little of the stuff. And then I am not ill, only weaker than I used to be. I was ridiculously strong and well when I lived at Walworth, and used to take long walks every day. Mother made me take those tramps to Dulwich or Norwood, for fear I should suffer from too much sewing-machine; sometimes—but very seldom—she went with me. She was generally toiling at home while I was enjoying fresh air and exercise. And she was very careful about our food—that, however plain it was, it should be always nourishing and ample. I owe it to her care that I grew up such a great, strong creature."

"You don't look great or strong now, you poor dear," said Lotta.

"I'm afraid Italy doesn't agree with me."

"Perhaps it is not Italy, but being cooped up with Lady Ducayne that has made you ill."

"But I am never cooped up. Lady Ducayne is absurdly kind, and lets me roam about or sit in the balcony all day if I like. I have read more novels since I have been with her than in all the rest of my life."

"Then she is very different from the average old lady, who is usually a slave-driver," said Stafford. "I wonder why she carries a companion about with her if she has so little need of society."

"Oh, I am only part of her state. She is inordinately rich—and the salary she gives me doesn't count. Apropos of Dr Parravicini, I know he is a clever doctor, for he cures my horrid mosquito bites."

"A little ammonia would do that, in the early stage of the mischief. But there are no mosquitoes to trouble you now."

"Oh, yes, there are; I had a bite just before we left Cap Ferrino."

She pushed up her loose lawn sleeve, and exhibited a scar, which he scrutinised intently, with a surprised and puzzled look.

"This is no mosquito bite," he said.

"Oh, yes, it is—unless there are snakes or adders at Cap Ferrino."

"It is not a bite at all. You are trifling with me. Miss Rolleston—you have allowed that wretched Italian quack to bleed you. They killed the greatest man in modern Europe that way, remember. How very foolish of you."

"I was never bled in my life, Mr Stafford."

"Nonsense! Let me look at your other arm. Are there any more mosquito bites?"

"Yes; Dr Parravicini says I have a bad skin for healing, and that the poison acts more virulently with me than with most people."

Stafford examined both her arms in the broad sunlight, scars new and old.

"You have been very badly bitten, Miss Rolleston," he said, "and if ever I find the mosquito I shall make him smart. But, now tell me, my dear girl, on your word of honour, tell me as you would tell a friend who is sincerely anxious for your health and happiness—as you would tell your mother if she were here to question you—have you no knowledge of any cause for these scars except mosquito bites—no suspicion even?"

"No, indeed! No, upon my honour! I have never seen a mosquito biting my arm. One never does see the horrid little fiends. But I have heard them trumpeting under the curtains, and I know that I have often had one of the pestilent wretches buzzing about me."

Later in the day Bella and her friends were sitting at tea in the garden, while Lady Ducayne took her afternoon drive with her doctor.

"How long do you mean to stop with Lady Ducayne, Miss Rolleston?" Herbert Stafford asked, after a thoughtful silence, breaking suddenly upon the trivial talk of the two girls.

"As long as she will go on paying me twenty-five pounds a quarter."

"Even if you feel your health breaking down in her service?"

"It is not the service that has injured my health. You can see that I have really nothing to do—to read aloud for an hour or so once or twice a week; to write a letter once in a way to a London tradesman. I shall never have such an easy time with anybody else. And nobody else would give me a hundred a year."

"Then you mean to go on till you break down; to die at your post?"

"Like the other two companions? No! If ever I feel seriously ill—really ill—I shall put myself in a train and go back to Walworth without stopping."

"What about the other two companions?"

"They both died. It was very unlucky for Lady Ducayne. That's why she engaged me; she chose me because I was ruddy and robust. She must feel rather disgusted at my having grown white and weak. By-the-bye, when I told her about the good your tonic had done me, she said she would like to see you and have a little talk with you about her own case."

"And I should like to see Lady Ducayne. When did she say this?"

"The day before yesterday."

"Will you ask her if she will see me this evening?"

"With pleasure! I wonder what you will think of her? She looks rather terrible to a stranger, but Dr Parravicini says she was once a famous beauty."

It was nearly ten o'clock when Mr Stafford was summoned by message from Lady Ducayne, whose courier came to conduct him to her ladyship's salon. Bella was reading aloud when the visitor was admitted; and he noticed the languor in the low, sweet tones, the evident effort.

"Shut up the book," said the querulous old voice. "You are beginning to drawl like Miss Blandy."

Stafford saw a small, bent figure crouching over the piled-up olive logs; a shrunken old figure in a gorgeous garment of black and crimson brocade, a skinny throat emerging from a mass of old Venetian lace, clasped with diamonds that flashed like fire-flies as the trembling old head turned towards him.

The eyes that looked at him out of the face were almost as bright as the diamonds—the only living feature in that narrow parchment mask. He had seen terrible faces in the hospital—faces on which disease had set dreadful marks—but he had never seen a face that impressed him so painfully as this withered countenance, with its indescribable horror of death outlived, a face that should have been hidden under a coffin-lid years and years ago.

The Italian physician was standing on the other side of the fireplace, smoking a cigarette, and looking down at the little old woman brooding over the hearth, as if he were proud of her.

"Good evening, Mr Stafford; you can go to your room, Bella, and write your everlasting letter to your mother at Walworth," said Lady Ducayne. "I believe she writes a page about every wild flower she discovers in the woods and meadows. I don't know what else she can find to write about," she added, as Bella quietly withdrew to the pretty little bedroom opening out of Lady Ducayne's spacious apartment. Here, as at Cap Ferrino, she slept in a room adjoining the old lady's.

"You are a medical man, I understand, Mr Stafford."

"I am a qualified practitioner, but I have not begun to practise."

"You have begun upon my companion, she tells me."

"I have prescribed for her, certainly, and I am happy to find my prescription has done her good; but I look upon that improvement as temporary. Her case will require more drastic treatment."

"Never mind her case. There is nothing the matter with the girl—absolutely nothing—except girlish nonsense; too much liberty and not enough work."

"I understand that two of your ladyship's previous companions died of the same disease," said Stafford, looking first at Lady Ducayne, who gave her tremulous old head an impatient jerk, and then at Parravicini, whose yellow complexion had paled a little under Stafford's scrutiny.

"Don't bother me about my companions, sir," said Lady Ducayne. "I sent for you to consult you about myself—not about a parcel of anaemic girls.

You are young, and medicine is a progressive science, the newspapers tell me. Where have you studied?"

"In Edinburgh—and in Paris."

"Two good schools. And you know all the new-fangled theories, the modern discoveries—that remind one of the medieval witchcraft, of Albertus Magnus, and George Ripley; you have studied hypnotism—electricity?"

"And the transfusion of blood," said Stafford very slowly, looking at Parravicini.

"Have you made any discovery that teaches you to prolong human life—any elixir—any mode of treatment? I want my life prolonged, young man. That man there has been my physician for thirty years. He does all he can to keep me alive—after his lights. He studies all the new theories of all the scientists—but he is old; he gets older every day—his brain-power is going—he is bigoted—prejudiced—can't receive new ideas—can't grapple with new systems. He will let me die if I am not on my guard against him."

"You are of an unbelievable ingratitude, Ecclenza," said Parravicini.

"Oh, you needn't complain. I have paid you thousands to keep me alive. Every year of my life has swollen your hoards; you know there is nothing to come to you when I am gone. My whole fortune is left to endow a home for indigent women of quality who have reached their ninetieth year. Come, Mr Stafford, I am a rich woman. Give me a few years more in the sunshine, a few years more above ground, and I will give you the price of a fashionable London practice—I will set you up at the West End."

"How old are you, Lady Ducayne?"

"I was born the day Louis XVI was guillotined."

"Then I think you have had your share of the sunshine and the pleasures of the earth, and that you should spend your few remaining days in repenting your sins and trying to make atonement for the young lives that have been sacrificed to your love of life."

"What do you mean by that, sir?"

"Oh, Lady Ducayne, need I put your wickedness and your physician's still greater wickedness in plain words? The poor girl who is now in your employment has been reduced from robust health to a condition of absolute danger by Dr Parravicini's experimental surgery; and I have no doubt those other two young women who broke down in your service were treated by him in the same manner. I could take upon myself to demonstrate—by most convincing evidence, to a jury of medical men—that Dr Parravicini has been bleeding Miss Rolleston, after putting her under chloroform, at intervals, ever since she has been in your service. The deterioration in the girl's health speaks for itself; the lancet marks upon the girl's arms are unmistakable; and her description of a series of sensations, which she calls a dream, points unmistakably to the administration of chloroform while she was sleeping. A practice so nefarious, so murderous, must, if exposed, result in a sentence only less severe than the punishment of murder."

"I laugh," said Parravicini, with an airy motion of his skinny fingers; "I laugh at once at your theories and at your threats. I, Parravicini Leopold, have no fear that the law can question anything I have done."

"Take the girl away, and let me hear no more of her," cried Lady Ducayne, in the thin, old voice, which so poorly matched the energy and fire of the wicked old brain that guided its utterances. "Let her go back to her mother—I want no more girls to die in my service. There are girls enough and to spare in the world, God knows."

"If you ever engage another companion—or take another English girl into your service, Lady Ducayne, I will make all England ring with the story of your wickedness."

"I want no more girls. I don't believe in his experiments. They have been full of danger for me as well as for the girl—an air bubble, and I should be gone. I'll have no more of his dangerous quackery. I'll find some new man—a better man than you, sir, a discoverer like Pasteur, or Virchow, a genius—to keep me alive. Take your girl away, young man. Marry her if you like. I'll write her a cheque for a thousand pounds, and let her go and live on beef and beer, and get strong and plump again. I'll have no more such experiments. Do you hear, Parravicini?" she screamed vindictively, the yellow, wrinkled face distorted with fury, the eyes glaring at him.

The Staffords carried Bella Rolleston off to Varese next day, she very loth to leave Lady Ducayne, whose liberal salary afforded such help for her dear mother. Herbert Stafford insisted, however, treating Bella as coolly as if he had been the family physician, and she had been given over wholly to his care.

"Do you suppose your mother would let you stop here to die?" he asked. "If Mrs Rolleston knew how ill you are, she would come post haste to fetch you."

"I shall never be well again till I get back to Walworth," answered Bella, who was low-spirited and inclined to tears this morning, a reaction after her good spirits of yesterday.

"We'll try a week or two at Varese first," said Stafford. "When you can walk half-way up Monte Generoso without palpitation of the heart, you shall go back to Walworth."

"Poor mother, how glad she will be to see me, and how sorry that I've lost such a good place."

This conversation took place on the boat when they were leaving Bellaggio. Lotta had gone to her friend's room at seven o'clock that morning, long before Lady Ducayne's withered eyelids had opened to the daylight, before even Francine, the French maid, was astir, and had helped to pack a Gladstone bag with essentials, and hustled Bella downstairs and out of doors before she could make any strenuous resistance.

"It's all right," Lotta assured her. "Herbert had a good talk with Lady Ducayne last night and it was settled for you to leave this morning. She doesn't like invalids, you see."

"No," sighed Bella, "she doesn't like invalids. It was very unlucky that I should break down, just like Miss Tomson and Miss Blandy."

"At any rate, you are not dead, like them," answered Lotta, "and my brother says you are not going to die."

It seemed rather a dreadful thing to be dismissed in that off-hand way, without a word of farewell from her employer.

"I wonder what Miss Torpinter will say when I go to her for another situation," Bella speculated ruefully, while she and her friends were breakfasting on board the steamer.

"Perhaps you may never want another situation," said Stafford.

"You mean that I may never be well enough to be useful to anybody?"

"No, I don't mean anything of the kind."

It was after dinner at Varese, when Bella had been induced to take a whole glass of Chianti, and quite sparkled after that unaccustomed stimulant, that Mr Stafford produced a letter from his pocket.

"I forgot to give you Lady Ducayne's letter of adieu!" he said.

"What, did she write to me? I am so glad—I hated to leave her in such a cool way; for after all she was very kind to me, and if I didn't like her it was only because she was too dreadfully old."

She tore open the envelope. The letter was short and to the point.

Goodbye, child. Go and marry your doctor. I enclose a farewell gift for
your trousseau.   ADELINE DUCAYNE.

"A hundred pounds, a whole year's salary—no—why, it's for a—A cheque for a thousand!" cried Bella. "What a generous old soul! She really is the dearest old thing."

"She just missed being very dear to you, Bella," said Stafford.

He had dropped into the use of her Christian name while they were on board the boat. It seemed natural now that she was to be in his charge till they all three went back to England.

"I shall take upon myself the privileges of an elder brother till we land at Dover," he said; "after that—well, it must be as you please."

The question of their future relations must have been satisfactorily settled before they crossed the Channel, for Bella's next letter to her mother communicated three startling facts.

First, that the enclosed cheque for £1,000 was to be invested in debenture-stock in Mrs Rolleston's name, and was to be her very own, income and principal, for the rest of her life.

Next, that Bella was going home to Walworth immediately.

And last, that she was going to be married to Mr Herbert Stafford in the following autumn.

"And I am sure you will adore him, mother, as much as I do," wrote Bella. "It is all good Lady Ducayne's doing. I never could have married if I had not secured that little nest-egg for you. Herbert says we shall be able to add to it as the years go by, and that wherever we live there shall be always a room in our house for you. The word 'mother-in-law' has no terrors for him."

1903

LUELLA MILLER

Mary E. Wilkins Freeman

C LOSE to the village street stood the one-storey house in which
Luella Miller, who had an evil name in the village, dwelt. She had
been dead for years, yet there were those in the village who, in spite
of the clearer light which comes on a vantage-point from a long-past danger,
half believed in the tale which they had heard from their childhood. In their
hearts, although they would scarcely have owned it, was a survival of the
wild horror and frenzied fear of their ancestors who had dwelt in the same
age with Luella Miller. Young people even would stare with a shudder at the
old house as they passed, and children never played around it as was their
wont around an untenanted building. Not a window in the old Miller house
was broken; the panes reflected the morning sunlight in patches of emerald
and blue, and the latch of the sagging front door was never lifted, although
no bolt secured it. Since Luella had been carried out of it, the house had had
no tenant except one friendless old soul who had no choice between that
and the far-off shelter of the open sky. This old woman, who had survived
her kindred and friends, lived in the house one week, then one morning no
smoke came out of the chimney, and a body of neighbours, a score strong,
entered and found her dead in her bed. There were dark whispers as to the
cause of her death, and there were those who testified to an expression of
fear so exalted that it showed forth the state of the departing soul upon
the dead face. The old woman had been hale and hearty when she entered
the house, and in seven days she was dead; it seemed that she had fallen a
victim to some uncanny power. The minister talked in the pulpit with covert

severity against the sin of superstition, still the belief prevailed. Not a soul in the village but would have chosen the almshouse rather than that dwelling. No vagrant, if he had heard the tale, would seek shelter beneath that old roof, unhallowed by nearly half a century of superstitious fear.

There was only one person in the village who had actually known Luella Miller. That person was a woman well over eighty, but a marvel of vitality and unextinct youth. Straight as an arrow, with the spring of one recently let loose from the bow of life, she moved about the streets, and she always went to church, rain or shine. She had never married, and had lived alone for years in a house across the road from Luella Miller's.

This woman had none of the garrulousness of age, but never in all her life had she ever held her tongue for any will save her own, and she never spared the truth when she essayed to present it. She it was who bore testimony to the life, evil, though possibly wittingly or designedly so, of Luella Miller, and to her personal appearance. When this old woman spoke, and she had the gift of description, although her thoughts were clothed in the rude vernacular of her native village, one could seem to see Luella Miller as she had really looked. According to this woman, Lydia Anderson by name, Luella Miller had been a beauty of a type rather unusual in New England. She had been a slight, pliant sort of creature, as ready with a strong yielding to fate, and as unbreakable as a willow. She had glimmering lengths of straight, fair hair, which she wore softly looped round a long, lovely face. She had blue eyes full of soft pleading, little slender, clinging hands, and a wonderful grace of motion and attitude. "Luella Miller used to sit in a way nobody else could if they sat up and studied a week of Sundays," said Lydia Anderson, "and it was a sight to see her walk. If one of them willows over there on the edge of the brook could start up and get its roots free of the ground, and move off, it would go just the way Luella Miller used to. She had a green shot silk she used to wear, too, and a hat with green ribbon streamers, and a lace veil blowing across her face and out sideways, and a green ribbon flyin' from her waist. That was what she came out bride in when she married Erastus

Miller. Her name before she was married was Hill. There was always a sight of 'l's' in her name, married or single. Erastus Miller was good lookin', too, better lookin' than Luella. Sometimes I used to think that Luella wasn't so handsome after all. Erastus just about worshipped her. I used to know him pretty well. He lived next door to me, and we went to school together. Folks used to say he was waitin' on me, but he wasn't. I never thought he was except once or twice when he said things that some girls might have suspected meant something. That was before Luella came here to teach the district school. It was funny how she came to get it, for folks said she hadn't any education, and that one of the big girls, Lottie Henderson, used to do all the teachin' for her, while she sat back and did embroidery work on a cambric pocket-handkerchief. Lottie Henderson was a real smart girl, a splendid scholar, and she just set her eyes by Luella, as all the girls did. Lottie would have made a real smart woman, but she died when Luella had been here about a year, just faded away and died: nobody knew what ailed her. She dragged herself to that school-house and helped Luella teach till the very last minute. The committee all knew how Luella didn't do much of the work herself, but they winked at it. It wasn't long after Lottie died that Erastus married her. I always thought he hurried it up because she wasn't fit to teach. One of the big boys used to help her after Lottie died, but he hadn't much government, and the school didn't do very well, and Luella might have had to give it up, for the committee couldn't have shut their eyes to things much longer. The boy that helped her was a real honest, innocent sort of fellow, and he was a good scholar, too. Folks said he overstudied, and that was the reason he was took crazy the year after Luella married, but I don't know. And I don't know what made Erastus Miller go into consumption of the blood the year after he was married: consumption wasn't in his family. He just grew weaker and weaker, and went almost bent double when he tried to wait on Luella, and he spoke feeble, like an old man. He worked terrible hard till the last trying to save up a little to leave Luella. I've seen him out in the worst storms on a wood-sled. He used to cut and sell wood, and he was hunched up on top lookin' more dead than alive. Once I couldn't stand it: I went over and helped him pitch some wood on the cart—I was always strong in my arms. I wouldn't stop for all he told me to, and I guess he was glad enough for the help. That was only a week before he died. He fell on the kitchen floor while he was gettin' breakfast. He always got the breakfast and let Luella lay a-bed. He did all the sweepin' and the washin' and the ironin' and most of the cookin'. He couldn't bear to have Luella lift her finger, and she let him do for her. She lived like a queen for all the work she did. She didn't even do her sewing. She said it made her shoulder ache to sew, and poor Erastus's sister Lily used to do all her sewin'. She wasn't able to, either; she was never strong in her back, but she did it beautifully. She had to, to suit Luella, she was so dreadful particular. I never saw anything like the fagottin' and hemstitchin' that Lily Miller did for Luella. She made all Luella's weddin' outfit, and that green silk dress, after Maria Babbit cut it. Maria she cut it for nothin', and she did a lot more cuttin' and fittin' for nothin' for Luella, too. Lily Miller went to live with Luella after Erastus died. She gave up her home, though she was real attached to it and wan't a mite afraid to stay alone. She rented it and she went to live with Luella right away after the funeral."

Then this old woman, Lydia Anderson, who remembered Luella Miller, would go on to relate the story of Lily Miller. It seemed that on the removal of Lily Miller to the house of her dead brother, to live with his widow, the village people first began to talk. This Lily Miller had been hardly past her first youth, and a most robust and blooming woman, rosy cheeked, with curls of strong, black hair overshadowing round, candid temples, and bright dark eyes. It was not six months after she had taken up her residence with her sister-in-law that her rosy colour faded and her pretty curves became wan hollows. White shadows began to show in the black rings of her hair, and the light died out of her eyes, her features sharpened, and there were pathetic lines at her mouth, which yet wore always an expression of utter sweetness and even happiness. She was devoted to her sister; there was no doubt that she loved her with her whole heart, and was perfectly content in her service. For it was her sole anxiety lest she should die and leave her alone.

"The way Lily Miller used to talk about Luella was enough to make you mad, and enough to make you cry," said Lydia Anderson. "I've been in there sometimes toward the last when she was too feeble to cook and carried her some blanc-mange, or custard—somethin' I thought she might relish, and she'd thank me, and when I asked her how she was, say she felt better than she did yesterday, and ask me if I didn't think she looked better, dreadful pitiful, and say poor Luella had an awful time takin' care of her, and doin' the work—she wan't strong enough to do anything—when all the time Luella wan't liftin' her finger, and poor Lily didn't get any care except what the neighbours gave her, and Luella eat up everythin' that was carried in to Lily. I had it real straight that she did. Luella used to just sit and cry, and do nothin'. She did act real fond of Lily, and she pined away considerable, too. There was those that thought she'd go into a decline herself. But after Lily died, her Aunt Abby Mixter came, and then Luella picked up and grew as fat and rosy as ever. But poor Aunt Abby begun to droop just the way Lily had, and I guess somebody wrote to her married daughter, Mrs Sam Abbot, who lived in Barre, for she wrote her mother that she must leave right away and come and make her a visit, but Aunt Abby wouldn't go. I can see her now. She was a real good lookin' woman, tall and large, with a big, square face and a high forehead that looked of itself kind of benevolent and good. She just tended out on Luella as if she had been a baby, and when her married daughter sent for her she wouldn't stir one inch. She'd always thought a lot of her daughter, too, but she said Luella needed her and her daughter didn't. Her daughter kept writin' and writin', but it didn't do any good. Finally she came, and when she saw how bad her mother looked, she broke down and cried and all but went on her knees to have her come away. She spoke her mind out to Luella, too. She told her that she'd killed her husband and everybody that had any-thin' to do with her, and she'd thank her to leave her mother alone. Luella went into hysterics, and Aunt Abby was so frightened that she called me after her daughter went. Mrs Sam Abbot she went away fairly cryin' out loud in the buggy. The neighbours heard her, and well she might, for she never saw her mother again alive. I went in that night when Aunt Abby called for me, standin' in the door with her little green checked shawl over her head. I can see her now. 'Do come over here, Miss Anderson,' she sung out, kind of gasping for breath. I didn't stop for anything. I put over as fast as I could, and when I got there, there was Luella laughin' and cryin' all together, and Aunt Abby trying to hush her, and all the time she herself was white as a sheet and shakin' so she could hardly stand. 'For the land sakes, Mrs Mixter,' says I, 'you look worse than she does. You ain't fit to be up out of your bed.'

"'Oh, there ain't anythin' the matter with me,' says she. Then she went on talkin' to Luella. 'There, there, don't, don't, poor little lamb,' says she. 'Aunt Abby is here. She ain't goin' away and leave you. Don't, poor little lamb.'

"'Do leave her with me, Mrs Mixter, and you get back to bed,' says I, for Aunt Abby had been layin' down considerable lately, though somehow she contrived to do the work.

"'I'm well enough,' says she. 'Don't you think she had better have the doctor, Miss Anderson?'

"'The doctor,' says I, 'I think you had better have the doctor. I think you need him much more than some folks I could mention.' And I looked right straight at Luella Miller laughin' and cryin' and goin' on as if she was the centre of all creation. All the time she was actin' so—seemed as if she was too sick to sense anythin'—she was keepin' a sharp lookout as to how we took it out of the corner of one eye. I see her. You could never cheat me about Luella Miller. Finally I got real mad and I run home and I got a bottle of valerian I had, and I poured some boilin' hot water on a handful of catnip, and I mixed up that catnip tea with most half a wineglass of valerian, and I went with it over to Luella's. I marched right up to Luella, a-holdin' out of that cup, all smokin'. 'Now,' says I, 'Luella Miller, *you swaller this!*'

"'What is—what is it, oh, what is it?' she sort of screeches out. Then she goes off a-laughin' enough to kill.

"'Poor lamb, poor little lamb,' says Aunt Abby, standin' over her, all kind of tottery, and tryin' to bathe her head with camphor.

"'*You swaller this right down*,' says I. And I didn't waste any ceremony. I just took hold of Luella Miller's chin and I tipped her head back, and I caught her mouth open with laughin', and I clapped that cup to her lips, and I fairly hollered at her: 'Swaller, swaller, swaller!' and she gulped it right down. She had to, and I guess it did her good. Anyhow, she stopped cryin' and laughin' and let me put her to bed, and she went to sleep like a baby inside of half an hour. That was more than poor Aunt Abby did. She lay awake all that night and I stayed with her, though she tried not to have me; said she wasn't sick enough for watchers. But I stayed, and I made some good cornmeal gruel and I fed her a teaspoon every little while all night long. It seemed to me as if she was jest dyin' from bein' all wore out. In the mornin' as soon as it was light I run over to the Bisbees and sent Johnny Bisbee for the doctor. I told him to tell the doctor to hurry, and he come pretty quick. Poor Aunt Abby didn't seem to know much of anything when he got there. You couldn't hardly tell she breathed, she was so used up. When the doctor had gone, Luella came into the room lookin' like a baby in her ruffled nightgown. I can see her now. Her eyes were as blue and her face all pink and white like a blossom, and she looked at Aunt Abby in the bed sort of innocent and surprised. 'Why,' says she, 'Aunt Abby ain't got up yet?'

"'No, she ain't,' says I, pretty short.

"'I thought I didn't smell the coffee,' says Luella.

"'Coffee,' says I. 'I guess if you have coffee this mornin' you'll make it yourself.'

"'I never made the coffee in all my life,' says she, dreadful astonished. 'Erastus always made the coffee as long as he lived, and then Lily she made it, and then Aunt Abby made it. I don't believe I *can* make the coffee, Miss Anderson.'

"'You can make it or go without, jest as you please,' says I.

"'Ain't Aunt Abby goin' to get up?' says she.

"'I guess she won't get up,' says I, 'sick as she is.' I was gettin' madder and madder. There was somethin' about that little pink-and-white thing standin' there and talkin' about coffee, when she had killed so many better folks than she was, and had jest killed another, that made me feel 'most as if I wished somebody would up and kill her before she had a chance to do any more harm.

"'Is Aunt Abby sick?' says Luella, as if she was sort of aggrieved and injured.

"'Yes,' says I, 'she's sick, and she goin' to die, and then you'll be left alone, and you'll have to do for yourself and wait on yourself, or do without things.' I don't know but I was sort of hard, but it was the truth, and if I was any harder than Luella Miller had been I'll give up. I ain't never been sorry that I said it. Well, Luella, she up an' had hysterics again at that, and I jest let her have 'em. All I did was to bundle her into the room on the other side of the entry where Aunt Abby couldn't hear her, if she wan't past it. I don't know but she was, and set her down hard in a chair and told her not to come back into the other room, and she minded. She had her hysterics in there till she got tired. When she found out that nobody was comin' to coddle her and do for her she stopped. At least, I suppose she did. I didn't pay much attention to her. I had all I could do with poor Aunt Abby tryin' to keep the breath of life in her. The doctor had told me that she was dreadful low, and give me some very strong medicine to give her in drops real often, and told me real particular about the nourishment. Well, I did as he told me real faithful till she wasn't able to swaller any longer. Then I had her daughter sent for. I had begun to realise that she wouldn't last any time at all. I hadn't before, though I spoke to Luella the way I did. The doctor he came, and Mrs Sam Abbot, but when she got there it was too late; her mother was dead. Aunt Abby's daughter just give one look at her mother layin' there, then she turned sort of sharp and sudden and looked at me.

"'Where is she?' says she, and I knew she meant Luella.

"'She's out in the kitchen,' says I. 'She's too nervous to see folks die. She's afraid it will make her sick.'

"The doctor he speaks up then. He was a young man. Old Doctor Park had died the year before, and this was a young fellow just out of college. 'Mrs Miller is not strong,' says he, kind of severe, 'and she is quite right in not agitatin' herself.'

"'You are another, young man; she's got her pretty claw on you,' thinks I, but I didn't say anythin' to him. I just said over to Mrs Sam Abbot that Luella was in the kitchen, and Mrs Sam Abbot she went out there, and I went, too, and I never heard anything like the way she talked to Luella Miller. I felt pretty hard to Luella myself, but this was more than I ever would have dared to say. Luella she was too scared to go into hysterics. She jest flopped. She seemed to jest shrink away to nothing in that kitchen chair, with Mrs Sam Abbot standin' over her and talkin' and tellin' her the truth. I guess the truth was 'most too much for her and no mistake, because Luella presently actually did faint away, and there wasn't any sham about it, the way I always suspected there was about them hysterics. She fainted dead away and we had to lay her flat on the floor, and the doctor he came runnin' out and he said something about a weak heart dreadful fierce to Mrs Sam Abbot, but she wan't a mite scared. She faced him jest as white-mad as even was Luella layin' there lookin' like death and the doctor feelin' of her pulse.

"'Weak heart,' says she, 'weak heart; weak fiddlesticks! There ain't nothin' weak about that woman. She's got strength enough to hang onto other folks till she kills 'em. Weak? It was my poor mother that was weak: this woman killed her as sure as if she had taken a knife to her.'

"But the doctor he didn't pay much attention. He was bendin' over Luella layin' there with her yellow hair all streamin' and her pretty pink-and-white face all pale, and her blue eyes like stars gone out, and he was holding onto her hand and smoothin' her forehead, and tellin' me to get the brandy in Aunt Abby's room, and I was sure as I wanted to be that Luella had got somebody else to hang onto, now Aunt Abby was gone, and I thought of poor Erastus Miller, and I sort of pitied the poor young doctor, led away by a pretty face, and I made up my mind I'd see what I could do.

"I waited till Aunt Abby had been dead and buried about a month, and the doctor was goin' to see Luella steady and folks were beginnin' to talk, then one evenin', when I knew the doctor had been called out of town and wouldn't be round, I went over to Luella's. I found her all dressed up in a pretty blue muslin with white polka dots on it, and her hair curled just as pretty, and there wasn't a young girl in the place could compare with her. There was somethin' about Luella Miller seemed to draw the heart right out of you, but she didn't draw it out of *me*. She was settin' rocking in the chair by her sittin'-room window, and Maria Brown had gone home. Maria Brown had been in to help her, or rather to do the work, for Luella wasn't ever helped when she didn't do anythin'. Maria Brown was real capable and she didn't have any ties; she wan't married, and lived alone, so she'd offered. I couldn't see why she should do the work any more than Luella; she wan't any too strong; but she seemed to think she could and Luella seemed to think so, too, so she went over and did all the work—washed, and ironed, and baked, while Luella sat and rocked. Maria didn't live long afterward. She began to fade away just the same fashion the others had. Well, she was warned, but she acted real mad when folks said anythin': said Luella was a poor, abused woman, too delicate to help herself, and they'd ought to be ashamed, and if she died helpin' them that couldn't help themselves she would—and she did.

"'I s'pose Maria has gone home,' says I to Luella, when I had gone in and sat down opposite her.

"'Yes, Maria went half an hour ago, after she had got supper and washed the dishes,' says Luella, in her pretty way.

"'I suppose she has got a lot of work to do in her own house tonight,' says I, kind of bitter, but that was all thrown away on Luella Miller. It seemed to her right that other folks that wan't any better able than she was herself should wait on her, and she couldn't get it through her head that anybody should think it *wasn't* right.

"'Yes,' says Luella, real sweet and pretty, 'yes, she said she had to do her washin' tonight. She has let it go for a fortnight along of comin' over here.'

"'Why don't she stay home and do her washin' instead of comin' over here and doin' *your* work, when you are just as well able, and enough sight more so, than she is to do it?' says I.

"Then Luella she looked at me like a baby who has a rattle shook at it. She sort of laughed as innocent as you please. 'Oh, I can't do the work myself, Miss Anderson,' says she. 'I never did. Maria *has* to do it.'

"Then I spoke out: 'Has to do it,' says I, 'has to do it? She don't have to do it, either. Maria Baker has her own home and enough to live on. She ain't beholden to you to come over here and slave for you and kill herself.'

"Luella she jest set and stared at me for all the world like a doll-baby that was so abused that it was comin' to life.

"'Yes,' says I, 'she's killin' herself. She's goin' to die just the way Erastus did, and Lily, and your Aunt Abby. You're killin' her jest as you did them. I don't know what there is about you, but you seem to bring a curse,' says I. 'You kill everybody that is fool enough to care anythin' about you and do for you.'

"She stared at me, and she was pretty pale.

"'And Maria ain't the only one you're goin' to kill,' says I. 'You're goin' to kill Doctor Malcom before you're done with him.'

"Then a red colour came flamin' all over her face. 'I ain't goin' to kill him, either,' says she, and she begun to cry.

"'Yes you *be*?' says I. Then I spoke as I had never spoke before. You see, I felt it on account of Erastus. I told her that she hadn't any business to think of another man after she'd been married to one that had died for her: that she was a dreadful woman; and she was, that's true enough, but sometimes I have wondered lately if she knew it, if she wan't like a baby with scissors in its hand cuttin' everybody without knowin' what it was doin'.

"Luella, she kept gettin' paler and paler, and she never took her eyes off my face. There was somethin' awful about the way she looked at me and never spoke one word. After awhile I quit talkin' and I went home. I watched that night, but her lamp went out before nine o'clock, and when Doctor Malcom came driving past and sort of slowed up, he see there wasn't any light, and he drove along. I saw her sort of shy out of meetin' the next Sunday too, so he shouldn't go home with her, and I begun to think mebbe she did have some conscience after all. It was only a week after that that Maria Baker died, sort of sudden at the last, though everybody had seen it was comin'. Well, then there was a good deal of feelin' and pretty dark whispers. Folks said the days of witchcraft had come again, and they were pretty shy of Luella. She acted sort of offish to the doctor and he didn't go there, and there wasn't anybody to do anythin' for her. I don't know how she *did* get along. I wouldn't go in there and offer to help her, not because I was afraid of dyin' like the rest, but I thought she was jest as well able to do her own work as I was to do it for her, and I thought it was about time that she did it and stopped killin' other folks. But it wasn't very long before folks began to say that Luella herself was goin' into a decline jest the way her husband, and Lily, and Aunt Abby, and the others had, and I saw myself that she looked pretty bad. I used to see her goin' past from the store with a bundle as if she could hardly crawl, but I remembered how Erastus used to wait and 'tend when he couldn't hardly put one foot before the other, and I didn't go out to help her.

"But at last one afternoon I saw the doctor come drivin' up like mad with his medicine chest, and Mrs Babbit came in after supper and said that Luella was real sick.

"'I'd offer to go in and nurse her,' says she, 'but I've got my children to consider, and mebbe it ain't true what they say, but it's queer how many folks that have done for her have died.'

"I didn't say anythin', but I considered how she had been Erastus's wife and how he had set his eyes by her, and I made up my mind to go in the next mornin', unless she was better, and see what I could do; but the next mornin' I see her at the window, and pretty soon she came steppin' out as spry as you please, and a little while afterward Mrs Babbit came in and told me that the doctor had got a girl from out of town, a Sarah Jones, to come there, and she said she was pretty sure that the doctor was goin' to marry Luella.

"I see him kiss her in the door that night myself, and I knew it was true. The woman came that afternoon, and the way she flew around was a caution. I don't believe Luella had swept since Maria died. She swept and dusted, and washed and ironed, wet clothes and dusters and carpets were flyin' over there all day, and every time Luella set her foot out when the doctor wasn't there there was that Sarah Jones helpin' of her up and down the steps, as if she hadn't learned to walk.

"Well, everybody knew that Luella and the doctor were goin' to be married, but it wan't long before they began to talk about his lookin' so poorly, jest as they had about the others; and they talked about Sarah Jones, too.

"Well, the doctor did die, and he wanted to be married first, so as to leave what little he had to Luella, but he died before the minister could get there, and Sarah Jones died a week afterward.

"Well, that wound up everythin' for Luella Miller. Not another soul in the whole town would lift a finger for her. There got to be a sort of panic. Then she began to droop in good earnest. She used to have to go to the store herself, for Mrs Babbit was afraid to let Tommy go for her, and I've seen her goin' past and stoppin' every two or three steps to rest. Well, I stood it as long as I could, but one day I see her comin' with her arms full and stoppin' to lean against the Babbit fence, I run out and took her bundles and carried them for her to the house. Then I went home and never spoke one word to her, though she called after me dreadful kind of pitiful. Well, that night I was taken sick with a chill, and I was sick as I wanted to be for two weeks. Mrs Babbit had seen me run out to help Luella and she came in and told me I was goin' to die on account of it. I didn't know whether I was or not, but I considered I had done right by Erastus's wife.

"That last two weeks Luella she had a dreadful hard time, I guess. She was pretty sick, and as near as I could make out nobody dared go near her. I don't know as she was really needin' anythin' very much, for there was enough to eat in her house and it was warm weather, and she made out to cook a little flour gruel every day, I know, but I guess she had a hard time, she that had been so petted and done for all her life.

"When I got so I could go out, I went over there one morning. Mrs Babbit had just come in to say she hadn't seen any smoke and she didn't know but it was somebody's duty to go in, but she couldn't help thinkin' of her children, and I got right up, though I hadn't been out of the house for two weeks, and I went in there, and Luella she was layin' on the bed, and she was dyin'.

"She lasted all that day and into the night. But I sat there after the new doctor had gone away. Nobody else dared to go there. It was about midnight that I left her a minute to run home and get some medicine I had been takin', for I begun to feel rather bad.

"It was a full moon that night, and just as I started out of my door to cross the street back to Luella's, I stopped short, for I saw something."

Lydia Anderson at this juncture always said with a certain defiance that she did not expect to be believed, and then proceeded in a hushed voice:

"I saw what I saw, and I know I saw it, and I will swear that I saw it on my death bed. I saw Luella Miller and Erastus Miller, and Lily, and Aunt Abby, and Maria, and the doctor, and Sarah, all goin' out of her door, and all but Luella shone white in the moonlight, and they were all helpin' her along till she seemed to fairly fly in the midst of them. Then it all disappeared. I stood a minute with my heart poundin', then I went over there. I thought of goin' for Mrs Babbit, but I thought she'd be afraid. So I went alone, though I knew what had happened. Luella was layin' real peaceful dead on her bed."

This was the story that the old woman, Lydia Anderson, told, but the sequel was told by the people who survived her, and this was the tale which has become folklore in the village.

Lydia Anderson died when she was eighty-seven. She had continued wonderfully hale and hearty for one of her years until about two weeks before her death.

One bright moonlight evening she was sitting beside a window in her parlour when she made a sudden exclamation, and was out of the house and across the street before the neighbour who was taking care of her could stop her. She followed as fast as possible and found Lydia Anderson stretched on the ground before the door of Luella Miller's deserted house, and she was quite dead.

The next night there was a red gleam of fire athwart the moonlight and the old house of Luella Miller was burned to the ground. Nothing is now left of it except a few old cellar stones, and a lilac bush, and in summer a help-less trail of morning glories among the weeds, which might be considered emblematic of Luella herself.

THE ROOM IN THE TOWER

E. F. Benson

I T is probable that everybody who is at all a constant dreamer has had at least one experience of an event or a sequence of circumstances which have come to his mind in sleep being subsequently realised in the material world. But, in my opinion, so far from this being a strange thing, it would be far odder if this fulfilment did not occasionally happen, since our dreams are, as a rule, concerned with people whom we know and places with which we are familiar, such as might very naturally occur in the awake and daylit world. True, these dreams are often broken into by some absurd and fantastic incident, which puts them out of court in regard to their subsequent fulfilment, but on the mere calculation of chances, it does not appear in the least unlikely that a dream imagined by anyone who dreams constantly should occasionally come true. Not long ago, for instance, I experienced such a fulfilment of a dream which seems to me in no way remarkable and to have no kind of psychical significance. The manner of it was as follows.

A certain friend of mine, living abroad, is amiable enough to write to me about once in a fortnight. Thus, when fourteen days or thereabouts have elapsed since I last heard from him, my mind, probably, either consciously or subconsciously, is expectant of a letter from him. One night last week I dreamed that as I was going upstairs to dress for dinner I heard, as I often heard, the sound of the postman's knock on my front door, and diverted my direction downstairs instead. There, among other correspondence, was a letter from him. Thereafter the fantastic entered, for on opening it I found inside the ace of diamonds, and scribbled across it in his well-known

handwriting, "I am sending you this for safe custody, as you know it is running an unreasonable risk to keep aces in Italy." The next evening I was just
preparing to go upstairs to dress when I heard the postman's knock, and did
precisely as I had done in my dream. There, among other letters, was one
from my friend. Only it did not contain the ace of diamonds. Had it done
so, I should have attached more weight to the matter, which, as it stands,
seems to me a perfectly ordinary coincidence. No doubt I consciously or subconsciously expected a letter from him, and this suggested to me my dream.
Similarly, the fact that my friend had not written to me for a fortnight suggested to him that he should do so. But occasionally it is not so easy to find
such an explanation, and for the following story I can find no explanation at
all. It came out of the dark, and into the dark it has gone again.

All my life I have been a habitual dreamer: the nights are few, that is to
say, when I do not find on awaking in the morning that some mental experience has been mine, and sometimes, all night long, apparently, a series of
the most dazzling adventures befall me. Almost without exception these
adventures are pleasant, though often merely trivial. It is of an exception that
I am going to speak.

It was when I was about sixteen that a certain dream first came to me,
and this is how it befell. It opened with my being set down at the door of a
big red-brick house, where, I understood, I was going to stay. The servant
who opened the door told me that tea was being served in the garden, and
led me through a low dark-panelled hall, with a large open fireplace, on to a
cheerful green lawn set round with flower beds. There were grouped about
the tea-table a small party of people, but they were all strangers to me except
one, who was a schoolfellow called Jack Stone, clearly the son of the house,
and he introduced me to his mother and father and a couple of sisters. I
was, I remember, somewhat astonished to find myself here, for the boy in
question was scarcely known to me, and I rather disliked what I knew of
him; moreover, he had left school nearly a year before. The afternoon was
very hot, and an intolerable oppression reigned. On the far side of the lawn

ran a red-brick wall, with an iron gate in its centre, outside which stood a walnut tree. We sat in the shadow of the house opposite a row of long windows, inside which I could see a table with cloth laid, glimmering with glass and silver. This garden front of the house was very long, and at one end of it stood a tower of three storeys, which looked to me much older than the rest of the building.

Before long, Mrs Stone, who, like the rest of the party, had sat in absolute silence, said to me, "Jack will show you your room: I have given you the room in the tower."

Quite inexplicably my heart sank at her words. I felt as if I had known that I should have the room in the tower, and that it contained something dreadful and significant. Jack instantly got up, and I understood that I had to follow him. In silence we passed through the hall, and mounted a great oak staircase with many corners, and arrived at a small landing with two doors set in it. He pushed one of these open for me to enter, and without coming in himself, closed it after me. Then I knew that my conjecture had been right: there was something awful in the room, and with the terror of nightmare growing swiftly and enveloping me, I awoke in a spasm of terror.

Now that dream or variations on it occurred to me intermittently for fifteen years. Most often it came in exactly this form, the arrival, the tea laid out on the lawn, the deadly silence succeeded by that one deadly sentence, the mounting with Jack Stone up to the room in the tower where horror dwelt, and it always came to a close in the nightmare of terror at that which was in the room, though I never saw what it was. At other times I experienced variations on this same theme. Occasionally, for instance, we would be sitting at dinner in the dining-room, into the windows of which I had looked on the first night when the dream of this house visited me, but wherever we were, there was the same silence, the same sense of dreadful oppression and foreboding. And the silence I knew would always be broken by Mrs Stone saying to me, "Jack will show you your room: I have given you the room in the tower." Upon which (this was invariable) I had to follow him up the oak staircase with many corners, and enter the place that I dreaded more and more each time that I visited it in sleep. Or, again, I would find myself playing cards still in silence in a drawing-room lit with immense chandeliers, that gave a blinding illumination. What the game was I have no idea; what I remember, with a sense of miserable anticipation, was that soon Mrs Stone would get up and say to me, "Jack will show you your room: I have given you the room in the tower." This drawing-room where we played cards was next to the dining-room, and, as I have said, was always brilliantly illuminated, whereas the rest of the house was full of dusk and shadows. And yet, how often, in spite of those bouquets of lights, have I not pored over the cards that were dealt me, scarcely able for some reason to see them. Their designs, too, were strange: there were no red suits, but all were black, and among them there were certain cards which were black all over. I hated and dreaded those.

As this dream continued to recur, I got to know the greater part of the house. There was a smoking-room beyond the drawing-room, at the end of a passage with a green baize door. It was always very dark there, and as often as I went there I passed somebody whom I could not see in the door-way coming out. Curious developments, too, took place in the characters that peopled the dream as might happen to living persons. Mrs Stone, for instance, who, when I first saw her, had been black-haired, became grey, and instead of rising briskly, as she had done at first when she said, "Jack will show you your room: I have given you the room in the tower," got up very feebly, as if the strength was leaving her limbs. Jack also grew up, and became a rather ill-looking young man, with a brown moustache, while one of the sisters ceased to appear, and I understood she was married.

Then it so happened that I was not visited by this dream for six months or more, and I began to hope, in such inexplicable dread did I hold it, that it had passed away for good. But one night after this interval I again found myself being shown out onto the lawn for tea, and Mrs Stone was not there, while the others were all dressed in black. At once I guessed the reason, and my heart leaped at the thought that perhaps this time I should not have to sleep in the room in the tower, and though we usually all sat in silence, on this occasion the sense of relief made me talk and laugh as I had never yet done. But even then matters were not altogether comfortable, for no one else spoke, but they all looked secretly at each other. And soon the foolish stream of my talk ran dry, and gradually an apprehension worse than anything I had previously known gained on me as the light slowly faded.

Suddenly a voice which I knew well broke the stillness, the voice of Mrs Stone, saying, "Jack will show you your room: I have given you the room in the tower." It seemed to come from near the gate in the red-brick wall that bounded the lawn, and looking up, I saw that the grass outside was sown thick with gravestones. A curious greyish light shone from them, and I could read the lettering on the grave nearest me, and it was, "In evil memory of Julia Stone". And as usual Jack got up, and again I followed him through the hall and up the staircase with many corners. On this occasion it was darker than usual, and when I passed into the room in the tower I could only just see the furniture, the position of which was already familiar to me. Also there was a dreadful odour of decay in the room, and I woke screaming.

The dream, with such variations and developments as I have mentioned, went on at intervals for fifteen years. Sometimes I would dream it two or three nights in succession; once, as I have said, there was an intermission of six months, but taking a reasonable average, I should say that I dreamed it quite as often as once in a month. It had, as is plain, something of nightmare about it, since it always ended in the same appalling terror, which so far from getting less, seemed to me to gather fresh fear every time that I experienced it. There was, too, a strange and dreadful consistency about it. The characters in it, as I have mentioned, got regularly older, death and marriage visited this silent family, and I never in the dream, after Mrs Stone had died, set eyes on her again. But it was always her voice that told me that the room in the tower was prepared for me, and whether we had tea out on the lawn, or the scene was laid in one of the rooms overlooking it, I could always see her gravestone standing just outside the iron gate. It was the same, too, with the married daughter; usually she was not present, but once or twice she returned again, in company with a man, whom I took to be her husband. He, too, like the rest of them, was always silent. But, owing to the constant repetition of the dream, I had ceased to attach, in my waking hours, any significance to it. I never met Jack Stone again during all those years, nor did I ever see a house that resembled this dark house of my dream. And then something happened.

I had been in London in this year, up till the end of the July, and during the first week in August went down to stay with a friend in a house he had taken for the summer months, in the Ashdown Forest district of Sussex. I left London early, for John Clinton was to meet me at Forest Row Station, and we were going to spend the day golfing, and go to his house in the evening. He had his motor with him, and we set off, about five of the afternoon, after a thoroughly delightful day, for the drive, the distance being some ten miles. As it was still so early we did not have tea at the club house, but waited till we should get home. As we drove, the weather, which up till then had been, though hot, deliciously fresh, seemed to me to alter in quality, and become very stagnant and oppressive, and I felt that indefinable sense of ominous apprehension that I am accustomed to before thunder. John, however, did not share my views, attributing my loss of lightness to the fact that I had lost both my matches. Events proved, however, that I was right, though I do not think that the thunderstorm that broke that night was the sole cause of my depression.

Our way lay through deep high-banked lanes, and before we had gone very far I fell asleep, and was only awakened by the stopping of the motor. And with a sudden thrill, partly of fear but chiefly of curiosity, I found myself standing in the doorway of my house of dream. We went, I half wondering whether or not I was dreaming still, through a low oak-panelled hall, and out onto the lawn, where tea was laid in the shadow of the house. It was set in flower beds, a red-brick wall, with a gate in it, bounded one side, and out beyond that was a space of rough grass with a walnut tree. The façade of the house was very long, and at one end stood a three-storeyed tower, markedly older than the rest.

Here for the moment all resemblance to the repeated dream ceased. There was no silent and somehow terrible family, but a large assembly of exceedingly cheerful persons, all of whom were known to me. And in spite of the horror with which the dream itself had always filled me, I felt nothing of it now that the scene of it was thus reproduced before me. But I felt intensest curiosity as to what was going to happen.

Tea pursued its cheerful course, and before long Mrs Clinton got up. And at that moment I think I knew what she was going to say. She spoke to me, and what she said was: "Jack will show you your room: I have given you the room in the tower."

At that, for half a second, the horror of the dream took hold of me again. But it quickly passed, and again I felt nothing more than the most intense curiosity. It was not very long before it was amply satisfied.

John turned to me.

"Right up at the top of the house," he said, "but I think you'll be comfortable. We're absolutely full up. Would you like to go and see it now? By Jove, I believe that you are right, and that we are going to have a thunderstorm. How dark it has become."

I got up and followed him. We passed through the hall, and up the perfectly familiar staircase. Then he opened the door, and I went in. And at that moment sheer unreasoning terror again possessed me. I did not know what I feared: I simply feared. Then like a sudden recollection, when one remembers a name which has long escaped the memory, I knew what I feared. I feared Mrs Stone, whose grave with the sinister inscription, "In evil memory", I had so often seen in my dream, just beyond the lawn which lay below my window. And then once more the fear passed so completely that I wondered what there was to fear, and I found myself, sober and quiet and sane, in the room in the tower, the name of which I had so often heard in my dream, and the scene of which was so familiar.

I looked around it with a certain sense of proprietorship, and found that nothing had been changed from the dreaming nights in which I knew it so well. Just to the left of the door was the bed, lengthways along the wall, with the head of it in the angle. In a line with it was the fireplace and a small bookcase; opposite the door the outer wall was pierced by two lattice-paned windows, between which stood the dressing-table, while ranged along the fourth wall was the washing-stand and a big cupboard. My luggage had already been unpacked, for the furniture of dressing and undressing lay orderly on the wash-stand and toilet-table, while my dinner clothes were spread out on the coverlet of the bed. And then, with a sudden start of unexplained dismay, I saw that there were two rather conspicuous objects which I had not seen before in my dreams: one a life-sized oil painting of Mrs Stone, the other a black-and-white sketch of Jack Stone, representing him as he had appeared to me only a week before in the last of the series of these repeated dreams, a rather secret and evil-looking man of about thirty. His picture hung between the windows, looking straight across the room to the other portrait, which hung at the side of the bed. At that I looked next, and as I looked I felt once more the horror of nightmare seize me.

It represented Mrs Stone as I had seen her last in my dreams: old and withered and white-haired. But in spite of the evident feebleness of body, a dreadful exuberance and vitality shone through the envelope of flesh, an exuberance wholly malign, a vitality that foamed and frothed with unimaginable evil. Evil beamed from the narrow, leering eyes; it laughed in the demon-like mouth. The whole face was instinct with some secret and appalling mirth; the hands, clasped together on the knee, seemed shaking with suppressed and nameless glee. Then I saw also that it was signed in the left-hand bottom corner, and wondering who the artist could be, I looked more closely, and read the inscription, "Julia Stone by Julia Stone".

There came a tap at the door, and John Clinton entered.

"Got everything you want?" he asked.

"Rather more than I want," said I, pointing to the picture.

He laughed.

"Hard-featured old lady," he said. "By herself, too, I remember. Anyhow she can't have flattered herself much."

"But don't you see?" said I. "It's scarcely a human face at all. It's the face of some witch, of some devil."

He looked at it more closely.

"Yes; it isn't very pleasant," he said. "Scarcely a bedside manner, eh? Yes; I can imagine getting the nightmare if I went to sleep with that close by my bed. I'll have it taken down if you like."

"I really wish you would," I said.

He rang the bell, and with the help of a servant we detached the picture and carried it out onto the landing, and put it with its face to the wall.

"By Jove, the old lady is a weight," said John, mopping his forehead. "I wonder if she had something on her mind."

The extraordinary weight of the picture had struck me too. I was about to reply, when I caught sight of my own hand. There was blood on it, in considerable quantities, covering the whole palm.

"I've cut myself somehow," said I.

John gave a little startled exclamation.

"Why, I have too," he said.

Simultaneously the footman took out his handkerchief and wiped his hand with it. I saw that there was blood also on his handkerchief.

John and I went back into the tower room and washed the blood off; but neither on his hand nor on mine was there the slightest trace of a scratch or cut. It seemed to me that, having ascertained this, we both, by a sort of tacit consent, did not allude to it again. Something in my case had dimly occurred to me that I did not wish to think about. It was but a conjecture, but I fancied that I knew the same thing had occurred to him.

The heat and oppression of the air, for the storm we had expected was still undischarged, increased very much after dinner, and for some time most of the party, among whom were John Clinton and myself, sat outside on the path bounding the lawn, where we had had tea. The night was absolutely dark, and no twinkle of star or moon ray could penetrate the pall of cloud that overset the sky. By degrees our assembly thinned, the women went up to bed, men dispersed to the smoking or billiard room, and by eleven o'clock my host and I were the only two left. All the evening I thought that he had something on his mind, and as soon as we were alone he spoke.

"The man who helped us with the picture had blood on his hand, too, did you notice?" he said.

"I asked him just now if he had cut himself, and he said he supposed he had, but that he could find no mark of it. Now where did that blood come from?"

By dint of telling myself that I was not going to think about it, I had succeeded in not doing so, and I did not want, especially just at bedtime, to be reminded of it.

"I don't know," said I, "and I don't really care so long as the picture of Mrs Stone is not by my bed."

He got up.

"But it's odd," he said. "Ha! Now you'll see another odd thing."

A dog of his, an Irish terrier by breed, had come out of the house as we talked. The door behind us into the hall was open, and a bright oblong of light shone across the lawn to the iron gate which led on to the rough grass outside, where the walnut tree stood. I saw that the dog had all his hackles up, bristling with rage and fright; his lips were curled back from his teeth, as if he was ready to spring at something, and he was growling to himself. He took not the slightest notice of his master or me, but stiffly and tensely walked across the grass to the iron gate. There he stood for a moment, looking through the bars and still growling. Then of a sudden his courage seemed to desert him: he gave one long howl, and scuttled back to the house with a curious crouching sort of movement.

"He does that half-a-dozen times a day," said John. "He sees something which he both hates and fears."

I walked to the gate and looked over it. Something was moving on the grass outside, and soon a sound which I could not instantly identify came to my ears. Then I remembered what it was: it was the purring of a cat. I lit a match, and saw the purrer, a big blue Persian, walking round and round in a little circle just outside the gate, stepping high and ecstatically, with tail carried aloft like a banner. Its eyes were bright and shining, and every now and then it put its head down and sniffed at the grass.

I laughed.

"The end of that mystery, I am afraid," I said. "Here's a large cat having Walpurgis night all alone."

"Yes, that's Darius," said John. "He spends half the day and all night there. But that's not the end of the dog mystery, for Toby and he are the best of friends, but the beginning of the cat mystery. What's the cat doing there? And why is Darius pleased, while Toby is terror-stricken?"

At that moment I remembered the rather horrible detail of my dreams when I saw through the gate, just where the cat was now, the white tomb-stone with the sinister inscription. But before I could answer the rain began, as suddenly and heavily as if a tap had been turned on, and simultaneously the big cat squeezed through the bars of the gate, and came leaping across the lawn to the house for shelter. Then it sat in the doorway, looking out eagerly into the dark. It spat and struck at John with its paw, as he pushed it in, in order to close the door.

Somehow, with the portrait of Julia Stone in the passage outside, the room in the tower had absolutely no alarm for me, and as I went to bed, feeling very sleepy and heavy, I had nothing more than interest for the curious incident about our bleeding hands, and the conduct of the cat and dog. The last thing I looked at before I put out my light was the square empty space by my bed where the portrait had been. Here the paper was of its original full tint of dark red: over the rest of the walls it had faded. Then I blew out my candle and instantly fell asleep.

My awaking was equally instantaneous, and I sat bolt upright in bed under the impression that some bright light had been flashed in my face, though it was now absolutely pitch dark. I knew exactly where I was, in the room which I had dreaded in dreams, but no horror that I ever felt when asleep approached the fear that now invaded and froze my brain. Immediately after a peal of thunder crackled just above the house, but the probability that it was only a flash of lightning which awoke me gave no reassurance to my galloping heart. Something I knew was in the room with me, and instinctively I put out my right hand, which was nearest the wall, to keep it away. And my hand touched the edge of a picture-frame hanging close to me.

I sprang out of bed, upsetting the small table that stood by it, and I heard my watch, candle, and matches clatter onto the floor. But for the moment there was no need of light, for a blinding flash leaped out of the clouds, and showed me that by my bed again hung the picture of Mrs Stone. And instantly the room went into blackness again. But in that flash I saw another thing also, namely a figure that leaned over the end of my bed, watching me. It was dressed in some close-clinging white garment, spotted and stained with mould, and the face was that of the portrait.

Overhead the thunder cracked and roared, and when it ceased and the deathly stillness succeeded, I heard the rustle of movement coming nearer me, and, more horrible yet, perceived an odour of corruption and decay. And then a hand was laid on the side of my neck, and close beside my ear I heard quick-taken, eager breathing. Yet I knew that this thing, though it could be perceived by touch, by smell, by eye and by ear, was still not of this earth, but something that had passed out of the body and had power to make itself manifest. Then a voice, already familiar to me, spoke.

"I knew you would come to the room in the tower," it said. "I have been long waiting for you. At last you have come. Tonight I shall feast; before long we will feast together."

And the quick breathing came closer to me; I could feel it on my neck.

At that the terror, which I think had paralysed me for the moment, gave way to the wild instinct of self-preservation. I hit wildly with both arms, kicking out at the same moment, and heard a little animal-squeal, and something soft dropped with a thud beside me. I took a couple of steps forward, nearly tripping up over whatever it was that lay there, and by the merest good-luck found the handle of the door. In another second I ran out on the landing, and had banged the door behind me. Almost at the same moment I heard a door open somewhere below, and John Clinton, candle in hand, came running upstairs.

"What is it?" he said. "I sleep just below you, and heard a noise as if— Good heavens, there's blood on your shoulder."

I stood there, so he told me afterwards, swaying from side to side, white as a sheet, with the mark on my shoulder as if a hand covered with blood had been laid there.

"It's in there," I said, pointing. "She, you know. The portrait is in there, too, hanging up on the place we took it from."

At that he laughed.

"My dear fellow, this is mere nightmare," he said.

He pushed by me, and opened the door, I standing there simply inert with terror, unable to stop him, unable to move.

"Phew! What an awful smell," he said.

Then there was silence; he had passed out of my sight behind the open door. Next moment he came out again, as white as myself, and instantly shut it.

"Yes, the portrait's there," he said, "and on the floor is a thing—a thing spotted with earth, like what they bury people in. Come away, quick, come away."

How I got downstairs I hardly know. An awful shuddering and nausea of the spirit rather than of the flesh had seized me, and more than once he had to place my feet upon the steps, while every now and then he cast glances of terror and apprehension up the stairs. But in time we came to his dressing-room on the floor below, and there I told him what I have here described.

The sequel can be made short; indeed, some of my readers have perhaps already guessed what it was, if they remember that inexplicable affair of the churchyard at West Fawley, some eight years ago, where an attempt was made three times to bury the body of a certain woman who had committed suicide. On each occasion the coffin was found in the course of a few days again protruding from the ground. After the third attempt, in order that the thing should not be talked about, the body was buried elsewhere in unconsecrated ground. Where it was buried was just outside the iron gate of the garden belonging to the house where this woman had lived. She had committed suicide in a room at the top of the tower in that house. Her name was Julia Stone.

Subsequently the body was again secretly dug up, and the coffin was found to be full of blood.

DRACULA'S GUEST

Bram Stoker

WHEN we started for our drive the sun was shining brightly on Munich, and the air was full of the joyousness of early summer. Just as we were about to depart, Herr Delbrück (the maître d'hôtel of the Quatre Saisons, where I was staying) came down, bareheaded, to the carriage and, after wishing me a pleasant drive, said to the coachman, still holding his hand on the handle of the carriage door:

"Remember you are back by nightfall. The sky looks bright but there is a shiver in the north wind that says there may be a sudden storm. But I am sure you will not be late." Here he smiled, and added, "for you know what night it is."

Johann answered with an emphatic, "Ja, mein Herr," and, touching his hat, drove off quickly. When we had cleared the town, I said, after signalling to him to stop:

"Tell me, Johann, what is tonight?"

He crossed himself, as he answered laconically: "Walpurgis nacht." Then he took out his watch, a great, old-fashioned German silver thing as big as a turnip, and looked at it, with his eyebrows gathered together and a little impatient shrug of his shoulders. I realised that this was his way of respectfully protesting against the unnecessary delay, and sank back in the carriage, merely motioning him to proceed. He started off rapidly, as if to make up for lost time. Every now and then the horses seemed to throw up their heads and sniffed the air suspiciously. On such occasions I often looked round in alarm. The road was pretty bleak, for we were traversing a sort of high, wind-swept plateau. As we drove, I saw a road that looked but little used, and which seemed to dip through a little, winding valley. It looked so inviting that, even at the risk of offending him, I called Johann to stop—and when he had pulled up, I told him I would like to drive down that road. He made all sorts of excuses, and frequently crossed himself as he spoke. This somewhat piqued my curiosity, so I asked him various questions. He answered fencingly, and repeatedly looked at his watch in protest. Finally I said:

"Well, Johann, I want to go down this road. I shall not ask you to come unless you like; but tell me why you do not like to go, that is all I ask." For answer he seemed to throw himself off the box, so quickly did he reach the ground. Then he stretched out his hands appealingly to me, and implored me not to go. There was just enough of English mixed with the German for me to understand the drift of his talk. He seemed always just about to tell me something—the very idea of which evidently frightened him; but each time he pulled himself up, saying, as he crossed himself: "Walpurgis-Nacht!"

I tried to argue with him, but it was difficult to argue with a man when I did not know his language. The advantage certainly rested with him, for although he began to speak in English, of a very crude and broken kind, he always got excited and broke into his native tongue—and every time he did so, he looked at his watch. Then the horses became restless and sniffed the air. At this he grew very pale, and, looking around in a frightened way, he suddenly jumped forward, took them by the bridles and led them on some twenty feet. I followed, and asked why he had done this. For answer he crossed himself, pointed to the spot we had left and drew his carriage in the direction of the other road, indicating a cross, and said, first in German, then in English: "Buried him—him what killed themselves."

I remembered the old custom of burying suicides at cross-roads: "Ah! I see, a suicide. How interesting!" But for the life of me I could not make out why the horses were frightened.

Whilst we were talking, we heard a sort of sound between a yelp and a bark. It was far away; but the horses got very restless, and it took Johann all his time to quiet them. He was pale, and said: "It sounds like a wolf—but yet there are no wolves here now."

"No?" I said, questioning him; "isn't it long since the wolves were so near the city?"

"Long, long," he answered, "in the spring and summer; but with the snow the wolves have been here not so long."

Whilst he was petting the horses and trying to quiet them, dark clouds drifted rapidly across the sky. The sunshine passed away, and a breath of cold wind seemed to drift past us. It was only a breath, however, and more in the nature of a warning than a fact, for the sun came out brightly again. Johann looked under his lifted hand at the horizon and said:

"The storm of snow, he comes before long time." Then he looked at his watch again, and, straightway holding his reins firmly—for the horses were still pawing the ground restlessly and shaking their heads—he climbed to his box as though the time had come for proceeding on our journey.

I felt a little obstinate and did not at once get into the carriage.

"Tell me," I said, "about this place where the road leads," and I pointed down.

Again he crossed himself and mumbled a prayer, before he answered: "It is unholy."

"What is unholy?" I enquired.

"The village."

"Then there is a village?"

"No, no. No one lives there hundreds of years." My curiosity was piqued: "But you said there was a village."

"There was."

"Where is it now?"

Whereupon he burst out into a long story in German and English, so mixed up that I could not quite understand exactly what he said, but roughly I gathered that long ago, hundreds of years, men had died there and been buried in their graves; and sounds were heard under the clay, and when the graves were opened, men and women were found rosy with life, and their mouths red with blood. And so, in haste to save their lives (aye, and their souls!—and here he crossed himself) those who were left fled away to other places, where the living lived, and the dead were dead and not—not something. He was evidently afraid to speak the last words. As he proceeded with his narration, he grew more and more excited. It seemed as if his imagination had got hold of him, and he ended in a perfect paroxysm of fear—white-faced, perspiring, trembling and looking round him, as if expecting that some dreadful presence would manifest itself there in the bright sunshine on the open plain. Finally, in an agony of desperation, he cried:

"Walpurgis nacht!" and pointed to the carriage for me to get in. All my English blood rose at this, and, standing back, I said:

"You are afraid, Johann—you are afraid. Go home; I shall return alone; the walk will do me good." The carriage door was open. I took from the seat my oak walking-stick—which I always carry on my holiday excursions—and closed the door, pointing back to Munich, and said, "Go home, Johann— Walpurgis-nacht doesn't concern Englishmen."

The horses were now more restive than ever, and Johann was trying to hold them in, while excitedly imploring me not to do anything so foolish. I pitied the poor fellow, he was so deeply in earnest; but all the same I could not help laughing. His English was quite gone now. In his anxiety he had forgotten that his only means of making me understand was to talk my language, so he jabbered away in his native German. It began to be a little tedious. After giving the direction, "Home!" I turned to go down the cross-road into the valley.

With a despairing gesture, Johann turned his horses towards Munich. I leaned on my stick and looked after him. He went slowly along the road for a while: then there came over the crest of the hill a man tall and thin. I could see so much in the distance. When he drew near the horses, they began to jump and kick about, then to scream with terror. Johann could not hold them in; they bolted down the road, running away madly. I watched them out of sight, then looked for the stranger, but I found that he, too, was gone.

With a light heart I turned down the side road through the deepening valley to which Johann had objected. There was not the slightest reason, that I could see, for his objection; and I daresay I tramped for a couple of hours without thinking of time or distance, and certainly without seeing a person or a house. So far as the place was concerned, it was desolation itself. But I did not notice this particularly till, on turning a bend in the road, I came upon a scattered fringe of wood; then I recognised that I had been impressed unconsciously by the desolation of the region through which I had passed.

I sat down to rest myself, and began to look around. It struck me that it was considerably colder than it had been at the commencement of my walk—a sort of sighing sound seemed to be around me, with, now and then, high overhead, a sort of muffled roar. Looking upwards I noticed that great thick clouds were drifting rapidly across the sky from North to South at a great height. There were signs of coming storm in some lofty stratum of the air. I was a little chilly, and, thinking that it was the sitting still after the exercise of walking, I resumed my journey.

The ground I passed over was now much more picturesque. There were no striking objects that the eye might single out; but in all there was a charm of beauty. I took little heed of time and it was only when the deepening twi-light forced itself upon me that I began to think of how I should find my way home. The brightness of the day had gone. The air was cold, and the drifting of clouds high overhead was more marked. They were accompanied by a sort of far-away rushing sound, through which seemed to come at intervals that mysterious cry which the driver had said came from a wolf. For a while I hesitated. I had said I would see the deserted village, so on I went, and presently came on a wide stretch of open country, shut in by hills all around. Their sides were covered with trees which spread down to the plain, dotting, in clumps, the gentler slopes and hollows which showed here and there. I followed with my eye the winding of the road, and saw that it curved close to one of the densest of these clumps and was lost behind it.

As I looked there came a cold shiver in the air, and the snow began to fall. I thought of the miles and miles of bleak country I had passed, and then hurried on to seek the shelter of the wood in front. Darker and darker grew the sky, and faster and heavier fell the snow, till the earth before and around me was a glistening white carpet the further edge of which was lost in misty vagueness. The road was here but crude, and when on the level its boundaries were not so marked, as when it passed through the cuttings; and in a little while I found that I must have strayed from it, for I missed underfoot the hard surface, and my feet sank deeper in the grass and moss. Then the wind grew stronger and blew with ever increasing force, till I was fain to run before it. The air became icy-cold, and in spite of my exercise I began to suffer. The snow was now falling so thickly and whirling around me in such rapid eddies that I could hardly keep my eyes open. Every now and then the heavens were torn asunder by vivid lightning; and in the flashes I could see ahead of me a great mass of trees, chiefly yew and cypress all heavily coated with snow.

I was soon amongst the shelter of the trees, and there, in comparative silence, I could hear the rush of the wind high overhead. Presently the blackness of the storm had become merged in the darkness of the night. By-and-by the storm seemed to be passing away: it now only came in fierce puffs or blasts. At such moments the weird sound of the wolf appeared to be echoed by many similar sounds around me.

Now and again, through the black mass of drifting cloud, came a straggling ray of moonlight; which lit up the expanse, and showed me that I was at the edge of a dense mass of cypress and yew trees. As the snow had ceased to fall, I walked out from the shelter and began to investigate more closely. It appeared to me that, amongst so many old foundations as I had passed, there might be still standing a house in which, though in ruins, I could find some sort of shelter for a while. As I skirted the edge of the copse, I found that a low wall encircled it, and following this I presently found an opening. Here the cypresses formed an alley leading up to a square mass of some kind of building. Just as I caught sight of this, however, the drifting clouds obscured the moon, and I passed up the path in darkness. The wind must have grown colder, for I felt myself shiver as I walked; but there was hope of shelter, and I groped my way blindly on.

I stopped, for there was a sudden stillness. The storm had passed; and, perhaps in sympathy with nature's silence, my heart seemed to cease to beat. But this was only momentarily; for suddenly the moonlight broke through the clouds, showing me that I was in a graveyard, and that the square object before me was a great massive tomb of marble, as white as the snow that lay on and all around it. With the moonlight there came a fierce sigh of the storm, which appeared to resume its course with a long, low howl, as of many dogs or wolves. I was awed and shocked, and felt the cold perceptibly grow upon me till it seemed to grip me by the heart. Then while the flood of moonlight still fell on the marble tomb, the storm gave further evidence of renewing, as though it was returning on its track. Impelled by some sort of fascination, I approached the sepulchre to see what it was, and why such a thing stood alone in such a place. I walked around it, and read, over the Doric door, in German—

COUNTESS DOLINGEN OF GRATZ

IN STYRIA

SOUGHT AND FOUND DEATH.

1801.

On the top of the tomb, seemingly driven through the solid marble—for the structure was composed of a few vast blocks of stone—was a great iron spike or stake. On going to the back I saw, graven in great Russian letters:

"The dead travel fast."

There was something so weird and uncanny about the whole thing that it gave me a turn and made me feel quite faint. I began to wish, for the first time, that I had taken Johann's advice. Here a thought struck me, which came under almost mysterious circumstances and with a terrible shock. This was Walpurgis Night!

Walpurgis Night, when, according to the belief of millions of people, the devil was abroad—when the graves were opened and the dead came forth and walked. When all evil things of earth and air and water held revel. This very place the driver had specially shunned. This was the depopulated village of centuries ago. This was where the suicide lay; and this was the place where I was alone—unmanned, shivering with cold in a shroud of snow with a wild storm gathering again upon me! It took all my philosophy, all the religion I had been taught, all my courage, not to collapse in a paroxysm of fright.

And now a perfect tornado burst upon me. The ground shook as though thousands of horses thundered across it; and this time the storm bore on its icy wings, not snow, but great hailstones which drove with such violence that they might have come from the thongs of Balearic slingers—hailstones that beat down leaf and branch and made the shelter of the cypresses of no more avail than though their stems were standing-corn. At the first I had rushed to the nearest tree; but I was soon fain to leave it and seek the only spot that seemed to afford refuge, the deep Doric doorway of the marble tomb. There, crouching against the massive bronze-door, I gained a certain amount of protection from the beating of the hailstones, for now they only drove against me as they ricochetted from the ground and the side of the marble.

As I leaned against the door, it moved slightly and opened inwards. The shelter of even a tomb was welcome in that pitiless tempest, and I was about to enter it when there came a flash of forked-lightning that lit up the whole expanse of the heavens. In the instant, as I am a living man, I saw, as my eyes were turned into the darkness of the tomb, a beautiful woman, with rounded cheeks and red lips, seemingly sleeping on a bier. As the thunder broke over-head, I was grasped as by the hand of a giant and hurled out into the storm.

The whole thing was so sudden that, before I could realise the shock, moral as well as physical, I found the hailstones beating me down. At the same time I had a strange, dominating feeling that I was not alone. I looked towards the tomb. Just then there came another blinding flash, which seemed to strike the iron stake that surmounted the tomb and to pour through to the earth, blasting and crumbling the marble, as in a burst of flame. The dead woman rose for a moment of agony, while she was lapped in the flame, and her bitter scream of pain was drowned in the thundercrash. The last thing I heard was this mingling of dreadful sound, as again I was seized in the giant-grasp and dragged away, while the hailstones beat on me, and the air around seemed reverberant with the howling of wolves. The last sight that I remembered was a vague, white, moving mass, as if all the graves around me had sent out the phantoms of their sheeted-dead, and that they were closing in on me through the white cloudiness of the driving hail.

Gradually there came a sort of vague beginning of consciousness; then a sense of weariness that was dreadful. For a time I remembered nothing; but slowly my senses returned. My feet seemed positively racked with pain, yet I could not move them. They seemed to be numbed. There was an icy feeling at the back of my neck and all down my spine, and my ears, like my feet, were dead, yet in torment; but there was in my breast a sense of warmth which was, by comparison, delicious. It was as a nightmare—a physical nightmare, if one may use such an expression; for some heavy weight on my chest made it difficult for me to breathe.

This period of semi-lethargy seemed to remain a long time, and as it faded away I must have slept or swooned. Then came a sort of loathing, like the first stage of sea-sickness, and a wild desire to be free from something—I knew not what. A vast stillness enveloped me, as though all the world were asleep or dead—only broken by the low panting as of some animal close to me. I felt a warm rasping at my throat, then came a consciousness of the awful truth, which chilled me to the heart and sent the blood surging up through my brain. Some great animal was lying on me and now licking my throat. I feared to stir, for some instinct of prudence bade me lie still; but the brute seemed to realise that there was now some change in me, for it raised its head. Through my eyelashes I saw above me the two great flaming eyes of a gigantic wolf. Its sharp white teeth gleamed in the gaping red mouth, and I could feel its hot breath fierce and acrid upon me.

For another spell of time I remembered no more. Then I became conscious of a low growl, followed by a yelp, renewed again and again. Then, seemingly very far away, I heard a "Holloa! holloa!" as of many voices calling in unison. Cautiously I raised my head and looked in the direction whence the sound came; but the cemetery blocked my view. The wolf still continued to yelp in a strange way, and a red glare began to move round the grove of cypresses, as though following the sound. As the voices drew closer, the wolf yelped faster and louder. I feared to make either sound or motion. Nearer came the red glow, over the white pall which stretched into the darkness around me. Then all at once from beyond the trees there came at a trot a troop of horsemen bearing torches. The wolf rose from my breast and made for the cemetery. I saw one of the horsemen (soldiers by their caps and their long military cloaks) raise his carbine and take aim. A companion knocked up his arm, and I heard the ball whizz over my head. He had evidently taken my body for that of the wolf. Another sighted the animal as it slunk away, and a shot followed. Then, at a gallop, the troop rode forward—some towards me, others following the wolf as it disappeared amongst the snow-clad cypresses.

As they drew nearer I tried to move, but was powerless, although I could see and hear all that went on around me. Two or three of the soldiers jumped from their horses and knelt beside me. One of them raised my head, and placed his hand over my heart.

"Good news, comrades!" he cried. "His heart still beats!"

Then some brandy was poured down my throat; it put vigour into me, and I was able to open my eyes fully and look around. Lights and shadows were moving among the trees, and I heard men call to one another. They drew together, uttering frightened exclamations; and the lights flashed as the others came pouring out of the cemetery pell-mell, like men possessed. When the further ones came close to us, those who were around me asked them eagerly:

"Well, have you found him?"

The reply rang out hurriedly:

"No! no! Come away quick—quick! This is no place to stay, and on this of all nights!"

"What was it?" was the question, asked in all manner of keys. The answer came variously and all indefinitely as though the men were moved by some common impulse to speak, yet were restrained by some common fear from giving their thoughts.

"It—it—indeed!" gibbered one, whose wits had plainly given out for the moment.

"A wolf—and yet not a wolf!" another put in shudderingly.

"No use trying for him without the sacred bullet," a third remarked in a more ordinary manner.

"Serve us right for coming out on this night! Truly we have earned our thousand marks!" were the ejaculations of a fourth.

"There was blood on the broken marble," another said after a pause—"the lightning never brought that there. And for him—is he safe? Look at his throat! See, comrades, the wolf has been lying on him and keeping his blood warm."

The officer looked at my throat and replied:

"He is all right; the skin is not pierced. What does it all mean? We should never have found him but for the yelping of the wolf."

"What became of it?" asked the man who was holding up my head, and who seemed the least panic-stricken of the party, for his hands were steady and without tremor. On his sleeve was the chevron of a petty officer.

"It went to its home," answered the man, whose long face was pallid, and who actually shook with terror as he glanced around him fearfully. "There are graves enough there in which it may lie. Come, comrades—come quickly! Let us leave this cursed spot."

The officer raised me to a sitting posture, as he uttered a word of command; then several men placed me upon a horse. He sprang to the saddle behind me, took me in his arms, gave the word to advance; and, turning our faces away from the cypresses, we rode away in swift, military order.

As yet my tongue refused its office, and I was perforce silent. I must have fallen asleep; for the next thing I remembered was finding myself standing up, supported by a soldier on each side of me. It was almost broad daylight, and to the north a red streak of sunlight was reflected, like a path of blood, over the waste of snow. The officer was telling the men to say nothing of what they had seen, except that they found an English stranger, guarded by a large dog.

"Dog! that was no dog," cut in the man who had exhibited such fear. "I think I know a wolf when I see one."

The young officer answered calmly: "I said a dog."

"Dog!" reiterated the other ironically. It was evident that his courage was rising with the sun; and, pointing to me, he said, "Look at his throat. Is that the work of a dog, master?"

Instinctively I raised my hand to my throat, and as I touched it I cried out in pain. The men crowded round to look, some stooping down from their saddles; and again there came the calm voice of the young officer:

"A dog, as I said. If aught else were said we should only be laughed at."

I was then mounted behind a trooper, and we rode on into the suburbs of Munich. Here we came across a stray carriage, into which I was lifted, and it was driven off to the Quatre Saisons—the young officer accompanying me, whilst a trooper followed with his horse, and the others rode off to their barracks.

When we arrived, Herr Delbrück rushed so quickly down the steps to meet me, that it was apparent he had been watching within. Taking me by both hands he solicitously led me in. The officer saluted me and was turning to withdraw, when I recognised his purpose, and insisted that he should come to my rooms. Over a glass of wine I warmly thanked him and his brave comrades for saving me. He replied simply that he was more than glad, and that Herr Delbrück had at the first taken steps to make all the searching party pleased; at which ambiguous utterance the maître d'hôtel smiled, while the officer pleaded duty and withdrew.

"But Herr Delbrück," I enquired, "how and why was it that the soldiers searched for me?"

He shrugged his shoulders, as if in depreciation of his own deed, as he replied:

"I was so fortunate as to obtain leave from the commander of the regiment in which I served, to ask for volunteers."

"But how did you know I was lost?" I asked.

"The driver came hither with the remains of his carriage, which had been upset when the horses ran away."

"But surely you would not send a search-party of soldiers merely on this account?"

"Oh, no!" he answered; "but even before the coachman arrived, I had this telegram from the Boyar whose guest you are," and he took from his pocket a telegram which he handed to me, and I read:

Bistritz.

"Be careful of my guest—his safety is most precious to me. Should aught happen to him, or if he be missed, spare nothing to find him and ensure his safety. He is English and therefore adventurous. There are often dangers from snow and wolves and night. Lose not a moment if you suspect harm to him. I answer your zeal with my fortune.—Dracula."

As I held the telegram in my hand, the room seemed to whirl around me; and, if the attentive maître d'hôtel had not caught me, I think I should have fallen. There was something so strange in all this, something so weird and impossible to imagine, that there grew on me a sense of my being in some way the sport of opposite forces—the mere vague idea of which seemed in a way to paralyse me. I was certainly under some form of mysterious protection. From a distant country had come, in the very nick of time, a message that took me out of the danger of the snow-sleep and the jaws of the wolf.

1939

THE CLOAK

Robert Bloch

THE sun was dying, and its blood spattered the sky as it crept into
its sepulchre behind the hills. The keening wind sent the dry,
fallen leaves scurrying toward the west, as though hastening them
to the funeral of the sun.

"Nuts!" said Henderson to himself, and stopped thinking.

The sun was setting in a dingy red sky, and a dirty raw wind was kicking
up the half-rotten leaves in a filthy gutter. Why should he waste time with
cheap imagery?

"Nuts!" said Henderson, again.

It was probably a mood evoked by the day, he mused. After all, this was
the sunset of Halloween. Tonight was the dreaded Allhallows Eve, when
spirits walked and skulls cried out from their graves beneath the earth.

Either that, or tonight was just another rotten cold fall day. Henderson
sighed. There was a time, he reflected, when the coming of this night meant
something. A dark Europe, groaning in superstitious terror, dedicated this
Eve to the grinning Unknown. A million doors had once been barred against
the evil visitants, a million prayers mumbled, a million candles lit. There was
something majestic about the idea, Henderson reflected. Life had been an
adventure in those times, and men walked in terror of what the next turn
of a midnight road might bring. They had lived in a world of demons and
ghouls and elementals who sought their souls—and by Heaven, in those
days a man's soul meant something. This new scepticism had taken a profound meaning away from life. Men no longer revered their souls.

"Nuts!" said Henderson again, quite automatically. There was something crude and twentieth-century about the coarse expression which always checked his introspective flights of fancy.

The voice in his brain that said "nuts" took the place of humanity to Henderson—common humanity which would voice the same sentiment if they heard his secret thoughts. So now Henderson uttered the word and endeavoured to forget problems and purple patches alike.

He was walking down this street at sunset to buy a costume for the masquerade party tonight, and he had much better concentrate on finding the costumer's before it closed than waste his time daydreaming about Halloween.

His eyes searched the darkening shadows of the dingy buildings lining the narrow thoroughfare. Once again he peered at the address he had scribbled down after finding it in the phone book.

Why the devil didn't they light up the shops when it got dark? He couldn't make out numbers. This was a poor, run-down neighbourhood, but after all—

Abruptly, Henderson spied the place across the street and started over. He passed the window and glanced in. The last rays of the sun slanted over the top of the building across the way and fell directly on the window and its display. Henderson drew a sharp intake of breath.

He was staring at a costumer's window—not looking through a fissure into hell. Then why was it all red fire, lighting the grinning visages of fiends?

"Sunset," Henderson muttered aloud. Of course it was, and the faces were merely clever masks such as would be displayed in this sort of place. Still, it gave the imaginative man a start. He opened the door and entered.

The place was dark and still. There was a smell of loneliness in the air—the smell that haunts all places long undisturbed; tombs, and graves in deep woods, and caverns in the earth, and—

"Nuts."

What the devil was wrong with him, anyway? Henderson smiled apologetically at the empty darkness. This was the smell of the costumer's shop, and it carried him back to college days of amateur theatricals. Henderson had known this smell of moth balls, decayed furs, grease paint and oils. He had played amateur Hamlet and in his hands he had held a smirking skull that hid all knowledge in its empty eyes—a skull, from the costumer's.

Well, here he was again, and the skull gave him the idea. After all, Halloween night it was. Certainly in this mood of his he didn't want to go as a rajah, or a Turk, or a pirate—they all did that. Why not go as a fiend, or a warlock, or a werewolf? He could see Lindstrom's face when he walked into the elegant penthouse wearing rags of some sort. The fellow would have a fit, with his society crowd wearing their expensive Elsa Maxwell take-offs. Henderson didn't greatly care for Lindstrom's sophisticated friends anyway; a gang of amateur Noel Cowards and horsy women wearing harnesses of jewels. Why not carry out the spirit of Halloween and go as a monster?

Henderson stood there in the dusk, waiting for someone to turn on the lights, come out from the back room and serve him. After a minute or so he grew impatient and rapped sharply on the counter.

"Say in there! Service!"

Silence. And a shuffling noise from the rear, then—an unpleasant noise to hear in the gloom. There was a banging from downstairs and then the heavy clump of footsteps. Suddenly Henderson gasped. A black bulk was rising from the floor!

It was, of course, only the opening of the trapdoor from the basement. A man shuffled behind the counter, carrying a lamp. In that light his eyes blinked drowsily.

The man's yellowish face crinkled into a smile.

"I was sleeping, I'm afraid," said the man, softly. "Can I serve you, sir?"

"I was looking for a Halloween costume."

"Oh, yes. And what was it you had in mind?"

The voice was weary, infinitely weary. The eyes continued to blink in the flabby yellow face.

"Nothing usual, I'm afraid. You see, I rather fancied some sort of monster getup for a party—Don't suppose you carry anything in that line?"

"I could show you masks."

"No. I meant, werewolf outfits, something of that sort. More of the authentic."

"So. The *authentic*."

"Yes." Why did this old dunce stress the word?

"I might—yes, I might have just the thing for you, sir." The eyes blinked, but the thin mouth pursed in a smile. "just the thing for Halloween."

"What's that?"

"Have you ever considered the possibility of being a vampire?"

"Like Dracula?"

"Ah—yes, I suppose—Dracula."

"Not a bad idea. Do you think I'm the type for that, though?"

The man appraised him with that tight smile. "Vampires are of all types, I understand. You would do nicely."

"Hardly a compliment," Henderson chuckled. "But why not? What's the outfit?"

"Outfit? Merely evening clothes, or what you wear. I will furnish you with the authentic cloak."

"Just a cloak—is that all?"

"Just a cloak. But it is worn like a shroud. It is shroud-cloth, you know. Wait, I'll get it for you."

The shuffling feet carried the man into the rear of the shop again. Down the trapdoor entrance he went, and Henderson waited. There was more banging, and presently the old man reappeared carrying the cloak. He was shaking dust from it in the darkness.

"Here it is—the genuine cloak."

"Genuine?"

"Allow me to adjust it for you—it will work wonders, I'm sure."

The cold, heavy cloth hung draped about Henderson's shoulders. The faint odour rose mustily in his nostrils as he stepped back and surveyed himself in the mirror. The lamp was poor, but Henderson saw that the cloak effected a striking transformation in his appearance. His long face seemed thinner, his eyes were accentuated in the facial pallor heightened by the sombre cloak he wore. It was a big, black shroud.

"Genuine," murmured the old man. He must have come up suddenly, for Henderson hadn't noticed him in the glass.

"I'll take it," Henderson said. "How much?"

"You'll find it quite entertaining, I'm sure."

"How much?"

"Oh. Shall we say five dollars?"

"Here."

The old man took the money, blinking, and drew the cloak from Henderson's shoulders. When it slid away he felt suddenly warm again. It must be cold in the basement—the cloth was icy.

The old man wrapped the garment, smiling, and handed it over.

"I'll have it back tomorrow," Henderson promised.

"No need. You purchased it. It is yours."

"But—"

"I am leaving business shortly. Keep it. You will find more use for it than I, surely."

"But—"

"A pleasant evening to you."

Henderson made his way to the door in confusion, then turned to salute the blinking old man in the dimness.

Two eyes were burning at him from across the counter—two eyes that did not blink.

"Good night," said Henderson, and closed the door quickly. He wondered if he were going just a trifle mad.

*

At eight, Henderson nearly called up Lindstrom to tell him he couldn't make it. The cold chills came the minute he put on the damned cloak, and when he looked at himself in the mirror his blurred eyes could scarcely make out the reflection.

But after a few drinks he felt better about it. He hadn't eaten, and the liquor warmed his blood. He paced the floor, attitudinising with the cloak— sweeping it about him and scowling in what he thought was a ferocious manner. Damn it, he was going to be a vampire all right! He called a cab, went down to the lobby. The driver came in, and Henderson was waiting, black cloak furled.

"I wish you to drive me," he said, in a low voice.

The cabman took one look at him in the cloak and turned pale.

"Whazzat?"

"I ordered you to come," said Henderson gutturally while he quaked with inner mirth. He leered ferociously and swept the cloak back.

"Yeah, yeah. O. K."

The driver almost ran outside. Henderson stalked after him.

"Where to, boss—I mean, sir?"

The frightened face didn't turn as Henderson intoned the address and sat back.

The cab started with a lurch that set Henderson to chuckling deeply, in character. At the sound of the laughter the driver got panicky and raced his engine up to the limit set by the governor. Henderson laughed loudly, and the impressionable driver fairly quivered in his seat. It was quite a ride, but Henderson was entirely unprepared to open the door and find it slammed after him as the cabman drove hastily away without collecting a fare.

"I must look the part," he thought complacently, as he took the elevator up to the penthouse apartment.

There were three or four others in the elevator; Henderson had seen them before at other affairs Lindstrom had invited him to attend, but nobody seemed to recognise him. It rather pleased him to think how his wearing of an unfamiliar cloak and an unfamiliar scowl seemed to change his entire personality and appearance. Here the other guests had donned elaborate disguises—one woman wore the costume of a Watteau shepherdess, another was attired as a Spanish ballerina, a tall man dressed as Pagliacci, and his companion had donned a toreador outfit. Yet Henderson recognised them all; knew that their expensive habiliments were not truly disguises at all, but merely elaborations calculated to enhance their appearance. Most people at costume parties gave vent to suppressed desires. The women showed off their figures, the men either accentuated their masculinity as the toreador did, or clowned it. Such things were pitiful; these conventional fools eagerly doffing their dismal business suits and rushing off to a lodge, or amateur theatrical, or mask ball in order to satisfy their starving imaginations. Why didn't they dress in garish colours on the street? Henderson often pondered the question.

Surely, these society folk in the elevator were fine-looking men and women in their outfits—so healthy, so red-faced; and full of vitality. They had such robust throats and necks. Henderson looked at the plump arms of the woman next to him. He stared, without realising it, for a long moment. And then, he saw that the occupants of the car had drawn away from him. They were standing in the corner, as though they feared his cloak and scowl, and his eyes fixed on the woman. Their chatter had ceased abruptly. The woman looked at him, as though she were about to speak, when the elevator doors opened and afforded Henderson a welcome respite.

What the devil was wrong? First the cab driver, then the woman. Had he drunk too much?

Well, no chance to consider that. Here was Marcus Lindstrom, and he was thrusting a glass into Henderson's hand.

"What have we here? Ah, a bogyman!" It needed no second glance to perceive that Lindstrom, as usual at such affairs, was already quite bottle-dizzy. The fat host was positively swimming in alcohol.

"Have a drink, Henderson, my lad! I'll take mine from the bottle. That outfit of yours gave me a shock. Where'd you get the make-up?"

"Make-up? I'm not wearing any make-up."

"Oh. So you're not. How silly of me."

Henderson wondered if he were crazy. Had Lindstrom really drawn back? Were his eyes actually filled with a certain dismay? Oh, the man was obviously intoxicated.

"I'll... I'll see you later," babbled Lindstrom, edging away and quickly turning to the other arrivals. Henderson watched the back of Lindstrom's neck. It was fat and white. It bulged over the collar of his costume and there was a vein in it. A vein in Lindstrom's fat neck. Frightened Lindstrom.

Henderson stood alone in the anteroom. From the parlour beyond came the sound of music and laughter; party noises. Henderson hesitated before entering. He drank from the glass in his hand—Bacardi rum, and powerful. On top of his other drinks it almost made the man reel. But he drank, wondering. What was wrong with him and his costume? Why did he frighten people? Was he unconsciously acting his vampire role? That crack of Lindstrom's about make-up, now—

Acting on impulse, Henderson stepped over to the long panel mirror in the hall. He lurched a little, then stood in the harsh light before it. He faced the glass, stared into the mirror, and saw nothing.

He looked at himself in the mirror, and there was no one there!

Henderson began to laugh softly, evilly, deep in his throat. And as he gazed into the empty, unreflecting glass, his laughter rose in black glee.

"I'm drunk," he whispered. "I must be drunk. Mirror in my apartment made me blurred. Now I'm so far gone I can't see straight. Sure I'm drunk. Been acting ridiculously, scaring people. Now I'm seeing hallucinations—or not seeing them, rather. Visions. Angels."

His voice lowered. "Sure, angels. Standing right in back of me, now. Hello, angel."

"Hello."

Henderson whirled. There she stood, in the dark cloak, her hair a shimmering halo above her white, proud face; her eyes celestial blue, and her lips infernal red.

"Are you real?" asked Henderson, gently. "Or am I a fool to believe in miracles?"

"This miracle's name is Sheila Darrly, and it would like to powder its nose if you please."

"Kindly use this mirror through the courtesy of Stephen Henderson," replied the cloaked man, with a grin. He stepped back a ways, eyes intent.

The girl turned her head and favoured him with a slow, impish smile. "Haven't you ever seen powder used before?" she asked.

"Didn't know angels indulged in cosmetics," Henderson replied. "But then there's a lot I don't know about angels. From now on I shall make them a special study of mine. There's so much I want to find out. So you'll probably find me following you around with a notebook all evening."

"Notebooks for a vampire?"

"Oh, but I'm a very intelligent vampire—not one of those backwoods Transylvanian types. You'll find me charming, I'm sure."

"Yes, you look like the sure type," the girl mocked. "But an angel and a vampire—that's a queer combination."

"We can reform one another," Henderson pointed out. "Besides, I have a suspicion that there's a bit of the devil in you. That dark cloak over your angel costume; dark angel, you know. Instead of heaven you might hail from my home town."

Henderson was flippant, but underneath his banter cyclonic thoughts whirled. He recalled discussions in the past; cynical observations he had made and believed.

Once, Henderson had declared that there was no such thing as love at first sight, save in books or plays where such a dramatic device served to speed up action. He asserted that people learned about romance from books and plays and accordingly adopted a belief in love at first sight when all one could possibly feel was desire.

And now this Sheila—this blond angel—had to come along and drive out all thoughts of morbidity, all thoughts of drunkenness and foolish gazings into mirrors, from his mind; had to send him madly plunging into dreams of red lips, ethereal blue eyes and slim white arms.

Something of his feelings had swept into his eyes, and as the girl gazed up at him she felt the truth.

"Well," she breathed, "I hope the inspection pleases."

"A miracle of understatement, that. But there was something I wanted to find out particularly about divinity. Do angels dance?"

"Tactful vampire! The next room?"

Arm in arm they entered the parlour. The merrymakers were in full swing. Liquor had already pitched gaiety at its height, but there was no dancing any longer. Boisterous little grouped couples laughed arm in arm about the room. The usual party gagsters were performing their antics in corners. The superficial atmosphere, which Henderson detested, was fully in evidence.

It was reaction which made Henderson draw himself up to full height and sweep the cloak about his shoulders. Reaction brought the scowl to his pale face, caused him to stalk along in brooding silence. Sheila seemed to regard this as a great joke.

"Pull a vampire act on them," she giggled, clutching his arm. Henderson accordingly scowled at the couples, sneered horrendously at the women. And his progress was marked by the turning of heads, the abrupt cessation of chatter. He walked through the long room like Red Death incarnate. Whispers trailed in his wake.

"Who is that man?"

"We came up with him in the elevator, and he—"

"His eyes—"

"Vampire!"

"Hello, Dracula!" It was Marcus Lindstrom and a sullen-looking brunette in Cleopatra costume who lurched toward Henderson. Host Lindstrom could scarcely stand, and his companion in cups was equally at a loss. Henderson liked the man when sober at the club, but his behaviour at parties had always irritated him. Lindstrom was particularly objectionable in his present condition—it made him boorish.

"M' dear, I want you t' meet a very dear friend of mine. Yessir, it being Halloween and all, I invited Count Dracula here, t'gether with his daughter. Asked his grandmother, but she's busy tonight at a Black Sabbath—along with Aunt Jemima. Ha! Count, meet my little playmate."

The woman leered up at Henderson.

"Oooh Dracula, what big eyes you have! Oooh, what big teeth you have! Ooooh—"

"Really, Marcus," Henderson protested. But the host had turned and shouted to the room.

"Folks, meet the real goods—only genuine living vampire in captivity! Dracula Henderson, only existing vampire with false teeth."

In any other circumstance Henderson would have given Lindstrom a quick, efficient punch on the jaw. But Sheila was at his side, it was a public gathering; better to humour the man's clumsy jest. Why not be a vampire?

Smiling quickly at the girl, Henderson drew himself erect, faced the crowd, and frowned. His hands brushed the cloak. Funny, it still felt cold. Looking down he noticed for the first time that it was a little dirty at the edges; muddy or dusty. But the cold silk slid through his fingers as he drew it across his breast with one long hand. The feeling seemed to inspire him. He opened his eyes wide and let them blaze. His mouth opened. A sense of dramatic power filled him. And he looked at Marcus Lindstrom's soft, fat neck with the vein standing in the whiteness. He looked at the neck, saw the crowd watching him, and then the impulse seized him. He turned, eyes on that creasy neck—that wabbling, creasy neck of the fat man.

187

Hands darted out. Lindstrom squeaked like a frightened rat. He was a plump, sleek white rat, bursting with blood. Vampires liked blood. Blood from the rat, from the neck of the rat, from the vein in the neck of the squeaking rat.

"Warm blood."

The deep voice was Henderson's own.

The hands were Henderson's own.

The hands that went around Lindstrom's neck as he spoke, the hands that felt the warmth, that searched out the vein. Henderson's face was bending for the neck, and, as Lindstrom struggled, his grip tightened. Lindstrom's face was turning, turning purple. Blood was rushing to his head. That was good. Blood!

Henderson's mouth opened. He felt the air on his teeth. He bent down toward that fat neck, and then—

"Stop! That's plenty!"

The voice, the cooling voice of Sheila. Her fingers on his arm. Henderson looked up, startled. He released Lindstrom, who sagged with open mouth.

The crowd was staring, and their mouths were all shaped in the instinctive O of amazement.

Sheila whispered, "Bravo! Served him right—but you frightened him!"

Henderson struggled a moment to collect himself. Then he smiled and turned.

"Ladies and gentlemen," he said, "I have just given a slight demonstration to prove to you what our host said of me was entirely correct. I *am* a vampire. Now that you have been given fair warning, I am sure you will be in no further danger. If there is a doctor in the house I can, perhaps, arrange for a blood transfusion."

The O's relaxed and laughter came from startled throats. Hysterical laughter, in part, then genuine. Henderson had carried it off. Marcus Lindstrom alone still stared with eyes that held utter fear. *He* knew.

And then the moment broke, for one of the gagsters ran into the room from the elevator. He had gone downstairs and borrowed the apron and cap of a newsboy. Now he raced through the crowd with a bundle of papers under his arm.

"Extra! Extra! Read all about it! Big Halloween Horror! Extra!"

Laughing guests purchased papers. A woman approached Sheila, and Henderson watched the girl walk away in a daze.

"See you later," she called, and her glance sent fire through his veins. Still, he could not forget the terrible feeling that came over him when he had seized Lindstrom. Why?

Automatically, he accepted a paper from the shouting pseudo-newsboy. "Big Halloween Horror," he had shouted. What was that?

Blurred eyes searched the paper.

Then Henderson reeled back. That headline! It was an *Extra* after all. Henderson scanned the columns with mounting dread.

"Fire in costumer's… shortly after 8 p.m. firemen were summoned to the shop of… flames beyond control… completely demolished… damage estimated at… peculiarly enough, name of proprietor unknown… skeleton found in—"

"No!" gasped Henderson aloud.

He read, reread *that* closely. The skeleton had been found in a box of earth in the cellar beneath the shop. The box was a coffin. There had been two other boxes, empty. The skeleton had been wrapped in a cloak, undamaged by the flames—

And in the hastily penned box at the bottom of the column were eyewitness comments, written up under scareheads of heavy black type. Neighbours had feared the place. Hungarian neighbourhood, hints of vampirism, of strangers who entered the shop. One man spoke of a cult believed to have held meetings in the place. Superstition about things sold there— love philtres, outlandish charms and weird disguises.

Weird disguises—vampires—cloaks—*his eyes!*

"This is an authentic cloak."

"I will not be using this much longer. Keep it."

Memories of these words screamed through Henderson's brain. He plunged out of the room and rushed to the panel mirror.

A moment, then he flung one arm before his face to shield his eyes from the image that was not there—the missing reflection. *Vampires have no reflections.*

No wonder he looked strange. No wonder arms and necks invited him. He had wanted Lindstrom. Good God!

The cloak had done that, the dark cloak with the stains. The stains of earth, grave-earth. The wearing of the cloak, the cold cloak, had given him the feelings of a true vampire. It was a garment accursed, a thing that had lain on the body of one undead. The rusty stain along one sleeve was blood.

Blood. It would be nice to see blood. To taste its warmth, its red life, flowing.

No. That was insane. He was drunk, crazy.

"Ah. My pale friend the vampire."

It was Sheila again. And above all horror rose the beating of Henderson's heart. As he looked at her shining eyes, her warm mouth shaped in red invitation, Henderson felt a wave of warmth. He looked at her white throat rising above her dark, shimmering cloak, and another kind of warmth rose. Love, desire, and a—hunger.

She must have seen it in his eyes, but she did not flinch. Instead, her own gaze burned in return.

Sheila loved him, too!

With an impulsive gesture, Henderson ripped the cloak from about his throat. The icy weight lifted. He was free. Somehow, he hadn't wanted to take the cloak off, but he had to. It was a cursed thing, and in another minute he might have taken the girl in his arms, taken her for a kiss and remained to—

But he dared not think of that.

"Tired of masquerading?" she asked. With a similar gesture she, too, removed her cloak and stood revealed in the glory of her angel robe. Her blond, statuesque perfection forced a gasp to Henderson's throat.

"Angel," he whispered.

"Devil," she mocked.

And suddenly they were embracing. Henderson had taken her cloak in his arm with his own. They stood with lips seeking rapture until Lindstrom and a group moved noisily into the anteroom.

At the sight of Henderson the fat host recoiled.

"You—" he whispered. "You are—"

"Just leaving," Henderson smiled. Grasping the girl's arm, he drew her toward the empty elevator. The door shut on Lindstrom's pale, fear-filled face.

"Were we leaving?" Sheila whispered, snuggling against his shoulder.

"We were. But not for earth. We do not go down into my realm, but up—into yours."

"The roof garden?"

"Exactly, my angelic one. I want to talk to you against the background of your own heavens, kiss you amidst the clouds, and—"

Her lips found his as the car rose.

"Angel and devil. What a match!"

"I thought so, too," the girl confessed. "Will our children have halos or horns?"

"Both, I'm sure."

They stepped out onto the deserted rooftop. And once again it was Halloween.

Henderson felt it. Downstairs it was Lindstrom and his society friends, in a drunken costume party. Here it was night, silence, gloom. No light, no music, no drinking, no chatter which made one party identical with another; one night like all the rest. This night was individual here.

The sky was not blue, but black. Clouds hung like the grey beards of hovering giants peering at the round orange globe of the moon. A cold wind blew from the sea, and filled the air with tiny murmurings from afar.

This was the sky that witches flew through to their Sabbath. This was the moon of wizardry, the sable silence of black prayers and whispered invocations. The clouds hid monstrous Presences shambling in summons from afar. It was Halloween.

It was also quite cold.

"Give me my cloak," Sheila whispered. Automatically, Henderson extended the garment, and the girl's body swirled under the dark splendour of the cloth. Her eyes burned up at Henderson with a call he could not resist. He kissed her, trembling.

"You're cold," the girl said. "Put on your cloak."

Yes, Henderson, he thought to himself. Put on your cloak while you stare at her throat. Then, the next time you kiss her you will want her throat and she will give it in love and you will take it in—hunger.

"Put it on, darling—I insist," the girl whispered. Her eyes were impatient, burning with an eagerness to match his own.

Henderson trembled.

Put on the cloak of darkness? The cloak of the grave, the cloak of death, the cloak of the vampire? The evil cloak, filled with a cold life of its own that transformed his face, transformed his mind, made his soul instinct with awful hunger?

"Here."

The girl's slim arms were about him, pushing the cloak onto his shoulders. Her fingers brushed his neck, caressingly, as she linked the cloak about his throat.

Henderson shivered.

Then he felt it—through him—that icy coldness turning to a more dreadful heat. He felt himself expand, felt the sneer cross his face. This was Power!

And the girl before him, her eyes taunting, inviting. He saw her ivory neck, her warm slim neck, waiting. It was waiting for him, for his lips.

For his teeth.

No—it couldn't be. He loved her. His love must conquer this madness. Yes, wear the cloak, defy its power, and take her in his arms as a man, not as a fiend. He must. It was the test.

"Sheila." Funny, how his voice deepened.

"Yes, dear."

"Sheila, I must tell you this."

Her eyes—so alluring. It would be easy!

"Sheila, please. You read the paper tonight."

"Yes."

"I… I got my cloak there. I can't explain it. You saw how I took Lindstrom. I wanted to go through with it. Do you understand me? I meant to… to bite him. Wearing this damnable thing makes me feel like one of those creatures."

Why didn't her stare change? Why didn't she recoil in horror? Such trusting innocence! Didn't she understand? Why didn't she run? Any moment now he might lose control, seize her.

"I love you, Sheila. Believe that. I love you."

"I know." Her eyes gleamed in the moonlight.

"I want to test it. I want to kiss you, wearing this cloak. I want to feel that my love is stronger than this—thing. If I weaken, promise me you'll break away and run, quickly. But don't misunderstand. I must face this feeling and fight it; I want my love for you to be that pure, that secure. Are you afraid?"

"No." Still she stared at him, just as he stared at her throat. If she knew what was in his mind!

"You don't think I'm crazy? I went to this costumer's—he was a horrible little old man—and he gave me the cloak. Actually told me it was a real vampire's. I thought he was joking, but tonight I didn't see myself in the mirror, and I wanted Lindstrom's neck, and I want you. But I must test it."

"You're not crazy. I know. I'm not afraid."

"Then—"

The girl's face mocked. Henderson summoned his strength. He bent forward, his impulses battling. For a moment he stood there under the ghastly orange moon, and his face was twisted in struggle.

And the girl lured.

Her odd, incredibly red lips parted in a silvery, chuckly laugh as her white arms rose from the black cloak she wore to circle his neck gently. "I know—I knew when I looked in the mirror. I knew you had a cloak like mine—got yours where I got mine—"

Queerly, her lips seemed to elude his as he stood frozen for an instant of shock. Then he felt the icy hardness of her sharp little teeth on his throat, a strangely soothing sting, and an engulfing blackness rising over him.

1941

OVER THE RIVER

P. Schuyler Miller

THE shape of his body showed in the frozen mud, where he had lain face down under the fallen tree. His footprints were sharp in the melting snow, and his feet had left dark, wet blotches where he had climbed the rock. He had lain there for a long time. Long enough it was for time to have lost its meaning.

The moon was coming up over the nearer mountain, full and white, etched across with the pattern of naked branches. Its light fell on his upturned face, on his sunken, brilliant eyes and the puffy blue of jowls on which the beard had started to grow, then stopped. It shone down on the world of trees and rocks of which he was a part, and gave it life.

The night was warm. In the valley the snow had long been gone. Flowers were pushing up through the moist earth; frogs were Pan-piping in every low spot; great trout stirred in the deep pools of the river. It was May, but on the mountain, under the north-facing ledges where the sun never came, the snow was still banked deep with an edge of blue ice, and needles of frost glistened in the black mud of the forest floor.

It was May. All through the warm night, squadrons of birds were passing across the face of the moon. All night long their voices drifted down out of the dark like gossip from another world. But to a listener in the night another voice was clearer, louder, more insistent—now like the striking of crystal cymbals, now like an elfin chuckling, always a breathless, never-ending whisper—the voice of running water.

He heard none of these things. He stood where he had first come into the full moonlight, his face turned up to receive it, drinking in its brightness. It tingled in him like a draught from the things he had forgotten, in another world. It dissolved the dull ache of cold that was in his body and mind, that stiffened his swollen limbs and lay like an icy nugget behind his eyes. It soaked into him, and into the world about him, so that every corner shone with its own pale light, white and vaporous, as far as he could see.

It was a strange world. What that other world had been like, before, he did not remember, but this was different. The moonlight flooded it with a pearly mist through which the columns of the trees rose like shadowy stalagmites. The light-mist was not from the moon alone; it was a part of this new world and of the things that were in it. The grey lichens under his feet were outlined with widening ripples of light. Light pulsed through the rough bark of the tree trunks and burned like tiny corpse-candles at the tip of every growing twig. The spruces and balsams were furred with silvery needles of light. A swirling mist of light hung ankle-deep over the forest floor, broken by black islands of rock. Light was in everything in this new world he was in, save only for the rock, and for himself.

He drank in the moonlight through every pore, and it burned gloriously in him and flowed down through every vein and bone of his body, driving out the dank cold that was in his flesh. But the light that soaked into him did not shine out again as it did from the budding trees, and the moss, and the lichens. He looked down at his swollen hands and flexed their puffed blue fingers; he moved his toes in their sodden boots, and felt the clammy touch of the wet rags that clung to his body. Under them, out of the moonlight, he was still cold with that pervading chill that was like the frozen breath of winter in him. He squatted in the pool of light that lay over the ledge and stripped them from him, clumsily and painfully, then lay back on the stone and stared up into the smiling visage of the moon.

Time passed, but whether it was minutes or hours, or whether there were still such things as minutes and hours, he could not have said. Time had no meaning for him in this new, strange world. Time passed, because the moon was higher and its light stronger and warmer on his naked flesh, but he did not sense its passage. Every part of the forest pulsed with its own inner light in response. As the feeling of warmth grew in him it brought another feeling, a dull hunger gnawing at his vitals, making him restless. He moved close to a great beech whose limbs reached high above the tops of the other trees around it, and felt the quick chill as its shadow fell across him. Then he had clasped it in both arms, his whole body pressing eagerly against its glowing trunk, and the light that welled out of it was thrilling through him like a flame, stirring every atom of him. He tweaked a long, pointed bud from a twig. It lay in his palm like a jewel of pale fire before he raised it to his mouth and felt its warmth spread into him.

He ate buds as long as he could find them, stripping them from the twigs with clumsy fingers, grubbing hungrily in the moss for the ones that fell. He crushed them between his teeth and swallowed them, and the fire that glowed in them spread into his chilled flesh and warmed it a little. He tore patches of lichen from the rock, but they were tough and woody and he could not swallow them. He broke off spruce twigs, needled with the life-light, but the resin in them burned his lips and tongue and choked him.

He sat, hunched against a rock, staring blindly into the glowing depths of the forest. The things he had swallowed had helped a little to alleviate the cold that was in his bones, but they did not dull the gnawing hunger or the thirst that was torturing him. They had life, and the warmth that was life, but not the thing he needed—the thing he must somehow have.

At the edge of his field of vision something moved. It drifted noiselessly through the burning treetops, like a puff of luminous cloud. It settled on a branch above his head, and he twisted his neck, back and stared up at it with hollow, burning eyes. The white light-mist was very bright about it. He could feel its warmth, even at this distance. And there was something more. The hunger gripped him, fiercer than ever, and thirst shrivelled his gullet.

The owl had seen him and decided that he was another rotting stump. It sat hunched against the trunk of the great spruce, looking and listening for its prey. Presently it was rewarded by some small sound or a wafted scent, and spread its silent wings to float like a phantom into the night. It did not see the misshapen thing, it had thought a stump, struggle to its feet and follow.

A porcupine, high in a birch, saw the owl pass and ignored it, as it well could. A roosting crow woke suddenly and froze on its perch, petrified with terror. But the great bird swept past, intent on other prey.

There were clearings in the forest, even this high, where trees had been cut off and brambles had followed. All manner of small creatures followed the brambles, and here was rich hunting for the owl and its kind.

He came to the edge of the clearing in time to see the owl strike and hear the scream of the hurt rabbit. To his eyes it was as though a bolt of shining fire had plunged through the night to strike a second ball of fire on the ground. Shambling forward, careless of the briars, he hurled himself on the two animals before the owl could free itself or take the air again.

The huge bird slashed at him savagely with beak and talons, laying open the puffy flesh of his face in great, curving gashes, but he bit deep into its breast, through feathers and skin, tearing at its flesh with his teeth and letting the hot, burning blood gush into his parched throat and spill over his cracked lips. His fingers kneaded and tore at its body, breaking it into bits that he could stuff into his mouth. Feathers and bone he spat out, and the rabbit's fur when the owl was gone, but the hollow in his belly was filled, and the thirst gone, and the aching cold in his numbed bones had been washed away. It seemed to him that his fingers were shining a little with the same wan light that emanated from the other things of the forest.

He hunted all that night, through the clearing and the nearby forest, and found and ate two wood mice and a handful of grubs and other insects. He found that the tightly coiled fiddle-heads of growing ferns were full of life and more palatable than buds or lichens. As the deadening cold left him he could move more freely, think more keenly, but the thirst was growing on him again.

Out of the lost memories of that world he had left, the murmur of running water came to him. Water should quench thirst. He could hear it below him on the mountainside, through the mist, plashing over bare stones, gurgling through tunnels in the roots and moss. He heard it in the distance, far below in the valley, roaring against boulders and leaping over ledges in foaming abandon. As he listened, a chill crept over him, as though a shadow were passing, but the feeling left him. Slowly and painfully he began to pick his way down the mountainside.

The water burst out at the base of a rock wall, lay for a little in a deep, clear pool under the cliff and then slipped away through the moss, twisting and turning, sliding over flat stones and diving into crevices, welling up in tiny, sparkling fountains and vanishing again under tangles of matted roots and fallen tree trunks, growing and running ever faster until it leaped over the last cliff and fell in a spatter of flashing drops into the valley. He saw it, and stopped.

Black vapour lay close over it like a carpet. It made a pathway of black, winding through the luminous mist that hung over the forest floor. Where the rill lay quiet in a pool it was thin, and the moonlight struck through and sparkled on the clear water, but where the little stream hurried over roots and stones, the black fog lay dense and impenetrable, dull and lifeless.

He licked his lips uneasily with his swollen tongue and moved cautiously forward. The chill had come on him again, numbing his nerves, dulling his labouring brain. Water quenched thirst; he still remembered that somehow, and this singing, shining stuff was water. At the base of the cliff, where the water welled up under the rock, the black fog was thinnest. He knelt and dipped his cupped hands into the water.

As the black mist closed over them, all feeling went out of his hands. Cold—terrible, numbing cold—ate its way like acid into his flesh and bones.

The mist was draining the warmth—the life—out of him, through his hands and arms—sucking him dry of the life-stuff he had drunk with the owl's blood and soaked in from the moon's white rays. He swayed to his feet, then collapsed in a heap beside the stream.

He lay there helpless for a long time. Little by little the moonlight revived him. Little by little the numbness went out of his muscles, and he could move his legs and grip things with his fingers. He pulled his legs under him and got to his feet leaning against the cliff for support. He stared with burning eyes at the water, and felt the first clutching at his gullet and the hunger gnawing in his vitals. Water was death to him. The black fog that lay close over running water was deadly, draining the life-force out of whatever touched it. It was death! But blood—fresh, burning, glowing blood was life!

Something rattled in the shadow of the cliff. His eyes found it—a lolloping bundle of fiery spines, humping along a worn path that led over the rocks to the little pool, a porcupine come to drink. He sensed the life in it, and hunger twisted his belly, but the black barrier of running water was between him and it.

It shambled down to the pool's edge and drank, the glow of its bristling body shining through the black fog over the water. It crossed the little rill where it was narrowest, below the pool, and came rattling up the path toward him, unafraid.

He killed it. His face and body were studded with quills before it was dead, but he tore open its body with his two numb hands and let its hot blood swill down his throat and give him back the warmth and life that the black mist had drained out of him. Blood was all he needed—he had learned that—and he left the porcupine's limp carcass by the path and turned back into the forest.

Water was everywhere, here on the lower slopes of the mountain. Its black runways ribbed the glowing floor of the forest on every side. It made a wall of cold about the place where he was, so that he had to climb back to the summit of the ridge and go around its sources.

The sun rose, bringing a scathing golden light that shrivelled his pallid flesh and brought the thirst up unbearably in his throat, driving him to the shelter of a cave. Blood would quench that awful, growing thirst, and drive out the cold that crept relentlessly over him, but it was hard to find blood. Other things would kill the cold—buds and growing things—but they could not quench the thirst or appease the savage hunger in him.

There was another night, at last, and he stood in the bright light of the shrinking moon, high on a bare spur overlooking the valley. All the world lay before him, washed in silver and lined with black. He could see mountain after mountain, furred with the light of growing trees, blanketed in the glowing mist, their bald black crowns outlined against the moonlit clouds. He could see the mountain torrents streaking down their flanks, like inky ribbons, joining, broadening, flowing down to join the river that roared sullenly under its black shroud in the valley at his feet.

The valley was full of life. It was alive with growing things, and the white mist that rose from them and clothed them filled it in the brim with a broth of light through which the river and its tributaries cut sharp black lines of cold. There were other lights—yellow constellations of lamplight scattered over the silver meadows. Many of them clustered at the mouth of the valley, where the mountains drew apart, but they grew fewer and fewer as they followed the black barrier of the river, and at the head of the valley below him one glowing spark burned by itself.

He stood with the moonlight washing his naked, dead-white body, staring at that speck of golden light. There was something he should know about it—something that was hidden in that other world he had been in. There was something that drew him to it—an invisible thread, stretched across space through the white night, binding him to it.

The next day he lay buried under a rotting log, halfway down the mountain. The following night, soon after moon-up, he came on a doe, its back broken, pinned under a fallen tree. He tore its throat out and drank the fuming blood that poured heat and life through his body, waking him, filling hint with vigour. The cold was gone, and he was sure now that his fingers were glowing with a light of their own. Now he was really alive!

He followed a ridge, and before sunrise he came to the river's edge. The blackness was an impenetrable wall, hiding the other shore. Through it he could hear the rush of running water over gravel, the gurgle of eddies and the mutter of rapids. The sound tormented him and brought the thirst back into his throat, but he drew back into the forest, for the sky was already brightening in the East.

When the moon rose on the fourth night he had found nothing to eat. Its light brought him down out of the forest again, to the river's edge, where it broadened into a quiet mill-pond. The black fog was thin over the glassy surface of the water, and through it he saw the yellow lamplight of the house that had drawn him down from the mountain.

He stood waist-deep in the weeds that bordered the pond, watching those two yellow rectangles. Back in the icy blankness of his mind a memory was struggling to be known. But it belonged to the other world, the world he had left behind, and it faded.

The reflection of the lights lay in the still water of the pond. So still was it that the mist was but a black gauze drawn across the lamplight, dulling it. The water lay like a sheet of black glass, hard and polished, with the phantoms of the pines on its other bank growing upside down in its quiet depths. The stars were reflected there in little winking spots, and the dwindling circle of the moon.

He did not hear the door slam, there among the pines. A new feeling was growing in him. It was strange. It was not thirst—not hunger. It submerged them in its all-powerful compulsion. It gripped his muscles and took them out of his control, forcing him step by step through the cat tails to the rivers' edge. There was something he must do. Something—

She came out of the shadows and stood in the moonlight on the other bank, looking up at the moon. The lamplight was behind her and the silver torrent of the moon poured over her slim, white body, over her shining black hair, caressing every line and curve of her long, slim figure. Her own light clung to her like a silver aura, soft and warm, welling out of her white skin and singing lovingly about her, cloaking her beauty with light. That beauty drew him—out of the shadows, out of the forest, into the moonlight.

She did not see him at first. The night was warm and there was the first perfume of spring in the air. She stood on a rock at the water's edge, her arms lifted, her hands clasping her flood of night-black hair behind her head. All her young body was taut, stretching, welcoming the moonlight and the touch of the night breeze that sent little cat's-paws shivering over the glassy water. The moon seemed to be floating in the water, there just beyond her reach. She knotted her hair in a bun behind her head and stepped down quickly into the water. She stood with it just above her knees, watching the ripples widen and break the mirror surface of the pond. She followed their spread across that glassy disc.

She saw him.

He stood there; his face half in shadow, hunched and naked. His arms were skeleton's arms and his ribs showed under skin that hung in flabby white folds from his shoulders. His eyes were black pits and a stubble of black beard was smeared across his sagging cheeks. The mark of the owl's claws was across his face and it was pocked with purple blotches where he had pulled out the porcupine quills. Some of them were still in his side, where the beast's tail had lashed him. His flesh was livid white in the moonlight, blotched and smeared with the dark stain of death.

She saw him and knew him. Her hand went to the little cross that glowed like a coal of golden fire in the hollow of her throat. Her voice rose and choked back:

"Joe! *Joe!*"

He saw her and remembered her. The thread he had felt on the mountain had been her presence, pulling him to her, stronger than thirst or hunger, stronger than death, stronger even than the black fog over the river. It was between them now, tightening, dragging him step by step into the silent water. Ripples broke against his legs and he felt the black mist rising from them, felt the numbness creeping into his feet, into his legs, up into his body. It was a day since he had killed the deer and had blood to warm him. He could not go on. He stood knee-deep, staring at her across the little space that separated them. He tried to speak, to call her name, but he had forgotten words.

Then she screamed and ran, a stream of white fire through the shadows, and he heard the house door slam after her and saw the shades come down, one after the other, over the yellow lamplight. He stood there, staring after her, until the cold crept up and began to choke him, and he turned and stumbled painfully ashore.

The sun found him high on the mountain, climbing from ledge to ledge, above the sources of the rushing torrents that walled him in, making his way toward the saddle that closed the valley's end. He could not cross running water, but he could go around it. He killed a rabbit and its blood helped him to go on, with the cold seeping up through his bones and hunger and thirst tearing at him like wild things. The new hunger, the yearning that drew him to the girl in the valley, was stronger than they. It was all that mattered now.

The moon was in the sky when he stood under the pines before the closed door of the house. Half the night was gone, and clouds were gathering, filling up the sky and strewing long streamers across the moon's shrunken face. In the East thunder muttered, rolling among the mountains until it died away beneath the sound of the river.

The tie that was between them was like a rope of iron, pulling him across the narrow clearing to the doorstep of the house. The door was closed and the shades drawn over the windows on either side of it, but yellow lamplight streamed out through cracks in its weathered panels. He raised a hand to touch it and drew back as he saw the pattern of crossed planks that barred him and his kind.

He whimpered low in his throat, like the doe he had killed. The cross wove a steel net across the doorway that he could not break. He stepped back, off the doorstep. Then the door opened. She stood there.

Her back was to the light and he could see only the slim silhouette of her body, with the cross of golden fire at her throat and the aura of silvery mist clinging about her, so warm and bright that he was sure it must drown out the moonlight. Even through the dress she wore the fire of her young vitality shone out. He stood bathing in it, yearning for it, as the hunger and thirst and aching longing welled up in him through the bitter cold.

It was a minute perhaps, or five minutes, of only seconds until she spoke. Her voice was faint.

"Joe," she said. "Joe dear. You're hurt. Come inside."

The pattern of the cross on the door could not bar him after her welcome. He felt the barrier dissolve as he stepped through. The clouds had drawn away and the moon made a bright spot through the open door. He stood in it, watching her, seeing the familiar room with its scrubbed board floor, its plastered walls, its neat, black stove—seeing them as if for the first time. They stirred no memory in him. But the girl drew him.

He saw her dark eyes blacken with horror and the blood drain out of her cheeks and lips as she saw him for the first time in the lamplight. He looked down at his hands—the flesh cheese-white and sloughing—at his naked, discoloured body, smeared with mud and stained with spilled blood. He whimpered, down in his throat, and took a stumbling step toward her, but her hand went up to the little crucifix at her throat and she slipped quickly around the table, placing it between them.

He stared at the cross. The golden fire that burned in it separated them as surely as the cold black fog of running water had done. Across the table he could feel its pure radiance, hot as the sunlight. It would shrivel him to a cinder. He whined again, in agony, like a whipped dog. The longing for her was sheer torment now, drowning out all else, but it could not force him nearer.

The girl followed his gaze. The crucifix had been his gift—before—in that other world. She knew that, though he did not. Slowly she unfastened the ribbon that held it and dropped it into his outstretched hand.

The cross burned into his flesh like a hot coal. He snatched back his hand but the burning metal clung. He felt the heat of it coursing up his arm, and hurled it savagely across the room. He seized the table with both hands and flung it out of his way. Then she was before him, her back against the wall, her face a mask of horror. He heard her scream.

In him the terrible yearning that had drawn him down from the mountain had submerged the hunger and thirst and cold that had been his only driving forces before he knew her. Now, as they stood face to face, the older, stronger forces surged up in him and took possession of his numbed mind. With her scream a dam in him seemed to burst. He felt her warm, slim body twisting and jerking under his tightening fingers. He sensed the fragrance that rose from her. He saw her eyes, mad with fear, staring into his.

When it was over the hunger was gone, and the thirst. The cold had gone out of his bones. His muscles were no longer cramped and leaden. The yearning was gone, too. He looked down incuriously at the heap of shredded rags on the floor and turned to go.

At that moment the storm broke. The door was still open, and as he turned it seemed to be closed by a curtain of falling water. The black fog swirled among the raindrops, blotting out the world. He thrust out an exploring hand, marked with the charred brand of the cross, and snatched it back as he felt the chill of the mist.

He heard their voices only a moment before they stood there—three men, dripping, crowded together in the doorway, staring at the thing on the floor—and at him. For a flicker he remembered: Louis—her brother—and

Jean and old Paul. The dogs were with them, but they slunk back, whining, afraid.

Louis knew him, as his sister had—as the others did. His whisper had hate in it as much as fear. It was on all their faces. They knew the curse that was on the unshriven of Joe Labatie's blood. They had known what it meant when he did not come down from the mountain on the night of the first storm. But only Louis, of them all, had seen the tree topple and pin him down. Louis it was who had made the mark of the cross in the snow that drifted over him and left him there. Louis Larue, who would not see the Labatie curse fall on his sister or her children after her.

It was old Paul whose gun bellowed. They saw the buckshot tear through that death-white body—saw the dark fluid that dripped from the awful wound—saw the dead thing that was Joe Labatie, his skull's eyes burning, as he surged toward them. They ran.

Louis held his ground, but the thing that rushed upon him was like a charging bear. It struck him and hurled him to the floor. Its slippery fingers bit into his shoulders; its hideous face hung close to his. But the crucifix at his throat saved him, as it might have saved her, and the thing recoiled and plunged out into the storm.

The rain was like ice on his naked body as he fled, rinsing the strength out of him as it might dissolve salt. The black mist filled the forest, blotting out the silver light of its living things. It closed over his body and sank into it, sucking out the unnatural life he had drunk in blood, draining it of warmth. He felt the great cold growing in him again. The moon was gone, and he was blind—cold and numb and blind. He crashed into a tree, and then another, and then his weakening legs buckled under him and he fell face down at the river's edge.

He lay in the running water, shrouded in the black fog, feeling them approach. He heard their footsteps on the gravel, and felt their hands on him, dragging him out of the water, turning him over. He saw them—three pillars of white light, the yellow fire of their crucifixes at their throats, the black mist billowing around their bodies as they stood staring down at him. He felt Louis' boot as it swung brutally into his side and felt the bones snap and the flesh tear, but there was no pain—only the cold, the bitter, freezing cold that was always in him.

He knew that they were busy at something, but the cold was creeping up into his brain, behind his eyes, as the rain wrapped him in its deadly mist. Perhaps when the moon rose again its light would revive him. Perhaps he would kill again and feel the hot blood in his throat, and be free of the cold. He could barely see now, though his eyes were open and staring. He could see that old Paul had a long stake of wood in his hands, sharpened to a point. He saw Louis take it and raise it in both hands above his head. He saw Louis' teeth shine white in a savage grin.

He saw the stake sweep down—

1975

THE LADY OF THE
HOUSE OF LOVE

Angela Carter

A T last the revenants became so troublesome the peasants abandoned the village and it fell solely to the possession of subtle and
vindictive inhabitants who manifest their presences by shadows
that fall almost imperceptibly awry, too many shadows, even at midday,
shadows that have no source in anything visible; by the sound, sometimes,
of sobbing in a derelict bedroom where a cracked mirror suspended from a
wall does not reflect a presence; by a sense of unease that will afflict the trav-
eller unwise enough to pause to drink from the fountain in the square that
still gushes spring water from a faucet stuck in the mouth of a stone lion. A
cat prowls in a weedy garden; he grins and spits, arches his back, bounces
away from an intangible on four fear-stiffened legs. Now all shun the village
below the chateau in which the beautiful queen of the vampires helplessly
perpetuates her ancestral crimes.

Wearing an antique bridal gown, the beautiful queen of the vampires
sits all alone in her dark, high house under the eyes of the portraits of her
demented and atrocious ancestors, each one of whom through her, projects
a baleful, posthumous existence; she is counting out the Tarot cards, cease-
lessly construing a constellation of possibilities as if the random fall of the
cards on the red plush tablecloth before her could precipitate her from her
chill, shuttered room into a country of perpetual summer and obliterate the
perennial sadness of a girl who is both death and the maiden.

Her voice is filled with distant sonorities, like reverberations in a cave.

Now you are at the place of annihilation, now you are at the place of annihilation. And she is herself a cave full of echoes; she is a system of repetitions, she is a closed circuit. "Can a bird sing only the song it knows or can it learn a new song?" She draws her long, sharp fingernail across the bars of the cage in which her pet lark sings, rousing in the metal a plangent twang like that of the plucked heartstrings of a woman of metal. Her hair falls down like tears.

The castle is mostly given over to ghostly occupants but she herself has her own suite of drawing room and bedroom. Closely-barred shutters and heavy, velvet curtains keep every leak of natural light out. There is a round table on a single leg covered with a red plush cloth on which she lays out her inevitable Tarot; this room is never more than faintly illuminated by a heavily shaded lamp on the mantelpiece and the dark red figured wallpaper is obscurely, distressingly patterned by the rain that drives in through the neglected roof and leaves behind it random areas of dreadful staining, ominous marks like those left on the sheets of beds of anthropophagous lovers. Depredations of rot and fungus everywhere. The unlit chandelier is so heavy with dust the individual prisms no longer show any shapes; industrious spiders have woven canopies in the corners of this ornate and rotting place, have trapped the porcelain vases on the mantelpiece in soft, grey nets. But the mistress of all this disintegration notices nothing. She sits in a chair covered in moth-ravaged burgundy velvet at a low, round table and distributes the cards; sometimes the lark sings, but more often remains a sullen mound of drab feathers. Sometimes the Countess will wake it for a brief cadenza by strumming the bars of its cage; she likes to hear it announcing how it cannot escape.

The querent approaches the arcana. She wakes up when the sun sets and goes immediately to her table, where she plays her game of patience until she grows hungry, until she becomes ravenous. She is so beautiful she is unnatural; her beauty is an abnormality, a deformity, for none of her features exhibit any of those touching imperfections that reconcile us to the imperfection of the human condition. Her beauty is a symptom of her disorder, of her soullessness.

The white hands of the tenebrous belle deal the hand of destiny. Her fingernails are longer than those of the mandarins of ancient China and each is pared to a fine point. These and teeth as fine and white as spikes of spun sugar are the visible signs of the destiny she wistfully attempts to evade via the arcana; her claws and teeth have been sharpened on centuries of corpses, she is the last bud of the poison tree that sprang from the loins of Vlad the Impaler who picnicked on corpses in the forests of Transylvania.

The walls of her bedroom are hung with black satin, embroidered with tears of pearl. At the room's four corners are funerary urns and bowls which emit slumbrous, pungent fumes of incense. In the centre is an exceedingly elaborate catafalque, in ebony, surrounded by long candles in enormous silver candlesticks. In a white lace negligee stained a little with blood, the Countess climbs upon the catafalque at dawn each morning and lies down to sleep in an open coffin.

A chignonned priest of the Orthodox faith staked out her wicked father at a Carpathian crossroad before her milk teeth grew. Now she possesses all the haunted forests and mysterious habitations of his vast domain; she is the hereditary commandant of the army of shadows who camp in the village below her chateau, who penetrate the woods in the form of owls, bats and foxes, who make the milk curdle and the butter refuse to come, who ride the horses all night on a wild hunt so they are sacks of skin and bone in the morning, who milk the cows dry and, especially, torment pubescent girls with fainting fits, disorders of the blood, diseases of the imagination.

But the Countess herself is indifferent to her own weird authority. She believes that, by ignoring it, she can abnegate it. More than anything, she would like to be human; but she does not know if that is possible. The Tarot always shows the same configuration: always she turns up La Papesse, Le Mort, Le Tour Abolie, wisdom, death, dissolution.

On moonless nights, her keeper lets her out into the garden. This garden, an exceedingly sombre place, bears a strong resemblance to a burial ground and all the roses her pathetic mother planted have grown up into a huge, spiked wall that incarcerates her in the castle of her inheritance. When the back door creaks open, the Countess will sniff the air and howl. She drops, now, on all fours. Crouching, quivering, she catches the scent of her prey. Delicious crunch of the fragile bones of rabbits and small, furry things she pursues with fleet, four-footed speed; she will creep home, whimpering, with blood smeared on her cheeks. She pours water from the ewer in her bedroom into the bowl, she washes her face with the wincing, fastidious gestures of a cat.

The voracious margin of huntress' nights in the gloomy garden, crouch and pounce, surrounds her habitual tormented somnambulism, her life, or imitation of life. The eyes of this nocturnal creature enlarge and glow. All claws and teeth, she strikes, she gorges; but nothing can console her for the ghastliness of her condition, nothing. She resorts to the magic comfort of the Tarot pack and shuffles the cards, lays them out, reads them, gathers them up with a sigh, shuffles them again, constantly constructing hypotheses about a future which is irreversible.

An old mute looks after her, to make sure she never sees the sun, that all day she sleeps in her coffin, to keep mirrors and all reflective surfaces from her—in short, to perform all the functions of the servants of vampires. Everything about this beautiful and ghastly lady is as it should be, queen of night, queen of terror, except her horrible reluctance for the role.

Nevertheless, if an unwise adventurer pauses in the square of the deserted village to refresh himself at the fountain, a crone in a black dress and white apron presently emerges from a house. She will invite you with smiles and gestures; you will follow her. The Countess wants fresh meat. When she was a little girl, she was like a fox and contented herself entirely with baby rabbits that squeaked piteously as she bit into their necks with a nauseated voluptuousness, with voles and field mice that palpitated for a bare moment between her embroideress' fingers. But now she is a woman, she must have men. If you stop too long at the giggling fountain, you will be led by the hand to the Countess' larder.

All day, she sleeps in her coffin in a negligee of blood-stained lace; when the sun drops behind the mountains, she yawns and stirs and puts on the only dress she has, her mother's wedding dress, to sit and read her cards until she grows hungry. She loathes the food she eats; she would have liked to take the rabbits home with her, feed them on lettuce, pet them and make them a nest in her red-and-black lacquer chinoiserie escritoire but hunger always overcomes her. She can eat nothing else. She sinks her teeth into the neck where an artery throbs with terror; she will drop the deflated skin from which she has extracted all the nourishment with a small cry of both pain and disgust. And it is the same with the shepherd boys and gypsy lads who, foolhardy or ignorant, come to wash the dust from their feet in the water of the fountain; the Countess' governess brings them into the drawing room where the cards on the table always show the Grim Reaper. She herself will serve them coffee in tiny, cracked cups of precious porcelain and little sugar cakes. The hobble-dehoys sit with a spilling cup in one hand and a biscuit in the other, gaping at the beautiful Countess in her satin finery as she pours from a silver pot and chatters distractedly to put them at their fatal ease. A certain desolate stillness of her eyes indicates she is inconsolable. She would like to caress their lean, brown cheeks and stroke their ragged hair. When she takes them by the hand and leads them to her bedroom, they can scarcely believe their luck.

Afterwards, her governess will tidy the remains into a neat pile and wrap it in its own discarded clothes. This mortal parcel she then discreetly buries in the garden. The blood on the Countess' cheeks will be mixed with tears; her keeper probes her fingernails for her with a little silver toothpick, to get rid of the fragments of skin and bone that have lodged there.

Fee fie fo fum
I smell the blood of an Englishman.

One hot, ripe summer in the pubescent years of the present century, a young officer in the British army, blond, blue-eyed, heavy-muscled, after a visit to friends in Vienna, decided to spend the rest of his furlough exploring the little-known uplands of Rumania. When he quixotically decided to travel the rutted cart-tracks by bicycle, he saw all the humour of it: "on two wheels in the land of the vampires." So, laughing, he sets out on his adventure.

He has the special quality of virginity, most and least ambiguous of states; ignorance, yet, at the same time, power in potentia, and, furthermore, unknowingness, which is not the same as ignorance. He is more than he knows—and has about him, besides, the special glamour of that generation for whom history has already prepared a special, exemplary fate in the trenches of France; history, then, is about to collide with the timeless Gothic eternity of the vampiress, for whom all is as it always has been and will be, whose cards always fall in the same pattern.

Although so young, he is also rational. He has chosen the most rational mode of transport in the world for his trip round the Carpathians. To ride a bicycle is in itself some protection against superstitious fears, since the bicycle is the product of pure reason applied to motion. Geometry at the service of man! Give me two spheres and a straight line and I will show you how far I can take them. Voltaire himself might have invented the bicycle, since it contributes so much to man's well-being and nothing at all to his bane. Beneficial to the health, it emits no harmful fumes and permits only the most decorous speeds. A bicycle is not an implement of harm.

A single kiss woke the Sleeping Beauty in the Wood.

The waxen fingers of the Countess, fingers of a holy image, turn up the card called L'Amoureux. Never, never before... never before has the Countess cast herself a fate involving L'Amoureux. She shakes, she trembles, her great eyes close beneath her finely veined, nervously throbbing eyelids; the lovely cartomancer has, this time, the first time, dealt herself a hand of love and death.

> Be he alive or be he dead
> I'll grind his bones to make my bread.

At the mauvish beginnings of evening, the English m'sieu toils up the hill to the village he glimpsed from a great way off; he must dismount and push his bicycle before him, the path too steep to ride. He hopes to find a friendly inn to rest the night; he's hot, thirsty, weary, dusty... at first, such disappointment to discover the roofs of all the cottages caved in and tall weeds thrusting through the piles of fallen tiles, shutters banging disconsolately from their hinges; an entirely uninhabited place. And the rank vegetation whispers, one could almost imagine twisted faces appearing momentarily beneath the crumbling eaves, if one were sufficiently imaginative... but the adventure of it all, and the comfort of the poignant brightness of the hollyhocks still bravely blooming in the shaggy garden, and the beauty of the flaming sunset, all these considerations soon overcome his disappointment, assuage the faint unease he'd felt. And the fountain where the village women used to wash their clothes still gushes out bright, clear water; he gratefully washes his feet and hands, applies his mouth to the faucet, lets the icy stream run over his face.

When he raised his dripping, gratified head from the lion's mouth, he saw, silently arrived beside him in the square, an old woman who smiled eagerly, almost conciliatorily, at him. She wore a black dress and a white apron, with a housekeeper's key-ring at the waist; her grey hair was neatly coiled in a chignon beneath the white linen headdress worn by elderly women of that region. She bobbed a curtsey at the young man and beckoned him to follow her. When he hesitated, she pointed towards the great bulk of the mansion above them, whose façade loured over the village, rubbed her stomach, pointed to her mouth, rubbed her stomach again and sighed, clearly miming an invitation to supper. Then she beckoned him again, this time turning determinedly on her heel as though she would brook no opposition.

A great, intoxicated surge of the heavy scent of red roses blew into his face as soon as they left the village, inducing a sensuous vertigo; a blast of rich, faintly corrupt sweetness strong enough, almost, to fell him. Too many roses. Too many roses bloomed on the enormous thickets of roses that lined the path, roses equipped with vicious thorns, and the flowers themselves, were almost too luxuriant, their huge congregations of plush petals somehow obscene in their excess, their whorled, tightly budded cores outrageous in their implications. The façade of the mansion emerged grudgingly from this jungle.

In the subtle and haunting light of the setting sun, that golden light rich with nostalgia for the day that is just past, the sombre visage of the place, part manor house, part fortified farmhouse, immense, rambling, a dilapidated eagle's nest atop the crag down which its attendant village meandered, reminded him of childhood tales on winter evenings, when he and his brothers and sisters scared themselves half out of their wits with ghost stories set in just such places, and then had to have candles to light them up the stairs to bed, so overworked had their imaginations become. He could almost have regretted accepting the crone's unspoken invitation; but now, standing before the great door of time-eroded oak while she selected a huge, iron key from the clanking ringfull at her waist, he knew it was too late to turn back and, besides, he was not a child any more, to be scared of bricks and mortar.

The old lady unlocked the door, which swung back on melodramatically creaking hinges, and fussily took charge of his bicycle, in spite of his vigorous protests; he felt a certain sinking of the heart to see his beautiful two-wheeled symbol of rationality vanishing into the dark entrails of the mansion, to some outhouse where they would not oil it or check the tyres. But, in for a penny, in for a pound—in his youth and strength and blond beauty, in the invisible, even unacknowledged pentacle of his virginity, the young man stepped over the threshold of Nosferatu's castle and did not shiver in the blast of cold air, as from the mouth of a grave, that emanated from the lightless, cavernous interior.

The crone took him to a little chamber where there was a black oak table spread with a clean white cloth and this cloth was carefully laid with heavy silverware, a little tarnished, as if someone with foul breath had breathed on it, but laid with one place only. Curiouser and curiouser; invited to the castle for dinner, now he must dine alone. Still, he sat down as she bade him. Although it was not yet dark outside, the curtains were closely drawn and only the sparing light trickling from a single oil lamp showed him how dismal his surroundings were. The crone bustled about to get him a bottle of wine and a glass from an ancient cabinet of wormy oak; while he bemus-edly drank his wine, she disappeared but soon returned bearing a steaming platter of the local spiced meat stew with dumplings, and a shank of black bread. He was hungry after his long day's ride, he ate heartily and polished his plate with the crust but this coarse food was hardly the entertainment he'd expected at such a mansion and he was puzzled by the assessing glint in the dumb woman's eyes as she watched him eating; but she darted off to get him a second helping as soon as he'd finished the first one and she seemed so friendly and helpful, besides, that he knew he could count on a bed for the night in the castle, as well as his supper, so he sharply reprimanded himself for his own sudden lack of enthusiasm for the eerie silence, the clammy chill of the place.

Then, when he'd put away the second plate, the old woman came and gestured he should leave the table and follow her once again. She made a pantomime of drinking; he deduced he was now invited to take after-dinner coffee in another room with some more elevated member of the household who had not wished to dine with him but, all the same, wanted to make his acquaintance.

He was surprised to find how ruinous the interior of the house was—cobwebs, worm-eaten beams, crumbling plaster; but the mute crone reso-lutely wound him on the spool of light she'd taken from the dining room down endless corridors, up winding staircases, through the galleries where the painted eyes of family portraits briefly flickered as they passed, eyes that belonged, he noticed, to faces one and all of a quite memorable beastliness. At last she paused and, behind the door where they'd halted, he heard a faint, metallic twang as of, perhaps, a chord struck on a harpsichord and then, wonderfully, the liquid cascade of the song of a lark, bringing to him, in the heart—had he but known it—of Juliet's tomb, all the freshness of morning. The crone rapped with her knuckles on the panels; the most beautiful voice he had ever heard in all his life softly called, in heavily accented French, the adopted language of the Rumanian aristocracy: "Entrez."

First of all, he saw only a moony gleam, a faint luminosity that caught and reflected from its tarnished surfaces what little light there was in the ill-lit room: of all things, a hoop-skirted dress of white satin draped here and there with lace, a dress fifty or sixty years out of fashion but once, no doubt, intended for a wedding; and its wearer a girl with the fragility of the skeleton of a moth, a being of such a famished leanness that the garment seemed to him to hang suspended, untenanted, in the dank air, a fabulous lending, a self-articulated gown. And then, as his eyes grew accustomed to the half-dark, he saw how beautiful and how very young the scarecrow inside the amazing dress was, and he thought of a child dressing up in her mother's clothes, perhaps a child putting on clothes of a dead mother in order to bring her, however briefly, to life again.

The Countess stood behind a low table, beside a pretty, silly, gilt-and-wire birdcage on a stand, in an attitude, distracted, almost of flight; she looked as startled by their entry as if she had not requested it. Only a low lamp with a greenish shade on a distant mantelpiece illuminated her so that, with her stark white face, her lovely death's head surrounded by long, dark hair that fell down as straight as if it were soaking wet, she looked like a shipwrecked bride. Her enormous, dark eyes almost broke his heart with their waif-like, lost look; yet he was disturbed, almost repelled by her extraordinarily fleshy mouth, a mouth with wide, full, prominent lips of a vibrant, purplish-crimson, a morbid mouth, even—but he put the thought away from him immediately—a whore's mouth. She shivered all the time, a starveling chill, a malarial agitation of the bones. He thought she must be only sixteen or seventeen years old, no more, with the hectic, unhealthy beauty of a consumptive. She was the chatelaine of all this decay.

The crone raised the light she held to show his hostess her guest's face and at that the Countess let out a faint, cawing cry and made a blind, appalled gesture with her hands, as if pushing him away, so that she knocked against the table and a butterfly dazzle of painted cards fell to the floor. Her mouth formed a round "o" of woe, she swayed a little and then sank into her chair, where she lay as if now scarcely capable of moving. A bewildering reception. Tsk'ing under her breath, the crone busily poked about on the table until she found an enormous pair of dark glasses such as blind beggars wear and perched them on the Countess' nose.

He went forward to pick up her cards for her from a carpet that, he saw to his surprise, was part rotted entirely away, partly encroached upon by all kinds of virulent-looking fungi. He retrieved the cards and shuffled them together; strange playthings for a young girl, grisly picture of a skeleton… he covered it with a happier one, two young, he supposed, lovers, smiling at one another, and put her toys back in a hand so slender you could almost see the frail net of bone beneath the translucent skin, hands with fingernails as long, as finely pointed as banjo picks. (She had been strumming on the birdcage again.)

At his touch, she seemed to revive a little and almost smiled, raising herself upright.

"Coffee," she said. "You must have coffee." And scooped up her cards in a pile so that the crone could set before her a silver spirit kettle, a silver coffee pot, cups, cream jug, sugar-basin, all on a silver tray, a strange touch of elegance, even if discoloured, in this devastated interior in which she ethereally shone with a blighted, submarine radiance.

The crone found him a chair and, tittering noiselessy, departed.

While the young lady attended to the coffee-making, he had time to contemplate with some distaste a further series of family portraits which decorated the stained and peeling walls of the room; these livid faces all seemed contorted with a febrile madness and the blubber lips, the huge, demented eyes they all held in common bore a disquieting resemblance to those of the hapless victim of inbreeding now patiently filtering her fragrant brew. The lark, its chorus done, had long ago fallen silent; no sound but the chink of silver on china. Soon, she held out to him a tiny cup of rose-painted china.

"Welcome," she said in her voice with the rushing sonorities of the ocean in it. "Welcome to my chateau. I rarely receive visitors and that's a misfortune, nothing animates me half as much as the presence of a stranger… This place is so lonely, now the village is deserted, and my one companion, alas, she cannot speak. Often I am so silent I think I, too, will soon forget how to talk."

She offered him a sugar biscuit from a Limoges plate; her fingernails struck carillons from the antique china. Her voice, issuing from those red lips like the obese roses in her garden, lips that do not move, her voice is curiously disembodied; she is like a doll, he thought, a ventriloquist's doll. And the idea she was an automaton, an ingenious construction of white velvet and black fur and crimson plush that could not move of its own accord never quite deserted him. The carnival air of her white dress emphasised her unreality, like a sad Columbine who lost her way in the wood a long time ago and never reached the fair.

"And the light, I must apologise for the lack of light… a hereditary affliction of the eyes…"

Her blind spectacles gave him his handsome face back to himself twice over; if he presented himself to her naked gaze, he would dazzle her like the sun she is forbidden to look at because it would shrivel her up at once, poor night bird. Night bird, butcher bird.

Vous serez ma proie.

You have such a fine throat, like a column of marble. When you came through the door retaining about you the golden light of the summer's day of which I know nothing, nothing, the card called "L'Amoureux" has just emerged from the tumbling chaos of imagery before me; it seemed to me you had stepped off the card into my darkness and, for a moment, I thought perhaps you might irradiate it.

I do not mean to hurt you. I shall wait for you in my bride's dress in the dark.

The bridegroom is come, he will go into the chamber which has been prepared for him.

I am condemned to solitude and dark; I do not mean to hurt you.

I will be very gentle.

(And could love free me from the shadows? Can a bird sing only the only song it knows, could I not learn a new song?)

See, how I'm ready for you, I've always been ready for you; I've been waiting for you in my wedding dress, why have you delayed so long... it will all be over very quickly.

You will feel no pain, my darling.

She herself is a haunted house. She does not possess herself; her ancestors sometimes come and peer out of the windows of her eyes and that is very frightening. She has the mysterious solitude of ambiguous states; she hovers in a no man's land between life and death, sleeping and waking, behind the hedge of spiked flowers, Nosferatu's sanguinary rosebud. The beastly forebears on the walls condemn her to a perpetual repetition of their passions.

(One kiss, however, and only one, woke up the Sleeping Beauty in the Wood.)

Nervously, to conceal her inner voices, she keeps up a front of inconsequential chatter in French while her ancestors leer and grimace on the walls; however hard she tries to think of any other, she only knows of one kind of consummation.

He was struck, once again, by the bird-like, predatory claws which tipped her marvellous hands; the sense of strangeness that had been growing on him since he buried his head under the streaming water in the village, since he entered the dark portals of the fatal castle, now fully overcame him. Had he been a cat, he would have bounced backwards from her hands on four fear-stiffened legs; but he is not a cat, he is a hero.

A fundamental disbelief in what he sees before him sustains him, even in the boudoir of Countess Nosferatu herself; he would have said, perhaps, that there are some things which, even if they are true, we should not believe possible. He might have said, it is foolish to believe one's eyes. Not so much that he does not believe in her; he can see her, she is real. If she takes off her dark glasses, from her eyes will stream all the images that populate this vampire-haunted land, but, since he himself is immune to shadow, due to his virginity—he does not yet know what there is to be afraid of—and due to his heroism, which makes him like the sun, he sees before him, first and foremost, an inbred, highly-strung girl-child, fatherless, motherless, kept in the dark too long and as pale as a plant that never sees the light, half-blinded by some hereditary condition of the eyes. And though he feels unease, he cannot feel terror; so he is like the boy in the folk-tale, who does not know how to shudder and not spooks, beasties, the Devil himself and all his retinue could do the trick.

This lack of imagination gives his heroism to the hero.

He will learn to shudder in the trenches. But this girl cannot make him shudder.

Now it is dark. Bats swoop and squeak outside the tightly shuttered windows that have not been opened for five hundred years. The coffee is all drunk, the sugar biscuits gone. Her chatter comes trickling and diminishing to a stop; she twists her fingers together, picks at the lace of her dress, shifts nervously in her chair. Owls shriek; the impedimenta of her condition squeak and gibber all around us. Now you are at the place of annihilation, now you are at the place of annihilation. She turns her head away from the blue beams of his eyes; she knows no other consummation than the only one she can offer him. She has not eaten for three days. It is dinner-time. It is bed-time.

Suivez-moi.
Je vous attendais.

Vous serez ma proie.

The raven caws on the accursed roof. "Dinner-time, dinner-time," clang the portraits on the walls. A ghastly hunger gnaws her entrails; she has waited for him all her life without knowing it.

The handsome bicyclist, scarcely believing his luck, will follow her into her bedroom; the candles around her sacrificial altar burn with a low, clear flame, light catches on the silver tears stitched to the wall.

> "My clothes have but to fall and you
> will see before you a succession of
> mysteries."

She has no mouth with which to kiss, no hands with which to caress, only the fangs and talons of a beast of prey. To touch the mineral sheen of the flesh revealed in the cool candle gleam is to invite her fatal embrace; in her low, sweet voice, she will croon the infernal liebestod of the House of Nosferatu.

Embraces, kisses; your golden head, of a lion although I have never seen a lion, only imagined one, of the sun, even if I've only seen the picture of the sun on the Tarot card, your golden head of L'Amoureux whom I dreamed would one day free me, this head will fall back, its eyes roll upward in a spasm you will mistake for that of love and not of death. The bridegroom bleeds on my inverted marriage bed. Stark and dead, poor bicyclist; he has paid the price of a night with the Countess and some think it too high a fee while some do not.

Tomorrow, her keeper will bury his bones under the roses. The food her roses feed on gives them their rich colour, their swooning odour that breathes lasciviously of forbidden pleasures.

Suivez-moi.

The handsome bicyclist, fearful for his hostess' health, her sanity, gingerly follows her into the other room; he would like to take her into his arms and protect her from the ancestors who leer down from the walls.

What a macabre bedroom!

His colonel, an old goat with jaded appetites, had given him the visiting card of a brothel in Paris where, the satyr assured him, ten louis would buy just such a lugubrious bedroom, with a naked girl upon a coffin; offstage, the brothel pianist played the *dies irae* on a harmonium and, amidst all the perfumes of the embalming parlour, the customer took his necrophiliac pleasure of a pretended corpse. He had good-naturedly refused the old man's offer of an initiation; how can he now take criminal advantage of the disordered girl with fever-hot, bone-dry, taloned hands and eyes that denied all the erotic promises of her body with their terror, their sadness, their dreadful, balked tenderness?

So delicate and damned, poor thing. Quite damned.

Yet I do believe she scarcely knows what she is doing.

She is shaking as if her limbs were not efficiently joined together. She raises her hands to unfasten the neck of her dress and her eyes fill with tears, they trickle down beneath the rim of her dark glasses. She can't take off her dress without taking off her glasses; when she takes off the dark glasses, they slip from her fingers and smash to pieces on the tiled floor. This unexpected, mundane noise breaks the wicked spell in the room, it disrupts the fatal ritual of seduction; she gapes blindly down at the splinters and ineffectively smears the tears across her face with her fist. When she kneels to try to gather the fragments of glass together, a shard pierces deeply into the pad of her thumb; she cries out. She kneels among the broken glass and watches the bright bead of blood form a drop. She has never seen her own blood before, not her own blood.

Into this macabre and lascivious room, the handsome bicyclist brings the innocent remedies of the nursery; in himself, by his presence, he is an exorcism. He gently takes her hand away from her and dabs away the blood with his own handkerchief, but still it spurts out; and so he puts his mouth to the wound, he will kiss it better for her.

All the silver tears fall from the wall with a flimsy tinkle. Her painted ancestors turn away their eyes and grind their fangs.

How can she bear the trauma of becoming human?

The end of exile, the end of being.

He was awakened by larksong. The shutters, the curtains, even the long-closed windows of the horrid bedroom were all opened up and light and air streamed into the room; now you could see how tawdry it was, how thin and cheap the satin, the catafalque not ebony at all but black-painted paper stretched on struts of wood, as in the theatre. The wind had blown droves of petals from the roses outside into the room and this ominous crimson residue swirled about the floor. The candles had blown out and the Countess' pet lark perched on the edge of the silly coffin and sang him an ecstatic morning song. His bones were stiff and aching; he'd slept on the floor, with his bundled-up jacket for a pillow, after he'd put her to bed.

But now there was no trace of her to be seen except, lightly tossed across the crumpled black satin bedcover, a lace negligee soiled with blood, as it might be from a woman's menses, and a rose that must have come from the fierce bushes nodding through the window. The air was heavy with incense and roses, it made him cough. The Countess must have got up early to enjoy the sunshine, slipped outside to pull him a rose. He got to his feet, coaxed the lark onto his wrist and took it to the window. At first, it exhibited the reluctance for the sky of a long-caged thing but, when he tossed it up onto the currents of the air, it spread its wings and was up and away into the clear, blue bowl of the heavens; he watched its trajectory with a lift of joy in his heart.

Then he padded into the boudoir, his mind occupied with plans. We shall take her to Zurich, to a clinic; she will be treated for nervous hysteria. Then to an eye specialist for her photophobia, and to a dentist to draw her teeth.

A manicurist, to deal with her claws… we shall turn her into the lovely girl she is, I shall cure her.

The heavy curtains are pulled back, to let in brilliant fusillades of early morning light; in the desolation of her boudoir, at her round table she sits, in her white wedding dress with the cards laid out before her. She has dropped off to sleep over the cards of destiny, the Lover, the Grim Reaper droop from her dreaming hand. Gently, a kiss upon her sleeping forehead…

She is not sleeping.

In death, she looked far older, less beautiful and so, for the first time, fully human.

I will vanish in the morning light, I was only an invention of the darkness.

And I give you as a souvenir the dark fanged rose I plucked from between my thighs, like a flower laid on a grave. On a grave.

My keeper will attend to everything.

Nosferatu always attends
his own obsequies.

After a search in some foul-smelling outhouses, he discovered his bicycle and, abandoning his holiday, rode directly to Bucharest where, at the post-restante, he found a telegram summoning him to rejoin his regiment at once; history asserted itself. Much later, when he changed back into uniform in his quarters, he discovered he still had the Countess' sad rose, he'd tucked it into the breast pocket of his tweed cycling jacket. Curiously enough, the flower did not seem quite dead and, on impulse, because the girl had been so lovely and her heart-attack so unexpected and pathetic, he decided to try to resurrect the rose; he filled his tooth-glass with water from the carafe on his locker and popped the rose into it, so that its shaggy head floated on the top.

When he returned from the mess that evening, the heavy fragrance of Count Nosferatu's roses drifted down the stone corridor of the barracks to greet him, and his spartan quarters brimmed lasciviously with the reeling odour of a glowing, velvet, monstrous flower whose petals had regained all their former bloom and elasticity, their corrupt and brilliant splendour.

Next day, his regiment embarked for France.

1984

THE MASTER OF
RAMPLING GATE

Anne Rice

R AMPLING Gate. It was so real to us in the old pictures, rising like a fairy-tale castle out of its own dark wood. A wilderness of gables and chimneys between those two immense towers, grey stone walls mantled in ivy, mullioned windows reflecting the drifting clouds. But why had Father never taken us there? And why, on his deathbed, had he told my brother that Rampling Gate must be torn down, stone by stone? "I should have done it, Richard," he said. "But I was born in that house, as my father was, and his father before him. You must do it now, Richard. It has no claim on you. Tear it down."

Was it any wonder that not two months after Father's passing, Richard and I were on the noon train headed south for the mysterious mansion that had stood upon the rise above the village of Rampling for 400 years? Surely Father would have understood. How could we destroy the old place when we had never seen it? But, as the train moved slowly through the outskirts of London I can't say we were very sure of ourselves, no matter how curious and excited we were.

Richard had just finished four years at Oxford. Two whirlwind social seasons in London had proved me something of a shy success. I still preferred scribbling poems and stories in my room to dancing the night away, but I'd kept that a good secret. And though we had lost our mother when we were little, Father had given us the best of everything. Now the carefree years were ended. We had to be independent and wise.

229

The evening before, we had pored over all the old pictures of Rampling Gate, recalling in hushed, tentative voices the night Father had taken those pictures down from the walls.

I couldn't have been more than six and Richard eight when it happened, yet we remembered well the strange incident in Victoria Station that had precipitated Father's uncharacteristic rage. We had gone there after supper to say farewell to a school friend of Richard's, and Father had caught a glimpse, quite unexpectedly, of a young man at the lighted window of an incoming train. I could remember the young man's face clearly to this day: remarkably handsome, with a head of lustrous brown hair, his large black eyes regarding Father with the saddest expression as Father drew back. "Unspeakable horror!" Father had whispered. Richard and I had been too amazed to speak a word. Later that night, Father and Mother quarrelled, and we crept out of our rooms to listen on the stairs. "That he should dare to come to London!" Father said over and over. "Is it not enough for him to be the undisputed master of Rampling Gate?"

How we puzzled over it as little ones! Who was this stranger, and how could he be master of a house that belonged to our father, a house that had been left in the care of an old, blind housekeeper for years?

But now after looking at the pictures again, it was too dreadful to think of Father's exhortation. And too exhilarating to think of the house itself. I'd packed my manuscripts, for—who knew?—maybe in that melancholy and exquisite setting I'd find exactly the inspiration I needed for the story I'd been writing in my head.

Yet there was something almost illicit about the excitement I felt. I saw in my mind's eye the pale young man again, with his black greatcoat and red woollen cravat, Like bone china, his complexion had been. Strange to remember so vividly. And I realised now that in those few remarkable moments, he had created for me an ideal of masculine beauty that I had never questioned since. But Father had been so angry. I felt an unmistakable pang of guilt.

It was late afternoon when the old trap carried us up the gentle slope from the little railway station and we had our first real look at the house. The sky had paled to a deep rose hue beyond a bank of softly gilded clouds, and the last rays of the sun struck the uppermost panes of the leaded windows and filled them with solid gold. "Oh, but it's too majestic," I whispered, "too like a great cathedral, and to think that it belongs to us!" Richard gave me the smallest kiss on the cheek. I wanted with all my heart to jump down from the trap and draw near on foot, letting those towers slowly grow larger and larger above me, but our old horse was gaining speed.

When we reached the massive front door Richard and I were spirited into the great hall by the tiny figure of the blind housekeeper Mrs Blessington, our footfalls echoing loudly on the marble tile, and our eyes dazzled by the dusty shafts of light that fell on the long oak table and its heavily carved chairs, on the sombre tapestries that stirred ever so slightly against the soaring walls.

"Richard, it is an enchanted place!" I cried, unable to contain myself. Mrs Blessington laughed gaily, her dry hand closing tightly on mine.

We found our bedchambers well aired, with snow-white linen on the beds and fires blazing cosily on the hearths. The small, diamond-paned windows opened on a glorious view of the lake and the oaks that enclosed it and the few scattered lights that marked the village beyond.

That night we laughed like children as we supped at the great oak table, our candles giving only a feeble light. And afterwards we had a fierce battle of pocket billiards in the games room and a little too much brandy, I fear. It was just before I went to bed that I asked Mrs Blessington if there had been anyone in this house since my father left it, years before.

"No, my dear," she said quickly, fluffing the feather pillows. "When your father went away to Oxford, he never came back."

"There was never a young intruder after that?..." I pressed her, though in truth I had little appetite for anything that would disturb the happiness I felt. How I loved the spartan cleanliness of this bedchamber, the walls bare of paper and ornament, the high lustre of the walnut-panelled bed.

"A young intruder?" With an unerring certainty about her surroundings, she lifted the poker and stirred the fire. "No, dear. Whatever made you think there was?"

"Are there no ghost stories, Mrs Blessington?" I asked suddenly, startling myself. Unspeakable horror. But what was I thinking—that that young man had not been real?

"Oh, no, darling," she said, smiling. "No ghost would ever dare to trouble Rampling Gate."

Nothing, in fact, troubled the serenity of the days that followed—long walks through the overgrown gardens, trips in the little skiff to and fro across the lake, tea under the hot glass of the empty conservatory. Early evening found us reading and writing by the library fire.

All our enquiries in the village met with the same answers: the villagers cherished the house. There was not a single disquieting legend or tale.

How were we going to tell them of Father's edict? How were we going to remind ourselves?

Richard was finding a wealth of classical material on the library shelves and I had the desk in the corner entirely to myself.

Never had I known such quiet. It seemed the atmosphere of Rampling Gate permeated my simplest written descriptions and wove its way richly into the plots and characters I created. The Monday after our arrival I finished my first real short story, and after copying out a fresh draft, I went off to the village on foot to post it boldly to the editors of *Blackwood's Magazine*.

It was a warm afternoon, and I took my time as I came back. What had disturbed our father so about this lovely corner of England? What had so darkened his last hours that he laid his curse upon this spot? My heart opened to his unearthly stillness, to an indisputable magnificence that caused me utterly to forget myself. There were times here when I felt

I was a disembodied intellect drifting through a fathomless silence, up and down garden paths and stone corridors that had witnessed too much to take cognisance of one small and fragile young woman who in random moments actually talked aloud to the suits of armour around her, to the broken statues in the garden, the fountain cherubs who had had no water to pour from their conches for years and years.

But was there in this loveliness some malignant force that was eluding us still, some untold story? Unspeakable horror… Even in the flood of brilliant sunlight, those words gave me a chill.

As I came slowly up the slope I saw Richard walking lazily along the uneven shore of the lake. Now and then he glanced up at the distant battlements, his expression dreamy, almost blissfully contented. Rampling Gate had him. And I understood perfectly because it also had me. With a new sense of determination I went to him and placed my hand gently on his arm. For a moment he looked at me as if he did not even know me, and then he said softly, "How will I ever do it, Julie? And one way or the other, it will be on my conscience all my life."

"It's time to seek advice, Richard," I said. "Write to our lawyers in London. Write to Father's clergyman, Doctor Matthews. Explain everything. We cannot do this alone."

It was three o'clock in the morning when I opened my eyes. But I had been awake for a long time. And I felt not fear, lying there alone, but something else—some vague and relentless agitation, some sense of emptiness and need that caused me finally to rise from my bed. What was this house, really? A place, or merely a state of mind? What was it doing to my soul?

I felt overwhelmed, yet shut out of some great and dazzling secret. Driven by an unbearable restlessness, I pulled on my woollen wrapper and my slippers and went into the hall.

The moonlight fell full on the oak stairway, and the vestibule far below. Maybe I could write of the confusion I suffered now, put on paper the inexplicable longing I felt. Certainly it was worth the effort, and I made my way soundlessly down the steps.

The great hall gaped before me, the moonlight here and there touching upon a pair of crossed swords or a mounted shield. But far beyond, in the alcove just outside the library, I saw the uneven glow of the fire, So Richard was there. A sense of well-being pervaded me and quieted me. At the same time, the distance between us seemed endless and I became desperate to cross it, hurrying past the long supper table and finally into the alcove before the library doors. The fire blazed beneath the stone mantelpiece and a figure sat in the leather chair before it, bent over a loose collection of pages that he held in his slender hands. He was reading the pages eagerly, and the fire suffused his face with a warm, golden light.

But it was not Richard. It was the same young man I had seen on the train in Victoria Station fifteen years ago. And not a single aspect of that taut young face had changed. There was the very same hair, thick and lustrous and only carelessly combed as it hung to the collar of his black coat, and those dark eyes that looked up suddenly and fixed me with a most curious expression as I almost screamed.

We stared at each other across that shadowy room, I stranded in the doorway, he visibly and undeniably shaken that I had caught him unawares. My heart stopped.

And in a split second he rose and moved towards me, closing the gap between us, reaching out with those slender white hands.

"Julie!" he whispered, in a voice so low that it seemed my own thoughts were speaking to me. But this was no dream. He was holding me and the scream had broken loose from me, deafening, uncontrollable and echoing from the four walls.

I was alone. Clutching at the door frame, I staggered forward, and then in a moment of perfect clarity I saw the young stranger again, saw him standing in the open door to the garden, looking back over his shoulder; then he was gone. I could not stop screaming. I could not stop even as I heard Richard's voice calling me, heard his feet pound down that broad, hollow staircase and through the great hall. I could not stop even as he shook me, pleaded with me, settled me in a chair.

Finally I managed to describe what I had seen.

"But you know who it was!" I said almost hysterically. "It was he—the young man from the train!"

"Now, wait," Richard said. "He had his back to the fire, Julie. And you could not see his face clearly—"

"Richard, it was he! Don't you understand? He touched me. He called me Julie," I whispered. "Good God, Richard, look at the fire. I didn't light it—he did. He was here!"

All but pushing Richard out of the way, I went to the heap of papers that lay strewn on the carpet before the hearth. "My story..." I whispered, snatching up the pages. "He's been reading my story, Richard. And—dear God—he's read your letters, the letters to Mr Partridge and Dr Matthews, about tearing down the house!"

"Surely you don't believe it was the same man, Julie, after all these years...?"

"But he has not changed, Richard, not in the smallest detail. There is no mistake, I tell you. It was the very same man!" The next day was the most trying since we had come. Together we commenced a search of the house. Darkness found us only half finished, frustrated everywhere by locked doors we could not open and old staircases that were not safe.

And it was also quite clear by suppertime that Richard did not believe I had seen anyone in the study at all. As for the fire—well, he had failed to put it out properly before going to bed; and the pages—well, one of us had put them there and forgotten them, of course... But I knew what I had seen.

And what obsessed me more than anything else was the gentle countenance of the mysterious man I had glimpsed, the innocent eyes that had fixed on me for one moment before I screamed.

"You would be wise to do one very important thing before you retire," I said crossly. "Leave out a note to the effect that you do not intend to tear down the house."

"Julie, you have created an impossible dilemma," Richard declared, the colour rising in his face. "You insist we reassure this apparition that the house will not be destroyed, when in fact you verify the existence of the very creature that drove our father to say what he did."

"Oh, I wish I had never come here!" I burst out suddenly.

"Then we should go, and decide this matter at home."

"No—that's just it. I could never go without knowing. I could never go on living with knowing now!"

Anger must be an excellent antidote to fear, for surely something worked to alleviate my natural alarm. I did not undress that night, but rather sat in the darkened bedroom, gazing at the small square of diamond-paned window until I heard the house fall quiet. When the grandfather clock in the great hall chimed the hour of eleven, Rampling Gate was, as usual, fast asleep.

I felt a dark exultation as I imagined myself going out of the room and down the stairs. But I knew I should wait one more hour. I should let the night reach its peak. My heart was beating too fast, and dreamily I recollected the face I had seen, the voice that had said my name.

Why did it seem in retrospect so intimate, that we had known each other before, spoken together a thousand times? Was it because he had read my story, those words that came from my very soul?

"Who are you?" I believe I whispered aloud. "Where are you at this moment?" I uttered the word, "Come."

The door opened without a sound and he was standing there. He was dressed exactly as he had been the night before and his dark eyes were riveted on me with that same obvious curiosity, his mouth just a little slack, like that of a boy.

I sat forward, and he raised his finger as if to reassure me and gave a little nod.

"Ah, it is you!" I whispered.

"Yes," he said in a soft, unobtrusive voice.

"And you are not a spirit!" I looked at his mud-splattered boots, at the faintest smear of dust on that perfect white cheek.

"A spirit?" he asked almost mournfully. "Would that I were that."

Dazed, I watched him come towards me; the room darkened and I felt his cool, silken hands on my face. I had risen. I was standing before him, and I looked up into his eyes.

I heard my own heartbeat. I heard it as I had the night before, right at the moment I had screamed. Dear God, I was talking to him! He was in my room and I was talking to him! And then suddenly I was in his arms. "Real, absolutely real!" I whispered, and a low, zinging sensation coursed through me so that I had to steady myself. He was peering at me as if trying to comprehend something terribly important. His lips had a ruddy look to them, a soft look for all his handsomeness, as if he had never been kissed. A slight dizziness came over me, a slight confusion in which I was not at all sure that he was even there.

"Oh, but I am," he said, as if I had spoken my doubt. I felt his breath against my cheek, and it was almost sweet. "I am here, and I have watched you ever since you came."

"Yes..."

My eyes were closing. In a dim flash, as of a match being struck, I saw my father, heard his voice. No, Julie... But that was surely a dream.

"Only a little kiss," said the voice of the one who was really here. I felt his lips against my neck. "I would never harm you. No harm ever for the children of this house. Just the little kiss, Julie, and the understanding that it imparts, that you cannot destroy Rampling Gate, Julie—that you can never, never drive me away."

The core of my being, that secret place where all desires and all commandments are nurtured, opened to him without a struggle or a sound. I would have fallen if he had not held me. My arms closed about him, my hands slipping into the soft, silken mass of his hair.

I was floating, and there was, as there had always been at Rampling Gate, an endless peace. It was Rampling Gate I felt enclosing me; it was that timeless and impenetrable secret that had opened itself at last... A power within me of enormous ken... To see as a god sees, and take the depth of things as nimbly as the outward eyes can size and shape pervade... Yes, those very words from Keats, which I had quoted in the pages of my story that he had read. But in a violent instant he had released me. "Too innocent," he whispered.

I went reeling across the bedroom floor and caught hold of the frame of the window. I rested my forehead against the stone wall.

There was a tingling pain in my throat where his lips had touched me that was almost pleasurable, a delicious throbbing that would not stop. I knew what he was!

I turned and saw all the room clearly—the bed, the fireplace, the chair. And he stood still exactly as I'd left him and there was the most appalling anguish in his face.

"Something of menace, unspeakable menace," I whispered, backing away.

"Something ancient, something that defies understanding," he pleaded. "Something that can and will go on." But he was shaken and he would not look into my eyes.

I touched that pulsing pain with the tips of my fingers and, looking down at them, saw the blood. "Vampire!" I gasped. "And yet you suffer so, and it is as if you can love!"

"Love? I have loved you since you came. I loved you when I read your secret thoughts and had not yet seen your face." He drew me to him ever so gently, and slipping his arm around me, guided me to the door.

I tried for one desperate moment to resist him. And as any gentleman might, he stepped back respectfully and took my hand.

Through the long upstairs corridor we passed, and through a small wooden doorway to a screw stair that I had not seen before. I soon realised we were ascending in the north tower, a ruined portion of the structure that had been sealed off years before.

Through one tiny window after another I saw the gently rolling landscape and the small cluster of dim lights that marked the village of Rampling and the pale streak of white that was the London road.

Up and up we climbed, until we reached the topmost chamber, and this he opened with an iron key. He held back the door for me to enter and I found myself in a spacious room whose high, narrow windows contained no glass. A flood of moonlight revealed the most curious mixture of furnishings and objects—a writing-table, a great shelf of books, soft leather chairs, and scores of maps and framed pictures affixed to the walls. Candles all about had dripped their wax on every surface, and in the very midst of this chaos lay my poems, my old sketches—early writings that I had brought with me and never even unpacked.

I saw a black silk top hat and a walking-stick, and a bouquet of withered flowers, dry as straw, and daguerreotypes and tintypes in their little velvet cases, and London newspapers and opened books. There was no place for sleeping in this room.

And when I thought of that, where he must lie when he went to rest, a shudder passed over me and I felt, quite palpably, his lips touching my throat again, and I had the sudden urge to cry.

But he was holding me in his arms; he was kissing my cheeks and my lips ever so softly.

"My father knew what you were!" I whispered.

"Yes," he answered, "and his father before him. And all of them in an unbroken chain over the years. Out of loneliness or rage, I know not which, I always told them. I always made them acknowledge, accept." I backed away and he didn't try to stop me. He lighted the candles about us one by one.

I was stunned by the sight of him in the light, the gleam in his large black eyes and the gloss of his hair. Not even in the railway station had I seen him so clearly as I did now, amid the radiance of the candles. He broke my heart. And yet he looked at me as though I were a feast for his eyes, and he said my name again and I felt the blood rush to my face. But there seemed a great break suddenly in the passage of time. What had I been thinking! Yes, never tell, never disturb… something ancient, something greater than good and evil… But no! I felt dizzy again. I heard Father's voice: Tear it down, Richard, stone by stone.

He had drawn me to the window, And as the lights of Rampling were subtracted from the darkness below, a great wood stretched out in all directions, far older and denser than the forest of Rampling Gate. I was afraid suddenly, as if I were slipping into a maelstrom of visions from which I could never, of my own will, return.

There was that sense of our talking together, talking and talking in low, agitated voices, and I was saying that I should not give in.

"Bear witness—that is all I ask of you, Julie."

And there was in me some dim certainty that by these visions alone I would be fatally changed.

But the very room was losing its substance, as if a soundless wind of terrific force were blowing it apart. The vision had already begun…

We were riding horseback through a forest, he and I. And the trees were so high and so thick that scarcely any sun at all broke through to the fragrant, leaf-strewn ground.

Yet we had no time to linger in this magical place. We had come to the fresh-tilled earth that surrounded a village I somehow knew was called Knorwood, with its gabled roofs and its tiny, crooked streets. We saw the monastery of Knorwood and the little church with the bell chiming vespers under the lowering sky. A great, bustling life resided in Knorwood, a thousand voices rising in common prayer.

Far beyond, on the rise above the forest, stood the round tower of a truly ancient castle; and to that ruined castle—no more than a shell of itself any more—as darkness fell in earnest we rode. Through its empty chambers we roamed, impetuous children, the horses and the road quite forgotten, and to the lord of the castle, a gaunt and white-skinned creature standing before the roaring fire of the roofless hall, we came. He turned and fixed us with his narrow and glittering eyes. A dead thing he was, I understood, but he carried within himself a priceless magic. And my companion, my innocent young man, stepped forward into the lord's arms.

I saw the kiss. I saw the young man grow pale and struggle and turn away, and the lord retreated with the wisest, saddest smile.

I understood. I knew. But the castle was dissolving as surely as anything in this dream might dissolve, and we were in some damp and close place.

The stench was unbearable to me; it was that most terrible of all stenches, the stench of death. And I heard my steps on the cobblestones and I reached out to steady myself against a wall. The tiny market-place was deserted; the doors and windows gaped open to the vagrant wind. Up one side and down the other of the crooked street I saw the marks on the houses. And I knew what the marks meant. The Black Death had come to the village of Knorwood. The Black Death had laid it waste. And in a moment of suffocating horror I realised that no one, not a single person, was left alive.

But this was not quite true. There was a young man walking in fits and starts up the narrow alleyway. He was staggering, almost falling, as he pushed in one door after another, and at last came to a hot, reeking place where a child screamed on the floor. Mother and father lay dead in the bed. And the sleek fat cat of the household, unharmed, played with the screaming infant, whose eyes bulged in its tiny, sunken face.

"Stop it!" I heard myself gasp. I was holding my head with both hands. "Stop it—stop it, please!" I was screaming, and my screams would surely pierce the vision and this crude little dwelling would collapse around me and I would rouse the household of Rampling Gate, but I did not. The young man turned and stared at me, and in the close, stinking room I could not see his face.

But I knew it was he, my companion, and I could smell his fever and his sickness, and the stink of the dying infant, and see the gleaming body of the cat as it pawed at the child's outstretched hand.

"Stop it, you've lost control of it!" I screamed, surely with all my strength, but the infant screamed louder. "Make it stop."

"I cannot," he whispered. "It goes on for ever! It will never stop!"

And with a great shriek I kicked at the cat and sent it flying out of the filthy room, overturning the milk pail as it went. Death in all the houses of Knorwood. Death in the cloister, death in the open fields. It seemed the Judgment of God—I was sobbing, begging to be released—it seemed the very end of Creation itself.

But as night came down over the dead village he was alive still, stumbling up the slopes, through the forest, towards that tower where the lord stood at the broken arch of the window, waiting for him to come. "Don't go!" I begged him. I ran alongside him, crying, but he didn't hear.

The lord turned and smiled with infinite sadness as the young man on his knees begged for salvation, when it was damnation this lord offered, when it was only damnation that the lord would give.

"Yes, damned, then, but living, breathing!" the young man cried, and the lord opened his arms.

The kiss again, the lethal kiss, the blood drawn out of his dying body, and then the lord lifting the heavy head of the young man so the youth could take the blood back again from the body of the lord himself.

I screamed, "Do not—do not drink!"

He turned, and his face was now so perfectly the visage of death that I couldn't believe there was animation left in him; yet he asked: "What would you do? Would you go back to Knorwood, would you open those doors one after another, would you ring the bell in the empty church—and if you did, who would hear?"

He didn't wait for my answer. And I had none now to give. He locked his innocent mouth to the vein that pulsed with every semblance of life beneath the lord's cold and translucent flesh. And the blood jetted into the young body, vanquishing in one great burst the fever and the sickness that had racked it, driving it out along with the mortal life. He stood now in the hall of the lord alone. Immortality was his, and the blood thirst he would need to sustain it, and that thirst I could feel with my whole soul.

And each and every thing was transfigured in his vision—to the exquisite essence of itself. A wordless voice spoke from the starry veil of heaven; it sang in the wind that rushed through the broken timbers; it sighed in the flames that ate at the sooted stones of the hearth. It was the eternal rhythm of the universe that played beneath every surface as the last living creature in the village—that tiny child—fell silent in the maw of time.

A soft wind sifted and scattered the soil from the newly turned furrows in the empty fields. The rain fell from the black and endless sky.

Years and years passed. And all that had been Knorwood melted into the earth. The forest sent out its silent sentinels, and mighty trunks rose where there had been huts and houses, where there had been monastery walls. And it seemed the horror beyond all horrors that no one should know any more of those who had lived and died in that small and insignificant village, that not anywhere in the great archives in which all history is recorded should a mention of Knorwood exist.

Yet one remained who knew, one who had witnessed, one who had seen the Ramplings come in the years that followed, seen them raise their house upon the very slope where the ancient castle had once stood, one who saw a new village collect itself slowly upon the unmarked grave of the old. And all through the walls of Rampling Gate were the stones of that old castle, the stones of the forgotten monastery, the stones of that little church.

We were once again back in the tower.

"It is my shrine," he whispered. "My sanctuary. It is the only thing that endures as I endure. And you love it as I love it, Julie. You have written it… You love its grandeur. And its gloom."

"Yes, yes… as it's always been…" I was crying, though I didn't move my lips.

He had turned to me from the window, and I could feel his endless craving with all my heart.

"What else do you want from me!" I pleaded. "What else can I give?"

A torrent of images answered me. It was beginning again. I was once again relinquishing myself, yet in a great rush of lights and noise I was enlivened and made whole as I had been when we rode together through the forest, but it was into the world of now, this hour, that we passed.

We were flying through the rural darkness along the railway towards London, where the night-time city burst like an enormous bubble in a shower of laughter and motion and glaring light. He was walking with me under the gas lamps, his face all but shimmering with that same dark innocence, that same irresistible warmth. It seemed we were holding tight to each other in the very midst of a crowd. And the crowd was a living thing, a writhing thing, and everywhere there came a dark, rich aroma from it, the aroma of fresh blood. Women in white fur and gentlemen in opera capes swept through the brightly lighted doors of the theatre; the blare of the music hall inundated us and then faded away. Only a thin soprano voice was left, singing a high, plaintive song. I was in his arms and his lips were covering mine, and there came that dull, zinging sensation again, that great, uncontrollable opening within myself. Thirst, and the promise of satiation measured only by the intensity of that thirst. Up back staircases we fled together, into high-ceilinged bedrooms papered in red damask, where the loveliest women reclined on brass beds, and the aroma was so strong now that I could not bear it and he said: "Drink. They are your victims! They will give you eternity—you must drink." And I felt the warmth filling me, charging me, blurring my vision until we broke free again, light and invisible, it seemed, as we moved over the rooftops and down again through rain-drenched streets. But the rain did not touch us; the falling snow did not chill us; we had within ourselves a great and indissoluble heat. And together in the carriage we talked to each other in low, exuberant rushes of language; we were lovers; we were constant; we were immortal. We were as enduring as Rampling Gate.

Oh, don't let it stop! I felt his arms around me and I knew we were in the tower room together, and the visions had worked their fatal alchemy.

"Do you understand what I am offering you? To your ancestors I revealed myself, yes; I subjugated them. But I would make you my bride, Julie. I would share with you my power. Come with me. I will not take you against your will, but can you turn away?"

Again I heard my own scream. My hands were on his cool white skin, and his lips were gentle yet hungry, his eyes yielding and ever young. Father's angry countenance blazed before me as if I, too, had the power to conjure. Unspeakable horror. I covered my face.

He stood against the backdrop of the window, against the distant drift of pale clouds. The candlelight glimmered in his eyes. Immense and sad and wise, they seemed—and oh, yes, innocent, as I have said again and again. "You are their fairest flower, Julie. To them I gave my protection always. To you I give my love. Come to me, dearest, and Rampling Gate will truly be yours, and it will finally, truly be mine."

Nights of argument, but finally Richard had come round. He would sign over Rampling Gate to me and I should absolutely refuse to allow the place to be torn down. There would be nothing he could do then to obey Father's command. I had given him the legal impediment he needed, and of course I told him I would leave the house to his male heirs. It should always be in Rampling hands.

A clever solution, it seemed to me, since Father had not told me to destroy the place. I had no scruples in the matter now at all.

And what remained was for him to take me to the little railway station and see me off for London, and not worry about my going home to Mayfair on my own.

"You stay here as long as you wish and do not worry," I said. I felt more tenderly towards him than I could ever express. "You knew as soon as you set foot in the place that Father was quite wrong." The great black locomotive was chugging past us, the passenger cars slowing to a stop. "Must go now, darling—kiss me," I said.

"But what came over you, Julie—what convinced you so quickly—?"

"We've been through all that, Richard," I said. "What matters is that Rampling Gate is safe and we are both happy, my dear."

I waved until I couldn't see him any more. The flickering lamps of the town were lost in the deep lavender light of the early evening, and the dark hulk of Rampling Gate appeared for one uncertain moment like the ghost of itself on the nearby rise.

I sat back and closed my eyes, Then I opened them slowly, savouring this moment for which I had waited so long. He was smiling, seated in the far corner of the leather seat opposite, as he had been all along, and now he rose with a swift, almost delicate movement and sat beside me and enfolded me in his arms. "It's five hours to London," he whispered.

"I can wait," I said, feeling the thirst like a fever as I held tight to him, feeling his lips against my eyelids and my hair. "I want to hunt the London streets tonight," I confessed a little shyly, but I saw only approbation in his eyes. "Beautiful Julie, my Julie..." he whispered. "You'll love the house in Mayfair," I said. "Yes..." he said.

"And when Richard finally tires of Rampling Gate, we shall go home."

ADVOCATES

Suzy McKee Charnas & Chelsea Quinn Yarbro

I T was shortly after teatime when the three Watchmen found the Renegade. He crouched over a tall, thin woman who layed sprawled on the floor. There was blood in her tangled hair, on the top of her dress, and on his mouth.

"Christ," whispered the biggest Watchman, who had never seen a vampire feeding in daylight before.

The other two Watchmen were silent, prepared to do battle.

The Renegade stepped back over the still-living body of his undead victim, ready to bolt.

"Stop him!" shouted the youngest Watchman as the Renegade sprang for the rusty door.

"Get him!" roared the biggest, plunging after the fleeing, bloodied figure.

As the Renegade seized the door handle it tore away, metal shrieking; he staggered back, slamming into the oldest Watchman.

At once the biggest Watchman lunged, catching the Renegade about the knees. The impact carried them all to the floor; the third Watchman landed on top of the pile with everything he had.

"Shit, he's strong," said the biggest as the Renegade struggled in silent desperation to get free.

"Get the Damper," gasped the youngest Watchman. "We can't hold him much longer."

"Where're the restraints?" yelled the man on top fumbling with a small spray can. He could not keep the fear out of his voice.

"In the truck," said the biggest. Only when the spray can had been fired into their captive's face and the powerful body relaxed did he dare to let go of the vampire's legs.

The man on the top climbed off. "Keep him out. Give him another inhale. I'll be right back." He did not walk quite steadily, and he was breathing too fast.

As the other two rose gingerly from the supine figure, the younger Watchman stared at the Renegade, his face pale. "I didn't believe it. I didn't really believe it."

"What?" asked the other Watchman. He stood straddling the unconscious Renegade, eager to kick him in the jaw if he regained consciousness. "What didn't you believe?"

The younger man shook his head, eyes haunted. "I didn't believe about the daylight. Fuck it! Who ever saw a vampire hunting in the daylight?"

Years ago the hotel had catered to the most affluent business travellers. The pillars and the floor in the lobby were green-veined marble, the sconces were solid brass, the carpets on the stairs and in the halls were from the finest Canadian mills. But it was no longer the splendid hostelry it had been; six years ago it was pressed into service as the Magistrates' Center. Now the carpets were worn, the brass was unpolished, and the tremendous wall mirrors were gone.

In the basement of the Magistrates' Center, four large storage rooms had been converted into holding cells. They brought the Renegade to the most remote of these, left him secured to metal cleats in the wall and hurried away; no one wanted to be there when he regained consciousness.

Inspector Frederick Samson had been awake less than half an hour when the three Watchmen brought him the good news.

"We found him by accident," the oldest admitted with a quick look of apology to the other two. "We heard a sound in a deserted warehouse. We didn't anticipate—"

The biggest Watchman nodded emphatically. "He'd got her."

"What about the… remains? Do we know who she is?" asked the inspector.

"Not yet. We brought it along. It's in the morgue," said the oldest.

"The Grand Ballroom," corrected the inspector. "With the others."

"And the Renegade's down in cell number four," said the youngest of the Watchmen, his eyes flicking nervously from the inspector to the other Watchmen. "The Damper'll wear off in about half an hour."

The inspector took a deep breath and straightened his immaculate black foulard vest. "That'll give me time to look at the victim before I talk to the Renegade. Good work. We couldn't have done it without you." He hesitated. "I don't suppose there's any chance you made a mistake?"

"Look at the victim: a remainder," said the biggest. "Same condition as all the others. Undead and comatose." He tried to suppress his shudder.

"That makes twenty-eight," said the youngest Watchman, and looked away from Frederick Samson as if the very number were a recrimination.

Half a dozen Cybertooths were waiting in the lobby, their studded black leather and chains no longer able to create the sensation they had once. The one called Demon Star strutted toward Samson as she caught sight of him, the jingle of her chains a counterpoint to the crack of her five-inch boot heels. "They say you found the guy who did the Renegade killings." Her voice grew derisive. "Someone you found in *daylight*."

"We're investigating," said Samson, trying not to glare at the statuesque figure with the white hair standing out in four-inch spikes around her head. "And until our investigation is completed, I have nothing more to say to you."

"You Beaux are all alike," jeered Demon Star, light shining from the red glitter on her eyelids. "I want to see this monster you've got in a cell in the basement."

"If he's the Renegade, he *is* a monster," said Samson, his manner quiet and serious. "And you're not going to see him."

"I have the right. He's cutting into our territory," said Demon Star. "And don't tell me he isn't cutting into your—"

Samson stood a little straighter "Is that all that concerns you—who's raiding your livestock?" He knew it was not wise to rise to the bait of these Cybertooths, but he could not stop himself issuing them a challenge. "Come with me," he said sharply. "I want you to see what the Renegade has done. Maybe that will give you some notion of the scope of our problem here."

Demon Star flung back her fantastical head and laughed. "Trying to shock us? Hey, drain a vein, who cares?" She signalled to the others with her to follow and began a loose-limbed saunter down the decaying elegance of the hall leading to the Grand Ballroom.

Half a dozen orderlies worked among the gurneys, tending to the victims of the Renegade. The latest victim was nearest the door. Her body was decently covered by a sheet, but her face was visible. Nothing had been done about the bloody mess in her hair.

"So?" said Demon Star as she nudged the latest victim with the riding crop she always carried. "Like the others. You got the right guy."

"In daylight," said Inspector Samson.

"Bullshit," answered Demon Star. "It was early evening. What's this plasma-pus about daylight?" She laughed again, even more theatrically.

"Twenty-eight vampires are… vegetables, thanks to the Renegade. They're too drained to ever be anything other than in a coma, but they have not died the true death." He made a gesture of helpless frustration. "Doesn't that mean anything to you?"

"It means she's a remainder, like all the rest." She shrugged so that the elaborate pattern of studs on her shoulder glistened in the light. "What else?"

Angrily Inspector Samson pushed by her back into the hall, not caring that the Cybertooths followed after him. He would have liked the luxury of yelling at them, but had given that up after the third victim had been brought to him.

"Squeamish about a remainder?" Demon Star taunted, but for once her brittle scorn rang false.

"Aren't you?" the inspector flung over his shoulder. He was so irritated that he almost ran into the black-clad clerk who hastened up to him holding out a sheet of paper.

"Inspector Samson, Inspector Samson," the clerk insisted as he turned in pursuit of the inspector. "Just a moment."

"Your flunkey wants you," called out Demon Star.

As much as he wanted to ignore her, Inspector Samson stopped and swung around to face the clerk. "What is it?" he demanded.

The clerk quailed. "It's… it's about the prisoner."

His wrath evaporated. "What about the prisoner?"

Now the Cybertooths came nearer, silent for once.

"We have a name for him, for the Renegade. That's all." The clerk looked from Inspector Samson to Demon Star and back. "We think we know who he is."

"And who's that?" asked Demon Star with such sardonic intent that it was not until later that Inspector Samson thought it had not been wise to permit the clerk to answer.

"Weyland," said the clerk eagerly. "Edward Lewis Weyland."

"They tell me you're a professor of anthropology," said Frederick Samson as he faced the Renegade across the cement floor of the holding cell.

Weyland gave a single, determined pull at his restraints.

"They tell me your name is Edward Lewis Weyland." He waited for a response.

"Who tells you this?" the Renegade said. His eyes locked on Samson's face.

Samson looked down at his glossy calf-high boots, deliberately avoiding the penetrating stare of his prisoner. "You're accused of preying on vampires, Weyland. Do you mind if I call you Weyland? For convenience?"

"Call me what you like, I can hardly prevent you," the other said. He turned his head and looked off into a corner of the cell as if the interview were over.

"How do you propose to answer the charge?" Samson inquired.

"I propose nothing," Weyland said. "I am not in a position to propose."

"There are over twenty vampires in our... morgue. They aren't truly dead. You've left them nothing but life enough to be in Hell." He had not intended this last to be so passionate.

"They were not vampires," Weyland said, "and I suspect that it is I who am in Hell."

Samson pushed himself away from the wall, his face rigid with the effort of mastering his revulsion. "We are better than that, Renegade. We do not prey on our own kind. We leave that to human beings."

"Perfectly appropriate," Weyland snapped. "You *are* humans, all of you. That is all you ever were, or ever can be. I hunt my prey, that is all."

For an instant Samson imagined the satisfaction of severing Weyland's head from his body, watching the blood run out of him. Then he looked down and fingered his lapels. "You will answer for what you did, Weyland. You will answer for what you *are*."

"I have already answered far too much," Weyland said. "You will get no more from me." He slumped against the wall and shut his eyes.

Samson accepted the impasse; he needed to consider what he would recommend to the Magistrates. Yet he permitted himself a parting shot. "I wouldn't wager on that."

The roll-up door of the loading dock was stiff and noisy with disuse.

"Keep it quiet!" hissed Demon Star, flicking her crop at the Cybertooth who had been foolish enough to let the door groan as it was opened halfway. "We don't want any Beaux finding us in here."

"I can't help it," said Dog, his tongue bright pink against his black-painted lips. "The thing's old."

She struck him again, harder. "That's for talking back," she said, then ducked down to slip inside the cellars of the Magistrates' Center. She took a moment to orient herself, the memorised cellar plans coming slowly to her mind. She cursed; it was getting late and she was growing lethargic. Dawn was only an hour away.

"Where to?" Dog whispered, motioning the other eight to come nearer.

"Left at the corner," she said. "There's a patrol due around in ten minutes. We have seven minutes to get to the Renegade's cell." She grabbed Dog's shoulder. "You stay here. I don't want anyone cutting off our way out."

"No one," Dog promised, kneeling to lick her hand.

There were few lights in the corridors—most had burned out long ago and there was no reason for vampires to replace them—and the cameras mounted to reveal intruders had not been modified to register those of their blood. "This way," Demon Star said, pointing toward the side-hallway where the holding cells were. "They post their human guards at dawn."

Slicker giggled. "We could grab one for a snack."

"We won't have room," Demon Star said. "Will we?"

They moved through the shadows making no particular effort to go undetected, for they had been told that at the slack end of the night these basement corridors were poorly guarded.

"That's the cell," said Sweet Blue, her cherub's face leering in anticipation.

Slicker had the crowbars for the locks, and between him and Long Poison the door was open in less than a minute.

"Don't bother to unhook him," said Demon Star as she shoved through the others into the cell. "Just do him."

The figure at the wall stood in a tense crouch, feet braced as widely as his chains allowed. He uttered no sound, and for an instant his stillness held them off, like a wall formed equally of his will and their apprehension. They had expected a cowering victim. They faced what appeared to be a desperate and resolute opponent.

"What are you waiting for?" Demon Star said with sudden force, and she caught Slicker by the arm and shoved him toward the Renegade, whipping along Sweet Blue and Hot Licks at the same time. They fell on the Renegade like a storm of leather and steel. He staggered beneath their weight. Hunched tightly against their onslaught, he lashed out with hands and feet to the extent that his restraints permitted. He caught Sweet Blue a crack in the face with his head that sent her reeling back with a yelp, both hands shielding her broken lips.

But the others bore him down in a heaving, cursing tangle, and Demon Star planted one boot against his shoulder and clawed at the side of his head, holding the curve of his throat taut and exposed for the plunging attacks of the others. He threshed and coiled under them like a python, but they clung hard, digging in with their fingers and their knees. They shoved each other and grunted in their eagerness to feed.

They were too embroiled to hear the hurried footsteps behind them, or see the beams of flashlights carried by half a dozen Watchmen.

"We'll cut you all down if we must!" shouted Inspector Samson. "Get away from him." His men crowded into the cell.

Demon Star turned toward the intruders. She bared her teeth, blood slathered over her face. "You're too late."

Samson advanced implacably. "Get away, all of you." He could barely control the distress he felt at the loss of his prisoner.

Sweet Blue broke and ran for the door, elbows up to shove the Watchmen out of the way. A sharp blow from a cudgel brought her down.

"*Fuckers!*" shrieked Demon Star, and her crop sliced the air toward Samson.

As he stepped back, the Cybertooths pushed past the door, Slicker scooping up Sweet Blue as he fled.

Samson issued a few terse orders, then moved forward to examine his prisoner. "Catch them if you can," he told the Watchmen, relieved that none of the Cybertooths had fallen to them. Only when they were gone did Samson kneel beside Weyland, expecting to find him as inert and drained as the undead husks in the Grand Ballroom.

To his amazement, Weyland was not sunk in unendable coma. The Renegade glared up at Samson, bloody faced, and croaked, "I told you—Hell."

Samson rose in silence, considering with rising excitement what nature of being he had confined in this basement cell.

On his desk only the formal memo from the Magistrates was out of place. Samson felt himself drawn to it again, trying to decide how to answer it.

We have decided that the Renegade's acts cannot go unpunished.

Samson agreed with them, but he could not second the Magistrates' demand for a summary execution. He had to find a way to keep Weyland alive, at least until he knew more about him. He picked up the memo again, as if in rereading it he would discover that the message had changed.

When he drew his own stationery from its case, he wrote out his response in his best hand, taking pains to make the memo as elegant as the one the Magistrates had sent him.

While I share the desire for justice, I believe that we cannot withhold some process of justice from the prisoner. An execution, ordered out-of-hand, would serve only to compound the crimes committed. It would subvert our order here; all later attempts at justice would be derided.

The prisoner has demonstrated certain characteristics that deserve our examination, and this will certainly not be possible if he is dispatched without recourse to a hearing to determine the most appropriate sentence.

I believe that no one in this city, vampire or human, can offer the prisoner the defence he must have if we are to conduct a hearing that is not a travesty. I volunteer to secure an advocate for him, one who will be acceptable to you Magistrates and to the great majority of our populace regarding the final disposition of the case, and to make every attempt to see that impartiality is maintained throughout the proceedings.

Would the Magistrates accept his proposal? he wondered. Never before had he been presented such an opportunity, never had he been given the chance to excel in his own area of science. Or would he lose the chance he had sought for so long, and that had been denied him.

Had he been human still, his pulse would have been racing as he reached for the telephone.

Samson was Beau enough to be disappointed by the advocate's appearance—his immaculate dark suit lacked a Beau's brass buttons and his cravat was merely a conservative silken burgundy—but he did his best to conceal this as he opened the inner door of the hotel suite. "We can make arrangements for a coffin if you prefer," he said as he indicated the bed.

"That won't be necessary," said the advocate. "My manservant will attend to it." He returned to the sitting room, gesturing toward the settee. "Please."

"I've brought the information you wanted," Samson told him as he took his seat. "And I'm delighted to answer any questions you might have."

The advocate gave a quick, ironic smile. "Are you?" He opened the case he carried and took out a sheaf of papers. "Then perhaps you wouldn't mind reviewing these?"

"What are they?" Samson asked, taken aback.

"Records," said the advocate as he settled back in the high-backed chair.

"Of what?" Samson had no idea how to respond to this sally. He looked at the neat stack. "Why?"

The advocate's dark eyes clouded. "Your city isn't the only one to have had this trouble," he said quietly. "There have been others. Yours is only the most recent."

Samson was shocked. "There are others like Weyland?"

"Or Weyland travels," said the advocate. "Let us hope."

The implication of this remark struck Samson forcibly. "But he couldn't get away with it, not for any length of time. Could he?"

"Tell me what you think after you read those records," the advocate recommended. "And while you are doing that," he said, rising, "I will have a word with my… client."

Weyland dozed fitfully on the iron bed they had given him after the Cybertooths' attack. Despite frequent draughts of blood brought him from the Center's stores, he was still subject to waves of weakness that terrified him, and he spent most of his time trying to conserve his strength for those dizzying moments.

Someone was coming, crisp steps in the corridor, accompanied by none of the grumble and chatter and whisper of the day guards which invariably raised the spectre of reprisal at the hands of his accustomed victims, now that he lay chained in their possession. So this would be one of the others, the humans who called themselves vampires, and who had themselves become his food.

With an effort he sat up, aware of thirst—for water only—and the ache in his throat where those phantasmagoric people had savaged him. Beneath the constant nagging apprehension, he felt the tingle of curiosity.

Though the cell was dark, the advocate had no difficulty in seeing Weyland. He came to the edge of the iron bed. "According to the reports, you drain vampires of their blood. Do you?"

Weyland said, "It's nothing to me what they tell you. Who are you and what do you want here?"

"I've been asked to represent you before the Magistrates; it seems they want to provide you a hearing." He did not flinch at the hard glare from Weyland.

"I haven't," Weyland said. "What would be the point? Here I am, and I will tell you this much frankly, here I expect to die, with a hearing—whatever that may mean—or without one."

"Then you might as well accept the hearing," said the advocate; at the back of his dark eyes was something too ancient to be understanding. He glanced toward the door. "Twenty-eight victims here—what do you call them?"

"I don't call them anything," Weyland retorted. "You people call them remainders, I believe; a usage with a certain morbid charm, to a former author of books. In this place and circumstance, I suppose I should appreciate any charm I can find."

"It might be wisest to leave aesthetics until later," said the advocate. "For now, our greatest concern must be those twenty-eight... remainders and why you attacked them." He gave a long, thoughtful look at Weyland. "Why remainders, and why other vampires? Do you have a reason?"

"Certainly," Weyland replied, moving to fold his arms across his chest but checked in this gesture by his chains. "Now explain to me precisely who you are and why you want to represent me at this so-called hearing, and I may choose to tell you my reasons, my secrets, my autobiography, my telephone number, and anything else you wish to know; or not."

The advocate did not answer at once, and when he did his voice was mild but precise. "You have been known as Edward Lewis Weyland, professor of anthropology. You have taught at Columbia and UCLA most recently. Your last known address was 153 Goethe Circle in Toronto. You have no records of spouses or long-term lovers. Most of your academic credentials are sham, and your childhood information a fiction. Your last known telephone number was 555-3881. Would you like me to continue?"

"'A hit; a very palpable hit,'" said Weyland drily, though his heart was beating hard. It was long since he had felt so exposed to unknown and dangerous factors. "But you most definitely have the advantage of me at the moment. My credentials may be largely fabricated, but at least I have them. What are yours? You seem unusually levelheaded for this place. You surely realise that I see no profit to myself in revealing any small rag of information about myself that I may still accurately call my own, if indeed such a thing exists."

"Humility doesn't become you, Professor," said his advocate lightly. "Still, I don't suppose it would hurt either of us for you to know that I am qualified to speak for you, by weight of years if nothing else. You see, little as I approve of what you have done, I do not want you or any other vampire made a scapegoat. Will that suffice?"

"No one is qualified to speak for me," Weyland said, feeling the onset of one of those dreaded waves of weakness, and with it the black hopelessness with which he had so far endured his days in this place. "Nothing will suffice, and no one who thinks I have anything in common with those who presently call themselves vampires can even begin to understand why."

"Those who presently call themselves vampires?" echoed his advocate. "That's an… interesting distinction. Are you willing to explain it?"

"To whom?" There was a rushing in Weyland's head and his chains were suddenly much heavier.

His advocate went to the door to summon help, then came back to the bedside. He stood watching Weyland for several seconds, and then, making up his mind, said, "Not that it will mean anything to you, Professor: for the present I answer to Saint-Germain."

It was nearing twelve, the busiest time of the night; Frederick Samson made a last careful adjustment of the discreet ruffles at his wrists before riding up four floors to the Magistrates' level. He carried a tooled leather case that contained all his files on Weyland as well as the additional material Saint-Germain had supplied. At the door of the Presidential Suite he stopped to permit a clerk to search his case and his jacket before being admitted to the chambers of Isodora Ruthven.

Near the window where the damask draperies were drawn open to the night was a tall stand, and on it a vase filled with white spider mums. The panelled walls glowed in the lantern light, though her desk—a high-fronted Victorian rolltop—was caught in the beam of two electric bulbs. As Samson looked around him, a door in the far wall swung wide and Isodora Ruthven stepped into the room.

Samson offered her a sociable bow before kissing her hand. "I'm—"

"Inspector Frederick Samson," said the Magistrate.

"Uh… yes." He felt the need to recover the initiative he had lost with her. "I realise you receive many petitions; this isn't one. I wouldn't have asked to see you unless I thought there was good reason to speak to you before the hearing of Professor Weyland's case begins."

She went to her desk, turning her chair around to face him before sinking into it. "Anything else would be a waste of time," she said cordially but with a clear warning in her tone.

"Exactly," said Samson, determined to gain her support. "I don't want to waste any time. That's why I thought it would be best to discuss the investigation with you." He indicated the case he carried. "There's a great deal of information in here."

"Condense it for me," said Magistrate Ruthven.

This was precisely what Samson wanted to hear. "I'll try," he said, and launched into his prepared discourse. "You know it started with these remainders. You've seen them in the Grand Ballroom. No one knows what to do about them. We've never had a vampire prey on vampires before, and we've never had to deal with the consequences."

Magistrate Ruthven toyed with the onyx inkwell on her desk. "One consequence," she observed coolly, "is a certain pruning back of our own numbers. There are some of us who feel that in the exuberance of our initial takeover, far too many human beings were carelessly added to our ranks. This Renegade has taken his prey largely from among newer vampires and older solitaries who have small tolerance even for our social system. There is something to be said for this. But it is not the sort of thing we would like to see continued; it sets a bad example. I think we will know what to do with your monster, Inspector."

"But you don't understand," said Samson, unable to control his agitation. "No other vampire has done what Weyland does."

"I'm aware of that. What's your point?" she inquired.

"We need to know why. It isn't enough just to execute him, Your Honour; we need to know why he can do what the rest of us apparently cannot." He said it in a rush, his enthusiasm undenied.

Magistrate Ruthven leaned back and looked at him, her body relaxed but her eyes snapping. "What makes you think we will find out?"

Samson was prepared to answer that. "I was a biochemist before I became a vampire. I worked for ten years on analysing the genetic makeup of variant forms of the same species of mammals. Politics and money made it impossible for me to go on then. I was gifted; that wasn't enough. But I know what someone like Weyland represents." He set down the case and walked toward her. "I know I'm rushing too fast. You may not be able to help me. But I want you to know that we could learn a tremendous amount from Weyland if we were given the chance."

Isodora Ruthven regarded him steadily. Then in a single fluid movement she rose from her chair. "You're suggesting that Weyland might be willing to enter into some sort of bargain with us?"

"It isn't impossible," said Samson carefully.

"Why should he?" She was standing by the vase with the mums, her pale hair as pretty as the flowers.

"Because he doesn't want to die," said Samson.

"Are you sure of that?" She lifted her head. "Why consult him at all? Why not make the terms of his condemnation be that he is placed in the hands of those prepared to do research?" Her smile was sensual and attractive so long as you did not look at her eyes. "There is no reason to negotiate with him when we can—"

Although this was what Samson wanted most, he could not conceal his shock. "How can you do that?"

She pulled a single mum from the vase. "Because I'm a Magistrate, Inspector, and the law is what I say it is."

*

At Saint-Germain's insistence a table had been brought into the cell. Like Weyland's iron bed, it was bolted to the floor, and the two chairs with it were lightweight moulded plastic, unable to inflict much damage if hefted or thrown.

"Here's the report on the remainders," he said, handing the pages to Weyland. "They'll be asking you about each of them. It might be helpful if you take the time to learn a few of the names, at least. The Magistrates are prepared to listen to your side if you don't fly in their faces."

Weyland spread the papers on the bed and scanned them. He glanced up at Saint-Germain. "Of course you realise that in the eyes of these people—your own kind, I assume—I have no justifiable 'side' to present."

"That might be our strategy," Saint-Germain said, his manner cool. As he shifted in the uncomfortable plastic chair he went on, "You may have contempt for those of us who were born as human as the rest of them and were changed later, but if there is any hope for you at all, it is at the undead hands of those you despise." He gestured toward the pages Weyland held. "I include those... remainders as well as the rest of us."

"I am relieved," Weyland responded. "You do seem to glimpse the gulf that yawns between myself and all of you; and by 'you' I mean both human beings and so-called vampires, since to me you are all the same. No, not quite the same—" His eyes narrowed, and he drew himself up with the air of one who had come to a conclusion. "Let me answer your original question. Then tell me about 'our' strategy, if you can. You ask why I attack vampires, by which you mean your kind. I assure you they are not my first choice, but since all of you have divided up the available ordinary population into herds, or protected allies, or fugitives too wary to tolerate my approach, nothing remains accessible to me but your kind, and I take you when opportunity offers, which is when you sleep. And that is because I am not of your kind, except in hunter's mimicry. I walk in sun or moonlight as I choose.

"Unfortunately the blood in your veins is, if you will pardon me a crude expression, only secondhand. It nourishes poorly. I need to drink more from your kind than from the common run of humans. You are easy prey, and at the moment the only regularly available prey, but believe me, you are not very satisfying food.

"And," he added, with a hard glance in which a flame of restrained rage burned, "because I loathe the whole squabbling lot of you, I am not particularly grieved to see you suffer as a consequence of my requirements."

Saint-Germain kept still for many seconds. "Well," he said quietly, "at least you are candid." He held out his hands for the papers. "I would say be grateful, but you cannot be grateful; I would say be reasonable, but you know no reason; and so I will say be prudent. Surely even you can appreciate prudence, and do not show your contempt to anyone but me, for that alone will condemn you."

"I see," said Weyland acidly, "that you take my point. And I trust that you do not hold yourself so high above your fellows as to imagine that no one else will. What makes you think, little man, that you can help me in any way?" He studied Saint-Germain with chilly speculation. "What makes you want to?"

Saint-Germain hesitated, then rose and bowed. "I doubt I could explain it to you. Were I like you, I would leave you to the wolves."

When the third day of the hearing concluded, both Weyland and Saint-Germain were irritated and tired. They emerged from the Florentine Room on the mezzanine to find a group of Fundamentalists waiting, all of them carrying the tall inverted black crucifixes that were the mark of their sect. The escort of Watchmen closed ranks in wedge-formation, but the fanatics pressed them hard, struggling to get through and touch him who had become the focus of their ardent attention.

"Free him!" shrieked a woman in blood red robes, "free the Annunciator of the Antichrist!"

"Give him to us, we are his people!" cried another, but this call was drowned out by a bellow from a large man with a shaven head.

"He *is* the Antichrist!" roared this individual, and at once two of his followers fell to struggling with the red-robes. "Free the Antichrist, he has come to lead us!"

"Keep them back, can't you?" Weyland snarled. "They'll be clipping bits of my ears off for talismans if you let them."

"Hurry up," panted one of the Watchmen, "there's more of them today."

"More every day," Weyland snapped. "If this is a sample of the public order you hope to create, Saint-Germain, I think I'd be better off dead. So don't worry yourself over the way things are going in that circus in there. I told you you'd be useless."

"In that case, would you prefer I leave?" His voice was even, his expression no more revealing than if he had been discussing the vandalism at the nearest school, but his purpose burned in his dark eyes.

Weyland shot him a cold look. "Ask me again in the solitude, such as it is, of my cell."

"If you like," said Saint-Germain, and turned as Inspector Samson hurried up to him. "Is anything the matter?"

"No." But he was clearly upset. "Just get him to the nearest elevator, and you come with me."

Saint-Germain's brows went up, but he said nothing. Instead he let the nearest Watchman take Weyland's arm and moved behind him. "All right," said Saint-Germain, deliberately standing so that few of the Fundamentalists could see their hero being hustled into the elevator surrounded by Watchmen. He met Samson's eyes. "What do you want to say to me?"

"I need to discuss something with you," said Samson with an uneasy look around the lobby.

"My suite, perhaps?" Saint-Germain suggested with a faint, sardonic smile.

"Yes, yes," said Samson. "In half an hour? Three o'clock?"

Saint-Germain shrugged. "If it is convenient." He looked toward the elevator in time to see the doors close on Weyland and the Watchmen.

*

As Saint-Germain came into the holding cell, he stopped, his shadow impinging on the early light. "I've had an offer," he said to Weyland.

"To sell me to those lunatics to be chopped into relics?" Weyland said bitterly.

"Nothing so extreme," said Saint-Germain, though his brow was creased with uncertainty. "No. What we have here is an offer to guarantee that you will be given into the keeping of Inspector Samson. He will be your jailer and he will conduct a series of experiments to determine how it is that you are so different. At least," he went on with a faint look of consternation, "that is what he claims."

Weyland's expression froze and his pale eyes widened.

"Oh, you child," he whispered. "You babe, you *human!* You have no idea what you are telling me, have you? No idea at all. And I have a certainty. First you brought this stupid, futile light of hope, damn you to Hell, I let you bring it. And now you bring the extinction of that light, and you only glimpse what it means, don't you? Go away, leave me alone, I don't want to look at you."

Saint-Germain put a single sheet of paper on the table. "I don't recall telling you I recommend accepting the offer," he said gently.

Slowly Weyland's shoulders loosened and his eyes grew shuttered and thoughtful. "Well, well," he murmured after a moment. "You are not so naive as I assumed. I think I have misjudged you. But don't you misjudge me. I would rather sit here in my damned chains and wait for destruction in full dark than spend my last days straining after phantom gleams of salvation like some witless fool. I would rather run my head against this wall until the bone cracks and leaks my life out than prance like a goat to disguised slaughter, all decked in garlands of either black roses or electrodes and monitor cables. Do you understand me? Is there the least possibility that you understand a tenth of what I say to you?"

"I think I can manage that," said Saint-Germain. He picked up the paper and returned it to his case. "Shall I refuse this out of hand, or would you prefer the door be kept open?"

Weyland smiled a slow, thin smile. "Refuse," he said, "of course. If they want me on their dissecting table, make them win me, fair and square."

On the eighth night, Fundamentalists testified fervently to the miracles they had seen since Weyland's activities had first been noticed in the city, and to the visions they had had of him. They swore they had seen him in solemn conversation with demons or new-raised spirits of the dead, transforming water into blood for hungry worshippers, and preaching his vision—described in voluminous and impassioned detail—of the New Order to come with the arrival of the Antichrist.

Saint-Germain patiently and persistently requested corroborating details, evidence, sometimes bare coherence. Weyland answered tersely the questions put directly to him, most of which required little but a simple no. It was a lurid session concluding when a group of Fundamentalists, those who called themselves Crux Tenebre, took over the hearing room and spent the last hour before dawn singing hymns to Weyland, imploring him to herald the coming of the Antichrist and to select one of them to despatch him as the sacrifice that would bring about that magnificent event.

At last Weyland rose in the dock and announced, "Unless you want to have to drag me in here tomorrow and try to obtain my cooperation by main force, you will keep these creatures out." He was escorted from the hearing room, his Watchmen guards hanging onto him like puppies.

The chief bailiff posted an order blocking the Crux members from the hearing until the verdict of the Magistrates was announced.

"That means nothing," declared Sister Marie LeMatte who stationed herself at the main entrance to the Magistrates' Center. "We will be here to revere the holy Weyland until he is hailed in Hell as the voice of salvation."

The chief bailiff heard her out, then assigned twice the number of Watchmen to the Cruxers as he had before.

Saint-Germain watched all this with apparent disinterest. "All they're doing is confusing the situation," he said to Samson as they approached the elevator. "They are like children who are enthralled by the latest fad, but dangerous children for all that."

Samson stared after the departing Cruxers with anxious eyes. "What if they break into Weyland's cell? They've said they want to bring him out, to offer him to his flock."

"Oh, yes," said Saint-Germain, his laughter short and irritated. "They would be delighted to venerate him... to pieces. And sell those pieces as holy relics." He was almost through the lobby when he stopped, his attention taken by figures across the street.

"What is it?" Samson asked.

Saint-Germain regarded the distant gathering, then, "Who are they?"

Samson followed his gaze and swore under his breath. "Damnit. We haven't been allowing any of them into the hearings, but they hang around outside every day. They're common men of the city, not undead; rebels and malcontents I think, though I can't prove anything. There's turmoil among our humans over all this. Weyland frightens them, but the really vengeful ones would like to see him free to go on doing what they want to do themselves—kill vampires. They even regard him as some sort of hero, like a lethal but useful god out of ancient myths."

"How do you deal with them?" Saint-Germain did not shift his gaze from the distant humans.

"I just try to keep them clear," Samson said. "I have my hands full with Cybertooths and Cruxers, and with these rebels besides—I don't want riots here." He motioned to some of his Watchmen to disperse the humans.

"No." Saint-Germain raised his hand to halt the half-dozen officers moving toward the revolving glass door. "Leave them alone. Our situation is too volatile already."

Samson stepped in front of him, and nodded to the Watchmen signalling them to carry out his orders. He said to Saint-Germain, "Pardon me, but this is my job."

"And my job—which you requested I do—is to protect Weyland." He saw that the officers were milling about near the door. "Let me have half an hour with them. As part of my job." With that, he moved past Samson and went directly out of the Magistrates' Center toward the shadowy humans.

They had lengthened Weyland's chains so that he could at least pace his cell. He paced, listening to the silence of the building around him and tasting the panic that periodically choked him. He paced to keep at bay the dark dizziness that still overwhelmed him without warning. He paced between boredom and the terrors of his own imagination and told himself he did it to keep his body strong, his sinews supple.

When the crisp footstep sounded in the hall, he turned almost eagerly. "You!" he said. "But it's daylight; the sun has been up for hours."

Saint-Germain, preoccupied and tired looking, let himself into the cell without more answer than "Indeed."

"I see no one here after sunrise but ordinary men," Weyland added tensely. "You're not like these Beaux, exactly, are you?"

"No," was the curt answer. He went to sit in one of the plastic chairs. "I've been outside, among the humans. Do you know that many of them sympathise with you?"

"Oh, them," said Weyland with exasperation. "They drop notes in through the ventilation grill, you'll find some in among the reports you brought me to study. It's all romantic nonsense, of course; or bait to draw me into a pretended escape in the course of which I could conveniently be killed."

"Nonsense or not, they have tried to contact you," Saint-Germain pointed out. "They want something from you."

"Everyone wants something from me," Weyland said. "But this lot is useless, they won't do anything. They're too frightened of all you undead, not to mention their terror of me—imagine, a vampire who hunts whomever he hunts in daylight! There can't be many of them who actually want me set free, outside of their own fantasies of power and revenge."

"Those few will be heard; not that their testimony will alter the final disposition, since vampires will judge you, and most of them think you are worse than a murderer. They want the Magistrates to order your death." His face was pale as he said this, and he looked down at the tabletop, ashamed.

Weyland studied him a moment. He returned to his bed and sat down, sifting a coil of chain between his hands. "Don't you?" he said in a conversational tone. "I half want it myself sometimes. My God, I never thought to hear myself say that! Are you listening? This is a historic moment for me. I am tired of this. I am tired to death of all of this, this place, these hearings, all of them—and you too, Saint-Germain. I am tired of not understanding you. I should have thrown myself into the claws of your saint-hungry friends out there last night. But you would like to prevent that, you want some other outcome that I can't even imagine. They want me dead. You don't. Will you tell me why?"

Saint-Germain sat quietly, paying no heed to the sudden attention Weyland riveted on him. "We cannot afford your caprice. Like it or not, we all must come to terms with one another, we must learn what it is to be civilised, to tolerate each other." He turned abruptly, catching Weyland with his compelling gaze. "You, and anyone like you, will be how we determine if we are hunting animals or creatures with… souls."

Weyland leaned his head back against the wall. "I am to be your lesson, then? Your example? Of the hunting animal you hope to transcend, surely. But what gives you the right to build your damned civilisation on my back, what gives you any rights regarding me at all?" He laughed and held up his fettered wrists which showed dark bruises where the steel had rubbed his skin. "An academic question, you understand. These give you the right, don't they?"

"No," said Saint-Germain wearily. "If anything, they support your view, I suspect." He was staring at the far side of the room now, but what he saw was far distant from that improvised cell. "Not that humanity offers any model much better than our own. But there have been times when there was compassion, and that is a start."

Weyland leaned forward intently. "How old are you? A hundred years? Six hundred? A thousand? I think I am thousands of years older than anything remotely akin to me on this planet. Don't talk to me about time. I am senior to you, I am your elder."

"You are what I was," said Saint-Germain, "more than four thousand years ago. But I have changed."

Demon Star sauntered through the lobby, serenely ignoring the stares of those who had just heard her testify before the five Magistrates. She had marked the occasion by painting a bloody heart on her cheeks and silvering the white spikes of her hair. Behind her the rest of her Cybertooths flocked, basking in her reflected glory.

Inspector Frederick Samson had waited for this moment. He had listened impatiently to her in the hearing room. He had to speak with her, to gain her support. Since he had so unexpectedly been given the approval of Magistrate Isodora Ruthven in the Weyland matter, he had developed a number of plans, and new information indicated that he had better act quickly on one that included the Cybertooths. He went after Demon Star, not too quickly, but fast enough to intercept her before she and her pack reached the door. "I have to speak with you, my lady," he said, having decided that Miss Demon Star sounded ridiculous even to his Beau ears.

Demon Star halted and raked her eyes over Samson. "The inspector. What do you want?" She held out her hand so he had to kiss it or be inexcusably rude; it was the hand with the riding crop.

"We need to talk," said Samson when he had—reluctantly—kissed her hand. "It's urgent, and it's in both our interests. If you don't speak with me, we may both be disappointed."

She cocked her head, looking more like an alien artifact than ever. "How do you mean, disappointed?" She made a sign to her followers and they drew back, huddled together and surrounded by those who had already left the hearing room.

"It might be best to go to my office," he suggested. "Not so many distractions."

"Beaux like you, in your elegant rigs, you mean, or those Cruxers?" Her laughter was loud and cutting, making itself heard throughout the lobby.

"I mean everything," Samson said through clenched teeth as he tried to remain polite. "Won't you come with me? It would be best if you do."

Demon Star contemplated the ceiling where the gilded scenes of frolicking gods were faded and watermarked. "I don't have anything to say I didn't tell the Magistrates, and you don't need to hear any more so-called testimony from anybody else, either. How long are you planning to drag this out, anyway? The Renegade was in our territory. He made remainders of some of my pack, he got some of our cattle. That's all there is to it. You turn him over to us. We'll handle him. We've got the right."

Samson grabbed her arm. "*Not here!*" he hissed.

She shrugged and strolled into the elevator ahead of him, carelessly signalling her pack to stay and await her return.

In Samson's office she took the one comfortable chair and adopted a pose of exaggerated patience while he moved nervously about the room moving papers and files from one place to another.

Finally he said, "I hear rumours. My Watchmen tell me that your gang and the Cruxers are talking together, about this animal Weyland. If this is true—"

"Sure it's true," Demon Star said lazily. "I'm gonna give them some style. Anybody with a pinch of guts could get off on being the leader of a cult, for as long as it was fun, anyhow."

"Don't do it" Samson said, facing her.

"Just like a cop—always telling everybody what kinds of fun they can have and what kinds they can't," she jeered.

"Don't get that rabble together to break in here and take him," Samson said. "You might be able to do it, all together you just might, I give you that, and then—you don't understand what's at risk here."

"Oh no," she drawled, "'course I don't. Nobody like me could ever understand anything so complicated, right? It's stamped all over your superior face, Inspector. You damn Beaux think you understand the whole damn world, which is why you're the ones who should hand out justice to everybody else."

"Listen!" he said. "I'm not talking about justice. I'm talking about walking around in daylight, so you never have to worry about anything like Weyland again, and you never have to go to sleep looking over your shoulder in case some stray human is sneaking up to slice your head off while you're helpless—"

"Cut to the suck," she said with sudden steel. "You're up to something. What?"

He hesitated, licking his dry lips and trying to decide how much to tell her. He circled behind his desk and sat down there, fortifying himself against her scorn. "All right. All right. I want to find out what it is in his makeup that allows him the same freedom as human beings. If I can work on him for a while, I can find answers that all of us can benefit from—but not all at once, do you see my meaning?" He leaned confidentially nearer and lowered his voice. "And if you wanted to be present, to be part of the proceedings, to learn for yourself what there is to be discovered in him, that could be arranged. But outside observation would be strictly limited."

"By you," she said, tapping the crop idly against her booted leg. "As the Renegade's keeper, is that what you're hoping for? Crap, Inspector. You Beaux stick together, you've got it all fixed up already. We all know that."

"Then you're wrong," Samson said forcefully, changing his tactics. "Would I talk to you about this if I didn't need your help? Which would you rather have, broken relics to string around your neck for decoration, or the secret of Weyland's strength and sunlight-tolerance?"

"What good would his secrets do for the rest of us?" she challenged.

He saw that he had her, or almost, and he relaxed slightly and glanced out of his window at the new-risen moon. "We have a little time till dawn," he said. "Let me tell you something about being a genius at science in a time when science was starving its young to death."

At least, Weyland thought, pacing, they were not starving him to death. Not yet. What they were doing filled him with despair and baffled rage, and in the daylight hours not spent in sleep to match the normal vampiric schedule now forced on him, he chewed this rage.

That there should be such a thing as a "normal" vampire had infuriated him from the start. Now the complexities of a world crowded with competitors had defeated him, and the defeat was bitter. He did not remember his previous lives, but he knew that each had ended in the small defeat of the long sleep. This ending now had the feel of something final, and not at the hands of some impersonal natural force or even a human being stumbling on his lair, but because of these swarms of undead in whose existence he had never even believed.

Only the daylight hours brought relief from the murmurings and howlings of his self-styled worshippers outside the high, barred vent to his cell. They sang and danced up there. They chanted prayers to raise him bodily into their hands, and they told him just how they would convert him into the centrepiece of the new religion, at least until the ritual of his death brought the One True Evil Presence palpably into the world.

He leaned his cheek against the cool cement wall and thought about death. Death at the hands of one mob or another, death under the knife of that eager-eyed inspector, death in some neatly "legal" form that would satisfy the more fastidious Beaux—he sweated and trembled, thinking of it, and somewhere in his thoughts the black surge of dizziness stirred threateningly. This new occupant of his mind was a lingering effect of that nightmarish moment of attack, when his had been the throat bared, his the wrenching terror as his own blood was drawn.

Perhaps they had contaminated him with some foulness of their own in that frightful moment. Perhaps even if he survived this mad trial, he was no longer fit to survive in their world.

In his thoughts, Death smiled. It had pursued him through lifetimes, and he, in a way, had pursued it.

What was it, after all? These undead didn't know that, not even this cool little man Saint-Germain; which was just as well since what he did know and deigned to try to communicate was curiously opaque and obscure.

Still, Weyland had come to enjoy their sparring matches, which were at least a diversion from the dreary night hours of the hearings and the empty ones of daylight. And Saint-Germain had a neat, well-cared-for look about him that Weyland approved of, however grudgingly. He knew himself at this point to be a rather shaggy, grimy figure, but found he no longer cared. Let this Saint-Germain keep up the sartorial standards.

Weyland found him puzzling. He was clearly trying to accomplish something that he felt to be of importance, with a minimum of the showy fuss that seemed so dear to these undead.

And here he was again, perhaps for the last time. Even the Magistrates were showing impatience with the process lately. Some sort of summation was in the offing, and then—a decision.

Weyland smoothed his hair back with his hands and composed himself for what he thought might be his last interview with Saint-Germain.

"They want to end the hearing tonight," he told Weyland as he came into the cell. He was dressed with more elegance than before, though in the same restrained un-Beauish style. Instead of the usual sheaf of papers, he now carried a small leather case embossed with a heraldic eclipse. "The Magistrates sent me word just after sundown."

"So this is my last chance to dazzle them with my virtue and brilliance?" Weyland raised a sarcastic eyebrow. "Or rather with yours, my advocate."

Saint-Germain dismissed his remarks with a shake of his head. "The Magistrates have announced they'll make a decision by sunrise. My summation will be tonight. I thought you'd like to know." He did not take a seat and his dark eyes seemed tired. "Is there anything you want?"

Weyland bit back the retort that sprang to his lips—there was, after all, quite a list of things he wanted—and concentrated on stilling the shaking of his hands. He looked Saint-Germain in the eye.

"Whatever you've been trying to do," he said slowly, "I have seen that your intention was clean and your execution, if I may be allowed the term, competent. Whatever happens, that must merit recognition." He shrugged. "Of course, there is no desirable outcome for me, so it's a good thing you have acted for your own aims all along. Mine were lost from the moment I woke in this Hellish version of the world. I will remember you, while I can."

Saint-Germain left without speaking.

Two of the large adjoining meeting rooms had been opened up to give more space in the Florentine Room to those who wanted to see the climax of the hearing. On one side, Demon Star and her pack gathered with other Cybertooths, all as touchy as cats. Across the room the Crux Tenebre cult sat among the many Fundamentalists, some of them singing, some praying, a few seemingly transfixed by visions. In the wedge between them, Beaux in their finery preened and waited for the final statements to begin. There were no humans present except the Watchmen who circulated through the aisles, determined and jittery.

Inspector Samson followed the five Magistrates toward the high-fronted desks that had been set up at the front of the room. He managed to exchange a single, speaking glance with Magistrate Ruthven before taking his place beside the bailiff.

Finally, when the crowd had been called to order, after a frenzied plea from the Cruxers and a sullen demand from the Cybertooths, Samson rose to speak. "All during these hearings, it has been my position that we are here to serve justice. Our justice must embrace the good of all the community if it is to have any meaning at all. We have been asked to free Edward Weyland, we have been asked to destroy Edward Weyland, we have even been asked to venerate him. But I have maintained that our cause can best be served if we *understand* Edward Weyland, and learn what it is about him that renders him so unlike the rest of us. I have submitted my proposals to you, Your Honours, and I ask that you consider them before you condemn him to any form of execution for his crimes."

He sat down, flushed with the excitement of the moment and heartened by the faint, approving nod from Magistrate Ruthven. With her help, he had a chance at last to prove his talents and his theories with discoveries that could change the nature and destiny of the entire vampire community.

For the moment, however, the hearing room was filled with whistles and catcalls and prayers in response to his remarks, and it took some little time for the Watchmen to restore quiet.

"Saint-Germain?" said the oldest Magistrate, a tall, cadaverous Beau with eyes like hot coals.

Saint-Germain did not rise at once. When he did, he came directly toward the Magistrates, locking eyes with each of them in turn. "Do you remember what it was like?" he asked, his voice low. "Do you remember how you had to live when we were few and people were many? Do you remember being called a monster and watching those of your blood die for being monsters? Do you remember?" He paused, watching them closely. "Do you remember having to hunt? Do you remember being a killer? Your Honour?" He addressed the oldest Magistrate.

The old man nodded. "I remember."

"Yes." Saint-Germain did not speak at once. "We all do. And that is what we are making of Edward Weyland. Everything we dreaded in humans we are now if we treat this vampire as we were treated." For the first time he turned away from the Magistrates and approached Weyland; his dark eyes were intent. "One of those... remainders is of my blood. She was a nurse, and she came to my life in eighteen-fifty-seven. You ended that for her, more surely than if you had cut her in pieces, and for that I loathe you, and will loathe you for all time."

Weyland, until now, a listless observer of the proceedings, started and seemed about to speak. But he sat back again in impassive silence.

Saint-Germain moved forward, forcing himself to address the Magistrates; he did not want to see Weyland's face now. "If it were only my need, I would roast him in hot coals. But that is him speaking in me, the beast we are, the thing that makes people call us creatures of death."

He looked around the crowded rooms. "But we do not kill. We instill life. Where death comes, we can banish it. Only those who see death as ultimately binding think us malign, and destroy us because of our life. If we accept the bond of blood, we accept the ties of life as well, and we revere it as no mortal human can. And it is for that reason," he went on, moving back toward Weyland once more, "for our cherished life that I ask you to treat this… this monster as the ghost of what we have been, that you do not condemn him to execution, either at the hands of his rivals"—he nodded toward the Cybertooths—"or his predators; that you free yourselves in freeing him." He swung his arm around, his small hand levelled at the Magistrates in order, binding them together invisibly. Only Magistrate Ruthven resisted his compelling gaze.

"Weyland cannot be forgiven, for what he has done is unforgivable. But we can, in mercy, pardon him. Find him a preserve where he can hunt or sleep, as he wishes. But do not give him up to death." The room had grown very still. "What are we: creatures of death or of life?" In the hush, he left the Florentine Room.

The moon had set, but the crowd remained. They milled and prowled around the walls of the Magistrates' Center, forming eddies of tense conversation and whorls of excited argument.

In his office Samson looked down at them, chewing his knuckles. If he had lost in the hearing room he had lost all, and his thoughts took him darkly down among the mob where he could lose himself, his office, and his failure if he must.

The basement cell was quiet. Weyland sat on the bed. He had not spoken for some time. At last, stretching his long legs out in front of him, he said, "Your story about the nurse; was it true?"

From his place by the door, Saint-Germain said, "Yes."

Weyland nodded, his dark-hollowed eyes steady on Saint-Germain. "Ah," he said. "Loyalty. I am familiar with the concept, though I don't see the point of making a fetish of it. But you humans do love to define some higher moral ground for yourselves and then twist yourselves and everyone else into knots trying to take that ground and hold it. I am not like you, I told you that at the start; my aspirations are not so high."

Saint-Germain looked out through the bars of the door. "Is that how it seems to you?" He did not expect an answer.

Weyland looked down at his fetters. "It will feel good to be free of these chains." He added in a distant tone, "How do you think they will decide."

After a moment Saint-Germain said, "I don't know."

LET THE OLD DREAMS DIE

John Ajvide Lindqvist

(For Mia. Still)

I WANT to tell you a story about a great love.
Unfortunately the story isn't about me, but I am part of it, and now
it's all over I want to bear witness for Stefan and Karin.

Bear witness. That sounds a bit grand, I know. Perhaps I am creating
exaggerated expectations about a story that is not in any way sensational, but
miracles are so few and far between in this world that you have to do your
best to make the most of them when they do appear.

I regard the love between Stefan and Karin as a miracle, and it is to this
miracle that I want to bear witness. You can call it an everyday miracle or a
conventional one, I don't care. Through getting to know them I was privi-
leged to be part of something that goes beyond our earthbound constraints.
Which makes it a miracle. That's all.

First of all, a little about me. Have patience.

I am part of the original population of Blackeberg. The cement was still
drying when my parents and I moved to Sigrid Undsets gata in 1951. I was
seven years old at the time, and all I really remember is that we had to trudge
all the way down to Islandstorget to catch the tram if we wanted to go into
town. The subway came the following year. I followed the building of the
station's ticket hall, designed by none other than Peter Celsing, which is still
a source of pride for many of us old Blackeberg residents.

I mention this because I actually spent a considerable portion of my life in this very station. In 1969 I began work as a ticket collector, and I stayed there until I retired two years ago. So apart from odd periods spent filling in for colleagues who were off sick from other stations along the green line, I have spent thirty-nine years of my working life inside Celsing's creation.

There are plenty of stories I could tell, and it's not that I haven't thought about doing so. I enjoy writing, and a modest little autobiography of a ticket collector might well find an audience. But this is not the appropriate forum. I just wanted to tell you a little bit about myself, so that you know who's telling the story. The anecdotes can wait.

I've heard it said that I am a person who lacks ambition. In a way this is true, if by "ambition" you mean a desire to climb the career ladder or the staircase of status or whatever you want to call it. But ambition can be so many things. My ambition, for example, has been to live a quiet, dignified life, and I believe I have succeeded.

I would probably have fitted in much better in Athens about two thousand five hundred years ago. I would have made an excellent Stoic, and much of the attitude to life I have been able to understand from the writings of Plato fits me like a glove. Perhaps I would have been regarded as a wise man in those days. Nowadays I tend to be regarded as a bore. That's life, as Vonnegut says.

I have dedicated my life to selling and punching tickets, and to reading. There's plenty of time to read when you work in the ticket office, particularly when you work nights as I have often done. Dostoevsky and Beckett are probably my favourites because both of them, although in very different ways, attempt to reach a point of—

Sorry, there I go again. "Stillness", I was going to say, but this is not the place to expand on my literary preferences. Enough about me, and over to Stefan and Karin.

*

Oh, but there must be just one more little diversion. Perhaps after all I was a little too ambitious in the conventional sense when I said I'd like to write my autobiography. I seem to find it difficult to organise my material. Oh well. You'll just have to put up with it, because I need to say a few words about Oskar Eriksson.

I don't know if you remember the case, but it attracted a great deal of attention and an enormous amount was written about it at the time, particularly out here to the west of the city. It's twenty-eight years ago now, and thank goodness nothing so tragic and violent has happened in Blackeberg since then.

A lunatic in the guise of a vampire killed three children in the old swimming baths—which is now a pre-school—and then abducted this Oskar Eriksson. The newspapers wallowed in what had happened for weeks and weeks, and many of those who were around at the time can barely hear the word "Blackeberg" without thinking of vampires and mass murder. What do you think of when I say "Sjöbo"? Integration and tolerance? No, I thought not. Places acquire a stigma, which then sits there like a nail stuck in your foot for years on end.

A lunatic in the guise of a vampire, I wrote, because I wanted to remind you of the image that was prevalent. However, I have had good reason to revise the account of what took place, but we'll get to that eventually.

What does this have to do with Stefan and Karin?

Well, the reason they moved to Blackeberg was that Karin was a police officer, and one of those responsible for the investigation into what was known as "the Swimming Pool Massacre in Blackeberg". To be more specific, she was actually involved in the section working on Oskar Eriksson's disappearance. Her enquiries meant that she spent a great deal of time in Blackeberg and she became very fond of the place, in spite of everything.

When she and her husband Stefan were looking for somewhere new to live a couple of years after the investigation had been put on the back burner, they came to Blackeberg, and so it was that they ended up moving into an apartment two doors down from me on Holbergsgatan in June 1987.

Under normal circumstances people come and go in the apartment blocks near me without my taking any notice at all. Even though I've lived here a long time, I'm not one of those who keeps an eye on things. But that summer I spent a lot of time on my balcony—I was ploughing through Proust's *In Search of Lost Time*—and I noticed the new arrivals for one very simple reason: they held hands with each other.

I estimated that the man was about my own age, and the woman a few years older—so well past the stage where most couples abandon that kind of physical closeness in public. There are exceptions, of course, but these days it seems as if not even young people bother holding hands any longer, at least not if they're over the age of ten.

But as soon as this middle-aged couple set foot outside the door they took each other by the hand, as if it were the most natural thing in the world. Sometimes of course they were alone, and they didn't always hold hands when they were walking together, but almost always. It made me feel happy, somehow, and I caught myself looking up from my book as soon as I heard their door open.

Perhaps it's a drawback of my profession, but I am in the habit of studying people, trying to guess who they are and putting two and two together from the various occasions on which I have the opportunity to observe them from my ticket booth.

Since the couple spent a great deal of time on their ground floor balcony that summer, I had plenty of chances to gather facts in order to draw my conclusions.

They often read aloud to one another, a virtually obsolete form of entertainment. The distance prevented me from hearing what they were reading, and I had to stop myself from fetching my binoculars when they left a book on the table. There is a difference between observation and spying. When a pair of binoculars enters the picture, that line has been crossed. So no binoculars.

They drank a fair amount of red wine, and they both smoked. One of them would roll a cigarette while the other was reading. Sometimes they stayed up quite late with a cassette player on the table between them. From what I could hear, they played mainly popular old songs. Siw Malmquist, Östen Warnerbring, Gunnar Wiklund. That kind of thing. And Abba. Lots of Abba.

Occasionally they would dance together for a little while in the limited space available, but when that happened I would look away and busy myself with my own affairs, because it felt as if that was *private* in a way I can't really explain.

OK. Let me tell you what conclusions I drew before I got to know them. I thought the man worked in some kind of service industry, and the woman was a librarian. I decided they had met at a mature age, and this was their first apartment together. I felt they had both had their own dreams, but now those dreams had been put on ice so that they could invest their energy in their relationship, their love.

Not bad, as you will see.

I was completely wrong on just one point, as you already know. The woman was a police officer, not a librarian. If someone had asked me to describe my idea of a female police officer, I would probably have said something about short black hair, prominent cheekbones and sinewy muscles. Karin didn't look like that. She had thick, fair hair that hung right down her back; she was comparatively short and very pretty in an appealing way, with lots of laughter lines. Just the kind of person you would happily ask for advice about which book to read next, in fact.

You could ask Karin that question, of course, but if she were really to be on home ground you would have to ask her about the development of scar tissue, the psychology of murderers and the density of ammunition in handguns. Her area of particular expertise was interrogating witnesses and the verbal collection of information, but she was also well versed in ballistics and blood-spatter analysis. "Although that's mainly just as a hobby," as she once explained.

I found out what Stefan did for a living at the same time as our embryonic friendship began.

After the Proust I turned to a biography of Edvard Munch. I had just finished it when my holiday started at the end of July, and I decided to take a trip to Oslo to visit the Munch museum. That's one of the advantages of being alone. You get an idea, and the very next day you can put it into practice.

I took the morning train so as to arrive in the afternoon, and when the ticket collector came along, who should I see decked out in his cap and full uniform but my new neighbour? So we had more or less the same profession. A profession that definitely counts as part of a *service industry*, wouldn't you say?

As I held out my ticket he frowned and looked at me as if he were searching for something. I helped him out.

"We're neighbours," I said. "And I'm on the ticket barrier at the station. In Blackeberg."

"That's it," he said, punching my ticket. "Thanks for telling me. I'd have been wondering all day otherwise."

There was a brief silence. I felt as if I wanted to say something more, but I couldn't come up with anything that wouldn't seem intrusive. I could hardly ask what books they read, or which was his favourite Abba track. He came to my rescue with the only neutral fact available at the time.

"So," he said. "You're off to Oslo?"

"Yes. I thought I'd go and have a look round the Munch museum. I've never been."

He nodded to himself, and I wondered if I should have specified *Edvard*. Perhaps he had no interest in art. So it came as a bit of surprise when he asked, "*The Kiss*. Have you seen that one?"

"Yes. But not the real thing."

"That's in the museum."

He looked as if he were about to say something else, but the passenger in front of me was waving his ticket. The man I would later come to know as Stefan clicked his hole punch a couple of times in the air and said, "It's a wonderful museum. Enjoy yourself," then carried on with his rounds.

When I visited the museum the following day I couldn't avoid paying particular attention to *The Kiss*, especially as it was already one of my favourites. As I have already said I have a tendency to speculate, and it was impossible not to interpret the painting in the light of what I thought I knew about my hand-holding neighbours.

It's more a matter of two bodies *melting together*, rather than a kiss. On the one hand the painting depicts the kiss above all other kisses, the union that makes two drift together and become one. On the other hand the painting is very dark, and there is something tortured about the position of the bodies, as if we are witnessing something inexorable and painful. Whatever it's about, it shows two people who are completely absorbed in one another and who have ceased to exist as separate individuals.

I thought I had learned something about my neighbours, but at the same time I told myself not to read too much into it. After all, even I had liked the picture, and I was all alone.

One amusing detail I would like to mention, in the light of what happened later: I spent a long time standing in front of the painting entitled *Vampire*. Here again we have a kind of kiss, bodies melting together. But is this about consolation, or a fatal bite? Is the woman's red hair enveloping the man in oblivion and forgiveness, or is it actually blood flowing? At any rate, we see the same faceless individuals as in *The Kiss*, the same blind and tortured symbiosis.

A few days after my return from Oslo, I passed the balcony where Stefan was sitting reading Dostoevsky's *The Idiot*. It would have been impolite not to speak, so I said something and he said something about Dostoevsky and I said something about Munch and he asked if I'd like a cup of coffee and that was how it started. To cut a long story short, there were more cups of coffee on other days, and in September I was invited to dinner.

I must apologise for this lengthy detour to Oslo with the sole aim of explaining how our friendship started, but as I said: with hindsight it doesn't seem to me to be entirely without significance. The end was already encapsulated in the beginning, so to speak.

It was easy to spend time with Stefan and Karin. We had similar interests, and more importantly the same sense of humour. Like me they enjoyed turning ideas and orthodoxies inside out, and for example we could spend a considerable amount of time speculating on what would happen if islands weren't fixed, but just floated around. How those in power would formulate their immigration policy, and so on and so on.

One evening when we were sitting on the balcony sharing a bottle of wine, I asked how they had met. They suddenly looked quite secretive, and glanced at one another with an expression that suggested they might be sharing a private joke. Eventually Karin said, "We met… during the course of the investigation."

"What investigation?"

"The one in Blackeberg."

"The swimming pool… incident?"

"Yes. Stefan was a witness and I interviewed him."

"A witness?" I looked at Stefan. "But you weren't living here then, were you?"

Stefan glanced at Karin as if he was requesting permission to talk about an ongoing investigation, and she gave a brief nod.

"Oskar Eriksson," said Stefan. "I punched his ticket. On the train. The day after it all happened. So I was kind of the last person who definitely saw him."

"Were there other people who saw him?"

"You'd have to ask Karin about that."

"Sorry," said Karin, pouring more wine into my glass by way of compensation. "It's an ongoing investigation and I can't... you understand."

"But I mean it's... what is it... five years ago?"

"It's an ongoing investigation."

And that was the end of that. For the time being.

This was an unusually striking example, because it was to do with a professional code of conduct, but I noticed that in general terms there were clear delineations with both of them when it came to boundaries. What they were prepared to say and what they were not prepared to say, particularly in matters to do with their relationship. During the twenty-three years of our friendship I never asked a question about their sex life, for example. The way they touched one another, the looks and the snatched kisses indicated that they probably had quite an active one, but I instinctively knew it wasn't something they wished to discuss with other people.

I have never met a couple with such integrity, such closeness as those two. They comprised their own little universe. I won't deny that I sometimes felt quite sad in their company, especially if we'd had a few glasses of wine. We would sit there having a lovely time, chatting and laughing, but I was the one who had to get up and go home alone at some point. However much we all liked each other, I was on the outside.

They weren't perfect by any means. More than once I thought that part of the reason they valued my company was that they wanted a witness. Someone who would gaze appreciatively at their love and confer the seal of approval. They lapped it up like cats when I said something about how terrific they were together, what a miracle it was that two people... and so on. A kind of vanity. Look how wonderful we are together.

But that's just a footnote. The love was there, and it was a great and true love, and even love can be permitted a certain amount of conceit, after all.

The years passed and we grew closer. They didn't spend much time with other people; they seemed perfectly content in each other's company, and I think I can say with confidence that I was the only one they let into their life to any extent.

In 1994 Karin retired. I apologise if that comes as something of a shock, but I felt the same when I found out about the age difference between them. Stefan was born in 1945, which meant he was a year younger than me, while Karin was born in 1929. My initial impression was that there were perhaps seven or eight years between them. But in fact it was sixteen. The combination of her bright eyes and long blonde hair had misled me, coupled with the fact that Stefan had something of the old man about him.

So Karin retired while Stefan carried on travelling around on the trains, principally the route from Stockholm to Oslo and back. As I said I worked mainly evenings and nights, so I had quite a bit of spare time during the day. Karin and I weren't quite as easy with each other when it was just the two of us as Stefan and I were, but after a year or so and a number of shared coffee breaks, we had reached a level with which we were both comfortable.

In fact it was while we were having coffee one day that she told me the Oskar Eriksson case was still occupying her mind, in spite of the fact that it was no longer her job. Perhaps because she had retired she felt able to disclose a little more.

"It's not true at all," she said. "The official version, it's not true at all."

"What do you mean?" I asked tentatively, anxious not to break the atmosphere that had led her to bring up the subject.

"First of all, there was blood on the ceiling in the swimming pool. On the *ceiling*. And it was directly above the water. Five metres above the water. Given the way it had spurted, someone would have had to climb up a ladder to splash it on the ceiling. A ladder that was standing in the actual pool. The blood came from the victim whose head was torn off."

"Chopped off, you mean?"

"No. Torn off. And you can't imagine the strength it would take to do that. Try pulling apart a Christmas ham with your bare hands—and you don't even have a skeleton to contend with in that case. You know the old custom of executing people by getting horses to pull them apart?"

"Yes."

"That's just a form of torture. Horses aren't capable of pulling off even an arm or a leg. You have to help out by chopping. And that's *horses*."

"Which are very strong animals."

"Yes. Elephants can do it. But not horses. And most definitely not people."

"So what did happen, then?"

Karin sat without speaking for a long time, gazing out of the window as if she was trying to use X-ray vision to penetrate the buildings that prevented her from looking into the boarded-up swimming pool four hundred metres away.

"There was a blow, a cut," she said eventually. "Which allowed the tearing-off process to begin, so to speak. But it wasn't done by a knife. We also found another victim, an elderly man, in an apartment…" The latter remarks were made mostly to herself, and she blinked a couple of times as if she were waking up. She looked at me. "Oskar Eriksson. You saw him once, didn't you?"

"Several times. He used to travel on the subway like everybody else."

"But there was one night…"

I had told Stefan and Karin about the incident several years ago when we had been chatting in general terms about the massacre in the swimming pool. I had been sitting by the ticket barrier at two o'clock in the morning reading Kafka's *Metamorphosis* when Oskar Eriksson came up from the subway. Some drunk over by the door was singing a song about Fritiof Andersson, and the boy… I told the story again.

"It was as if a great feeling of happiness suddenly came over him as he stood there. I had been on the point of asking if he was OK, what such a young lad was doing out so late at night, but as he stood there with the drunk singing, it was as if… he started to smile with his whole face and then he *rushed* out of the building as if he was in a tremendous hurry to get to whatever was making him so happy. And then the drunk started pissing in a rubbish bin and—"

"So what was it? What made him so happy?"

"No idea. And I wouldn't have given it a thought if he hadn't hit the headlines a couple of weeks later."

"What could make a twelve-year-old boy so happy?"

"I don't know. I was pretty gloomy at that age. Are you still working on this?"

"I think I always will be."

During the years that followed Karin would occasionally let slip some further snippet of information. For example, Oskar Eriksson had lived next door to the person who took him away from the swimming pool, and there was also evidence which indicated that Oskar had been in this person's apartment on at least one occasion.

Some of the odd characters Karin had questioned at the time, the ones who still hung out in the Chinese restaurant or pizzeria as they had done in those days, had said that the dead man who was found in the apartment next door to Oskar had been looking for a child, a youngster who he insisted had killed his best friend. Who was in fact the same man who had been cut out of the ice down below the hospital with a tremendous amount of commotion.

It was a hell of a mess, and the more Karin dug around and puzzled over the case, the more connections she found to other unsolved and inexplicable murders and in the end, just before she retired, she had put forward the only theory that made all the pieces fit: "What if it really was a vampire?"

The Chief of Police had tilted his head to one side and asked, "What do you mean?"

"Exactly what I say. That the perpetrator really was a creature with supernatural strength, a creature that needs to drink blood in order to survive. It's the only thing that makes everything fit."

"I still don't understand what you mean."

Karin had given up at that point. Of course she didn't believe in the existence of vampires any more than anyone else did, it was just that... it would explain everything. On the other hand, there were plenty of unsolved cases that could be neatly tied up if you just accepted the idea of a supernatural perpetrator. Police work didn't sit well with superstition.

During Karin's final weeks at work she began to think that the counter-argument was weak. The reason why so many complex cases could be solved if a mythological figure was the perpetrator could simply be because *that was exactly what had happened.*

She didn't breathe a word of this to her colleagues or her superiors. However, the Chief of Police had a certain amount of trouble keeping things to himself, and when Karin retired she thought she sensed an air of relief through the celebratory drinks and speeches at the thought of getting rid of somebody who had gone a bit soft in the head in her old age, and sure enough some bastard made a comment about making sure she ate plenty of garlic.

During her last few years at work she had been allowed to spend time on the Oskar Eriksson case only as a concession. When she retired it was regarded as done and dusted, something of a hobby for Karin and nothing more. She would still ring her former colleagues from time to time just to check if anything new had come in, but it never had. The case was dead. Or so everyone thought.

My friendship with Stefan and Karin took a new direction in 1998, when Stefan's father died. At the age of seventy-eight he had gone out in his skiff to lay nets, fallen in the water and been unable to get out. Stefan inherited a cosy house and a summer cottage in Östernäs on Rådmansö.

The summer cottage had been available to rent for next to nothing, and Stefan and Karin decided to sell it. The cottage was in a very pretty spot up on the cliffs overlooking a cove, and the bidding went mad. Stefan ended up with just under three million kronor.

They told me all this during one of our evenings on the balcony, and then they dropped a bombshell: they were planning to move to Östernäs. I muttered something about Stefan's job and the difficulty of commuting, but they had worked it all out and come to the conclusion that the inheritance and Karin's pension would be enough to keep them afloat for as long as they wanted to stay afloat.

That same autumn I helped them load up the removal van. Then I stood at my window and watched them drive away, feeling as if an era of my life was at an end. Of course we had parted with promises to meet up often, it was only a hundred kilometres after all, there was always a place for me to stay and so on. It was a nice thought, but nothing would be the same from now on.

However, my worst fears came to nothing. Their open invitation really was exactly that, and about once a month I would go over to visit them, staying overnight and travelling back the next day. Sometimes, particularly in the summer, I thought it wasn't too bad having friends with a veranda overlooking the sea where you could sit drinking wine and chatting into the small hours. It could have been worse. I could have had no friends at all.

Their apartment on Holbergsgatan was taken over by a man from Norrland who had a big dog. I assume he was from Norrland, because that's what his dialect sounded like when he talked to the dog, which he did quite often. He never spoke to me, nor I to him.

By the time Stefan and Karin had been living on Rådmansö for a couple of years, everything was more or less chugging along as it had always done, by which I mean as it had done before they moved to Blackeberg in 1987. In 2000 I was fifty-six years old, and as I worked my way through *In Search of Lost Time* once more, it struck me that the title of the book doesn't chime with my perception of time at all.

Time neither flies nor flows nor crawls along. Time stands completely still. We are the ones who move around time, like the apes around the mon-olith in the film 2001. Time is black, hard and immovable. We circle around it, and eventually we are sucked into it. I don't really know what I mean, but that's how it feels, and you may or may not believe this, but it's an uplifting feeling.

Speaking of 2001, I celebrated the millennium with Stefan and Karin. The much-vaunted computer chaos didn't happen, and time gazed blindly at us as we entered a new millennium. Age had begun to take its toll on Karin. She suffered from dizzy spells, and the least exertion wore her out. When she fetched champagne from the cellar she had to sit down and recover for a long time before she was able to come out onto the veranda with us to drink a toast as fireworks lit up the winter sky.

In spite of the fact that I fear neither time nor the ageing process—as befits a stoic—it was somewhat painful to see the change in Karin. To me she had always been the very picture of how to grow old attractively, and it cut me to the heart to see her leaning against the oven or bending over the table to recover after doing something as simple as putting more wood on the fire.

If Stefan found it painful too, he never showed it. He would take over some task as if in passing when Karin faltered, and would put his arm around her waist as if in fun, supporting her without making a fuss about it. I left with a good feeling in my heart in spite of everything.

Oh, that heart.

A month later Stefan rang to tell me that Karin had suffered a heart attack. They had spent three days at the hospital in Danderyd, and Karin was due to have an operation a couple of hours later. The coronary arteries were severely affected by atherosclerosis and she needed a major bypass, which was by no means guaranteed to succeed.

"What do you mean?" I asked. "What do you mean, not guaranteed to succeed?"

Stefan took a deep breath, and I could tell he was forcing himself not to cry. "There's a risk that she could die. If the operation fails, then... Karin will die."

"Do you want me to come?"

"Yes. Please."

I made a few calls and called in a couple of favours to cover my shift that evening and the next, if it should prove necessary. Then I took the subway. As I sat alone in a block of four seats I felt empty-handed. At first I thought it was because I hadn't got a present with me, but when I changed at Central Station and took the red line I realised the feeling went deeper than that.

I was empty-handed because I had nothing with me that could help or save Karin. I *should* have had something. Stefan had called me, and I had immediately rushed to his rescue. I should be the one who came along with the solution, the one who made everything all right. And I had nothing. Nothing. My own impotence made my lungs ache.

I found my way through the immense hospital complex and found Stefan sitting alone in a waiting room on the third floor. A green linoleum floor with metal-framed chairs and tables dotted around. Our fate is determined in rooms that must be easy to clean. Stefan was slumped over the arm of a two-seater sofa. When I sat down beside him I could see that his skin was grey and his hands were shaking.

"Thanks for coming," he whispered.

I rubbed his back and took his hand, which was dry and unnaturally hot. We sat like that and after a minute or so Stefan started to stroke the back of my hand with the fingers of his other hand. I don't think he was aware of what he was doing, or whose hand he was holding, because he suddenly stiffened in mid-movement, squeezed my hand and then let go of it.

"That's how Karin and I met," he said. "We were holding hands."

There was a faint hint of something more cheerful in Stefan's voice, and I tried to play along. "People usually hold hands *after* they've met."

"Yes. But that's how it was. It happened when we were holding hands."

"Tell me."

Stefan straightened up, and the ghost of a smile flitted across his lips.

"It was during the investigation. Into the Oskar Eriksson case. The police called me in, and Karin was conducting the interview. I think I can say that as soon as I sat down in that room, opposite this woman, I…"

Stefan's gaze wandered to some closed double doors at the end of the corridor, and I sensed that somewhere behind those doors the doctors were trying to save the life of the woman he was talking about.

"I had information, you see. That's what she wanted, and I was under no illusions about anything else. Or… I don't know. Karin has said that she felt something too when I walked into the room. But it wasn't until we held hands that it… blossomed."

"I still don't understand. Why were you holding hands? It's not usually part of a police interview, as far as I know."

Stefan gave a snort and a little of the greyness in his skin disappeared; there was a slight pinkness in his cheeks.

"No, sorry. I'll have to tell you the story. The story I told Karin at the time."

Stefan had punched the boy's ticket and wondered about his luggage, but hadn't given the matter any more thought because the boy had told him he would have help later on. Stefan had finished his shift in Karlstad and spent an hour or so in the staffroom at the station while he waited for the train back to Stockholm.

Fifteen minutes before the train was due he went for a stroll around the station to get some air in his lungs in the chilly November evening before spending several hours in the stale air on the train.

That's when he spotted the boy again. Next to the station there was a small grove, an open space surrounded by deciduous shrubs where people could wait for the train in the summer. The grove was illuminated by a single floodlight, and Stefan saw Oskar Eriksson sitting on the trunk he had had with him on the train. A girl with black hair was sitting beside him.

"And of course I reacted because the girl was only wearing a T-shirt, even though it was well below freezing. The boy, Oskar, was fully dressed in a jacket and everything. But they were sitting side by side on that trunk. And they were holding hands. Like this."

Stefan held up his right hand, then gently took my left wrist and raised my hand to his, weaving our fingers together and rubbing our palms together before letting go.

"It was when I was telling Karin about the children sitting there holding hands. She didn't understand what I meant. So I had to show her, just as I showed you. And that was when it happened. As we sat there with our hands joined just like the children, that was when... we looked into each other's eyes and that was when... it started."

Stefan's voice had grown weaker and weaker, and as he uttered the final words he collapsed and began to weep. He bent over his knees, the sobs tearing his body apart as he whispered, "Karin, Karin, Karin. My darling, darling Karin, please don't die..."

My hands were empty, and all I could do with them was to stroke his back as he continued to whisper his prayer beneath the cold, indifferent fluorescent light. There should be storm-lashed rocks or the hall of the Mountain King. But our lives are weighed in cold, white light, and is it even possible to imagine that anyone hears our prayers?

The doors at the end of the corridor opened and a man of about our age dressed in a white T-shirt and green scrubs came towards us. Stefan didn't see him, and I tried to read the man's expression to work out what Stefan could expect. It was completely neutral, and I couldn't prepare myself one way or the other.

The man nodded to me and said, "Larsson? Stefan Larsson?"

Stefan gave a start and turned his tear-stained face to the man, who smiled at long last.

"I just wanted to tell you that the operation went extremely well. No complications, and I think I can promise that your wife will experience a considerable improvement in her quality of life once she gets through the rehabilitation stage."

I put my arm around Stefan's shoulders, but his mouth was hanging open and he didn't seem to understand what he had been told.

"It went… well?"

"As I said, it went extremely well. The blood vessels we took from your wife's leg to replace those that were damaged were of a surprisingly high quality for a woman of her age. In all probability her heart will work much better in a couple of months than it did before." The doctor held up a warning finger. "But the smoking. The smoking…"

Stefan leapt to his feet and looked as if he might be on the point of giving the doctor a hug, but he came to his senses and merely grabbed his upper arms.

"She's not going to so much as look at a cigarette packet from now on, and neither am I! Thank you, doctor! Thank you! Thank you!"

The doctor gave a brief nod and said, "She's in the recovery room at the moment, but you can see her in a couple of hours. We'll be keeping her in for a few days."

"You can keep her for a month as long as she gets better."

"She's going to be fine."

The doctor's predictions were correct. Two days after the operation Karin was allowed to go home, and after only three weeks she was able to go for walks in a way that had been impossible for her for years. It wasn't so much the weakness of her heart as the pain from the scars on her legs that prevented her from going even further, but after another month those too had healed.

Walking became a new passion for both of them. Karin started walking with Nordic poles, Stefan beside her. Sometimes he would read aloud from a poetry anthology as they walked. Both of them gave up smoking, apart from the odd evening on the veranda when they might smoke *one* cigarette each if for some reason the atmosphere was particularly festive.

*

This story is beginning to draw to its conclusion. I began by saying that I was going to tell you about a great love, and I don't know whether you think I have fulfilled that promise. Perhaps you are disappointed? Perhaps you were expecting something more dramatic?

All I can say in response is that for one thing you haven't heard the end of my story yet, and for another I feel that I have carried out my duty to bear witness, as I promised to do.

Because how do you picture a great love?

Perhaps it's something along the lines of *Gone with the Wind* or *Titanic* that immediately springs to mind. But those aren't really about love as such, they are about the context. Everything seems grander when it happens against the background of a civil war, a shipwreck or a natural disaster. But that's like judging a painting by its frame. Like saying the *Mona Lisa* is a masterpiece mainly because of the ornate carvings surrounding it.

Love is love. In those dramatic stories the main characters are willing to give up their life for the other person on a purely practical level, but that's exactly what happens in an everyday love story that is also a great love. You give your lives to one another all the way, every day, unto death.

Perhaps it's true that we recognise great love by the fact that the people involved could easily have been actors in some major drama, if only the circumstances had been different. If Stefan had been a Montague from Ibsengatan and Karin a Capulet from Holbergsgatan, perhaps they might have woven their escape plans behind my ticket booth. To run away means life, to linger means certain death. I'm sorry, I'm losing the plot here. But I think you know what I mean.

Love is love. The way it is expressed changes.

I thought a lot about what Stefan had told me at the hospital, picturing the situation. The two of them in a bare, sterile interview room—at least that was how I imagined it. Gripping each other's hands to re-create the scene between the two children in Karlstad, something that would last their whole lives beginning in that moment.

It was a pleasant thought, but Stefan had been interrupted in his narrative, and it would be some years before I was given the full picture.

Perhaps that was a contributing factor in Karin's refusal to give up on her investigation into what happened to Oskar Eriksson—it was this case that had brought her and Stefan together. Perhaps it had a special place in her heart, which was now functioning perfectly.

When we celebrated Karin's seventy-fifth birthday in April 2004, she told me that at the very beginning of the investigation the police had received a great deal of information, mainly from people claiming to have seen Oskar Eriksson in various places in Sweden and even abroad. His picture had been all over the press, and in a case like that it was normal for people to see the missing person in every conceivable place. But none of the leads had produced any results.

It was on a number of these loose threads that Karin was still working some twenty-two years later. She rang people in the places where Oskar had allegedly been seen, carefully read photocopies of old newspapers. But nobody knew anything, and if they had known anything, they'd forgotten it.

Karin sighed and shook her head as we sat on the patio beneath the infra-red heaters, took a decent swig of her wine—good for the circulation—and said, "I think it might be time to give up. Start doing crosswords or something instead."

"You already do crosswords," said Stefan.

"Do more crosswords, then."

That evening I had the opportunity to look around Karin's study properly. She had kitted out a spare room upstairs with bookshelves and a desk. Dozens of files were lined up on the shelves, and the desk was piled high with papers, maps and printouts. Karin waved her hand and said, "The nerve centre. All this to investigate *one* case, and do you know what the only practical result of the whole lot has been?"

"No."

"The fact that Stefan and I met."

Stefan walked over and weighed a bundle of papers in his hand; he shook his head gloomily and said, "A singles night for the more mature individual would have been simpler, there's no denying that."

"True," said Karin. "But then neither of us would ever have gone to such a thing."

"No. You're right. So it was all worth it, wasn't it?"

They gave each other one of those looks that still had the ability to send a pang of sorrow through my heart, even after all these years. If I had been different, if life had been different. If anyone had ever looked at me that way.

Then the stoic in me took over. Socrates was able to stand on guard in the bitter cold for hours on end without uttering one word of complaint, and he emptied his cup of hemlock in one draught. He took his place within me, and the sorrow abated.

The following year Karin devoted no time to the investigation, apart from making one phone call to police headquarters every six months to check if there was anything new. There wasn't.

The final phase in my story begins in the summer of 2007. I had noticed that Stefan was sitting in an odd position when we were out on the veranda, as if he couldn't get comfortable. When we rowed out in the skiff to lay some nets, he pulled a face when he grabbed the oars, and allowed me to take over for once.

"Are you OK?" I asked as we headed out towards Ladholmen. "Are you in pain?"

"My back hurts," he said. "And my stomach. It's as if there's something… I don't know… inside. Don't say anything to Karin."

"But she's bound to notice."

"I know. But I want to tell her myself. I think it's something… that's not good news."

Stefan and I had once talked about the age difference between him and Karin, about the fact that statistically she was likely to die several years before him, and about his feelings. As Stefan doesn't exactly have the same controlled attitude to life as I do, and tends to get worked up about things or to sink into a trough of despair, his answer surprised me.

"That's just the way it is," he said. "She's my life, she's my story. If part of the story is that I end up alone for a few years at the end, then so be it. There's no alternative. And when there's no alternative, there's no point in brooding on things. That's just the way it is."

I imagine I would have said something similar if I had been in Stefan's shoes, and we ended the conversation with some jokey comment on how he and I could always sit around throwing bread to the pigeons until the grim reaper put a stop to our activities.

But that's not how things turned out.

Stefan's pains grew worse over the next few days, and Karin drove him to the hospital in Norrtälje, which referred him to Karolinska Hospital in Stockholm. After a series of tests it was established that Stefan was suffering from pancreatic cancer. I remember with perfect clarity the day Karin rang to tell me.

I stood there with the phone in my hand, looking out of my window at what used to be their apartment. The flowerbeds were magnificent in shades of green and pink. Some children were sitting on the climbing frame with their heads close together and everything was summer and life as Karin uttered the words: "Cancer. Of the pancreas."

I knew. I'd read enough books and was generally well-informed enough to know. But I asked the question anyway: "What are they going to do?"

"There's nothing they can do. They can slow it down slightly with radio-therapy and so on. But there's no cure."

I couldn't form the words. "How... how...?"

"In the worst case scenario a few months. At best a year. No longer."

There wasn't much more to say. I put the phone down and looked over at what I still thought of as their balcony, their door. I remembered how I had noticed them because they held hands, the pop music they used to play, the faint sound of their voices on distant summer evenings. In search of lost time.

The tumour in Stefan's pancreas had spread to his liver, and barely responded to the radiotherapy. When I visited them in October he had been given a morphine pump so that he could administer his own pain relief. I had thought that he would look terrible, but sitting there on the veranda with a blanket over his legs, he looked healthier and more at ease than he had done in August.

When I mentioned this to him he gave a wry smile and clicked the pump a couple of times. "It's just because the pain has gone. I actually feel OK. But it's gnawing away inside me, I know that. It's a matter of months now."

"It seems so bloody unnecessary. Looking at you today."

"Yes. We've both said the same. But there's nothing that can be done. That's just the way it is."

Karin was sitting next to him, and he reached for her hand. They sat there holding hands and gazing out to sea. I had two years left to my retirement, and I couldn't remember when I last cried. But I cried then.

Silently I wept, and when Stefan and Karin noticed they put their arms around me to console me, absurdly enough. That made me cry even more. For them. For myself. For everything.

Stefan's liver could no longer cope with alcohol, but as we sat on the veranda that evening he made up for it by smoking more than ever. Karin drank wine and smoked, since it no longer mattered. We talked about what had happened when Karin had her heart attack, how she had felt ever since that she was living on borrowed time. She sighed and stroked Stefan's arm. "I just never thought it would have to be paid back."

"Don't think like that," said Stefan. "I could have been dead twenty-five years ago if what you believe is true."

"What do you mean?" I asked.

And that was when I was given the final piece of the information available on Oskar Eriksson. Stefan went back to what he had told me at the hospital, about the two children holding hands, which in turn had become the beginning of Stefan and Karin's story.

"But that wasn't quite all. The girl was about to kill me." He stole a glance at his wife. "According to Karin."

"It's just a theory," she said. "Which very few people would subscribe to."

"Anyway," said Stefan. "The children were sitting on the trunk rubbing their hands against each other's. I was on my way over to say something, since the girl was so inadequately dressed, and then... she turned to face me."

Stefan grimaced with pain and clicked the morphine pump a couple of times; he took a deep breath and slowly let it out again, closing his eyes. A couple of minutes passed without anyone saying anything; the only sound was the lapping of the waves on the shore and the faint ticking of the infrared heater. I had started to think he wasn't going to say any more when Stefan exhaled once again and went on:

"So. I know this sounds strange. She was a child of perhaps twelve, thirteen, but when our eyes met I felt two things, as clear as a revelation: firstly that she intended to kill me, and secondly that she was capable of doing so. Because I had disturbed them. When she jumped off the trunk and I saw that she had a knife in her hand, the feeling didn't exactly diminish. We were standing a couple of metres apart. I looked at her and the boy, saw what they were up to. The girl looked as if she was on the point of hurling herself at me when the guard shouted that my train had arrived. I think that saved me. I backed away, and she stayed where she was with the knife in her hand."

Stefan lit a cigarette and sighed with pleasure as he inhaled deeply. He looked at the cigarette and shook his head. "Being able to smoke again. It's almost worth it."

Karin thumped him on the shoulder. "Don't say that, silly."

"So what were they up to?" I asked. "The children?"

Stefan ran his index finger down his palm.

"She'd cut her hand. So that it bled. He'd done the same. They were sitting there mixing their blood. That was why they were holding hands like that. And that's why Karin has her theory. Which isn't exactly popular with the police."

"We know so little, we human beings," said Karin. "We know almost nothing."

We gazed out over the sea and considered this while Stefan sucked on his cigarette. When he had stubbed it out he said, "Do you know what the worst thing is? It's not the fact that I'm going to die. It's all the dreams I had. Which have to die. Which will never be fulfilled. On the other hand…" Stefan looked at Karin's hand, which was resting on the table. "On the other hand there are so many that have been fulfilled. So perhaps it doesn't really matter."

I don't remember what else was said that evening, but it was to be the last time I saw Stefan and Karin. At that stage Stefan's condition had been critical but stable, and the doctors believed he had at least a few months left, so when we said goodbye there was nothing to suggest that it would be forever.

But something intervened.

When I rang on the Monday a couple of weeks later, no one answered the phone. When there was no answer the following day either, I started to worry. On the Wednesday I received a card with a Stockholm postmark. It was a picture of Arlanda airport, and on the back it said, "Let the old dreams die. We are dreaming new ones. Thank you for everything, dearest friend. Stefan and Karin."

I turned the postcard over and over, but I was none the wiser. Arlanda? Let the old dreams… had they gone abroad? Was there some new treatment available elsewhere? It seemed highly unlikely. After all, that was why I had taken the news so hard; I knew as well as they did that pancreatic cancer was untreatable. Anywhere.

I was free on the Saturday and caught the bus to Östernäs. I had a spare key to their house and permission to use the place whenever they were away. However, I still felt uncomfortable as I unlocked the front door and called out, "Hello? Anyone home?" As if I were barging into something private. But I had to find out.

The house had recently been cleaned, and a faint smell of detergent lingered in the wooden floor. There wasn't a sound, and it was obvious that no one was at home. But still I crept through the hallway as if I were afraid of disturbing some delicate balance.

The fridge had been emptied and the water heater switched off. No radiators were on, and it was quite cold inside the house. When I opened Stefan's wardrobe to borrow a sweater, I saw that quite a lot of his clothes were missing. They had gone away, that much was clear. I pulled on a yellow woollen cardigan with big buttons that Stefan loathed; he had kept it only because I used to borrow it when we were sitting on the veranda.

I went through the house and found more signs of a well-organised but definitive departure. The few photograph albums they owned were gone, along with a number of favourite albums from the CD rack. Eventually I found myself standing outside Karin's study. If the answer wasn't in there, then there was no answer to be found. I cautiously opened the door.

Yes, I might as well admit it. With every door I opened I was afraid I would find the two of them in a deathly embrace, in the best-case scenario achieved with an overdose of Stefan's morphine, in the worst-case with more obvious means.

But there were no beautiful corpses in Karin's study either. There was, however, a printout of a receipt, along with an envelope containing a photograph. Both were neatly laid out on the desk, as if they had been placed there so that I would find them.

The receipt was for plane tickets. Two one-way tickets to Barcelona, four days earlier. So far so good. They had gone to Spain. The photograph, however, made no sense at all. It showed a group of people who were presumably a family. Mother, father and two children standing on a street at night, brightly lit by the camera's flashbulb. The signs around them were in Spanish and Catalan, so it wasn't a great stretch to assume they were in Barcelona.

I looked at the envelope. It had been sent by the National Police Board a week earlier, and was addressed to Karin. Right down in the bottom corner someone had written "Something for you, maybe?" and drawn a smiley. When I looked inside the envelope again I found a short letter from someone who lived in Blackeberg and had known Oskar Eriksson very well. He apologised for wasting police time, said the whole thing was completely crazy of course, but he asked them to look carefully at the enclosed photograph.

I did as the letter asked, and took a closer look at the picture. I thought I knew what he meant, but looked around on the desk for a magnifying glass. Instead I found an enlargement of the relevant part of the picture, which Karin had presumably printed out herself.

There was no doubt. Once I had seen the enlargement, it was as clear as day on the first picture too. To one side behind the family were two people who happened to have been caught in the camera flash. One was Oskar Eriksson, and the other was a slender girl with long, black hair. In spite of the fact that the photograph must have been taken immediately after his disappearance, Oskar had changed his hairstyle; it was cut short in a way that was more fashionable among young people today.

I remembered him as a chubby child, but the boy in the picture was considerably slimmer, and as he had been caught on the run, so to speak, he actually looked quite athletic. I looked at the enlargement again, and Stefan's story about what had happened in Karlstad came back to me. There was something vaguely menacing about the way the two children were moving behind the smiling, unsuspecting family. Like predators.

Then I spotted something that made me gasp. The father of the family was holding a mobile phone, and not just any mobile phone, but an iPhone. How long had they been around? A year? Two years?

I turned the photograph over and read the words in the bottom right-hand corner.

Barcelona, September 2008.

The photograph had been taken barely a month ago.

I sat at Karin's desk for a long time, looking from the receipt for the plane tickets to the photograph of Oskar Eriksson and the girl with black hair, moving through the night. And I thought about how the end can be encapsulated in the beginning, and I thought about Stefan and Karin, my dearest friends.

It's been two years now. I haven't heard if they're alive, but nor have I heard that they're dead.

Let the old dreams die. We are dreaming new ones.

I hope they found what they were looking for.